Watching You

Watching You

Michael Robotham

W F HOWES LTD

This large print edition published in 2013 by
W F Howes Ltd
Unit 4, Rearsby Business Park, Gaddesby Lane,
Rearsby, Leicester LE7 4YH

1 3 5 7 9 10 8 6 4 2

First published in the United Kingdom in 2013
by Sphere

A CIP catalogue record for this book is available
from the British Library

ISBN 978 1 47124 663 0

Typeset by Palimpsest Book Production Limited,
Falkirk, Stirlingshire
Printed and bound by
CPI Group (UK) Ltd, Croydon, CR0 4YY

For Charlotte

BOOK I

Yesterday, upon the stair,
I met a man who wasn't there
He wasn't there again today
I wish, I wish he'd go away.
When I came home last night at three
The man was waiting there for me
But when I looked around the hall
I couldn't see him there at all!
Go away, go away, don't you come back
    any more!
Go away, go away, and please don't slam
    the door . . .

William Hughes Mearns (1875–1965)

I fell in love and I followed her, that's all you need to know. She had hair the colour of bottled honey and wore different ribbons to school every day, even though most girls her age had grown out of wearing ribbons. Winter had made her beautifully pale but the cold had rouged her cheeks. She pushed her hair back behind her ears and shifted her satchel between shoulders, right to left.

She didn't see me. She didn't even know I existed. I didn't duck into doorways or press myself against walls. I didn't slow when she slowed, or speed up as she turned the corners. I was like a shadow, following in her footsteps, looking at the world through her eyes. She wore a navy blazer and a tartan skirt that swayed against her thighs and little white ankle socks that peeked out of her polished black shoes.

We caught the train at East Didsbury and got off at Burnage station. Then we took a bus along Fog Lane as far as Wilmslow Road. At Claremont Grove she bought hot chips at the Butty Full Café, sucking vinegar and salt from her fingers, her nails bitten to the quick.

It was Marnie Logan who triggered the fitful birth

of my imagination. It was Marnie Logan who gave my life meaning when my days were darkest and I could see no hope at all.

I still have the souvenirs – the strands of her hair, a ribbon, a used lip-gloss, an earring and a leather bangle from Morocco – all of which I keep in a polished wooden box. Piled together these objects look like random flotsam left behind by houseguests or bric-a-brac discovered down the side of the sofa. Yet each of them tells a story and is testament to the close shaves, the small triumphs, the fleeting moments of pure exhilaration. I cannot explain the feelings I have when I look at them, the pride, the shame, the tenderness and the joy.

I am the most important figure in Marnie's life, but she doesn't know it yet. I am the half-figure at the edge of her photographs and the shadow in the corner of her eye that vanishes each time she turns her head. I am the ghost that dances behind her closed lids and the darkness that blinks when she blinks. I am her nameless champion, her unheralded hero and the conductor of her symphony. I am the one who watches.

CHAPTER 1

When Marnie Logan was fourteen she dreamed of marrying Johnny Depp or Jason Priestley and living happily ever after in a house with a Gone-with-the-Wind staircase and a double-fridge full of Mars Bars. When she was twenty-five she wanted a house with a small mortgage and a big garden. Now she'd take a flat on the ground floor with decent plumbing and no mice.

Pausing on the landing, she swaps two plastic bags of groceries between her hands, flexing her fingers before continuing the climb. Elijah is ahead of her, counting each step.

'I can count to a hundred,' he tells her, putting on his serious face.

'What about a hundred and one?'

'Nope.'

'Why not?'

'That's too many.'

Elijah knows how many steps there are from the lobby to the top floor of the mansion block (seventy-nine) and how long it takes for the electronic timer to flick off, plunging the stairwell into darkness (sixty-four) unless you run really fast; and how to unlock the front door using two different keys, the gold one at the top and the big silver one at the bottom.

He pushes open the door and runs down the hallway to the kitchen, calling Zoe's name. She doesn't answer because she's not at home. She'll be at the library or at a friend's house, hopefully doing her homework, more likely not.

Marnie notices an envelope on the doormat. No stamp or address. It's from her landlords, Mr and Mrs Brummer, who live downstairs on the second floor and who own four other flats in Maida Vale. This makes them rich, but Mrs Brummer still collects coupons and holds up the queue at the supermarket by counting out coppers that she keeps in little reusable plastic bags.

Marnie puts the letter in a drawer with the other final demands and warnings. Then she unpacks the groceries, the cold items first, restocking the fridge. Elijah taps his finger on the fishbowl where a lone goldfish, stirred from indolence, circumnavigates his universe and comes to rest. Then he runs to the front room.

'Where's the TV, Mummy?'

'It's broken. I'm getting it fixed.'

'I'm going to miss *Thomas*.'

'We'll read a book instead.'

Marnie wonders when she learned to lie so easily. There is a gap in the corner of the room where the TV used to be. Cash Converters gave her ninety pounds, which paid for the groceries and the electricity bill, but not much more. After unpacking the bags, she mops the floor where the freezer has leaked. A mechanical beep tells her to close the door.

'The fridge is open,' yells Elijah, who is playing in her wardrobe.

'I got it,' she replies.

After wiping the speckled grey bench tops, she sits down and takes off her sandals, rubbing her feet. What's she going to do about the rent? She can't afford the flat, but she can't afford anywhere else. She is two months behind. Ever since Daniel disappeared she's been living off their limited savings and borrowing money from friends, but after thirteen months the money and favours have been exhausted. Mr Brummer doesn't wink at her any more or call her 'sweetie'. Instead he drops around every Friday, walking through the flat, demanding that she pay what's owed or vacate the premises.

Marnie goes through her purse, counting the notes and coins. She has thirty-eight pounds and change – not enough to pay the gas bill. Zoe needs extra phone credit and new school shoes. She also has an excursion to the British Museum next week.

There are more bills – Marnie keeps a list – but none of them compare to the thirty thousand pounds she owes a man called Patrick Hennessy, an Ulsterman with malice in every lilt and cadence of his accent. It was Daniel's debt. The money he

7

lost before he went missing. The money he gambled away. According to Hennessy, this debt didn't disappear when Daniel vanished. And no amount of crying poor or begging or threatening to tell the police will wipe it out. Instead the debt is handed down like a genetic trait through a person's DNA. Blue eyes, dimples, fat thighs, thirty thousand pounds: from father to son, from husband to wife . . . In Marnie's worst dreams, the Ulsterman is a distant light, hurtling towards her down a long narrow tunnel, miles away, but getting closer. She can feel the rumbling beneath her feet and the air pressure changing, unable to move, locked in place.

Hennessy visited her two weeks ago, demanding to see Daniel, accusing Marnie of hiding him. Forcing his foot in Marnie's door, he explained the economics of his business, while his eyes studied the curves of her body.

'It's a basic human trait, the desire to live in the past,' he told her, 'to spend a few harmless hours pretending that everything will be as it used to be, but the Tooth Fairy and the Easter Bunny aren't real, Marnella, and it's time for big girls to grow up and take responsibility.'

Hennessy produced a contract signed by Daniel. It named Marnie as being equally liable for his debts. She pleaded ignorance. She tried to argue. But the Ulsterman only saw things in black and white – the black being the signature and the white being a sheet covering Marnie's body if she failed to pay.

'From now on you work for me,' he announced, pinning her neck against the wall with his outspread fingers. She could see a stray piece of food caught between his teeth. 'I have an agency in Bayswater. You'll go on their books. Half of what you earn will come to me.'

'What do you mean, an agency?' croaked Marnie.

Hennessy seemed to find her naïvety amusing. 'Keep that up. It'll play well with the punters.'

Marnie understood. She shook her head. Hennessy raised his other hand and used his thumb to press against her neck below her earlobe right behind her jawbone, finding the nerve.

'It's called the mandibular angle,' he explained as the blinding pain detonated down Marnie's right side, making her vision blur and her bowels slacken. 'It's a pressure point discovered by a martial arts professor. The police use it to control people. Doesn't even leave a bruise.'

Marnie couldn't focus on his words. The hurt robbed her of any other sense. Finally, he released her. 'I'll send someone to pick you up tomorrow. Get some photos taken. How does that sound?' He forced her head up and down. 'And don't even think of going to the police. I know the name of the nursing home where you keep your father and where your children go to school.'

Pushing the memory aside, Marnie fills the kettle and opens the fridge, removing a Tupperware container of gluten-free Bolognese, which is pretty much all Elijah eats these days. He's happy. He doesn't cry. He smiles all the time. He just won't put on any weight. 'Failure to thrive,' is what the doctors call it; or more technically he has coeliac disease. If he doesn't eat he can't grow and if he doesn't grow . . .

'I have to go out tonight,' she tells him. 'Zoe will look after you.'

'Where is she?'

'She'll be home soon.'

Her daughter is fifteen. Independent. Strong-willed. Beautiful. Rebellious. Hurt. Adolescence and hormones are difficult enough without tragedy. All children destroy their own childhoods by wanting to grow up too quickly.

Tonight Marnie will make five hundred pounds. Hennessy will take half the money. The rest will pay the bills and be gone by tomorrow afternoon. Her cash doesn't circulate so much as spiral down the drain.

Standing at the sink, she looks down at the garden below, which has a paddling pond and a broken set of swings. A gust of wind rocks the branches, sending leaves into a spin. She doesn't know most of her neighbours in the mansion block. That's what happens when you live on top of people and beside them and opposite them, but never *with* them, not together. She might never meet the person on the other side of the plastered wall, but she will hear their vacuum cleaners knocking against the skirting boards and their petty arguments and favourite TV shows and bedheads bashing against common wall. Why does sex sound like someone doing DIY?

On the far side of the garden, beyond the laneway and the lock-up garages, there is another garden and an identical mansion block. Mr Badger lives on the fifth floor. Elijah gave him the name because his grey streak of hair reminded him of Badger in *Wind in the Willows*. Marnie came up with another name after seeing Mr Badger standing naked at his kitchen window with his eyes half-closed and his hand moving frantically up and down.

A few days ago somebody passed away in the mansion block next door. Marnie had been looking out the window when she saw the ambulance pull up and collect the body. According to Mrs Brummer, who knows everybody in Maida Vale, it was an old woman who'd been sick for a long time. Shouldn't I have known her, wondered Marnie? Did she die alone like one of those forgotten old people whose partially decomposed bodies are found months afterwards when a neighbour finally complains about the smell?

When Elijah was born Daniel put a baby monitor near his cot and they discovered almost immediately how many other parents in the neighbourhood had bought the identical monitor broadcasting on the same channel. They heard lullabies and music boxes and mothers breastfeeding and fathers falling asleep in their baby's room. Marnie felt as though she was spying on complete strangers, yet oddly in touch and connected with these people who were unknowingly sharing their experiences.

Elijah has stopped eating. Marnie tries to coax another mouthful, but his lips tighten into a single line. She lifts him down from his booster seat and he follows her into the bedroom, where he watches her getting ready. He holds her lingerie up to the light with his hand under the fabric.

'You can see right through it,' he says.

'You're supposed to be able to.'

'Why?'

'You just are.'

'Can I zip up your dress?'

'This dress doesn't have a zip.'

'You look very pretty, Mummy.'

'Why thank you.'

She looks in the mirror and turns sideways, sucking in her stomach, holding her breath, causing her breasts to stick out.

Not bad. Nothing has started to sag or wrinkle. I've put on a little weight, but that's OK, too.

On other days she will look at the same reflection and hate the harshness of the lighting or find faults where she could be kinder.

Along the hallway she hears the front door open and close. Zoe dumps her schoolbag in the corner of her bedroom and kicks off her shoes. She goes to the kitchen where she opens the fridge and drinks milk straight from the container. Wiping her mouth, she pads barefoot to the living room. Shouting.

'Where is the *fucking* TV?'

'Mind your language,' says Marnie.

'It's broken,' says Elijah.

Zoe is still shouting. 'It's not broken, is it?'

'We can do without a TV for a few weeks.'

'Weeks?'

'When the insurance money comes in we'll get a new one, I promise. A big flat-screen TV with cable and all the movie channels.'

'It's always about the insurance money. We're not going to get the insurance.'

Marnie emerges from the bedroom, holding her shoes. Zoe is still staring at the empty corner where the TV once sat. Her blonde curls are flying loose, as though twisting towards the light.

'You can't be serious.'

'I'm sorry,' says Marnie, trying to give her daughter a hug.

Zoe shrugs her away. 'No you're not. You're useless!'

'Don't talk to me like that.'

'We don't have a computer. We don't have the internet. And now we don't have a fucking TV!'

'Please don't swear.'

'Weeks?'

'I said I was sorry.'

Zoe spins away in disgust and slams her bedroom door. Elijah has gone quiet. He coughs and his whole body shakes. His chest has been jumping all day. Marnie feels his forehead. 'Is your throat sore?'

'No.'

'Tell Zoe to take your temperature.'

'Can I stay up?'

'Not tonight.'

'How long will you be?'

'Not long.'

'Will I be awake when you get home?'

'I hope not.'

The doorbell rings. Marnie presses the intercom button. A small screen lights up. Quinn is standing on the front steps.

'I'm on my way,' she tells him, grabbing her purse and keys. She knocks on Zoe's door and presses her face near the painted wood.

'I'm going now. Dinner is on the stove.'

She waits. The door opens. Zoe is wearing shorts and a singlet-top. One ear-bud is wedged in her ear, the other dangles. They hug. It lasts a beat longer than usual. An apology.

Elijah pushes past Marnie and launches himself into his sister's arms. Picking him up easily, Zoe settles him on her hip and blows a raspberry into his neck. She carries him to the living room and looks out the large bay window overlooking the street.

'You must be the only waitress in London who gets picked up in a fancy car.'

'It's a bar, not a restaurant,' says Marnie.

'With a chauffeur?'

'He works on the door.'

'A bouncer?'

'I guess you could call him that.'

Marnie checks the contents of her bag. Mobile phone. Lipstick. Eyeliner. Mace. Keys. Emergency numbers. Condoms.

'Take Elijah's temperature and give him Calpol if he has a fever. And make sure he does a wee before you put him to bed.'

Walking down the stairs, she hoists her dress higher on her hips to make it easier. As she reaches the foyer, she tugs it down again. A door opens. Trevor peers from inside his flat and opens the door wider.

'Hi, Marnie.'

'Hi, Trevor.'

'Going out?'

'Yep.'

'Work?'

'Uh huh.'

In his early thirties, Trevor has a skinny chest and widening waist, freckles across his nose and cheeks. Headphones are hooked over his neck and the cord dangles between his knees.

Marnie glances at the exterior door. Quinn doesn't like to be kept waiting.

'I've bought some new music,' Trevor says. 'Would you like to hear it?'

'I don't have time right now.'

'Maybe later.'

Marnie is at the door. 'Maybe.'

'Have a good night,' he shouts.

'You, too.'

She feels guilty. Trevor is always asking her to listen to his music or watch a DVD. She sometimes borrows his computer to send emails or look up information, but doesn't linger. Trevor is the care-taker who looks after the gardens and general maintenance. He's also what Daniel used to call 'a drainer': someone who sucks the energy from a room. Other people are 'heaters' because they give warmth and make you feel energised and happy around them.

Quinn crushes a cigarette beneath a polished black brogue. He doesn't open the door for Marnie. Instead he slips behind the steering wheel and guns the engine. Sullen. Silent. Marnie's stomach rumbles emptily. The booker at the agency told her not to eat before working because it would make her feel bloated.

Reaching Harrow Road, Quinn weaves aggressively through the traffic.

'I told you seven o'clock sharp.'

'Elijah has a cold.'

'Not my problem.'

Marnie knows three things about Quinn. He has a Geordie accent, he keeps a tyre-iron in the door pocket next to his seat and he works for Patrick Hennessy. This is only Marnie's third night. Each time she has felt her stomach churning and her palms grow damp.

'Is he a regular?'

'A newbie.'

'Has he been vetted?'

'Of course.'

Marnie's best friend Penny had told her to ask questions like this. Penny had experience. After university, she worked as an escort in between modelling assignments because the latter couldn't cover her credit card bills or fund her taste in designer clothes. Marnie was shocked at the time. She asked Penny what the difference was between being an escort and a prostitute.

'About four hundred pounds an hour,' Penny replied, making it sound so obvious.

Marnie pulls down the sun visor and checks her make-up in the mirror. Is this my life now, she wonders? Opening my legs for money. Making small talk with rich businessmen, pretending to be dazzled by their charm and wit. Paying back Patrick Hennessy one trick at a time. It's not what she expected or imagined, not when she was Zoe's age, or when she married Daniel, or when she lost him so suddenly. When she was seventeen she was going to be a journalist, writing feature stories for *Tatler* or *Vogue*. She settled for a job in advertising and was a junior copywriter. Loved it. Fell pregnant. Left.

Not in her worst nightmares did she imagine working for an escort agency. And no matter how often she told herself that it wasn't for ever, just a few more weeks, just until she gets the insurance money, it didn't stop the butterflies doing power dives in her stomach.

Only two people knew – Penny and Professor

O'Loughlin, the psychologist that Marnie has been seeing. The rest of her friends and family think she has a new job, working as a part-time manager at an upmarket restaurant. And when these same friends drag out clichéd analogies of 'whoring themselves' in their corporate jobs, Marnie just nods and commiserates and thinks, 'you wankers'.

The car pulls up on The Aldwych opposite Bush House. A hotel doorman crosses the footpath and opens Marnie's door. She holds up two fingers, wanting him to wait. The doorman retreats, glancing at her legs, his eyes drawn upwards from her ankles to the edge of her dress.

Quinn makes a call.

'Hello, sir, just confirming that Marnella will be with you shortly . . . sorry for the delay . . . Room 304 . . . Cash up front . . . Five hundred for the hour . . . Yes, sir, have a nice evening.'

Marnie checks herself again, running her fingers through her hair, thinking she should have washed it.

'How old did he sound?'

'Over eighteen.'

'Where will you be?'

'Close.'

Marnie nods and crosses the pavement, keeping her head down, holding her breath. The doorman ushers her inside, wishing her a good evening. Escorts aren't welcome in high-class hotels, but are tolerated as long as they dress elegantly and don't solicit in the foyer or the bar. There are protocols. Don't linger. If the lifts aren't obvious, keep walking and give the impression that you know where you're going. Quinn told her these things, along with the other rules: get the money first; keep your phone close; no bondage unless the client is getting tied up; extra time, extra money.

On the third floor, she studies the numbers. Pausing outside the door, she tries to relax, telling herself she can do this. She knocks lightly with just a knuckle. The door opens immediately.

She smiles demurely. 'Hello, I'm Marnella.'

The client is in his late forties with a narrow face and a strangely old-fashioned hairstyle, parted on the right. Barefoot, he's wearing casual clothes.

'Owen,' he says uncertainly, opening the door wider.

Marnie takes off her coat, playing a role now. Quinn had told her to be confident and take charge. Don't let the client know she's nervous or new to the game. Owen is trying not to stare. He takes her coat, his hands trembling. He fumbles with a hanger and forgets to close the wardrobe door.

'Would you like a drink?'

'Sparkling water.'

Crouching on his haunches, he opens the mini-bar. She can see the pale skin above his heels, streaked with veins.

'I can never find the glasses.'

'On the top shelf,' says Marnie.

'Ah, yes.' He raises them aloft. 'You must know your way around a place like this.'

'Pardon?'

'Hotel rooms.'

'Oh, yes, I'm an expert.'

'I'm sorry, I didn't mean . . .'

'I know you didn't.' She gives him her painted-on smile and sips her drink. 'Listen, Owen, before we start I have to collect the money. That's one of the rules.'

'Of course.'

He reaches for his wallet, which is worn smooth and curved by the shape of his backside.

Marnie feels nauseous. She hates this part. The sex she can make believe is simply sex, but the money turns it into something tawdry, brutish and ancient. It shouldn't be a commercial transaction when bodily fluids and hotel rooms are involved. Owen counts out the cash. Marnie crosses the room and slips the bundle of banknotes into her coat pocket. She notices a plastic dry-cleaning bag hanging in the wardrobe.

Smoothing down the front of her dress, she turns back to Owen, waiting for him to make a start. He gulps his drink and suggests some music, turning on the CD player. It's an old song. When he looks back, Marnie is undressing.

'You don't have to do that.'

'We only have an hour,' she says.

'I know, but we could talk a bit.'

She nods and sits down on the edge of the

mattress, feeling self-conscious in her lingerie. Owen sits next to her, a foot distant. He's a thin man with large hands.

'I haven't done this before,' he says. 'I'm not saying that I haven't done *this* . . . . It's not like I'm gay or anything . . . I'm straight. I've been with plenty of women. I'm a father, which is why this is difficult for me . . . seeing you.'

'Of course,' says Marnie.

'My mother just died,' he blurts.

'I'm sorry to hear that. Had she been sick?'

'For a long while . . . cancer.'

Marnie doesn't want to hear his life story or to compare notes.

Owen stares at the backs of his hands as though counting the freckles. 'I've wanted to do this for a long while, but my mother wouldn't have understood. And she always seemed to know when I was lying to her. It's not easy caring for someone.'

'I understand,' says Marnie.

'Do you?'

Marnie pats the bed beside her, motioning him to come closer.

'Would you dance with me?' he blurts.

'I'm not a very good dancer.'

'I can show you.'

Owen stands and holds out his arms. Marnie puts her left hand on his shoulder and feels his hand close around her waist. Next thing they're dancing, hipbone to hipbone, her long pink fingernails disappearing in his fist. Spinning. Floating.

It's not a big room, but they don't crash into furniture.

Marnie feels small in his arms, like a grown-up niece dancing with her uncle.

'I haven't danced since my wedding day,' she laughs. 'But my father was never this good a dancer.'

Owen tips her backwards with a flourish, smiling at her smile.

Marnie straightens and they share a moment, unsure of how to proceed. Marnie lets the straps of her negligee slip from her shoulders, pooling at her ankles. About now she normally gets complimented on her breasts, but Owen hasn't reacted. Wrinkles seem to enclose his eyes. He turns away. Something has altered between them. His nerve has failed him.

'Please get dressed.'

Embarrassed, Marnie covers herself and goes to the mini-bar. She pours herself a drink, a Scotch this time, drinking it neat.

'You don't have to stay,' Owen says.

'You've paid.'

'I know, but you don't have to stay.'

'Why don't you go to the bathroom and splash water on your face? You'll feel better.'

When the door closes, Marnie pulls back the bedding. She takes a condom from her purse and puts it on the bedside table. It's her third night and she's learning that every client is different. Her first was a businessman from the Midlands in

London for a trade fair at the Earl's Court Exhibition Centre. Her second was a posh-sounding thirty-something from the City with a wife and two kids at home in Hertfordshire. Now she has a middle-aged man with a mother fixation, riddled with guilt. Worse still, his guilt has become infectious and increased her own sense of shame.

She notices a plastic shopping bag tucked beneath the bed. Nudging it open with her toe, she sees a pair of polished black leather shoes and two envelopes. The first is marked: *Last Will and Testament*. The second: *To whom it may concern*.

Both envelopes are unsealed. Marnie opens the flap and can make out a line below the fold.

I'm sorry to take the coward's way out, but I have lost someone I love very much and can't think of any other way out of my suffering. Please look after my children . . .

Marnie's eyes flash around the room. The dry-cleaned suit. The shoes.

Owen is standing in the bathroom door.

'What are you doing?'

Marnie is holding the letter. 'Is this a suicide note?'

'You shouldn't open other people's mail. How much did you read?'

'Enough,' Marnie says, refolding the letter. 'Are you going to kill yourself?'

'That's none of your business.'

'This is wrong. Things are never as bad as you think.'

He laughs wryly. 'Now I'm getting emotional advice from a prostitute.'

Marnie's body stiffens.

'You can leave now,' he says.

'I'm not leaving until you promise me you won't do it.'

'You've known me less than an hour,' says Owen. 'How could you possibly understand?'

Marnie argues the point, finding the words, telling him that life is a gift and a privilege and it shouldn't be wasted. Things can change.

'And tomorrow is another day,' he says sarcastically.

'What about your children? What sort of message are you sending to them? I've felt like you do,' she says. 'I've thought about suicide.'

'This isn't a contest about who has the shittiest life.'

'I didn't give up. I survived.'

She tells him about Daniel disappearing and raising two children on her own. He's standing at the window with his back to her, looking at the lights of Waterloo Bridge.

'How?' she asks.

'The river.'

'So you were going to fuck me and then jump off a bridge?'

'No, I was going to wait till after my mother's funeral.'

Marnie's mouth opens in shock.

'I can't swim,' he explains.

'That's not a very nice way to die.'

'It isn't supposed to be nice.'

Marnie's mobile is ringing. It's Quinn. If she doesn't answer, he'll be knocking on the door.

'*You OK?*' he asks.

'Yeah. It's taking a little longer.'

'*Is he paying extra?*'

'It's not that simple.'

'*You're on the clock. Make him pay.*'

He hangs up. Marnie looks at Owen across the bed. There is a long pause and in that awkward moment she feels like she's pulling him back or maybe he's pulling her closer. She thinks of Daniel and it makes her angry.

'You will not do this. You will not disappear. You will not kill yourself. You will stay and you will fight and you will live . . . Promise me,' she says.

'Why does it matter to you?'

'Because I've lost my husband and I have a little boy at home and I don't want him to think the world is such a terrible place.'

'You care that much?'

'Yes.'

He smiles at her. It's almost a laugh. 'I've only paid for an hour.'

'That's not the point. I'm not leaving. I'm going to stay here until you promise.'

'You would stay with me?'

'Not for sex, only until you promise.'

Owen gazes at her with a mixture of admiration and yearning. Marnie puts on her dress and shoes,

25

balling up her lingerie and shoving it into the pocket of her overcoat. She feels the wad of cash.

'I'll give you back your money.'

'What?'

'Take the money. Do something nice for yourself.'

He doesn't take it straight away. Marnie peels back his fingers and presses the bundle of banknotes into his palm.

'Keep the money,' he says.

'No.'

'You need it.'

Marnie shakes her head. 'This way I'll know you won't do it because you'll owe me. Do we have a deal?'

He nods.

Owen is sitting on the bed, legs splayed, elbows on his knees. Marnie has nothing in common with this man, not money, or class, or education, or age, or interests. She doesn't even know his surname, but somehow she has touched a chord within him or made a connection. It's a strange feeling, watching a man do something because of her.

'When is the funeral?'

'Tomorrow morning.'

'What time?'

'Nine o'clock.'

'I want you to phone me afterwards. I'll give you my number.'

Marnie writes her number on a hotel pad. Owen

takes it without looking at her face. 'Would you come with me?'

'To the funeral?'

'It would mean a lot.'

'I have an appointment.'

He nods.

'Listen to me, Owen. You're going to get through this. I'll help you. Call me tomorrow.'

He looks at Marnie's note. 'I thought escorts were supposed to use fake names.'

'I'm not a very good escort.'

Owen laughs to himself.

'What's so funny?'

'You read stories, don't you.'

'Stories?'

'About hookers with a heart of gold.'

'It's not gold,' she says.

'You're right,' he replies. 'It's more precious than that.'

As Marnie reaches the revolving door, she's already beginning to panic about what Quinn will say. The black Audi is parked illegally in a narrow alley behind the hotel, nearer to Covent Garden. Quinn is leaning on the bonnet, smoking a cigarette. The streetlight behind his head creates a silhouette and throws a shadow on the cobblestones like a dark path leading to his polished shoes.

Marnie keeps the car between them, holding her coat closed as though wishing it could protect her.

'Did he pay extra?' Quinn asks.

'There was a problem. He was going to commit suicide.'

'And you fell for that?'

'It's true.'

Quinn moves towards her, his reflection sliding across the bonnet of the Audi. She tries not to back down, but her throat is thickening and she wants to hide somewhere. He flicks the cigarette aside and pushes Marnie hard against the car.

'Where's the fucking money?'

'I didn't take it.'

'So you fucked him for free?'

'We didn't do it.'

He laughs again, more sarcastically this time, forcing his knee between her legs. One hand is holding her throat while the other feels between her legs, looking for proof. The roughness of his fingers makes her wince. Humiliated. Angry.

'Satisfied?'

Her tone ignites him. One punch, delivered low down in the swell of her stomach, doubles her over. She wants to fall, but he's holding her there, pushing her up against the vehicle. A second punch lands. Her lungs have no more air to give. He won't hit her face. Bruises are a liability when you're selling a woman's body. He pulls his fist back and swings it into her stomach again. Her limbs jerk. The world flushes up and down in her eyes.

There is a brutal poetry to his movements, each blow delivered with a minimum of effort for the maximum of damage. Quinn takes a thick handful of her hair and puts his mouth to her ear.

'Are you frightened?' he whispers, seeming to savour the moment. He looks along the street. A black cab has rounded the corner, the headlights rising and falling over a speed bump. The cab pulls up. The driver's window slides down.

'Is everything all right?' he asks.

'Fine and dandy,' says Quinn, supporting Marnie with his arm around her waist. 'She had a little too much champagne.'

The driver looks at Marnie. 'Are you OK, miss?'

She nods.

The cab moves away. Quinn opens the door of the Audi and pushes Marnie onto the back seat. She drops her bag, scattering the contents into the footwell. She gathers them up.

'The boss isn't going to be happy,' says Quinn. 'You understand that, don't you?'

CHAPTER 2

The pain wakes Marnie before the sun does. Peering through cracked lids, not daring to move, she wonders if her ribs could be broken. Maybe Quinn went too far. Opening her eyes wider, she tries to focus on a framed photograph on her bedside table. In the picture she's sitting on Daniel's lap, wearing her wedding dress, laughing as he tips her backwards. His hand is cupped behind her head, her lips open, a kiss coming.

Most of her wedding photographs were too stiff and formal with people shepherded into place; the men desperate for a drink or to loosen their top buttons; and the women growing tired of sucking in their stomachs. This one was spontaneous and full of passion and emotion. Happiness trapped by the blink of a shutter.

When Marnie thinks of Daniel it's the small almost incidental memories that catch in her throat. Watching him shave; smelling his hair after a shower; curling up in the crook of his arm on the sofa; seeing him dressed in a frilly apron as he made pancakes on Sunday mornings . . .

Now he's gone. Absent. Missing. For more than a year she has heard nothing. No phone calls, no emails, no sightings, no text messages, no bank withdrawals. His passport hasn't been used, his credit cards, his gym membership, his mobile phone . . .

For most of that time she's clung to the belief that he's still alive. She has jumped at every phone call and checked her messages constantly and called the police every few days. She has said her prayers and studied passing cars and opened her post box with anticipation. But now she can't afford to hang on. She needs money and the only way to unlock Daniel's remaining assets is for him to walk through the door or for his body to be found. There is nothing in between, no compromises or half-measures.

Up until now, her rational voice has been drowned out by her longing. She has read those stories of people who never give up hope, who never stop believing their loved ones are alive under the rubble or clinging to wreckage or being raised by someone else. Marnie has tried to be one of them, but reality keeps intervening. Nobody simply disappears, not without trace, not when we have mobile phones, electronic banking, passports and Facebook accounts. The police spent months looking for Daniel. They searched for an electronic footprint. They sent his photograph around the world through Interpol and Europol and missing person agencies, but there have been no sightings.

For thirteen months Marnie has made excuses. Daniel must be lying in a coma or being held hostage. Perhaps he lost his memory or is part of a witness protection programme waiting to give evidence. The one thing she hasn't been able to countenance is the obvious – he's not coming home because he can't. She swallows hard and opens her mouth, trying to say the sentence: *my . . . husband . . . is . . . dead.*

Elijah is still asleep, wrapped in the duvet, a mound of boy smells and snuffles. She promised him waffles for breakfast. Then she'll walk him to his nursery and make her appointment with Professor O'Loughlin at eleven.

Ever since Daniel went missing, Marnie has been seeing the professor twice a week, Tuesdays and Fridays. The NHS is picking up the bill. Perhaps they have a special fund for women whose husbands disappear. She couldn't afford a clinical psychologist otherwise.

Her anxiety attacks are less frequent, but she still has blackouts and missing periods of time, some lasting a matter of minutes and others for hours, where she wakes as if from a dream with no memory of what's happened. Professor O'Loughlin doesn't use words like 'cure'. Instead he talks about 'coping' as though that's the best she can hope for. Cure would be good. Coping is OK.

She has been through this before, counselling and

therapy sessions. As a child she saw a psychiatrist who became like a second father to her, but she hasn't told the professor this and she doesn't know precisely why. Embarrassment. Irrelevance. She doesn't want him to think she's a hopeless case.

Joe O'Loughlin is a good listener. Most people don't know how to listen. Usually they're just waiting for the other person to shut up so they can start talking again, but the professor hangs on every word like she's preaching from a holy book. When she gets to the bad parts and can't find the language, he doesn't push her. He waits.

Marnie looks at the photograph again. Daniel's hair is teased with gel and his gold wedding band catches the light. Laughter creases his eyes and she can almost feel his kiss. She raises her fingers to her lips and tries to recreate the moment. It was such a carefree, careless time. No fear, no worries, no petty squabbles. She was pregnant with Elijah but wouldn't know it for another few weeks when she peed on a stick. She had never been so happy or inspired or in love. Together they could conquer the world.

Swinging her legs out of bed, she winces and shuffles gingerly to the bathroom, staring at her naked reflection. The bruises have already begun to show, discolouring her pale skin with variegated yellow and blue blotches. It triggers a flashback and she remembers the beating, how her joints seemed to unglue and loosen, how the pain travelled through her in waves.

Quinn said something to her as she was doubled over.

'Your husband was a coward,' he whispered.

What did he mean?

She couldn't ask. She couldn't breathe. She's going to demand to know next time, but there won't be another one. She can't go back. Last night she threw away the dress and lingerie, burying them deep in the communal rubbish bins. This was evidence of her intent, proof of her determination. Touching her stomach, she runs her fingers over the discoloration, noticing her broken nail. She lost it last night, along with her dignity and her last remaining shred of self-respect.

Turning on the tap, she splashes cold water on her face until her eyes sting. Then she pulls on her dressing gown and goes to the kitchen. Zoe is eating toast over the pages of her biology folder.

'You're up early.'

'Exam.'

'What have you done to your hair?'

'Nothing.'

'It has a blue streak.'

'So?'

'It looks awful.'

'Thanks, Mum, you look like shit too.'

Marnie sighs. 'Can we start again?'

Zoe holds up her hands, accepting the truce.

'Good morning, daughter of mine, love of my life, you look like you have spilled Blue Loo on your head, but it's *your* head and *your* hair and you have the right to ruin it any way you wish.'

'Thank you, mother of mine, can I have some money?'

'Why?'

'Ancient history – the British Museum trip, the permission slip is due in today.'

'How much?'

'Ten quid.'

'Do I sign a something?'

'I forged your signature.'

Zoe scoffs the last mouthful of toast and picks up her schoolbag.

'Later, Mother.'

'Wait!'

'What?'

Marnie points to her cheek. 'Even to the post office.'

Zoe rolls her eyes and plants the kiss. 'Even to the post office.'

Marnie puts on her blue summer dress and a cardigan. It's the prettiest thing she has and it makes her feel better. The dress has small white flowers stitched around the neck and reminds her of her honeymoon in Florence when she bought a similar dress at the open-air market in San Lorenzo.

Elijah is dressed and most of his gluten-free waffles consumed. They leave on time for once. Halfway down the stairs Marnie's legs almost buckle and she grabs the banister, sitting for a moment.

'Are you all right, Mummy?'

'I'm fine.'

'Why is you sitting?'

'I'm resting.'

It's a sunny morning late September. The trees looking tired. Wilting. Elijah skips along the pavement, jumping over the cracks. His SpongeBob SquarePants satchel contains a volcanic egg from Mount Vesuvius (*he pronounces it Venus*), which he's taking to school for show-and-tell for the twentieth time. Marnie can imagine an audience of preschoolers rolling their eyes and muttering, 'Please, God, not again.'

As they reach Warrington Crescent she gets a familiar feeling, the weight of eyes upon her. She can't explain the jittery, crawling sensation across the back of her neck as if she were being spied upon or quietly laughed at.

Sometimes she looks over her shoulder or steps into a doorway, looking for somebody, but the street is always empty. No eyes. No footsteps. No shadows.

Elijah's nursery is an old rectory attached to the church. Smelling of crayons and poster paint, the playroom is furnished with miniature plastic tables and chairs. Marnie hangs Elijah's satchel on a hook and signs her name into the book. Elijah hugs her twice but doesn't cry. Those days are long gone.

Mrs Shearer wants a word. 'It's the end-of-year

concert,' she says. 'We're doing a song about fathers but I thought of Elijah.'

'What about him?'

'Given the circumstances, I thought it might make him sad.'

'Sad?'

'By bringing up painful memories.'

'He has only good memories.'

Mrs Shearer smiles stiffly. 'Of course, yes, very good.'

Marnie should be more forgiving, but she can't bear the expressions of sympathy from people or ignore the conversations that she knows are going on behind her back. Gossip. Asides. She couldn't keep her husband. He ran off. Abandoned her. Now she's a single mother. The worst comments are those about 'moving on'. What does that even mean? She's moving. The earth is turning. The sun rises and sets.

Her mobile is vibrating. She touches the screen but doesn't recognise the number.

'Is that Marnella?'

She recognises the voice.

'Hello, Owen, how was the funeral?'

'Awful.'

'Where are you now?'

'I'm at Paddington station.'

'Why?'

'I thought I might take a day trip up north. Would you like to come?'

'I'm pretty busy just now, but it's a nice day for a train trip.'

'Yes it is. I'm going to keep my promise, Marnella, but perhaps you'd do something for me.'

'What's that?'

'Nice girl like you shouldn't be having sex with strangers.'

'I don't think you're in any position to lecture me, Owen.'

'Maybe not, but I wonder what your mother would say.'

'My mother is dead,' says Marnie, trying not to sound annoyed.'

A platform announcement is being made in the background.

'I guess I'd better go,' says Owen. 'It was nice meeting you, Marnella.'

'You too, Owen, but since we're on the subject of favours, I want you to keep crossing those bridges.'

He chuckles. 'You too.'

CHAPTER 3

Joe O'Loughlin takes his regular table at the café, ordering his usual breakfast from a waitress who famously never smiles. Every morning he tries to coax some semblance of good cheer from her, using his best lines and trying to engage her in conversation. Each time she curls her top lip and says, 'Will that be all, sir?'

He prefers an outside table, where he can read the morning papers and watch commuters walking purposefully towards the train station – women with wet hair and matching skirts and jackets, men in suits carrying briefcases or satchels. Where are they going, all these people, he wonders? To work in boxes, stacking boxes, ticking boxes.

He missed London when he moved to the West Country and now he misses the West Country, most notably Julianne and his daughters, Charlie and Emma. Sometimes he tries to convince himself that he's only living in London during the week and commuting back to Wellow on weekends, but that's been happening less and less. Home is a hard place to define when you're separated. His marriage lasted nearly twenty years; the separation has stretched to five. It doesn't feel like a divorce, not yet, and sometimes it can still seem like they're together, particularly on those mornings when he wakes and imagines that he can hear Julianne downstairs, making breakfast and answering Emma's questions. Emma is only seven and she will be a lawyer or a scientist. A lawyer because she argues and a scientist because she explores every answer, demanding to see the evidence. His other daughter, Charlie, wakes early and leaves for school before Julianne gets up. She will have skipped breakfast, but put a cereal bowl in the sink to make her mother think otherwise.

Joe's coffee has arrived – a double espresso, muddy and strong. Breakfast comes soon afterwards: poached eggs on sourdough toast. He's nothing if not a creature of habit. Unfurling the morning paper, he glances at the headlines of the day. So much of what passes as newsworthy makes him feel defeated because the stories never change, only the names and the places. Particular newspapers will favour the left or the right of the political spectrum, reflecting the wishes of their proprietors and pandering to prejudices of their readers rather than moderating them. Meanwhile the columnists will insult those who disagree with their opinions, conflating gossip with real news and amplifying their anger until they sound increasingly like angry wasps buzzing in a jar.

Joe doesn't have his first patient until eleven o'clock. Marnie Logan. This café is where they

40

first met, which is a coincidence that should not be mistaken for irony. Marnie had been working as a waitress – one who knew how to smile – and she saw Joe drawing circles around 'To Let' advertisements.

'Are you looking for a house or a flat?' she asked.

'A flat.'

'How many bedrooms?'

'Two.'

'I know a place.' She jotted down the address. 'It's about half a mile from here, just off Elgin Avenue in Maida Vale. My landlords are looking for someone.'

Two weeks later he moved into his flat. He went back to the café to thank Marnie, but she wasn't there. He dropped by again and the café owner told him that she'd quit because her husband had gone missing.

Joe left a note for Marnie thanking her and adding a message: *If ever you need to talk to someone here is my phone number.*

He didn't expect to hear from her again. He *hoped* that she didn't need him. Now he sees her twice a week, talking through issues of grief and abandonment.

'I'm planning to kill myself,' Marnie told him when she came to her first session.

'How will you do it?' he asked.

'I want to choose a way that isn't messy.'

'There's no neat way of dying.'

'You know what I mean.'

She described her physical symptoms – the heart palpitations and tremors, the clamminess and gulping of air. She was suffering from an existential anxiety that was so profound it went right to her core. Some people suffer from phobic anxieties, fearing things like spiders or heights or confined spaces. These are easier to treat because they have a specific focus. Existential anxiety is more difficult because the reasons aren't obvious and the magnitude confounds everything in their lives.

Marnie's problem went beyond a missing husband, Joe realised. Something else haunted her – a sense of dread that filled her like a dark liquid. Hours would disappear. Fugues. Lapses. Mind slips. Joe had spent months trying to discover the reason, but areas of Marnie's mind were closed to him.

Finishing his breakfast, he folds the newspaper beneath his arm and gets to his feet, arching his back to prevent his stooped walk. Then he looks at his shoes, wiggling his toes and issuing instructions. One of the side effects of Parkinson's is a tendency to trip over when he starts walking, or to move in the wrong direction. His brain can send the message but it doesn't always arrive. He has learned over the years how to hot-wire his system and overcome the false starts.

Walking confidently now, he checks to make sure both his arms are swinging and his shoulders are back. Just another pedestrian, he thinks. Not a cripple. Not an invalid. Just a man on his way to work.

Joe's secretary buzzes him through the door, because he sometimes struggles with keys and locks. She takes his jacket.

'What a lovely morning? Did you walk?'

'Yes I did.'

'This needs dry-cleaning. I'll take it today.'

'You really don't have to bother.'

'It's only downstairs.'

Carmen is in her late forties, divorced with grown-up children and the singsong voice of a kindergarten teacher (her previous career). She has great legs, a fact she celebrates by wearing shortish dresses and skirts.

'If you've got 'em, flaunt 'em,' she once told him, when she caught him looking. Joe apologised. Carmen said she was flattered. Joe told himself this wasn't going to work out.

'Mrs Duncan has cancelled her twelve o'clock, but Mr Egan called, wanting an appointment. I took the liberty . . .'

'Thank you.'

The intercom buzzes. Marnie pushes through the door and walks straight into Joe's office. She takes a seat and grimaces slightly, clearly in pain. Joe doesn't ask about it immediately. He'll give her time. She sits in a closed way, anchored to the chair as though scared the world might shift suddenly beneath her. Marnie steels herself for these sessions. Survival first. Revelation second.

Joe takes his seat and spends a moment studying Marnie.

'How have you been?'

'Good.'

'Any anxiety attacks?'

'No.'

Marnie interrupts before he speaks again. She has a story for him. She starts twice and goes back, looking for the right words. When they come it's in a rush of breathless descriptions and recounted conversations.

'So I stopped someone committing suicide,' she says proudly, folding her arms in satisfaction.

Joe nods, not showing any emotion. 'You can see the irony, of course.'

'What irony?'

'You told a man to look at the positives.'

'I don't see why a person can't contemplate suicide yet talk someone else out of it. They're not mutually exclusive emotions.'

'That sounds like self-justification.'

'It's better than self-pity.'

'Do as I say, don't do as I do.'

'Exactly.'

Marnie laughs. It doesn't happen often. Normally she's always holding something in reserve. Once or twice Joe has pondered whether she's been through this process before – therapy or psychoanalysis. She seems to predict many of his questions before he asks them.

Lying is almost expected in clinical psychology. People lie to avoid embarrassment, conflict and shame, to protect their image and to gain reward.

They lie to friends and family, but mostly to themselves. It has always been so, from the cradle to the grave. But with Marnie it is different. Behind her grey-green eyes and pale skin he senses something coiled and caged. Not caged in a way that it wants to come out. Caged in a way that it's too dangerous to be released.

Marnie shifts in her chair, wincing.

'You're hurt.'

'It's nothing.'

'Your ribs are bruised.'

'How do you know that?'

'I did three years at medical school.'

'Could they be broken?'

'You should see a doctor.'

'But you could tell me.'

'I'm not allowed to do that.'

Marnie stands. 'Just take a quick look. Tell me if I need an X-ray.'

Grabbing the hem of her dress, she pulls it over her hips, bunching it around her breasts. Joe can feel himself blushing. The dark bruises reach across her stomach and almost to the edge of her panties.

'What happened?'

'I ran into a fist.'

'Repeatedly?'

Joe knows about Marnie's escort work. He tried to talk her out of it and then gave her chapter and verse about taking precautions. Vetting clients. Emergency numbers. Operating a call-back system.

'For a psychologist you seem to know a lot about sex work,' Marnie told him.

'I've known a lot of sex workers,' he replied, 'but not in the biblical sense.'

'What does that mean – the biblical sense?'

'It means to know someone completely: physically *and* emotionally.'

'No one-night stands?'

Joe hesitates and summons a memory of a former prostitute called Eliza who almost cost him his marriage, but doomed it anyway, just as certainly as *he* cost Eliza her life.

Marnie is still talking, telling him that she's not going back to the agency. She'll find another way to repay Daniel's debts. She's holding her dress under her arms.

Joe presses his fingertips against the darkest of the bruises. 'Are you having trouble breathing?'

'Only when I bend or move too quickly.'

'I don't think anything is broken, but you should rest up for a few days. Did you go to the police?'

'I'd rather talk about something else.' Marnie pulls her dress over her hips and brushes the creases with her hands, more self-conscious now that she's covered.

'What was the scar just above your navel?' he asks.

Marnie rolls her eyes, playfully. 'You were supposed to be looking at my ribs.'

Joe doesn't play along.

Marnie shrugs ambivalently. 'I fell off a horse and ruptured my spleen.'

'How old were you?'

'Thirteen.'

'Why have you never talked about it?'

'What's there to talk about? The horse got spooked and threw me onto a fence. I stopped riding after that.'

Marnie has retaken her seat and crossed her arms as though closing the subject. Joe moves on and asks about Daniel. 'Have you had any news?'

'He's dead.'

'So the police have . . .?'

'I just know it's true.'

Marnie leans forward and begins explaining her reasoning, talking as though she's been rehearsing the speech in her head.

'I have to get on with my life. I need to sort out Daniel's affairs . . . talk to the bank . . . a lawyer. Daniel had an insurance policy. The money can pay off our debts. We can start again.'

'How are you going to do that?'

'I don't know yet, but things are going to change. I'm sick of living like this.' She pauses, frowning. 'Why are you grinning?'

'It's good news.'

Shaking her head, she smiles shyly before another silence settles upon them. Marnie sits very still, waiting for the professor to speak.

'Tell me how you met Daniel?'

'You know that story.'

'I want to hear it again.'

Marnie sighs and begins explaining how it

happened. She was twenty-nine years old and six years divorced after a brief and disastrous first marriage. Zoe must have been eight or nine. They went back to Manchester to visit her father and arrived to find a domestic crisis. A water pipe had burst in the street, flooding the basement of her father's cottage. He was wearing wellingtons and a storm jacket, looking like a North Sea fisherman.

'Nothing but mud and misery down there,' he said, before winking at her. 'But I have a couple of nice young lads from over the road who are lending me a hand. One of them is a journalist. He's the one with the smile. You're going to like him.'

Marnie took no notice of her father. Thomas Logan had a way of acting like a schoolboy, despite being sixty-two. She watched him disappear downstairs and resume dragging sodden boxes and rolls of carpet into the garden. After a while she took them mugs of tea and a packet of biscuits. That's when she saw Daniel. He was covered in mud with a shirt plastered to his chest. Then he smiled.

'I know it sounds corny,' Marnie says, looking up at Joe, 'but it was like one of those things you see on TV, where the room goes dark except for a single spotlight beaming right down on him. I didn't hear angels singing, but everything seemed to slow down and his beautiful mouth opened.'

'Fancy a roll in the mud?' he'd said, in an Aussie accent that made her ovaries tingle.

'Where did you get that lovely accent?' she asked.
'Sydney.'

'Damn, I need to move to Australia.'

Thomas Logan came out of the basement and introduced them. Later, when she was cleaning up in the kitchen, Marnie said to him, 'That's the man I am going to marry, Daddy.'

And he said, 'I knew you were going to love that smile.'

CHAPTER 4

There is a man sitting in a car outside Marnie's flat with a hat tilted over his eyes as though he's fallen asleep. A newspaper rests on his lap with a crossword showing and a pen poised above the grid. Marnie walks past the car and up the steps, hearing the driver stir and the car door close.

'Excuse me, ma'am.'

Marnie slides her key into the lock. He's wearing a lightweight suit and holding his hat.

'I'm Detective Inspector Gennia of the Metropolitan Police.'

A jangle of alarm runs through Marnie. She thinks of Elijah, cataloguing possible disasters. Kidnapping. Choking. Meningitis. Electrocution. Drowning. How could he possibly drown at day care?

'Your little boy is fine,' says the detective, reading her thoughts.

'Is this about Daniel?'

'No, ma'am.'

The detective is holding his hat with both hands,

pushing a dent out in the crown. He glances skywards. 'Looks like we might get some rain.'

'You didn't come here to discuss the weather.'

'Where were you last night between nine o'clock and midnight?'

Marnie won't meet his eyes. It's an uncomfortable thing to lie to someone when you fear they know the truth.

'I was at home.'

'All night?'

'Yes.'

'Can anyone vouch for that?'

'My daughter and son were home.'

The detective nods. His hazel eyes seem to blink very slowly. He has thick lashes like a woman and a strange haircut, but everything else about his face is chiselled and angular with skin stretched tightly over his bones.

He's wearing a wedding ring. Marnie wonders when she began noticing such things. He's not handsome, but she's fascinated by the way his lips barely move as he speaks.

'Is that all?' she asks.

'I'm giving you a little time.'

'Pardon?'

'You answered so quickly I thought maybe you didn't take time to think. So I'm giving you a chance to change your story.'

'You think I'm lying?'

'I don't know *what* I think,' he replies, giving her

his boyish smile. 'It's like these shoes I'm wearing. I don't know if they match this suit or if they make me look like a fashion victim, but I want to believe they're not completely naff.'

Marnie glances at his needlepoint boots.

'They're not.'

'Mmmmm,' he says, rocking onto his heels. 'Most comfortable shoes I've ever owned . . . . the leather is so soft.'

He takes a stick of chewing gum from his coat pocket, unwrapping the silver foil and folding the gum against his tongue. Chewing pensively, he gazes up at the block of flats.

'I know you weren't home last night. Where did you go?'

'I met a friend for a drink.'

'What time?'

'Early.'

'Does your friend have a name?'

'Does it matter?'

'I talked to your caretaker, Trevor. He said you didn't get home until after midnight.'

'He made a mistake.'

The detective's eyes move through a range of emotions from scepticism to sadness. Taking out a notebook, he jots something down.

'What are you writing?'

'Just making a note.'

He puts the pen away. 'Do you have a good lawyer, Miss Logan?'

'Why?'

'In case I come back with an arrest warrant.'

DI Gennia turns and skips down the steps, putting on his hat and running a finger over the brim.

'Wait!' says Marnie.

The detective pauses.

'Why is it so important to know what I was doing last night?'

'We fished a body out of the river this morning. He was carrying a mobile phone. We traced the last number he called.'

Marnie shakes her head. 'That's not right. He called me this morning.'

'Who?'

'Owen.'

'Who's Owen?'

'The friend I met last night. He . . . he was depressed. His mother had just died. He was planning to commit suicide but I talked him out of it.'

'What is Owen's last name?'

'I don't know.'

'And he's a *friend* of yours?'

Marnie doesn't like Gennia's sarcasm and she's annoyed at telling him anything.

'He was an acquaintance rather than a friend. I only met him last night. He was going to jump off Waterloo Bridge.'

Gennia looks puzzled. 'The man we found was stabbed to death. His body was discovered shortly before seven this morning floating next to Execution Dock in Wapping. We found his car three hours later, two miles further east, a black Audi.'

Marnie's breath catches inside her throat like a bubble that won't break.

The detective is studying her. 'We haven't released the name of the dead man. Perhaps you know it already. The last call made from his mobile was to your number at 8.46 p.m. last night. The call lasted forty-seven seconds.'

Marnie opens the door.

'Why was he calling you?'

She pushes it closed.

'You're making a mistake,' yells the detective. 'You should talk to me.'

Some people's lives make good movies. Some people's lives make bad movies. The vast majority lead existences that are so mind-numbingly banal they would have an audience chewing on their chairs. Instead of romantic comedies or soaring love stories, they get kitchen-sink dramas and trite tragedies.

Shakespeare was right about the world being a stage and all of us being mere players, but most people can't act even when they're typecast as themselves. They lack verisimilitude or they come up with their best lines after the event.

I am the director of Marnie's life. I don't write the script, but I set the scenes and let the actors ad-lib their lines. The detective is a new character. I don't like that he's watching. I'm not being selfish or hypocritical, but I've been doing this for a long time and I have come to regard Marnie as mine.

There is a nice symmetry to where the police found Quinn. The incoming tide carried him as far as Execution Dock. Back in the nineteenth century this was where they brought the condemned prisoners by cart from Marshalsea Prison and paraded them in front of the crowds who gathered along the banks of the river or chartered boats to get a better view. Murderers. Pirates. Deserters. Mutineers. The hangmen from Tyburn or Newgate prisons would do the honours, shortening the rope for acts of piracy so that death came more slowly, which is why they called it the 'Marshal's dance' because their limbs would jerk and spasm as they slowly asphyxiated.

I remember how Quinn looked at me last night, rubbing his eyes to make sure. Then he told me to 'fuck off' with so much malice, I wondered where his bravery came from.

For a moment he contemplated putting his foot hard on the accelerator, taking his chances, but chose instead to negotiate because I held a knife against his neck.

'Where did you get that?' he asked, feeling the blade against his skin.

'I came prepared.'

'Can we talk?'

'Keep driving, both hands on the wheel. Let's talk about men who hit women. Did it make you feel more like a man? Do you feel like a man now?'

He shook his head slowly. 'You're creeping me out.'

'Is that all you have to say?'

'I'm sorry. Really I am.'

'What are you sorry for?'

'Call it a blanket apology.'

I laughed.

'What's so funny?'

'Saying you're sorry without being specific is like

telling a woman you have a big cock. Everybody knows you're lying.'

He glanced in the rear-view mirror. His lips were compressed, downturned at the corners.

'Do you always hit women?'

'Sometimes I forget my own strength.'

'I forget myself too sometimes. People often misjudge me, but only the once.'

'What are you going to do?'

'I haven't decided yet.'

Quinn followed my instructions. Driving carefully. We reached an area of waste ground, flanked by warehouses on two sides and the river on a third. A narrow canal ran through the middle of the weeds and rubble. Large metal doors sealed off the canal from the river, the weight of the water holding them closed. Small rivulets leaked through the seals and rust stained the cables and hinges.

I have often wondered if London should make more of its canals. Most are bleak, boring, lonely, occasionally menacing places. Perhaps they could be planted and refurbished like the High Line in Manhattan, or dotted with bohemian shops and bars, or purified to create urban swimming holes. Gentrified, in other words. Or perhaps they're better as they are; under-appreciated, under-explored ribbons of old industry through the heart of a modern city.

I touched the side of Quinn's head and ran one finger behind his ear in a romantic way. He didn't move. I dropped a plastic cable tie onto his lap.

'Loop it over your hands and pull the end with your teeth . . . Tighter.'

He looked in the mirror, trying to see the future in my eyes.

'Listen, just take the motor.' He motioned to his pocket. 'My wallet – you can have it.'

Before he could finish the statement I had slid the knife across his throat. Not deep because the knife wasn't particularly sharp. I felt the blood between my thumb and forefinger and smelled the urine soaking his trousers. The car door opened. He tried to run, holding his throat, but he couldn't yell for help.

At the edge of the canal, he looked at the water below, so black it could have been sump oil or boiling tar. He sobbed and knelt down, pleading with me. I took hold of his hair, tilting his face to mine.

'When you hurt Marnie, you hurt me.'

He gave me a puzzled look before toppling forward.

CHAPTER 5

Sitting at the kitchen table, Marnie tries to steady her heartbeat. What should she have told the detective? Once she started, where would she have stopped? She'd have had to tell him about working as an escort. He would have called child protection and she'd be knee-deep in social workers, threatening to take Zoe and Elijah away from her. How much further would she have to go – telling them about the gambling debts and Patrick Hennessy's threats and Daniel's disappearance? So she said nothing and made herself look guilty.

Marnie can't remember Quinn dropping her home. She recalls getting rid of her clothes and curling up in bed, nursing her ribs, but not the details of the drive and what Quinn said to her when they reached Maida Vale and she opened the car door. Professor O'Loughlin has a special word for these absences, but to Marnie they're like dropped stitches in the fabric of her day; lapses that she glosses over because she's too busy or too frightened to do anything else.

She'd wished Quinn dead. Now he is. He was a

thug and a bully; he worked for Hennessy, pimping women and collecting debts. He must have had enemies.

Right now Marnie doesn't have time to think about it. She has an important meeting. Straightening her clothes, she does her make-up. Not too much. She glances at the window. Rain rattles against the pane like thrown rice. What happened to the sunshine? She'll have to run to the tube station.

She takes two painkillers from a foil packet and washes them down. Then she pours a mouthful of frozen vodka into a glass and swallows it, feeling the liquor scald her throat.

Breathe. You can do this.

Trevor intercepts her as she reaches the ground floor.

'I collected your post,' he says, holding up the envelopes.

'You shouldn't have bothered.'

'No trouble.'

Bare-armed, he's wearing a Rolling Stones T-shirt and a pair of ripped jeans over combat boots.

'A man was looking for you earlier. He said he was a detective.'

'I talked to him.'

'He asked me if I saw you come in last night. Is everything OK?'

'Everything is fine.'

Marnie hurries to leave, ignoring a comment on the weather. She wrestles with her umbrella on the front steps and notices a cab coming along the road. She can't afford the fare, but she's late. She raises her hand. The cab pulls up. A couple run across the pavement and open the doors.

'Hey! That's my cab,' she shouts.

A man and woman look up. She's seen them before. He's always dressed in a nice suit. Charcoal grey. The woman is less familiar. She has a little girl about Elijah's age and sometimes goes to the park. She's one of those irksome mothers who appear perfectly groomed even when they're feeding ducks or pushing a swing.

'We hailed it first,' says the woman, disappearing inside.

'I'm running so late,' Marnie replies, exasperated.

'Where are you heading?' he asks.

'Tottenham Court Road.'

'We can share.'

'Now we're going to be late,' the woman says. She has a wheedling voice.

'We'll be fine,' he says, pushing down the rear-facing seat. He makes the introductions. His name is Craig Bryant. His wife is Eleanor. They moved into the area a year ago, but Eleanor spends most of her time in the country at 'the big house'.

'Eleanor doesn't like London very much.'

'I am *here*,' she says, still annoyed.

'You have a daughter,' says Marnie, trying to break the ice. 'I've seen you at the park.'

'Gracie,' he says.

'I have a little boy. Elijah. He's about the same age.'

Bryant's mobile is ringing. He checks the screen. Answers.

'Tell Anthony not to be so precious . . . we hate ALL our clients. That's why we can overcharge them and still sleep at night . . . I'm on my way to the office now . . . see if you can schedule a consult. Ask Ginny to check my diary . . . I'll see you in fifteen.'

He apologises. Smiles. He has a great smile. Marnie can see the child in it. Eleanor begins asking about schools and nurseries, all of them too expensive for Marnie to even consider.

'Where do you send Elijah?'

'He goes to the church playgroup in the park.'

'You're religious?'

'No, it's cheap.'

That should suffocate the conversation, thinks Marnie, but Eleanor carries on. 'What does your husband do?'

'He's a journalist.'

Eleanor perks up. 'Does he work for a newspaper?'

'He's not around at the moment.'

'Is he on assignment?'

'No.'

Bryant puts a hand on his wife's knee. 'I think she means that they're not together.'

'He's missing,' says Marnie, making it sound like

something that happens to everyone occasionally and can't be helped.

Eleanor looks at her husband and back to Marnie. 'What happened?'

'He just disappeared.'

'When?'

'Last summer.'

'And you have no idea . . .?

'Not a clue.'

'The police?'

'Have given up looking.'

The cab has pulled up. Marnie juggles with her dripping umbrella, looking for money. 'How much do I owe you?'

'I'll get this,' says Bryant.

'Are you sure?'

'Absolutely. Good luck with your interview.'

'How do you know . . .?'

He points to the creased letter in Marnie's hand. The masthead is from the insurance company. 'I guessed.' He hands Marnie his business card. 'Should you ever need a lawyer . . .'

His wife admonishes him. 'Not everyone is a potential client, Craig.'

'Maybe I'll see you in the park,' says Marnie, trying to be cordial.

'I'm rarely in London,' replies Eleanor, making no attempt to reciprocate.

Marnie steps into the downpour, pleased to be outside. Dodging the spray from passing traffic, she runs along the street, counting down the numbers. The building is a 1920s six-storey office block, with a pillared porte cochère over the main entrance. Standing in the marbled foyer, Marnie looks down the list of company names. Life General is on the fifth floor. She takes the lift and pushes through a heavy glass door into a reception area that is half the size of her flat.

'Didn't you see the stand outside?' says a receptionist, who is pointing at Marnie's dripping umbrella as though it's nuclear run-off.

'I'm sorry.'

The receptionist is pregnant, squeezed into a skirt that must be constricting blood flow to her legs. It could explain her mood. She answers a phone. There is a script and a tone: *Good afternoon, Life General, can I help you?*

Marnie uses a tissue to mop up the puddle on the floor.

The receptionist comes back to her, peering over the edge of her desk. 'Who do you wish to see?'

'Mr Rudolf.'

'Do you have an appointment?'

'Sort of.'

'What does that mean?'

'I told him I was coming.'

The receptionist punches keys on her computer and picks up the phone. Marnie takes a seat, glancing at her watch. She has to pick up Elijah from nursery in under an hour.

Fifteen minutes go by. She asks the receptionist to call him again.

'I'm here,' says Mr Rudolf, emerging from a swinging glass door. A lean, sharp-featured man in his mid thirties, he's wearing a navy suit, white shirt and crimson club tie. Marnie follows him to an office with a large picture window that looks across the street. He doesn't close the door. A blue foolscap folder is centred on his desk.

'How can I help you today?'

'I wanted to ask about claiming on my husband's life insurance.'

'I thought I explained the situation on the phone.'

'Yes, but I don't think you understood . . .'

'Has your husband been found?'

'No, but I *know* he's dead.'

'You *know*.'

'Yes.'

'How?

'It's obvious. Nobody has sighted him. He hasn't touched his bank accounts or turned on his mobile phone or contacted his friends or family. The police have stopped looking. Don't you think Daniel would have contacted someone if he were still alive?'

Mr Rudolf takes a deep breath and holds it for a moment before releasing it in a long sigh. 'Under the terms of our life policies we don't assume a missing person is dead until seven years have passed and only then when all proper avenues of investigation have been exhausted.'

'What avenues?'

'The usual ones.'

'Where do you think my husband is?'

'I don't know.'

'Do you think he's alive?'

'That's not my area of expertise.'

'So what you're saying is that I must keep paying premiums on a policy that I cannot claim for seven years unless I can produce my husband's body?'

'We cannot settle your claim without a death certificate.'

Marnie looks at her hands. She feels dizzy. It's as though she's stood up too quickly from a hot bath.

'Do you have children, Mr Rudolf?'

'Yes.'

'Is your life insured?'

'Of course.'

'If something happened to you, would you want your wife to be kept waiting for seven years?'

'I hardly think that's the—'

'I can't access his bank accounts. I can't cancel his gym membership. I'm still paying his annual credit card fees. I can't stop his direct debits. I can't divorce him. I can't mourn him. I can't change his address or redirect his mail or wind up his investments. I was married to him for five years, but I don't have any rights because he disappeared instead of dropping dead in front of me. I have two children. I'm trying to feed them and keep a roof over their heads. I'm begging you . . . please.'

Mr Rudolf won't look at her.

'Can I get some sort of advance payment?'

'We don't make advance payments.'

'I'm owed three hundred thousand pounds. We paid our premiums every year. This isn't right! You're trying to take our money.'

'This isn't my decision. We have rules. We have formulas—'

'Formulas?'

'We cannot pay a claim without a death certificate.'

'How do I get that?'

'Talk to a lawyer.'

Mr Rudolf shuffles paper now, wishing to end the conversation. Marnie's voice grows louder, but she doesn't realise that she's shouting until a security guard comes to the door. Marnie tries to hold on to the arms of her chair, but her fingers are prised loose and she's forced to her feet and frogmarched along the corridor to the lift.

It's not until she's outside that she remembers her umbrella. They won't let her back inside. She blinks and looks at the puddle lapping over her shoes. Pedestrians flow around her, dashing between doorways as if they're stealing bases, ignoring her tears, which look like raindrops.

CHAPTER 6

Joe O'Loughlin wakes when it's still dark outside. He seldom sleeps well. Mr Parkinson snores and snuffles, nudging him awake, wanting to be entertained. Sometimes he tries to avoid going to bed, dozing off in front of the TV or reading a book, waking hours later, feeling victorious because half the night is already gone and he's stolen sleep like a thief.

His dreams have changed. In the nightmares of his childhood he was always running, trying to escape a monster or a rabid dog or perhaps a Neanderthal second-rower with no front teeth and cauliflower ears. When he married, his nightmares involved his wife and children in danger, always out of reach.

Now he has a different recurring dream. He imagines standing in an attic room, aiming a gun at a man's forehead, screaming at him to let a girl go. Begging him. Pleading. Then the gun jumps in his hand and seems to rip organs loose in his chest.

The memory is like a strip of film that plays on a loop. He can't expunge it from his unconscious or drown it with alcohol. Instead he is forced to watch every frame through his eyelids, night after night, pulling the trigger, feeling the spray of blood and seeing dull black dead eyes staring at him triumphantly.

He killed someone. Not an innocent man, not a saint, but a monster who had done terrible things. None of this seemed to ease Joe's conscience or make his dreams any less vivid. Nor could he confess his sins or seek forgiveness or assuage his guilt in other ways. Although not a believer in heaven or the concept of an afterlife, Joe often wondered why people thought they have to die to go to hell.

His left arm is jerking and his head seems to move in sympathy. He fumbles for his pills, knocking over the bottle, scattering the contents across the wooden floor. Scrambling on his hands and knees, he tries to retrieve them. Pills have rolled under the dresser and the bed.

Sitting on the edge of the mattress, his hands are clenched between his knees to stop them shaking and he's filled with a self-loathing that he will not show to anyone except himself. The world will think him stoic and brave; facing adversity with grace and good humour, never weeping with despair or railing at the injustice. Joe doesn't subscribe to the theory that we get the luck we deserve. Fairness is a hair colour not something to be balanced on a set of scales.

Charlie is sleeping in the spare room. She's off

school for the week and visiting her dead-old dad, but going home in two days. Why do expensive private schools have the longest holidays? Quality must beat quantity or it's wasted money.

Joe dresses in a tracksuit and running shoes. He kisses his daughter on the forehead before leaving, telling Charlie he'll be home early. She stirs and rolls over, mumbling something that sounds more like a protest than a goodbye.

At a quarter past seven the sun has risen above the rooftops and painted the highest leaves on the tallest trees in Kensington Gardens. Joe used to laugh at people who exercised every morning: the joggers and gym rats clad in Lycra and expensive trainers, sweating their way to a longer life. Now the muscle memory of youth has faded and Mr Parkinson is dancing through his joints, exercise and diet have become more important. He has lost twenty pounds since he moved back to London. Before he could pinch the fat above the waistband of his boxer shorts, but now he's leaner and fitter. A man has to look his best if he's going to win back his wife.

A young woman jogs past him. He follows her tightly clad bottom and quickens his stride. When he lived in Wellow he walked a dog every morning, a grey Labrador called Gunsmoke, who chased rabbits and caught them only in his dreams. Gunsmoke is dead. Joe's marriage is over. His own dreams are works in progress.

His walk ends in Westbourne Grove. He'll shower

at the office and grab a coffee before his first patient arrives. As he turns the corner he becomes conscious that something is wrong. Carmen is standing on the footpath, chatting to the owner of the Laundromat downstairs.

Spying Joe, she lets out a sympathetic hiccup and hugs him. 'Someone broke in,' she says in a dramatic whisper. 'They made such a mess.'

Joe holds her away and glances at the outer door, which shows no signs of damage. 'Have you called the police?'

She nods.

'Did you touch anything?'

'No.'

Joe sends Carmen home, ignoring her protests. Then he climbs three flights of stairs, stepping over broken glass outside his office door. On the opposite side of the corridor is a bathroom. A wet stain leaks across the carpet. Joe pushes open the door. The cistern has been kicked from the wall and papers are wedged into the toilet bowl.

Entering the office, he finds more damage. Carmen's Ficus tree is lying on its side, the clay pot shattered, spilling soil onto the carpet. His matching leather armchairs have been slashed open, gaping like carcasses at a slaughterhouse. The glass coffee table is undisturbed but has been decorated with a brown turd that curls like a cinnamon scroll.

Files are scattered across the floor. Joe steps over them and takes a handkerchief from his pocket. He covers his fingers and lifts the catch on the window, sliding it upwards. Leaning out, he looks at the fire escape and a rear courtyard full of rubbish bins and flattened cardboard boxes. A lone pigeon flutters from the rooftop. Joe turns and studies the office again. As each moment passes the scene appears more like a reproduction, skilfully done, the details exact yet lacking authenticity.

Retreating downstairs, he waits two hours for the police. In the meantime he calls a locksmith and a glazier and a cleaning company, putting them on standby. The two constables introduce themselves as Collie and Denholm. Barely out of probation, they're wearing new uniforms, yet have an end-of-shift weariness, as though they've seen a dozen burglaries since breakfast.

Joe follows them upstairs, listening to the squeaking of their leather belts that dangle with police paraphernalia. One of them takes notes and the other has a digital camera.

'Has anything been taken, sir?' asks Collie.

'I don't know.'

'Cash?'

'I don't keep money on the premises.'

'Maybe they were looking for drugs.'

'I'm not a doctor.'

'Kids are so dumb they don't know the difference.'

'You think it was kids?'

Denholm has black button-shaped eyes like a sparrow. 'We see a lot of burglaries like this, sir.

Kids get excited. They trash the place for no reason. They shit. They're like dogs, leaving their mark.'

'I don't think it was kids,' says Joe.

The constable seems surprised to be contradicted. 'You have a different theory?'

'Whoever did this came up the fire escape and through the window.'

'What about the office door?' asks Denholm.

'It was broken afterwards. Half the glass is lying outside, which means the door was partially open.'

Joe takes them to the office window, sliding it upwards. Stepping onto the narrow fire escape, he crouches and points to the edge of the window where the paint has been broken.

'Someone used a gemmy or a crowbar. You can see how the top latch has been bent and re-attached. You might pull fingerprints from the fire escape but he probably wore gloves.'

'Gloves?'

'Yes. I think the burglar *wants* us to assume it was kids because he was looking for something specific. He only trashed my office once he'd found it.'

'But you said nothing was missing,' says PC Denholm.

Joe points to the spilled files. 'These were taken out and searched at the desk. They were only scattered after he'd finished, which is why they've fallen like cards from a dealer's shoe. The flooded bathroom and faeces were afterthoughts, attempts to misdirect. You might get DNA from the faeces, although it's difficult to single out individual DNA because of the bacteria. More likely it's not human. He picked it up in a park.'

The constables look at each other. Neither of them wants to collect a sample.

'What was he looking for?' asks Denholm.

'I don't know. I'll have to go through the files.'

'Did you have them backed up?'

'Of course.'

PC Collie is being summoned on his shoulder radio. He turns his head into the microphone. They're wanted on a more urgent job. The constables make appropriate noises about catching the perpetrator, but Joe knows that's unlikely. There is a protocol with crimes like this one. They're only investigated if deemed solvable using 'proportionate resources'. That means there must be clear evidence pointing to a suspect, such as fingerprints or CCTV footage, which makes an arrest likely. Without these factors, this robbery will be written up, filed and forgotten.

After they've gone, Joe clears a space on his desk and starts sorting through the files. Someone broke into his office and tried to cover their tracks. He won't know what they were searching for until he knows what's missing.

CHAPTER 7

Marnie measures time differently now. There is the period *before* Daniel and the period *after*. She has drawn up a list of resolutions since yesterday. Number one: change the answering machine message. This might not seem like an especially important resolution, but she's been listening to that outgoing message for more than a year just to hear Daniel's voice. Nursing the machine on her lap, she presses the button again.

Hello, you've reached Daniel and Marnie. We can't come to the phone just now, but leave a message after the tone.

Raising her finger she hits delete and follows the instructions to record a new message:

Hi, this is Marnie. Leave a message at the beep.

Short. Unoriginal. Functional.

She sets the machine to ring eight times before it answers. That way she can screen out the prank callers and nutjobs who think it's funny to abuse her or pretend they have information. One in particular likes calling her – a man with a raspy thin voice, who sounds like he smokes too much.

'I know where your husband is,' he says. 'I know where you buried him.'

Another caller asks if she's lonely and what she's wearing. His voice is vaguely familiar and she can hear his fist furiously working.

Marnie hangs up on them, but dutifully records the date, time and content of the calls so that she can tell her police liaison officer, PC Rhonda Firth. Rhonda told Marnie to note every phone call because it might be important. She also told her not to give up hope, but now Marnie wonders what 'hope' is supposed to look like. She imagines it as a small animal – a bird perhaps – perched in her ribcage, fluttering occasionally.

Not surprisingly, Marnie was a suspect for a while, although nobody told her that officially or unofficially. Nor did they apologise for the awkward questions and the DNA tests and the vital days that were lost. The police think an apology is an admission of failure, but sorry can just mean sorry.

On Daniel and Marnie's first date they argued about politics. Daniel thought the British Royals were an anachronism.

'That's because you're Australian,' Marnie told him.

'What's that got to do with it?'

'You're still smarting about our ball-and-chain tourism policy.'

'So you're starting already with the convict jokes.'

'I could have started with foreplay jokes.'

Then he smiled. 'You're making fun of me.'

'Are you upset?'

'I'll get over it.'

They went to dinner at a cute Italian restaurant in Hampstead. Daniel began talking about sport. Marnie flicked him hard on the right ear.

'What was that for?'

'You can watch sport and play sport and talk about it with your friends, but when you're with me we talk about something else.'

'That doesn't seem very fair.'

'I have no-go areas,' she said. 'If I talk about shoes or period cramps you can pull me up.'

'So what do we talk about?'

'Feminism. The single currency. *Coronation Street*. Are you the sort of journalist who makes up lies?'

'No.'

'Good.'

Daniel looked back at her for a full ten seconds. 'You're truly something.'

'Yes I am,' said Marnie, feeling pleased with herself. 'There's something else you should know about me. I have a daughter.'

'Oh.'

'Is that a problem?'

'I don't eat children, if that's what you're worried about.'

'Good to know.'

Later that night she kissed him on the doorstep. He wanted to come inside. 'Another time,' she said, before closing the door.

Marnie paid Zoe's babysitter and walked her down the stairs. Daniel was still waiting outside.

'You're still here.'

'I'll still be here tomorrow morning,' he replied.

She invited him inside, whispering for him to be quiet. Before she could shut the door his hands were on her body. They had sex. Later, they had sex again. Sleeping with a man on the first date was something Marnie had promised herself she would never do. In the morning Daniel left early for a skiing holiday in Italy with three of his mates. Pre-planned. Booked. Paid for.

'I'll call you when I get back,' he told her.

'Yes, you will,' she said.

Only he didn't call. She waited a month. Heard nothing. She went from angry to furious and then hating him and then chastising herself for being so naïve as to confuse flirtation and sex with anything deeper. And then he turned up one day at her father's house, asking for her number. She didn't return his calls. He sent her flowers. She didn't respond. One lunch hour she was sitting in the spring sunshine in Green Park, with her skirt pulled up to get some colour into her legs, when Daniel sat down next to her.

'I'm here to apologise.'

'You've done that already.'

'I'm really, really sorry.'

'So you said.'

He told her the story of the accident. He shattered his knee on a black run and had to be stretchered off the mountain and airlifted to hospital. He showed her the scars from his surgery.

'I've forgotten you,' she said.

'I'd have done the same.'

'How is your knee?'

'It's fine. I'm cycling to get fit.' He tried to take her hand. 'That's why you didn't hear from me. I was concussed. I was hurt. Then I had weeks in a wheelchair and on crutches. I figured you wouldn't want a boyfriend who was a cripple.'

'You could have called.'

'I lost your number.'

'You knew my father's address.'

'I know, but I wanted two legs so I could sweep you off your feet.'

She stood up. 'I have to go to work.'

'Can I see you?'

'You can meet me here tomorrow for lunch.'

Daniel grinned.

'It's a sandwich not a date,' she said.

And that's how it began. It was another month before Marnie allowed him into her bed, but they didn't make love. She slept with her arm around him and her face pressed into his neck. In the morning they each averted their eyes as the other one dressed.

On the second night she let him kiss her. On the third night she let him take off her clothes. On the fourth night she opened her heart. Marnie had been married once before when barely out of her teens; but had no idea she was capable of being so ridiculously in love. She was full up with it. Overflowing. Daniel was the boy she should have waited for the first time. Gorgeous, funny, adventurous, romantic, smart, uncomplicated and laid-back, he was her big handsome Aussie bloke, her surf lifesaver, her Crocodile Dundee.

The sex was equally great. They collected locations: on a beach (Turkey), in a deck chair (Green Park), on the front seat of a Mini Cooper (not easy), in a rowing boat next to a herd of cows (uncomfortable) and in a medieval church during a rainstorm (sacrilegious).

They married at a registry office in Chelsea in the summer of 2008. Zoe was bridesmaid. Although it was the second time around for Marnie, it felt completely different because she had found a man who made up for all the things she didn't like about herself.

Daniel had been in London for three years, working casual shifts for various newspapers. Soon after the wedding he was offered a full-time job with the *Sunday Telegraph*, news rather than features, but that was OK. He loved working for a Sunday paper – the extra challenge of predicting where a big story would be by the weekend. He reported stories and broke them, always searching for the next exclusive.

He didn't have hobbies. When he opened his eyes every morning, he turned on the radio and listened to the news. Then he collected the papers from the doorstep, reading them over breakfast, cutting out paragraphs and tearing off pages as he constantly made notes.

A year after they married, Daniel was promoted to features editor, a meteoric rise, everybody said. He bought champagne for the staff and later trawled the casinos in Covent Garden and Soho. The promotion meant more money. They could save a bigger deposit and get a nicer house, perhaps in Clapham or Kingston.

Marnie knew she shouldn't make Daniel out to be perfect. He could be abrasive, opinionated, pig-headed and cruel. He hated when she pointed out his flaws, particularly his gambling, but he didn't go to the casino very often – normally only to celebrate a big exclusive or to commiserate about a story lost to the competition.

Unbeknown to Marnie, there were more lows than highs. The world of newspapers had begun changing. Readers were deserting 'dead-tree technology', fleeing to the internet where they expected to pay nothing for their news. Advertisers followed, chasing 'clicks' and certainty. Circulations crumbled. Budgets were slashed.

Daniel used to rail against the 'bean-counters' who were cutting expenses and curtailing overseas travel. They were hiring casuals instead of experienced journalists; buying agency copy instead of using staffers. These were publicly listed companies, answerable to shareholders, who were more inter-ested in the bottom line than breaking big stories and winning awards.

Management started laying people off. Daniel would call Marnie and say that he'd survived to fight another day. 'I'm just taking a few of the lads out for a farewell drink.'

These were colleagues. Mates. They went to the pub and then to a nightclub and at some point Daniel would find his way to the casino, playing cards or roulette. He would stumble home at three a.m. reeking of beer and curry, tip-toeing past the bedroom, trying not to wake the kids. Then he'd sit in the dark, watching TV.

'Come to bed,' she'd say.

'When the room stops spinning,' he'd reply, nursing a pint glass of water on his chest.

Marnie would watch him for a minute, her stomach in knots, wanting to say something, but not wanting to be the wife who nags.

'I know things are difficult right now.'

'You have no idea.'

'Tell me.'

'It's fine for you. You sit at home all day. I'm the one who has to earn the money.'

'I'm working.'

'Part-time. You're a waitress.'

'I'll go back full-time . . . get a job in advertising.'

'There are no jobs in advertising.'

When they fought it was over money. Daniel loved Zoe and Elijah, but seemed to resent how much they cost. He acted as though Marnie had never had a job, but that wasn't true. Before Elijah came along she was writing copy and earning almost as much as Daniel, but he didn't think her job was as important as his.

The final nail in his newspaper coffin was self-inflicted. Daniel thought he could take voluntary redundancy and 'walk across the road' into another job. *The Times* would snap him up or the *Guardian*, but none of them were hiring, not even the trade magazines he once laughed at.

For the first few months he tried to freelance, selling occasional pieces for shitty money. Marnie tried to be supportive, but Daniel would pick fights with her. He imagined her tallying up his short-comings, when in reality her heart was breaking for him. Her big Aussie bloke with the killer smile had become bitter and brittle, knotted inside like an overwound clock, angry with himself and everyone else.

His redundancy money should have lasted six months. Daniel gambled it away in two. He told Marnie he was paying contacts and researching stories that would get him 'back in the game'. One morning she picked up his wallet from the floor. It was bulging with receipts and ATM dockets. She searched through the cash withdrawals and noticed how many ATMs were adjacent to a casino. Five hundred pounds had been withdrawn the evening before. Forty pounds was all that was left.

Marnie could picture Daniel spending up big at the casino, splashing money around, big-noting himself. She found another piece of paper with a phone number and the name, 'Sam'. She pictured some firm-breasted TOWIE with a postage stamp dress and a be-jazzled vagina, pressing herself against Daniel, putting her glossy lips to his ear.

Then she told herself she was being ridiculous. 'Sam' was a man's name. Daniel would never have been unfaithful. When he married Marnie he said he was 'over the bullshit'. He had met the woman he wanted to spend the rest of his life with.

She shouldn't have mentioned the phone number. She could have kept quiet. Instead she opened her mouth. Daniel accused her of jumping to conclusions and acting like a shrill fishwife. Marnie hated quarrelling. She had seen other couples pick apart each other's flaws like carrion, but she and Daniel had never gone to bed without making up after an argument.

That day it changed. She didn't back down. Daniel didn't suffer in silence. Glass was broken. Tears were spilled. He grabbed his coat and stormed out. He didn't come home for two days.

'You don't understand,' he said, trying to apologise. 'I've been working since I was fourteen: every weekend, holidays, when I finished school . . . at university . . . I've always worked . . .'

'And you'll work again.'

'I had to try so much harder than anyone else to succeed. I was an outsider. I had to prove myself.'

'And you did!'

Things were better after that. Daniel took a part-time job teaching journalism at London College. Marnie imagined his classes were full of girls called Jacinta and Charlotte who dreamed of working for glossy magazines and dashing around Soho in designer heels, hailing cabs with a latte in one hand and mobile phone in the other. Why does everybody still want to be a journalist, she wondered. Thousands of bright young things were doing media courses and studying journalism when the jobs were disappearing and none of them actually read the publications they dreamed of working for.

Marnie talked of writing copy again, but who would look after Elijah? Maybe if he'd been healthier or once he started school, said Daniel. So he kept teaching (and secretly gambling) while their savings shrank in fits and bursts, tumbling through his fingers like discarded playing cards.

On the day he went missing, Marnie came home and found a half-filled vase in the sink and a bunch of flowers still wrapped in cellophane. A mug sat on the kitchen bench, instant coffee spooned inside, milk waiting, the kettle grown cold. It was as though he'd been interrupted in mid-thought and simply forgotten where to pick up the thread.

Marnie called his mobile. She kept calling. The next morning she phoned the police. A constable asked her if there was evidence of violence.

'What would that be?' she asked.

'Did you find blood or signs of a break-in?'

'No.'

'How long has he been missing?'

'Since yesterday.'

'We can't report someone missing until it's been forty-eight hours.'

'Why?'

'That's the rule.'

'It's a pretty stupid rule. What if something has happened to him? What if he's hurt?'

'He might have wanted to get away for a few days.'

The constable was younger than Marnie. He told her that most missing husbands turn up eventually, making Daniel sound like a stray dog being fed by a neighbour.

Two more days passed. By then Marnie had called every number in her contacts list, along with hospitals, clinics, homeless shelters and casinos. That's when the police assigned PC Rhonda Firth to keep her informed. The big-hipped black woman had hair woven into Rastafarian plaits, pinned tightly to her scalp. Smart, sturdy and good-natured, Rhonda was the sort of woman that Marnie once wished she could have as a friend because she didn't have any black friends and she thought it reflected badly on her.

Rhonda took notes and collected photographs, asking about Daniel's daily routines. Did he have any hobbies? Could he have been seeing someone else? Do you have his passport?

Marnie mentioned the gambling and casinos. She thought maybe Daniel had been followed home and mugged. Rhonda thought it unlikely. Already she seemed to have passed judgement, dismissing Daniel as a problem gambler who had abandoned his wife and children.

'Why aren't you out there looking for him?' Marnie asked. 'Why isn't his photograph all over the news?'

Rhonda smiled as though dealing with a child. 'We have to take into consideration Daniel's feelings.'

'His feelings?'

'What if he meant to run away? He might need some time to think. Maybe he's feeling emotionally fragile. If we plaster his face all over the news, it might make him do something foolish.'

'He's not going to kill himself,' said Marnie, growing frustrated. 'He's the least suicidal person you'll ever meet.'

Rhonda asked about their sex life. Did Marnie and Daniel have arguments? *Yes.* Had he ever been violent towards her? *No.* Was disappearing like this out of character? *Yes.* Could he have been having an affair? *No.*

Marnie heard herself answering, but couldn't make herself sound convincing.

'No offence,' said Rhonda, 'but sometimes the spouse is the last to know.'

'No offence,' replied Marnie, 'but more often they're the *first.*'

'Did your husband ever borrow money to gamble?'

Marnie hesitated. 'I don't think so. He was going to meetings.'

'What sort of meetings?'

'Gamblers Anonymous.'

'Could he have met someone there?'

'I'm sure he meets lots of people.'

'Someone special?'

The answer was still no.

Marnie remembered the name and phone number she found in Daniel's wallet, but she didn't mention the incident to Rhonda. Nor did she say how secretive Daniel had become, keeping odd hours and taking phone calls into other rooms. Instead Marnie sat on the sofa, bottling up her fear, one foot jittering up and down, listening to the policewoman talk about circulating Daniel's photograph and checking his mobile phone records.

'You want my advice,' said Rhonda as she was leaving. 'Pour yourself a glass of wine, take a long hot bath and call a girlfriend. Your husband is a big boy – he'll find his way home.'

CHAPTER 8

The *Evening Standard* has two paragraphs at the bottom of page four.

Police divers have spent a second day scouring the Thames beneath a pier at Wapping where the body of a security guard was pulled form the river on Tuesday morning. Niall Quinn, 35, a father of two from Kilburn, was found with his throat cut and hands bound with a plastic cable tie.

An incident room has been set up and police are asking for anyone with information to call their local Crimestoppers number.

Marnie reads the story again. She had no idea Quinn was married. He didn't wear a wedding ring. He'd never mentioned a wife or children. Their only conversations were about pick-up times and money. Perhaps 'security guard' is a euphemism for pimp or minder.

Penny is reading over her shoulder, holding the stem of a wine glass between her thumb and two manicured fingers. 'It's cocktail hour somewhere,' she told Marnie, when she arrived with the bottle. She finishes reading and dismisses the story with a *pfffft* sound.

'He had his throat cut,' says Marnie.

'He stomped all over you, the sadistic bastard, I'm glad he's dead.' Penny sets down her wine glass. 'Let me see.'

'I'm fine.'

'Show me.'

Marnie raises her blouse. Penny brushes her fingertips across the bruises. Even the slightest touch hits fresh sharp notes of pain.

She looks at Marnie guiltily. 'I should never have got you involved in this.'

'It's not your fault.'

She puts her arms around Marnie, who flinches.

'Too soon?'

'Still tender.'

The two of them have been friends since their second year at university. Drugs. Parties. Festivals. Holidays. Marnie had been the sensible, normal one, while Penny partied for England and tried to bed the entire team. Penny dropped out of university to become a model, but not one anyone will remember. She did a few Littlewoods catalogues and a shampoo commercial where they had her standing under a waterfall in Sweden. She nearly froze to death, she said, 'my nipples were like bullets'. That was the highlight of her career – a week in Stockholm, the Four Seasons Hotel, all

90

expenses paid, sleeping with the director. Penny was philosophical about her lack of subsequent success. She didn't have the height for the catwalk or the breasts for glamour modelling, but she'd fallen in love with the lifestyle by then.

She stopped working as an escort when she met Keegan – one of her better clients, she said, because he was single, sober and showered regularly. He was fifteen years older and slightly overweight, but he fell madly in love with Penny, whom he called his 'Pretty Woman'. Nobody else knew about her past except for Marnie. And Daniel, of course, who got quite turned on by the fact that Marnie's best friend had once been a prostitute.

So they married and Penny put away her condoms and slutty lingerie and became the corporate wife: beautiful, doting and expensive to keep. Motherhood wasn't quite so seamless. She fell pregnant unexpectedly and complained for the duration about stretch marks, water retention and being 'too fat to fuck'. She gave up smoking (ish) and drinking (ish) and demanded a Caesarean because 'the Kegster doesn't drive a big enough car for me to need a bigger garage'.

Since Abigail was born, Marnie and Penny haven't seen as much of each other, but they still talk on the phone every few days, less and less about Daniel, whom Penny calls a 'shitty husband' and a 'fuck-up' for abandoning his family.

Penny's legs are entwined, one foot hitched behind an ankle. She notices the bottle of painkillers on the counter. 'Ooh, blue ones and yellow ones. Lucky old you!'

Marnie doesn't laugh because it hurts. She changes the subject quite suddenly, as though afraid that she might lose the courage if she doesn't act immediately.

'I'm going to have him declared dead.'

Penny is holding the wine glass to her lips. She lowers it again. 'Can you do that?'

'I have to do something.'

'What about Hennessy?'

'If I get the insurance money, I can pay him back.'

'You go, girl!' Penny slurs. 'It's about time.'

Marnie gazes across the table, not wanting to ask. 'I don't have any money.'

Penny's fingers are fidgeting on the stem of her glass. She begins speaking rapidly, stumbling over words.

'The Kegster has me on a tight leash at the moment. There wasn't a Christmas bonus last year. He said I couldn't give you any more money.'

'Of course,' says Marnie, 'I understand.'

'I would if I could.'

'I know.'

'I feel terrible.'

'Don't.'

The atmosphere has changed. Warmth has been swept away by guilt. Penny blinks, her eyes less bright, and looks at her watch. 'The nanny leaves at five. I should get home.'

At the door they touch cheeks. Penny's long

slender fingers make a peculiar gesture, moving sideways and up as though imparting some sort of blessing.

'He didn't deserve you,' she says. 'If he comes back, I'll kill him personally.'

Marnie searches for the business card that the lawyer gave her, fearing she may have lost it. She tips the contents of her bag onto the table. The card is stuck to a sweet wrapper.

Craig Bryant
G.K. & Associates
Barristers and Solicitors
34 Bank Chambers
Pryce Street, London

'Should you ever need a lawyer,' he had said to her in the cab. She needs one now.

They meet at the Cheshire Cheese in Fleet Street, a landmark pub from the days when printing presses rumbled in nearby basements and convoys of liveried trucks took bundles of newspapers on a race around the country to news-stands and corner shops. Daniel brought Marnie here once and spoke in hushed, almost reverential tones about the famous journalists and writers associated with the pub, like Dickens and Twain and Tennyson. There were other names she didn't recognise but they rolled off Daniel's tongue as though she should have known them.

'This place is older than European settlement in Australia,' he said. 'Makes me realise that we have no history.'

'Give it a few more centuries,' she told him.

Alone at a table, Marnie glances at the door, practising what she's going to say to Craig Bryant. She sees him first. He's standing on the far side of the road, holding up his mobile phone as though taking a photograph.

Tall and loose-limbed, the lawyer is dressed in the same dark suit but today has a tie the colour of a cut watermelon. Crossing the road, he jinks between traffic and acknowledges her with a smile. Wide. White. He's like a model in a commercial for toothpaste, minus the toothbrush and the jingle.

'So who did you kill?' he asks, pulling up a chair.

Marnie flinches.

'Hey, I'm only joking.'

She smiles tightly and her stomach flips over.

'Have you ordered something? What would you like? Wine? Beer?'

'Nothing. I'm fine.'

'Please don't let me drink alone.'

'White wine.'

'I know just the one.'

Bryant goes to the bar and orders two glasses. Marnie watches the way his suit hangs from his shoulders. Well cut. Expensive. She feels frumpy and out of practice.

When the lawyer returns, he sets down her wine. She holds the glass in both hands. Sips.

'Is this Cloudy Bay?'

'You like it?'

'It's my favourite.'

Bryant raises his glass. 'Great minds.'

Unbuttoning his suit jacket, he lets it flare out as he leans back in his chair.

'So what can I do for you, Marnie Logan?'

'I want my husband declared dead.'

The statement arrives at a lull in the background noise. People turn from nearby tables. Marnie feels her cheeks grow hot, but looks up and meets their stares as though challenging them. People look away.

Bryant brushes his fingers against her hand. Her eyes return to his.

'You believe he's dead?'

'Yes.'

'Do you have any evidence?'

Marnie fidgets with the strap of her shoulder bag and relates the details of Daniel's disappearance and the police investigation. She tries not to leave anything out – mentioning the gambling debts and Patrick Hennessy.

'And you've told the police this?'

Marnie hesitates.

'They know most of it.'

The lawyer lets her answer hang in the air for a moment. He seems to make a decision. 'Normally you have to wait seven years to have a missing person declared dead.'

'I know.'

'Why is it so important. Why now?'

'Daniel had a life insurance policy and the company won't pay out unless I produce a death certificate.'

'So it's about the money?'

Marnie is tired of feeling guilty. 'I'm not trying to steal from anyone. I can't even change Daniel's direct debits or access the little money in his accounts. I'm getting legal letters. The Inland Revenue claim he owes money. I tried to explain that he was missing, but they accused me of lying. Three days ago I sold the TV. I've borrowed from everyone I know. Friends. Family. They don't return my calls any more.'

Bryant runs his finger down the edge of the glass. 'It's not my field.'

'Please?'

'From what I've read it's a crazy paving of legislation, all sorts of statutory and non-statutory provisions. Under normal circumstances the courts assume a person to be dead when there's no evidence of his or her continued existence.'

'For seven years?'

'Yes, but that's a common law presumption. It can sometimes be rebutted with the right evidence.'

'What evidence?'

'You have to convince a judge that your husband can't possibly be alive.'

'How do I do that?

'You exhaust every avenue. You get statements from people, his family, friends, colleagues; you tick the boxes. Then we go to court and see what happens.'

Bryant takes out a yellow legal notepad from his briefcase.

'I can't afford to pay you,' says Marnie.

'You don't know how much I cost.'

'More than I can afford.'

He reaches across the table and takes her hand, lacing his fingers in hers.

'We'll work it out later.'

Something shifts inside her stomach. 'But I don't want—'

'You're going to do most of the work, Marnella.'

'How do you know my name?'

'I figured Marnie was short for something.'

Blinking away a film of moisture, she watches him writing notes on the pad.

'Did Daniel have mental problems?'

'No.'

'Was he depressed?'

'No.'

'You said he had gambling debts.'

'Yes.'

'OK. You need to get affidavits from Daniel's parents and his closest friends, saying they're convinced he's dead – all the people who knew him best. How old is your eldest daughter?'

'Fifteen.'

'Get an affidavit from her.'

'I haven't told her yet.'

'Well she needs to know.'

Bryant jots another note to himself. 'We can try an application under the Non-Contentious Probate Rules. It allows a judge to grant an applicant leave to swear to the death of a person to the best of his or her information or belief.'

'Will that work?'

'It's sometimes granted in cases where a death is presumed rather than proven, but I can't promise anything. Best-case scenario, a judge will grant probate, allowing you to administer your husband's affairs, but it still won't guarantee that your insurance company will pay up.'

'Why?'

'They might not accept the order. How much is the policy worth?'

'Three hundred thousand pounds. I don't need it all,' says Marnie, self-consciously.

'You deserve it.'

'I mean . . .'

'Your husband is dead. You're owed the money.'

Marnie nods gratefully.

Bryant stands and hovers over Marnie for a few seconds. 'Do you need money now?'

'No, you've done enough.'

'Do you still have my business card?' He takes it from her and writes his mobile phone number on the back. He returns the card. 'If you need anything.'

'Why are you doing this?' she asks, moved by his kindness.

The lawyer opens his palms. 'We're neighbours.'

CHAPTER 9

Joe O'Loughlin lifts his head from his desk and glances at his vandalised office. The blinds are open and afternoon sunlight slants diagonally across the floor, painting a bright rhombus on the stained rug.

He has spent the past six hours rescuing files, collating the scattered pages, creating some semblance of order. Rising from his desk he goes to the bathroom and splashes water on his face, drinking every second mouthful.

A file is missing, his clinical notes on Marnie Logan. A tiny metronome of concern ticks within him, rocking from side to side in his mind. Something familiar. Something unbidden.

His left arm is jerking and his body begins to gyrate and twist. Joe takes a small pillbox from his pocket and swallows his medication. Then he waits for his brain to acknowledge the drugs. He imagines how forces of good are meeting the enemy in his cerebral cortex, circling like fighting fish, calling a truce. Mr Parkinson is a patient man. He knows that science moves slower than the disease.

Back in his office, Joe picks up the phone and

calls Paddington police station. He asks to speak to PC Denholm or PC Collie. Waiting, he watches the sun slip drunkenly behind the rooftops, stretching shadows from chimney pots and TV aerials.

Denholm answers. 'Professor O'Loughlin, what can I do for you?'

'You asked if anything was missing. A file was taken. Clinical notes for one of my female patients.'

'Her name?'

'Marnella Logan.'

'What was in the file?'

'I can't discuss that.'

'What use would it be to anyone?'

'I don't know.'

The constable sighs, bored rather than frustrated. 'Thank you for your help, Professor.'

Vincent Ruiz sits on the edge of the Thames, watching the river turn various shades of gold before its features blend into the darkness. The former detective has always had a soft spot for London, which wears its history like a tattered cloak. The city is a motley collection of villages full of people with various accents, who support opposing football teams, pay assorted rates and vote for different political parties. How is it possible to travel by black cab between Brick Lane and Richmond? Surely it should involve an ocean voyage or jetlag.

Solid rather than overweight, Ruiz has maintained

many of his routines since he retired from the Metropolitan Police. He doesn't drink before six in the evening unless he has company. He doesn't watch daytime TV or anything masquerading as being based on reality. He reads the newspapers, does the *Times* crossword and fishes from a deckchair without any bait on his hook. More importantly, he doesn't argue or try to contend with the nature of the world. He prefers to appear ambivalent, as though he no longer gives a shit.

His mobile phone is ringing. He ignores it.

From across the road he hears the sound of a garage band rehearsing, displaying more volume than talent. That's another sign of age, he thinks, believing that each new generation of music is inferior to the one before. And while the eternal song in Ruiz's heart puts him at forty, the reality of his birth certificate puts him closer to a free bus pass. This doesn't make him old – not in his own mind. Instead the years have brought a mixed bag – greater wisdom, less patience and more bad memories than any man needs.

His phone rings again.

'Greetings, Professor.'

'Are you busy?'

'I'm flitting to and fro.'

'You're in the pub?'

'Heading there now.'

'I was robbed this morning.'

'Mugged?'

'Burgled. The office. A patient's file was taken.'

'Any idea why?'

'None.'

'What about the police?'

'Next to useless – no offence.'

'None taken.'

Ruiz takes a tin of boiled sweets from his pocket and unscrews the lid. Choosing a coloured rock between his thumb and forefinger, he pops it into his mouth, enjoying the sweetness on his tongue and how it rattles against his teeth.

'And you called me because . . .?'

'The team needs you.'

'What team?'

'Pick a team – it needs you.'

'Do I have a choice?'

'Sure you do – you can say *yes* any way you like. You can do it in a funny voice if you want to.'

'Very droll, for that you can buy me dinner, but it can't be tonight. I'm otherwise engaged.'

'Tomorrow then.'

CHAPTER 10

Marnie waits until Elijah is asleep and Zoe is doing homework before she phones Daniel's parents in Australia. She closes the door and sits on the sofa, drawing her legs beneath her.

The time difference is nine hours, which means she's contacting people who have already woken tomorrow. Rosemary and Norman Hyland live in one of those gated-style resort communities on the Gold Coast with man-made canals, security patrols, hundreds of by-laws and nothing but white, tanned faces.

Normally she calls Daniel's parents once a week and puts Elijah on the phone to say hello to his grandparents. The conversations are polite and trivial with no mention made of Daniel until the very end because the news doesn't change.

The phone is ringing. Marnie can picture the scene – the sunshine, pastel colours and lawns that look like golfing greens. Norman will be dressed in long shorts, boating shoes and a polo shirt. Rosemary plays tennis every day and looks like she's slowly petrifying. Marnie knows what they think of her. She is the uppity English princess who stole their son's heart and kept him away from Australia to punish them. She is also bossy, demanding, whiny, needy – everything she fights so hard not to be.

When Daniel went missing, Marnie waited forty-eight hours before she called them. In those days she could never get the time difference right and there is no harmless reason for calling someone at 3.00 a.m.

Rosemary answered the phone. 'What is it?' she asked. 'Is it one of the kiddies?'

'No.'

'Let me talk to Daniel.'

Marnie's throat closed. 'Have you heard from him?'

'No. Why?'

'I should have called sooner.'

'What's happened?'

'He's missing. Nobody has seen him for two days.'

'Oh my God. Norman. Wake up. Wake up. It's Daniel.'

They barked questions down the phone. Marnie managed to keep her calm. She comforted them. She gave them a number for the police liaison officer. Before she hung up, she heard her father-in-law's voice, saying, 'It's all that bitch's fault – he should never have been in England.'

A week later they flew to London. Marnie met them at Heathrow, but they didn't want to stay at the flat. Instead they took a hotel room around the corner. Norman talked to the police directly. He told Marnie he'd 'put a rocket under them'.

Rosemary couldn't understand why the British newspapers were ignoring the story. Why wasn't Daniel front-page news?

Rhonda Firth tried to explain. 'Do you know how many people go missing every year in this country: two hundred thousand. Most of them don't make the headlines because they turn up eventually.'

But Daniel wasn't just *anyone*. Norman stalked the streets like a vengeful boxer and put the police offside by accusing them of being idiots. Meanwhile, Rosemary rediscovered her English accent and added her middle name when she introduced herself to people. She came to the flat every day, baked and ironed, fussed over the children, told Zoe she was too pale and needed to spend some time in Australia. Marnie felt like a guest in her own flat.

She hated the way her in-laws talked to each other. Norman rarely used Rosemary's first name. He called her 'woman' or 'wife' and disparaged her when she offered an opinion he didn't agree with. 'What would you know, woman?' he'd say, or 'You're talking nonsense, woman.' Or Marnie's favourite: 'Make yourself pretty, wife, and leave the thinking to me.'

After a month in London they flew back to Australia. Neither of them said goodbye or offered

Marnie any words of encouragement. The gambling issue was the catalyst. Norman and Rosemary refused to believe their blue-eyed boy could have racked up such debts. They accused Marnie of lying or spending the money herself. It was only later that Marnie discovered that her in-laws had given a statement to the police before leaving, accusing her of having murdered Daniel. It was obvious, they said, because she 'wasn't crying enough'.

Despite her hurt and anger, Marnie hasn't stopped calling them or sending them photographs of Elijah and Zoe. Twice she has asked them for money and each time Norman has lectured her about being more careful with her pennies, suggesting that they move to Australia.

The phone is still ringing. Rosemary answers.

'Hello, it's Marnie.'

'I'll get Norman.'

'Actually I wanted to talk to you.'

'Me?'

'Yes.'

'Will it take long? I'm playing tennis this morning.'

'It won't take a minute.'

The line has a delay, which echoes Marnie's voice back to her. She's planned what she's going to say, but it comes out in a rush, sounding too strident and desperate.

'I talked to a lawyer today about how I can access Daniel's life insurance. We need the money. Elijah isn't putting on weight. He needs to see a specialist.' This bit isn't a complete lie but Marnie still feels guilty. 'The lawyer said it might be possible to get a court to declare Daniel dead if enough people swear to the fact. If a judge grants probate, I can administer Daniel's affairs. I can access his bank accounts and get the insurance money.'

'You want his money?'

Marnie can hear a click. Someone has picked up the extension.

'It's a life insurance policy. Daniel set it up for the family. I think he'd want us to have—'

Norman has been listening. 'So this is your new plan? You want to steal his money.'

'It's not *his* money.'

'Found a new boyfriend, have you? Want a divorce?'

'No, no, it's nothing like that.'

'He's our son and he's not dead until we say he's dead. You hear me? You try a stunt like this and I'll fucking destroy you. I'll sue for custody. I'll take my grandchildren away from you. Are you listening?'

'I'm sorry,' says Marnie, her heart hammering. 'I didn't mean . . . I was trying to think of Zoe and Elijah.'

'Don't you dare use our grandchildren as an excuse! We always knew what you were like. What he ever saw in you – God only knows!'

Marnie's throat is closing. She can't talk. Norman is still yelling at her. She hangs up. Shaking.

Zoe is standing in the doorway, framed by the light. She's wearing three-quarter-length pyjama bottoms and Daniel's old pyjama top. The sight of it plucks at something in Marnie, an invisible string seems to vibrate against her heart.

'Why were you talking about Dad being dead?' Zoe asks.

'I'm trying to make things right.'

'How?'

'If a judge says he's dead, the insurance company will pay out.'

Zoe's hair is flattened by the humidity. Her hands are resting defiantly on her hips. 'You think he's dead!'

'Daniel wouldn't just leave us like this. He loved us too much.'

'That doesn't mean he's dead.'

'I'm trying to be realistic.'

'You're giving up on him.'

'No.'

'Bullshit! You want to take the cash and forget all about him.'

'That's not true.'

Zoe is a physical girl, quick to anger, quick to forgive. In the space of a heartbeat her expression changes. It's like a curtain being drawn across her eyes or something darker taking control. 'How long have you been planning this?'

'I saw a lawyer today.'

'You said you wouldn't keep things from me.'

'I was going to tell you.'

'You can't just do this. You can't randomly decide to have him declared dead.'

'Where do you think he is, Zoe?'

'I don't know.'

'The police have looked. Interpol. Immigration. Nobody has heard from him.'

'It's only been—'

'Thirteen months.'

'So that's it! Fuck off, Dad! Get out of our lives.'

'That's not what I said.'

'But that's what you mean.'

'Daniel had debts. He borrowed a lot of money from a gangster and I'm supposed to pay it back or something bad is going to happen.'

'Tell the police.'

'It's not that simple.'

'You're making it harder.'

'With the insurance money we can start again. I can get Elijah well. You can have a laptop. We can get another TV.'

'I don't give a shit about a TV.'

Zoe's eyes are brimming. Marnie hasn't seen her cry since . . . since . . . she can't remember. Crossing the room, she holds out her arms, wanting to hold her.

Zoe shrugs her away. 'Have you found someone else? Is it that guy who picks you up in his car?'

'It's nothing like that.'

'I've seen the condoms in your bag. You take them with you when you go out. Are you sleeping with him?'

109

'I'm not seeing anyone else.'

'You're a liar!'

Zoe spins away, sucking in loud gulps of air, her face mottled with anger. Marnie tries to stop her, but Zoe ducks under her arms. Marnie tries again, hugging her like a drunken dance partner.

'Let me go!'

'Just listen to me.'

'Let me go or, I swear I'll . . .'

Zoe drops her head. It feels like an act of surrender. Marnie relaxes. Zoe uses the moment, jerking her head upwards. The back of her skull smashes into Marnie's chin. Her teeth crunch together. Her lip is caught in between, punctured, bleeding.

Zoe slips away, slamming her bedroom door. Marnie goes to the kitchen and takes ice from the freezer, wrapping it in a washcloth and holding it against her lip until the bleeding stops.

There used to be a cinema on Oldham Road called the Empress Electric Theatre, although most people called it the Old Empress. It was a Grade II listed building until it burned down in 2006. When I was growing up, before I started school and afterwards during the holidays, my mother would drop me at the cinema every morning, buying a ticket and telling me to stay there until she came back. If I hid between sessions, avoiding the ushers and the projectionists, I could spend all day watching the same films over and over, sucking on sweets that fell between the seats.

I saw King Kong tumble from the Empire State Building and David Bowie fall to earth. I saw Sandy turning slutty for Danny, De Niro doing his best De Niro, Peter Finch getting mad as hell and Ripley in her little white knickers nursing a cat while battling an alien. I saw sex movies and horror movies, psychopaths and heroes, killer sharks, mass murderers, bumbling detectives, adventurers, vampires, zombies, body snatchers, cowboys, Indians, boxers, prostitutes, gunslingers, gangsters, princesses, witches, wizards, dragons and dragon slayers. I saw all life and death, love and hate, ruin and redemption.

One day I grew bored of seeing the same movie, so I sat in the orchestra pit with my back to the screen, watching the audience. I could see the front few rows, the wide eyes and pale faces, chewing on their popcorn and sipping their drinks with their faces canted backwards a little, lips parted, lost in blissful ignorance of self, of surroundings, of me . . .

After that I didn't bother with the movies any more. I spent every possible moment with my back to the screen, watching people as they watched. The twitchy light slid across their faces and the images flashed in their eyes, as the projector spun in the small room above their heads, creating a beam of light that caught the dust motes and cigarette smoke. I saw them laugh at the wisecracks, sob at the sad endings and scream as they peeked through their chinked fingers. I saw them pashing, fingering and fucking. I saw a Tuesday pensioner close her eyes and not wake up; and a woman go into labour, her waters breaking on an upper aisle. I saw the dirty old men playing pocket billiards in their overcoats and prostitutes giving blow-jobs in the back row.

I have been back to that old cinema, which is now a pile of rubble behind a wooden fence dotted with flyers and posters. I have walked along the familiar streets, standing in all weathers to watch the places that punctuated my childhood. Most remain painfully recognisable. At one house in Manchester I carved my name in a Jacaranda tree. It's still there. I've checked.

I have ridden the same buses looking through dirty windows at the same schools, recognising every change of gear by the dip of the clutch and the sound of the engine. My life is like that. I listen for the vibrations and know where I am. Once I knocked on one of the doors and heard someone shuffling down the corridor. I felt myself straighten. My insides held. An old woman appeared. I thought for a moment I was going to recognise her. I thought she might recognise me. But it wasn't anyone I knew. The family had moved on, she said. I looked hard at her faded blue eyes, seeing if she was lying.

When you watch someone like I do, you learn to read their moods and mannerisms, spotting the lies they tell and the ways they disguise the truth. Ever since I can remember I have seen how people lived and died, fellated and fornicated, loved and lost. I have followed their lives like I'm watching a soap opera – my own version of *Coronation Street or EastEnders or Days of Our Lives*.

Mrs Ferndale, a woman who lived two streets away, caught me looking through the window when I was eleven and beat me with a wooden spoon. Mum said she'd 'tear the bitch a new one' if she ever touched me again. Then she hit me herself for being 'a little pervert'. I had to look 'pervert' up in the dictionary. It said I was someone whose sexual behaviour is regarded as abnormal and unacceptable. I didn't understand. I didn't care about sex. I simply wanted to watch.

CHAPTER 11

Marnie walks through the arched portico into the College Building at City University. As she passes the reception desk, she flashes Daniel's employee lanyard, giving the security guard no chance to study the photograph. Instead, she pretends to be chatting on her mobile, too busy to stop.

She's almost at the stairs.

'Excuse me, miss?'

She turns. The security guard approaches. Tall. Black. 'You dropped this,' he says, handing her Daniel's office key.

Marnie accepts it, still holding the lanyard tightly in her fist.

'You're new around here.'

'Just started,' she says. 'Library services.'

'You've come through the wrong door.'

'I have to see Professor Bradshaw.'

'Second floor. Have a good day.'

She wants to say, 'You, too,' but can't get the words out.

Climbing the stairs, she steps aside for students who are too busy typing text messages or dialling up music to watch where they're going. One boy bumps into her and reacts as though he's been infected.

The last time Marnie visited the university she had argued with the vice-chancellor, who threatened to have her arrested for trespassing. Her request for Daniel's personal effects had been passed between various departments, up the chain of command, until it reached the vice-chancellor. She waited four hours. The message came back. The locker was her husband's private property and couldn't be opened without a warrant or approval from the University Executive Team.

'You could make a written application,' she was told. 'Provide us with evidence.'

'What sort of evidence?'

'A letter from your husband.'

'My *missing* husband?'

'I can see that might be a problem,' said the vice-chancellor, who refused to give way.

Now she's back again, without a warrant or a letter, taking matters into her own hands. On reaching the third floor, she stops outside an office door, unsure if she's in the right place. She only visited Daniel once after he took a job at the university. She and Elijah decided to surprise him, bringing him his favourite iced coffee. They spied him on the stairs, surrounded by bright young things, girls with wedged haircuts, skinny-legged jeans and tight tops who talked in breathless sentences, using the word 'like' as a punctuation point. Daniel was telling them newspaper stories, colourful, behind-the-scenes anecdotes and untold truths that couldn't be written because of libel laws or public sensibilities.

He looked so relaxed. Happy. Handsome. And these young wannabes were hanging on his every word. Marnie could picture them, flirting with Daniel, leaning over his desk. He had such an easy smile, which is why he was so successful as a journalist. People opened their doors, invited him inside and poured out their hearts.

Marnie had felt a pang of jealousy. These girls would make him happy. They would laugh at his jokes and give him sex when he wanted. They would straddle him on the sofa at halftime during the football and fetch him beers from the fridge and blow him when it was their time of the month. They wouldn't have two children or stretch marks or grey roots poking through their fringe.

She remembered how he used to be; how he'd come home after the Saturday-night deadline, hyped about an exclusive story, beer-loose and horny. He'd squeeze her in his strong arms. Fondle her breasts.

'God, I love you,' he'd say.

'We have to wait until Zoe is asleep.'

'She won't hear us.'

Marnie would let him kiss her. Feel his hands slide lower, his fingers searching. His hardness.

She tries to remember the last time something like that happened – spontaneous, sweaty, passionate sex – but can't fix it in her mind. So much about their lives had become routine. Days rolled into weeks and months and then blended to form one amorphous mass that felt like existence rather than living.

All of these things ran through her mind as she watched the girls flirting with her husband, but she forced the images away and scolded herself for being stupid. Guiding the pushchair along the corridor, she called Daniel's name and waved.

Instead of being pleased to see her and Elijah, he reacted strangely, as though embarrassed about having a wife and a child. Marnie felt a pang of hurt.

The office door is locked. Trying the key, the handle turns and she peers inside. There are two desks. Daniel used to share the office with another part-time lecturer. Boxes of books and papers are stacked like bricks to form a precarious wall between two filing cabinets and matching lockers. Old newspapers have been collected in the corner, yellowing at the edges, rising towards the windowsill as though searching for the light.

Daniel's desk is nearest the window. Marnie notices the dirty coffee cup and a photograph of a different family. Someone else has been using it.

'Can I help you?'

A man is standing in the doorway. Marnie vaguely recognises him from somewhere. Perhaps Daniel introduced them.

'I'm Marnie Logan,' she says. 'Daniel's wife.'

'Of course you are,' he replies, not giving his

name. 'I didn't realise you were coming.' He is still in the doorway. 'Is everything all right? Have you heard any news?'

'No news.'

'Oh.'

'I'm here to pick up Daniel's things.'

'Right. Well. Don't let me stop you.'

He has a narrow face and thick eyebrows that look glued on rather than natural. He's holding his cigarettes and is redolent with the after-effects of a visit to the pavement or the roof.

'I never got a chance to say how much we miss Daniel,' he says. 'I wanted to call. I didn't know what to say.'

'That's OK.'

'Must be hard – not knowing.'

'Yes.'

'Am I talking too much? You're probably sick of people asking you questions.'

'You're fine. About Daniel's things . . .?'

'They've been moved.'

'His locker?'

'I cleared that out too,' he says. 'The department needed the space. I put them in a box. They're in the storeroom.'

Typical, thought Marnie. The university had refused her access on privacy grounds and then dumped her husband's things in a storeroom.

'I was wondering when someone would call you,' he says, opening his desk drawer and rummaging inside. 'You have children, don't you?'

'A boy and a girl.'

Another nod.

'I'm sorry, I don't remember your name,' says Marnie.

The man blinks at her and frowns as though searching for his name. 'Jeremy,' he says eventually, adding his surname as an afterthought. 'Holland.'

He holds the set of keys aloft, surprised at having found them.

'The storeroom is just down the corridor.'

Marnie follows him, answering his questions with nods and murmurs rather than risk telling an outright lie. He unlocks the door. Triggers the light. There are metal shelves on three walls rising to the ceiling. A cleaner's trolley is parked in the centre, sprouting brooms and mops.

'I'm sure I put it somewhere back here.'

Squeezing between the shelves and the trolley, he begins moving cartons and equipment aside.

'Ah, here it is.'

He lifts a box free and carries it into the corridor.

'Do you have a car?'

'I came by train.'

'How are you going to get this home?'

'I'll manage.'

Marnie holds out her arms and takes the box, staggering slightly under the weight.

'Maybe I'll sort through it here,' she says.

'Of course, you can use the office.'

Back at Daniel's old desk, she slices open the

packing tape and folds back the cardboard flaps. Jeremy sits at his desk, pretending to mark papers, but sneaking glances at Marnie, looking at her legs. He mumbles something that Marnie can't quite hear.

'Pardon?' she asks.

'What?'

'You said something.'

'No, I mean, I don't think I did. I'm sorry.' Jeremy fumbles in his drawer for his cigarettes. 'I'm just going to pop outside. Won't be long.'

Marnie continues sorting through the contents, putting the personal items into a pile, including a framed photograph of the children that Zoe gave Daniel for Father's Day. There is a desk calendar, a diary and notebooks. A piece of fabric is tucked into the corner of the box. She pulls it free – a pair of women's underwear. Lacy. Black. Not hers. Marnie feels her throat constrict.

There are innocent explanations: a joke, a secret admirer, a souvenir confiscated from a male student, but Marnie has been here before. Zoe's father was a serial offender. Unfaithful. Unreliable. Dishonest. Daniel was different, she tells herself, holding the panties between her thumb and forefinger. She wants to drop them in the nearest wastepaper bin, but instead she puts them back in the box.

She finds Daniel's diary and address book. Flicking through the pages, she scans the names, numbers, notes and dates. Setting the diary aside, she lifts several magazines from the box. It takes her a moment to realise what they are – her old school year books as well as copies of a campus newspaper she edited in her last year before graduating.

At the bottom of the box is a cloth-covered album, once white, now a faded yellow. It's Marnie's baby book. Her birth certificate is glued to the first page, along with the hospital bracelet she wore when she was born. Weight charts. Vaccination certificates. Hearing tests. The rest of the book is taken up by dozens of photographs. Holidays. Picnics. Birthdays. Easter egg hunts. Her mother has written captions beneath the earliest images. Her stepmother was less diligent later.

Marnie's entire childhood is documented, every accomplishment noted. Report cards. Concert programmes. Diplomas. A Red Cross resuscitation course. Her bronze medallion. There are shots of Marnie in drama performances, playing hockey and dressed up for her graduation dance. The final two items in the box are a large red photo album and a compact digital recorder. The cover of the album is embossed in swirling gold letters, saying: 'This Is Your Life.'

Marnie remembers the TV show when Michael Aspel would surprise celebrities with the 'Big Red Book', gathering old friends and colleagues to tell stories. Opening the front page, Marnie sees her name and a photograph of her as a baby. Daniel's handwriting is underneath.

Marnella Louise Logan, it all began at St Mary's Hospital in Manchester on 20 June 1978, when you arrived in a screaming hurry in the wee hours of the morning. You couldn't even wait for the obstetrician to arrive.

There are more words and photographs. Chapter headings. Quotes. One picture shows Marnie in a pink tutu and ballet tights, aged six. In another she's playing Snow White in a school play. Daniel put this book together. This must have been why he had been so secretive, staying late at work and taking phone calls in other rooms. He was calling her old friends, tracking people from her past and collecting photographs. Jeremy has arrived back. He stands silently at the door.

'Find anything interesting?'

Marnie holds up the album. 'Did you know about this?'

'He wanted to surprise you.'

Marnie begins imagining the work involved and how the idea might have formed. She remembers the fight she had with Daniel a month before he went missing. She accused him of gambling away their future; losing the deposit they were saving. She went to bed. Daniel stayed up. Later she felt him come to bed. He pulled aside the strap of her nightdress and kissed her shoulder. He whispered that he was sorry, but Marnie pushed the blankets and sheets between them, not wanting him to touch her.

Later, she heard him get up and go the bathroom. He closed the door. After a long while she got out bed and tiptoed across the bedroom, pressing her ear to the bathroom door. She heard a sound like an animal in pain. Whimpering. Humiliated.

CHAPTER 12

It's five o'clock and the library is almost deserted. Unpacking her schoolbag, Zoe settles at her favourite desk. She likes how the light shines through the large arched windows and throws patterns on the parquet floor. Across the road, she can see some boys from school. They're sipping on cans of high-energy cola and smoking outside the off-licence run by Mr Patel, a Sikh who sometimes gives out free packets of biscuits that are past their expiry date.

Ryan Coleman is among the boys. He's seventeen and Zoe is pretty sure that he likes her because he teases her so much and everyone knows that teasing is a form of flirting. She hates being made fun of, but she likes Ryan.

A few weeks ago he stopped Zoe outside the school gates and commented on the punk cover she'd drawn on her music book. He said he liked the Ramones more than The Clash. Zoe told him he was talking out of his arse. Ryan laughed.

After that she burned him a CD of classic punk anthems and slipped it into his schoolbag without a note. Since then she's heard nothing. Maybe he's avoiding her. Maybe she scared him off. Zoe doesn't get on with many people at school. The girls in her class don't like her because she doesn't watch *X Factor* or *The Voice* and she doesn't wear make-up or try to sneak alcohol into parties.

Ryan Coleman is with his best mate, Dean Hancock, who has a roll of fat on his neck that is dotted with pimples. Zoe doesn't like Dean. When he teases her it doesn't seem like flirting.

Turning away from the window, she sits at a nearby computer, logging into her Facebook account. She reads her latest messages. She has three new 'friend' requests – two from people she's never heard of. She ignores them and updates her status.

I have a sodding cold! I do NOT have time to be sick!!!

Then she logs in to a second Facebook page with a banner photograph and the headline:

HELP: My Dad Is Missing.

Beneath is a short description.

My dad (really my stepdad), Daniel William Hyland, sometimes known as Danny, has been missing for more than a year. He was last seen on 4 August 2012 in Maida Vale, London, and we haven't heard from him since.

He is six feet tall with greeny-blue eyes and brown shoulder-length hair and a goofy smile. Has anyone seen him? Do you have any ideas? I am fifteen and I miss my Dad. I want to know he's OK. Please help me find him. Share this link with your friends.

People have left comments. A woman in North Carolina has written that nobody has seen her husband for three years. And another from Belgium writes that her father disappeared in October 1965.

He just walked out saying he was going to a local bar and never came back. You never give up hope, even after forty years. If you continue to have faith you will find the answers.

Zoe clicks on the 'photo' link where there are more images of Daniel. She has added them over the months, along with descriptions of his clothes, his favourite foods and his taste in music. Back on the main page, she updates her status, typing the words 'Still Missing'.

This is Zoe's secret project. She hasn't told Marnie about the webpage because her mum doesn't *get* social networking and says things like, 'In my day we had *real* friends', not understanding her own lameness. Zoe felt so helpless when Daniel disappeared, but this is how she coped. She set up her own search, creating a Facebook page and joining chatrooms where she could spread the word. If Marnie knew, she would argue it was pointless or warn Zoe about exposing private details to strangers on the internet, but she has no right to lecture Zoe about Daniel, not after the other night.

Logging off, Zoe moves through the shelves, looking at the titles, imagining other lives. She chooses two textbooks on Shakespeare and goes back to her desk, quickly glancing out the window. The boys have gone.

Opening the first of the books, she runs her finger down the index. A movement distracts her. A man passes her desk and leans towards the window, tilting his head as though checking out the weather.

'What are you studying?' he asks.

'Shakespeare.'

'Which one?'

'*Othello*.'

'Ah, the jealous Moor.'

The man has a narrow face and is over-dressed for the weather in a coat and heavy boots. Zoe isn't good at estimating ages when people get past forty because they all look old to her. And she doesn't want to make eye contact in case it encourages him. The library seems to attract weirdos and wackjobs, the homeless, unemployed and unemployable, who use it like a halfway house, particularly in the winter. This one seems to be watching her, glancing in her direction each time she turns a page. Maybe she's imagining it. A voice interrupts her thoughts.

'Ah, here she is, the punk princess,' says Dean Hancock, talking too loudly. He snatches the book from under Zoe's hand. 'What you reading?'

'Give it back.'

He holds it above his head where she can't reach it. Ryan Coleman isn't with him. Instead there are two other boys from school and a girl with ratty hair and a tight skirt that she tugs down over her thighs.

Hancock has a nasally voice. 'Why are you locked away in here, Princess? We got beer. We got weed. This evening has potential. It's pregnant with possibilities.'

He produces a can of lager from the inside pocket of his jacket and takes a swig, wiping his mouth. He has an ugly seed wart on the side of his ring finger and a homemade blue tattoo on his right wrist.

'You like Shakespeare? To be or not to be, that is the question. To shag or not to shag, to surf or turf.'

'Give it back.'

'Say please.'

'Please.'

'Maybe you'd prefer to read what's tattooed on my cock?'

'Only with a magnifying glass,' says Zoe.

The girl laughs. Hancock glares at her.

He's a foot taller and twice Zoe's weight. 'Give me a kiss and you can have your book back.'

'Fuck off!'

'Oops!' He rips a page out. 'Now look what you've made me do.'

'Please don't.'

Another page is torn away and floats to the floor.

Zoe doesn't see exactly what happens next. Dean Hancock seems to shudder before dropping to his knees. He's winded, lungs empty, eyes bulging. The girl lets out a high-pitched squeak and his two mates vanish like popped bubbles.

Hunched over, Hancock is breathing in quick gasps, trying to get oxygen.

The man from the window is next to him. He has rescued Hancock's can of lager, which he hands to Zoe, asking her to hold it. Then he hooks an arm around the teenager's waist, helping him to walk out of the library, past the information desk.

'I think this lad is going to be sick,' he tells the librarian. 'He needs some fresh air.'

Half carrying him through the double doors, he lowers him onto the steps, sitting next to him like they're old friends. The man takes the cigarette from behind Hancock's ear and pops it between his lips. The girl has followed them out.

'What did you do to him?' she asks.

'I stopped him being a complete dickhead.'

'Is he going to be OK?'

'Hard to say.'

He helps Hancock to his feet and down the remaining stairs, where he passes him over to the girl, who sags under the teenage boy's weight.

'He's all yours,' he says, 'but you could do a lot

better.' The girl doesn't answer as she wobbles along the footpath in her high heels.

The man returns to the steps and lights the cigarette, drawing smoke deep into his lungs.

Zoe watches from the doorway. 'Where are they?'

'Gone.'

She notices a bead of blood the size of a ladybird on the man's neck. He must have cut himself shaving without noticing. The man takes another drag, stretching his legs down the steps. He dabs a finger on his neck, smearing the bead of blood. He looks at his fingertip, seemingly puzzled and then sucks on the finger.

'Was he a friend of yours?'

'No.' Zoe sits on the steps next to him and stares at her feet.

'I'm Ruben,' he says, holding out his hand. Zoe stares at it for a moment, unsure of what to do. She shakes his hand. He turns her palm upwards.

'Hmm.'

'What?'

'I can read palms.'

'Really?'

Something happened to you when you were seven. You got sick.'

'I had glandular fever – how did you know?'

'I know everything.'

'Really. What's that like?'

'Not all it's cracked up to be.'

She smiles wryly. 'What else can you tell?'

'You're worried about someone – a parent maybe. You haven't seen them for a while.'

Zoe doesn't react. They sit in silence. The cigarette is finished. He crushes the butt and drops it into the garden.

'You should get back to your homework. *Othello*. The black guy who smothers his wife with a pillow because he thinks she's having an affair with his best friend, a prize wanker called Iago, who couldn't lie straight if you ran him over with a steam roller.'

'Is that all you got?'

'That's all you need.'

Zoe laughs properly this time. 'Are you making fun of me?'

'I would never do that. What do you take me for?' He glances at the trees. 'So why do you do your homework in the library?'

'I don't have a computer at home.'

'What sort of person doesn't have a computer?'

Zoe doesn't answer.

'So what are you going to do when you finish school?'

'Go to university, I guess. I thought I might study philosophy. When I work out the meaning of life I'm going to tell my mum.'

'Good plan.'

Ruben stands. 'Well, I got to be going.' He brushes down the back of his trousers and takes about five paces before turning. 'Do you want a laptop?'

'Pardon?'

'I have an old laptop. It still works. I don't use it any more. Sits in a cupboard.'

'We don't have wi-fi at home.'

'Yeah, but you can use it at the library or piggyback off an open network.'

'Mum wouldn't let me.'

'Suit yourself.'

Ruben turns and continues walking. Zoe watches him, wanting to say something. He turns at the last moment, catching her looking.

'Nice meeting you, Zoe.'

'How did you know my name?'

'Like I said, I know everything.'

CHAPTER 13

Marnie is almost at the stairs when she hears a door open. Trevor is dressed in an apron that says, *Grill Sergeant – I don't take orders, I give them.* He's holding a set of barbecue tongs. A pocket of air is trapped in his cheek.

'Let me help you.'

'I can manage.'

But Trevor has already seized the box. He climbs ahead of her, turning back occasionally as though worried she might get lost. Why does he always smell of urinal soap, she wonders.

'Somebody left a package for you,' he says. 'I put it outside the flat.'

'Thank you.'

'And Mr Brummer came round earlier to collect the rent. He said he was going to come back.'

'OK.'

'That detective was also here. I saw him waiting in his car.'

They've reached her door. Trevor steps back. Marnie bends to pick up a padded brown envelope on the welcome mat. It has her name but no address or postmarks. The words are written in dark felt-tipped pen. Capitals. She tucks the envelope under her arm and fishes her keys from her shoulder bag.

The door swings inwards. She turns to take the box, but Trevor has already pushed past her into the flat. He walks to the kitchen and sets down the box on the counter, sneaking a glance inside. Elijah comes running to greet Marnie. He's been playing in her wardrobe again.

Zoe pokes her head out of her bedroom, but retreats when she sees Trevor.

'I'm having a barbecue,' he explains. 'You should come down. I have loads of food. Elijah can run around the garden.'

'Zoe has homework.'

'She doesn't have to come.'

Elijah has picked up the padded envelope. 'Is that a present for me?'

'No, it's for Mummy.'

'Can I open it?'

Marnie ignores him and tells Trevor, 'Perhaps another time. I have work to do.' She points to the box.

Trevor frowns and gives her a sidelong glance. Marnie doesn't like the way his pale tongue flicks out and disappears again, wetting his bottom lip. Elijah has managed to peel back a corner of the envelope. He grits his teeth, pulling it harder. The envelope rips open and a bundle of cash drops onto the floor with a thud. Twenties. Fifties. Held together with a rubber band. It must be thousands of pounds.

Marnie stares at the money. Elijah looks disappointed. Trevor whistles under his breath.

'Somebody likes you.'

'Did you do this?'

'Me?'

Her mind flashes through the possibilities. Who would give her this? Penny, perhaps, but she said Keegan had put her on a budget. Who else? Not Daniel's parents, they hate her.

Trevor has picked up the torn envelope, looking for a note. Marnie takes it from him but finds nothing. 'Did you see who it was?'

Trevor shakes his head.

Elijah reaches for the money. 'Don't touch it, sweetheart.'

'Why?'

'It doesn't belong to us.'

'But your name is on the envelope,' says Trevor.

'Please, go.'

Trevor pouts at her. 'I did the right thing. I could have taken that money.'

'It was addressed to me.'

'Even so.'

'Leave.'

Grudgingly, he obeys. Complaining. Nasal-voiced. 'I made extra potato salad.'

Marnie takes the money and counts it, laying each note on the table. It's exactly five thousand pounds.

She puts the cash in a new envelope after taking two hundred pounds and pushing it deep into the pocket of her jeans where she can feel it beneath the denim. Somebody is helping her, but what do they want in return? She's not going to worry about that now. She can pay rent and buy a TV. She can stock the pantry and fill the empty freezer.

She makes a list and then taps on Zoe's door. 'I'm going to the shops. Will you look after Elijah?'

'I looked after him all afternoon.'

'Just for a while longer.' Marnie rests her head against the smooth wood. 'What would you like for dinner? Anything you want.'

'Do we have money?'

'We do.'

'Did you borrow it from Trevor?'

'No.'

'Can we get some Ben and Jerry's Cookie Dough ice cream?'

'You got it.'

Marnie unchains her bicycle from the side path and slips a reflective vest over her blouse. Pushing off, she rises onto the pedals and straightens, finding her balance. The bike has a toddler seat behind the saddle and a basket that rattles above her front wheel.

Riding along Elgin Avenue, she passes Maida Vale station and the small strip of shops and restaurants, before turning left onto Kilburn Road. Following the bus lane, she passes three tower blocks and Zoe's school and climbs the rise into Kilburn. She chains the bike to a fence outside an estate agents and crosses the parking area to the supermarket. There are cheaper places, but today she doesn't have to worry about comparative pricing, home brands or what time of day they discount their meat.

The doors open automatically and she uncouples a trolley, steering it between battlements of sanitary napkins, toilet rolls, disposable nappies and dog biscuits. At the deli counter she takes a number and buys a whole rotisserie chicken. She gets Zoe's ice cream and some gluten-free treats for Elijah, along with the staples.

Glancing at her list, she turns a corner and collides with another trolley.

'I'm so sorry,' she says, crouching to pick up a fallen box of cereal.

'You should be more careful.'

Marnie raises her eyes. Patrick Hennessy is smiling at her, without showing his teeth. His hair is pushed back in a greasy wave and his eyes are pale brown, the whites looking almost jaundiced.

'You did that on purpose.'

'Don't be so harsh. It scratches your pretty face.'

Marnie ignores him. Her knuckles are white on the trolley's handle. She walks straight to a checkout. Hennessy is behind her. Another cashier motions him to change aisles.

'I'm fine just here,' he says, standing so close to Marnie she can smell his cologne. She spins and confronts him. 'Leave me alone or I'll scream for help.'

'No you won't,' he replies.

The composition of his face surprises her, the thin lips, pink cheeks and strange hair. His eyes seem to sweep the entirety of her, noting the loops of sweat beneath her arms and the curve of her breasts.

She bags her groceries and walks quickly across the parking area, not looking behind her. After putting her shopping in the basket of the bike, she uncouples the security chain.

'We either talk here, or I follow you home,' says Hennessy, blocking her way. He's wearing the fixed expression of a fairground clown. 'What happened to Quinn?'

'I don't know.'

'You do know he's dead.'

Marnie doesn't answer. Hennessy pinches the bridge of his nose. 'He took you on a job the other night. He didn't call me afterwards. What happened?'

'Nothing.'

Hennessy wraps his fingers around her handlebars. He raises the front tyre a few inches and drops it. The basket rattles.

'Concentrate on me, Marnie, no more lies.'

'Quinn gave me a beating. He almost broke my ribs.'

'And now he's dead. See how it looks?'

'I didn't kill him.'

'I think you know something.'

'He dropped me home. That's the last time I saw him.'

Hennessy sighs. 'I have a dilemma, Marnie. You see, Quinn was more than an employee. My youngest sister married him – not her finest moment, I'll admit – but now she's bending my ear about finding out who killed him.'

'I don't know what happened.'

'What did you tell the police?'

'Nothing.'

'But they've talked to you?'

'I didn't mention you.'

'I want to believe you.' Hennessy looks down at her groceries, opening one of the bags with his thumb and forefinger. 'Found some money have we?'

Marnie doesn't reply.

'Or maybe you've found your husband?'

'No.'

'Pity.'

Marnie recognises something new in his eyes.

'Life is pretty simple when you think about it,' he says. 'We both want the same things – to be happy, raise a family, pay our bills, set a little aside for a rainy day . . . ' He lets go of the handlebars and strokes his chin. 'In the great circle of life everything is interrelated. It's like a daisy chain and I'm not talking about flowers. You owe me money. I owe people money. *They* owe people money. Understand? I bankrolled your husband.

The O'Hara clan bankrolled me. They're like the royal fucking family of criminals – each one madder than the next – and they don't just leave bruises. Understand?'

Marnie doesn't answer.

'I'm giving you the benefit of the doubt over Quinn, but if I find out you killed him, I'm going to be surprised on the one hand – perhaps even a little impressed – then I'm going to kill you. Otherwise my sister will never shut up. Blood is thicker than water and it's also a fuck of a lot harder to get out of a white shirt.'

Hennessy has moved around the bike. He cups Marnie's chin with his right hand, letting his eyes drift downwards.

'One way or another, I'm going to get what's owed to me. You pay in cash or you pay in kind.'

Marnie's hand slips into the basket. Hennessy traces a line down her throat, letting the tips of his thumb and forefinger brush over her right nipple. Without a word, she raises a can of insecticide and sprays it directly into his eyes. He reels away, clutching his face. Two figures are running towards her across the parking area: Hennessy's men.

Up on the bike, pushing hard on the pedals, she rides across the footpath and bounces over the gutter. A car swerves and blasts its horn. Pedalling furiously, she weaves between stationary traffic at a pedestrian crossing.

Stupid cow! Stupid cow! Stupid cow!

She's angry with herself . . . angry with Daniel. Look at what he's done to her.

Turning right, she takes the back streets, avoiding traffic lights. Terraced houses stretch in both directions. Occasionally, she risks looking over her shoulder. It's getting dark.

Stupid cow! Stupid cow!

Reaching Elgin Avenue, she's not far from home. A truck passes her and she gets a backwash of fumes from the exhaust. Another vehicle is behind her. Marnie slows, breathing hard, and looks for a gap between the parked cars. The footpath will be safer. She risks glancing over her shoulder and sees the headlights of a dark-coloured Land Cruiser. She veers towards the gutter, giving it room to pass. It accelerates. At the last possible moment the passenger door opens, striking her handlebars. The bike is tossed sideways. Tumbling. Head. Heels. Head. Marnie lands on asphalt and slides before hitting something solid and sinking into a moaning place. Darkness.

CHAPTER 14

Joe O'Loughlin didn't expect Ruiz to come to Maida Vale. He thought they'd meet somewhere halfway at a restaurant or a pub that served real ale and carbohydrates. But the big man wanted to see Joe's new flat, which isn't so new any more. He's been in London for over a year.

'Like what you've done with the place,' Ruiz says, facetiously. 'It's going to look even better when you finish unpacking.'

There are still boxes in the spare bedroom and lined up along the hallway. Apart from the high ceilings and a bay window, the flat doesn't have anything else that you might call a 'feature'. The living room has a mismatched sofa and armchairs, cluttered bookshelves and wilting plants on either side of the fake gas fireplace. A large desk takes up the width of the bay window.

'It has a sort of bachelor-academic chic,' says Ruiz, winking at Charlie, who is sitting opposite. She likes Vincent. He's like a pseudo-uncle who tells jokes and has loads of cool stories, most of them age-inappropriate.

'I'm not used to having visitors,' yells Joe, who

is in the kitchen trying to chisel a tray of ice from the freezer using a knife.

'He's a hermit,' whispers Charlie.

'I heard that,' says Joe. He hits the handle of the knife with his palm and a tray seems to explode out, scattering ice cubes across the floor. 'Some people are very comfortable living on their own,' he says, looking at the mess.

'Lonely people,' says Charlie.

'Who are independent.'

'Or sad.'

He emerges from the kitchen and hands Ruiz a Scotch on the rocks. 'J. D. Salinger lived on his own.'

'So did the Unabomber,' says Ruiz.

'You're not helping.'

Ruiz raises the glass and takes a rattling sip.

'Can I have one?' asks Charlie.

'Sure,' says Ruiz.

'No,' answers Joe. 'And don't you go encouraging her.'

'I don't see why not. Most girls her age are binge-drinking by now.'

'I don't binge-drink,' protests Charlie.

'That's because you're like your father and have no friends.'

She knows he's teasing her. Ruiz swirls the ice cubes in the glass. 'Where are we going for dinner?'

'Can I come?' asks Charlie.

'I've made you something in the fridge,' says Joe.

'Macaroni bake?'

'You *like* my macaroni bake.'

'Slightly more than starvation.'

Ruiz is looking settled on the sofa. He suggests takeaway. He looks at Charlie. 'Your choice, madam.'

'Don't call me madam.'

'Princess.'

'That's worse.'

'You want to eat or what?'

Charlie chooses Indian and orders by phone. The restaurant is only on the corner. Joe opens his wallet and gives her the cash. Ruiz issues the instructions. 'Make sure I get my chutney and lime pickle and don't break the poppadums.' Joe holds the money above her head, just out of Charlie's reach. 'And don't you go talking to any strange boys.'

'As if.'

After she's gone, Ruiz pours himself another drink and shakes his head.

'Two daughters – you poor bastard.'

Marnie opens her eyes. The darkness is different now. Softer. Quieter. There's no crunching of metal or spinning wheels. She's lying in a gutter that smells of vomit and dog shit. Above her head she can see rags of clouds in a darkening sky . . . and faces. People are scrambling from cars and craning to see what's happened. A large man toils towards her at a bow-legged run, stopping abruptly.

'Are you all right, dear?' asks an elderly woman, who appears in Marnie's field of vision.

The question seems funny in the circumstances, but Marnie tries not to laugh. Moving her head slowly, she takes an inventory, bending her fingers and toes. Nothing broken. A wave of nausea rises in her stomach and she shuts her eyes again. Someone is holding her hand. For a moment she thinks it might be Daniel and almost bursts into tears.

She turns her head. Her bike is lying on its side. Her shopping has spilled onto the road and rolled under nearby cars. The foil bag with the roast chicken has split and a dog nuzzles the brown bird. She remembers the Land Cruiser. Hennessy. The supermarket.

'Can you hear me, missy?' asks the woman, who is clutching a dog lead.

'You came off yer bike,' says a man, who has a moustache like a circus ringmaster.

The woman speaks again. 'Harold called an ambulance. You should lie still, missy, you might have hurt your spine.'

'Or you could be concussed,' says Harold.

Ignoring the advice, Marnie hauls herself onto her hands and knees, the gravel sharp under her palms. Carefully, she inspects the grazes on her thigh and left shoulder.

'I'm fine. Really.'

The woman is collecting her groceries. A can of tomatoes has rolled out of reach beneath a car chassis. The chicken can't be salvaged.

'Come inside and clean up,' says the woman. Her front door is open. Light shines from inside.

Marnie stands, gritting her teeth.

'I have to call my daughter.' The words catch in her throat. 'She'll be worried about me.'

Ruiz pours himself another drink and fishes ice from a tall glass that Joe has left on the counter. 'You mentioned a file was taken from your office.'

Joe nods.

'What was in it?'

'Nothing that warranted the effort, but someone tried very hard to conceal their purpose.'

'A professional?'

'Above average intelligence, forensic awareness, nothing rushed, no sign of panic.'

'What was in the file?'

'Clinical notes on a female patient.'

'What's her problem?'

Joe hesitates. 'I can't talk about her treatment, but she's in trouble. Her husband disappeared a year ago. Vanished. Not a trace. She can't touch his bank accounts or open his gym locker or cancel direct debits. She can't mourn him or bury him or move on with her life. I thought maybe you could . . .'

'Help?'

'Yeah.'

'I can't prove the man is dead.'

'I know.'

Ruiz pauses. Closes his eyes. 'How well do you know this woman? Maybe she killed her husband.'

'I don't believe that.'

The two men sit in silence for a while. Ruiz stretches his legs, putting the heel of one shoe on the toe of the other. He studies the professor without making it obvious. 'You still having the nightmare?'

Joe wets his lips and shifts in his chair. 'Sometimes.'

'The same one?'

'Pretty much.'

Ruiz scratches the stubble on his top lip as though stroking a moustache. 'You shot a madman. You saved a girl. End of story.'

'The rational side of me knows that.'

'You're a rational man.'

Joe's eyes are glistening. Ruiz can see the depths of his pain.

'You're not a killer, Joe. Not in your heart. Not where it matters. You're made differently from most men. Maybe it happened in the womb. You understand more than most people. You look harder. You care more. You let things bruise your soul and question what's wrong with humanity, but don't ever doubt yourself.'

Joe squeezes his eyes shut as though fighting with an emotion he doesn't plan to discuss. 'I'm all right, Vincent. You don't have to worry.'

The two men share the silence for a while, enjoying the peace.

'So how are things with Julianne?' asks Ruiz.

'Fine.'

'They say absence makes the heart grow fonder.'

'We're not sleeping together.'

'Not even accidentally bumping into each other in the dark?'

'Afraid not.'

Marnie presses the intercom.

Joe answers. 'Have you forgotten your key?'

'Professor?'

'Who is this?'

'Marnie.' Her voice is trembling. 'I'm sorry. I know I shouldn't bother you at home . . .'

'Are you all right?'

'No.'

Moments later she's sitting at the kitchen table, still apologising. Joe is crouched at her feet, examining the grazes on her shoulder and the blood leaking through her torn jeans. He's not alone. A big man is standing the doorway, holding a glass of Scotch.

'Fill the kettle,' Joe says to him. 'Top cupboard, beside the fridge, second shelf, you'll find cotton swabs and disinfectant.'

Perched on the edge of the chair, Marnie squeezes her hands between her knees. 'I didn't know where else to go.'

'What happened?'

'I was knocked off my bike.'

Joe makes her flex her fingers and bend her limbs. 'Nothing seems to be broken. Where are your children?'

'Zoe is looking after Elijah. I've called her. They're fine.'

'This is my friend, Vincent Ruiz,' says Joe. Marnie nods.

'Did you see the vehicle?' asks Ruiz.

'It was big and dark . . . a four-wheel drive.'

'Get a number?'

'No.'

Joe fills a bowl with warm water and adds a splash of disinfectant. After soaking balls of cotton wool, he dabs at the graze, cleaning away blood and dirt and small fragments of gravel from Marnie's forearm and shoulder. His left hand has started shaking.

'You're not hurting me,' she says. 'If that's worrying you.'

'I have Parkinson's,' Joe replies, making it sound like a character trait rather than a disease.

'How long?'

'Eight years.'

'I didn't know.'

Marnie has never seen Joe away from his consulting room except for when she worked at the café. She's surprised at how different he seems, less aloof, more ordinary. She had always regarded him as a shaggy-headed academic type whose clothes never seemed to fit him properly. But he has a younger man's face and strong hands.

Joe turns her leg a fraction. 'You should take off your jeans. I'll find you something else to wear.'

Marnie goes to the bathroom and changes, rolling her jeans into a tight bundle before putting on a dressing gown. She silently thanks her mother for always telling her to wear decent underwear in case of an accident. As she opens the bathroom door, she can hear Joe and Ruiz talking.

'Who is she?'

'That patient I mentioned.'

'Now there's an interesting happenstance. Has she been here before?'

'No.'

'But she knows your address?'

'She helped me find this place.'

Marnie reappears and Ruiz holds off asking any more questions. She tries to sit demurely with one leg higher than the other as Joe cleans the grazes on her thigh and hip. She tells them about Quinn and Hennessy and the police. It comes as a relief to unburden herself. Halfway through the story, the door opens and Charlie appears carrying bags of takeaway. She takes in the scene: Marnie in underwear and a dressing gown, her leg exposed, her father kneeling on the floor.

'I go away for twenty minutes,' she says incredulously.

'This is Marnie,' says Joe. 'She's one of our neighbours . . . almost.'

'How can someone be *almost* a neighbour?'

'I live around the corner,' says Marnie. 'I had an accident.'

Charlie leans closer. 'Nasty.'

'I really should be leaving. Thanks for patching me up.'

'Stay for dinner,' says Ruiz. 'We ordered plenty.'

150

Charlie screws up her face.

'I have my own kids to feed,' says Marnie, standing gingerly.

Joe empties the bowl of bloody water, watching it swirl in pink circles down the drain.

'You can't wear that home. Charlie will lend you some clothes.'

Marnie notices another pout from the teenage girl. 'You don't really have to,' she says, trying to make amends.

'Nonsense. She has loads of clothes.'

Marnie gets changed in the spare room, spotting the suitcase beside the bed and the teenage mess. She had often wondered if the professor had a wife and family. He has never mentioned them, not even in passing.

The others are eating. Ruiz and Charlie are laughing.

Joe is waiting for her. 'I'll walk you home.'

'No, you stay and finish. I'll manage.'

'I insist. Where's your bike?'

'Downstairs. I don't think it's salvageable.'

They walk side by side with Marnie limping slightly. Joe carries her groceries. The ice cream has melted and the fruit will be bruised.

'Where is your wife?' she asks.

'She lives in the West Country.'

'You live apart.'

'We're separated. Charlie is going back tomorrow. I see her every second weekend and during the holidays.'

'Your only child?'

'I have Emma. She's almost seven.'

Marnie nods. Questions are chorusing in her head.

'About tonight,' says Joe. 'You have to talk to the police.'

'I can't be certain Hennessy was in the car.'

'Did he threaten you?'

'Yes, but he'll deny it.'

'So what are you going to do?'

'I'm going to try to prove my husband is dead and collect the insurance money. Then I can pay Hennessy and start again.'

'You make it sound so easy.'

'I don't have a choice.'

'People often say that, but it's rarely true. Vincent used to be a detective. He knows people. He can help you.'

'Why would he do that?'

'He's a good man.'

Marnie turns. She's standing beneath a streetlight, wearing one of Charlie's over-sized sweaters. Is there such a thing as 'a good man', she wonders. So few people have stayed with her. Friends have stopped calling. Invitations have dried up. Bad luck is like a contagion.

'I went to Daniel's office today,' she says. 'I went through his things and found the proof that he still loved me.'

'Proof?'

'He was planning a surprise for my birthday: a

big red album like on *This is Your Life*. He contacted all my old friends, getting them to record messages and send photographs.' Marnie wants Joe to be excited. 'I have his diary. It shows what he was doing, who he was meeting . . . Maybe someone knows what happened to him.'

'Why haven't they come forward by now?'

'I don't know. Maybe they don't realise.' She touches his forearm. 'He made me a DVD. I haven't watched it yet. I don't have a TV.'

'What about a computer?'

Marnie shakes her head.

'I could lend you my laptop.'

'Will you watch it with me?'

Joe hesitates.

'It doesn't have to be tonight,' she adds.

'Wouldn't you rather see it in private?'

'No.'

Without her having to explain, Joe seems to sense the reason. Despite her previous certainty, Marnie is frightened the DVD could hold Daniel's farewell message.

'So you'll come.'

'Yes.'

'When?'

'Tomorrow.'

She feels a weight lifting from her chest. Someone has set out a roadmap. She can only see a little way ahead, but that's all right. Even the longest and darkest of journeys can be made in the glow of the headlights.

Standing outside the mansion block, she raises her eyes to the top floor, where every window is lit up.

'Charlie seems nice.'

'She is.'

'Are you going to get back together with your wife?' Her head is cocked to one side, studying him like a portrait painter.

'That ship might have sailed.'

Unexpectedly, Marnie puts her arms around him, tilting her head up to peck him on the lips, but letting her lips stay there, parting slightly. Then she hugs him tightly to her chest.

He pulls away. She laughs. 'You're not a hugger?'

'Out of practice.'

'Maybe you think it's inappropriate.'

'I haven't worked that out yet.'

CHAPTER 15

Elijah has been vomiting since midnight. Marnie changes his pyjamas and sheets, but he keeps throwing up on the half-hour until she's run out of clean clothes and he falls asleep. At nine o'clock she phones her GP, but can't get an appointment until Monday. Instead she dresses Elijah in one of Zoe's old T-shirts and takes him to West Hammersmith Hospital.

The A&E department is already busy, full of the stabbed, burned, broken and scraped. The overworked registrar takes Elijah's details and tells Marnie that she'll have to wait until the paediatrician finishes his rounds.

'When will that be?'

'I can't tell you.'

There is a TV in the waiting room playing cartoons and showing advertisements for nappies and toys. All the TV babies are giggling and happy and the mothers are pretty and wholesome. Marnie doesn't envy them. She hates them.

Dr Vallery arrives just after midday, breezing through the swinging doors, sharing a joke with one of the prettier nurses. 'I'd better get back to work,' he says.

Arsehole!

The nurse calls Elijah's name. Marnie feels his body stiffen on her lap. There have been too many hospitals, too many tests; too many conversations that begin with 'This is the very last time . . .'

The paediatrician is tall and pale with a floppy fringe. A tiny scale of glitter blinks on his cheek, the remnant of a daughter's goodbye hug. He studies Elijah, mentally noting his clothes, as though deciding what kind of mother Marnie presents. Meanwhile, she's trying to explain.

'He was diagnosed with coeliac disease. He had a biopsy on his small intestine.'

'Who diagnosed him?'

'A specialist . . . he has an Irish name . . . I can't remember.' She tries again. 'He has an office in Harley Street.'

Why does this man make her feel so useless?

'He's been on a gluten-free diet,' says Marnie.

'For how long?'

'Five months.'

'Was he tested for cystic fibrosis?'

'Yes.'

Dr Vallery sits Elijah on an examination table and goes through the usual tests: eyes, ears, throat, 'Say ahhhh', 'Step on the scales'.

'He was born six weeks early,' says Marnie, trying to be helpful.

'What was his birth weight?'

156

'Almost five pounds.'

Dr Vallery drapes a stethoscope over his neck and takes a seat, leaning back in his chair, studying Marnie.

'This is your ninth visit to the hospital with Elijah.'

'I haven't been counting.'

'Each time you've managed to have more tests ordered.'

Marnie doesn't grasp his point.

'What do you want me to do?' he asks.

'Pardon?'

'You're here – what would like to me to do?'

'I don't understand.'

'Do you want me to admit Elijah? Arrange an operation?'

Marnie stares at him, not comprehending. Then it hits her – he thinks she *wants* Elijah to be sick; that she's some sort of Mommy Dearest, Munchausen-by-proxy nutcase who is .seeking attention by making her son unwell and dragging him between specialists so he can be pricked and prodded.

Never in her life has Marnie wanted to throw herself across a table and hurt a medical professional. Chewing her rage, she tries to control the vibration in her voice.

'I don't want my boy to be admitted. I don't want him operated upon. I want him to be healthy.'

Dr Vallery doesn't reply, but has grown less confident. He avoids Marnie's glare and makes another note. He explains that Elijah is being referred to a specialist at Great Ormond Street Children's Hospital. Marnie feels a grip of panic. Another appointment. More tests. She has grown to hate hospitals. It's a setback, she tells herself. He'll bounce back. Everything will be fine. What else can she say?

After it's over they take the tube from White City to Oxford Circus before changing onto the Bakerloo Line. Hot and crowded, the carriage is polluted by discarded copies of *Metro* and the aural fuzz of leaking headphones. People ignore each other, disparate and self-interested, grumpy yet normally civil. Elijah points out things he recognises, re-assured by the familiar.

'Dog,' he says. 'Bus. Petrol station.'

As they walk along Elgin Avenue, Marnie notices a car parked opposite the flat. Detective Inspector Gennia is sitting inside with the door propped open, one leg on the footpath as though it needed stretching.

'Are you waiting for me?' she asks.

'I was hoping we could talk.'

'We have nothing to talk about.'

Elijah has run on ahead. Marnie calls to him to wait. She turns back to the detective, whose face looks scrubbed awake. Freshly shaved. He's wearing jeans today instead of a suit, but has the same needlepoint boots. Maybe it's his day off. For some reason Marnie feels sorry for him. He looks lonely. Like a new kid at school hoping to meet a friend.

'I promised Elijah I'd push him on the swing,' she says, without making it sound like an invitation.

'I'll walk with you.'

Gennia talks about the weather. His voice has something familiar about it, an accent that she recognises or a tone, but she doesn't like the way he studies her, taking note of every detail right down to her bare shins and sandals. When they reach Paddington Rec, Elijah runs to the climbing frame. A handful of mothers are picnicking on the grass, spooning mush into the mouths of babies.

Gennia has slung his jacket over his shoulder. When he talks his eyes keep darting over Marnie with a fascinated intensity, as though he's putting her together piece by piece like a jigsaw puzzle.

'You have lovely fingernails,' he says, looking at her hands. 'You've broken one of them. What happened?'

'I can't remember.'

'Shame.'

Reaching into his pocket, he produces a small ziploc bag and holds it up to the light. Marnie can see it contains a fragment of fingernail; polished, peach-coloured, trapped within the clear plastic.

'It's amazing what they can tell from something this small,' he says. 'I'm not just talking about DNA – that's a given – but nowadays they can identify if someone is a smoker or if they're in good health.'

Elijah is swinging on a bar, feeling for the ground with his outstretched toes. He's taken off his shoes and socks.

'We found this in Niall Quinn's car,' says Gennia, turning the bag in his fingers. 'Care to explain?'

'I've told you everything I know.'

'No, you've lied to me.'

Marnie doesn't answer. She's jittering from one foot to the other, feeling slightly dazed and disbelieving.

'We also traced the signal from Quinn's mobile phone. He was in the West End that night. A CCTV camera picked up his car at the Strand. He dropped a woman at a hotel.'

'I didn't kill him.'

'You were in his car.'

'I was meeting someone else. Quinn drove me.'

'Who were you meeting?'

'The one I told you about – he wanted to commit suicide.' Marnie doesn't look at Gennia's face. 'He was a client.'

'What do you mean, "a client"?'

'Do I have to spell it out?'

The information registers.

'Quinn was your pimp.'

'We don't really call them pimps.'

'What do you call them?'

She recognises the sarcasm in his question and refuses to answer.

160

'How long had you worked for him?' asks Gennia.

'I didn't work for him. I was employed by an agency. I only did it for three nights.'

'Really?'

'Yes.'

Marnie wants to quantify and mitigate; to make it sound less sordid. Up until she married Daniel, she had slept with exactly four men, including her first husband. That's seven in total, which shouldn't make her a slut or a nymphomaniac, yet one payment made her a whore.

She contemplates telling Gennia about Patrick Hennessy and Daniel's gambling debts, but she has vowed not to apologise for her husband and she remembers the Ulsterman's threats. Instead she recounts half the story, explaining how she arrived at the hotel and met with Owen.

'You had sex with him.'

'No. He just wanted company.'

The detective looks at her sceptically.

'But you were paid?'

'No, I felt sorry for him. I didn't take his money.'

'How did Quinn feel about that?'

Marnie gazes around the playground. Undoing the lowest two buttons of her blouse, she lifts the fabric above her midriff. The bruise is now marbled with purple and yellow.

'He did that?'

Marnie nods.

'So you cut his throat?'

'No!'

Gennia leans towards her. His hairline seems to slide backwards when he raises his eyebrows. 'In my experience, people turn themselves into suspects because they try to be too clever.'

'I'm not being clever.'

Elijah has left the climbing frame and run to the slippery dip.

Gennia is still talking. 'We haven't found the murder weapon. According to the pathologist, we're looking for a five-inch blade, single-sided, sharp, fairly standard in most kitchens.'

Elijah is standing at the base of the slippery dip, staring up at the ladder. Marnie yells out to him. 'Remember last time.'

Ignoring her, Elijah begins climbing; hand over hand, not looking down.

'He doesn't like heights,' she explains, already moving.

Gennia follows her. 'Your husband is missing.'

'Yes.'

'Is that why you're working as an escort?'

'My business – not yours.'

'If you're in some sort of trouble, you should talk to me.'

Elijah has stopped at the top of the slide. Children are queuing behind him, yelling at him to move, but he's frozen, his hands gripping the sides. Knuckles white. Eyes round.

One of the bigger boys climbs past the others. He screams at Elijah, whose small pale body is shaking. Marnie is running. She can see the boy prying Elijah's fingers loose. Elijah won't say anything.

He's falling. Not sliding. Sideways. Gennia reaches him first, catching Elijah before his body crumples onto the artificial turf. Elijah reaches for Marnie, clinging to her. Then he points to the swing.

'You promised, Mummy.'

CHAPTER 16

Marnie sits on the floor next to the open box, staring at the contents as though looking at the pieces of a puzzle that she had once been able to complete but has since forgotten where to start. Showered, wearing fresh clothes, she can feel painkillers dissolving in her stomach.

Zoe is at the library and Elijah is playing with his trains in the wardrobe. Marnie can hear him talking to himself, having one-sided conversations. Marnie once asked Professor O'Loughlin if it was healthy for a four-year-old to have a make-believe friend and he told her that Elijah would grow out of it eventually.

Joe is with her now, leaning forward from the sofa. It's strange seeing him here. Normally they're in Joe's consulting room, sitting opposite each other in big matching armchairs. At their first session Marnie had felt like an eleven-year-old about to get the facts-of-life speech from her father. In reality her father didn't give her such a speech. Instead he knocked on her bedroom door one day and said, 'Marnie, do I have to tell you about the birds and the bees?'

'Please don't.'

'So you're up to speed?'

'Totally.'

Marnie takes the Big Red Book from the box and traces her fingers over the gold letters of the title. Daniel was always one for grand gestures. On their first wedding anniversary he covered the bedroom walls with hundreds of sticky notes, each with a reason that he loved her. Another time he wrote a series of cryptic clues, which took her cycling around Regent's Park and finished at a picnic spot where he and Zoe were waiting.

Marnie opens the album. The first few pages are photographs of her as a baby. Most of them are captioned. She recognises her father's handwriting:

You were so beautiful. I would go to the hospital nursery to look at you and find your crib empty. The nurses were passing you around. They had seen lots of babies, but you were special.

Her mother had four miscarriages and tried for ten years before Marnie was born. She never gave up hope and she refused to let science intervene. It would happen naturally or not at all, she said. Later she changed her mind and tried for a second child using IVF – a brother or sister for Marnie – but a car accident intervened and Marnie remained an only child.

'You were a miracle,' her mother said, 'a gift

from God.' And she baptised Marnie within hours, convinced that God might take his gift away.

Turning the next page, there is a new series of photographs: Marnie as a toddler, her face smeared with chocolate; Marnie feeding the ducks; Marnie riding a bike. Her baby fat had dropped away, her wispy hair had grown thick and her dimples were deep enough to hold raindrops. One picture shows her sitting between a man and a woman on a porch swing. The man has long hair and a beard, while the woman is dressed in a patchwork skirt and cheesecloth top with a macramé headband round her forehead.

'Your parents?' asks Joe.

'Uh-huh.'

'You've never talked about your mother.'

'I can barely remember her. She died when I was four.'

'What happened?'

'It was a car accident. She was driving. I was strapped in the back seat. Nobody knows how I got out.' Marnie points to another photograph. 'Dad remarried about two years after Mum died. That's my stepmother.'

The woman looks like a young Margaret Thatcher, wearing an apron and brandishing a ladle, waving it at the camera because she doesn't want to be photographed. There are other children at the kitchen table.

'I thought you were an only child,' says Joe.

'We used to take in foster kids. Dad called them strays. Usually they stayed for a few days or weeks. We had plenty of room.'

The memories come back to Marnie, including some of their names; the bed-wetters, biters, screamers, cutters, scratchers and mutes. Some wanted to be left alone, while others clung to her as if she was a piece of wreckage that might carry them to safety. She hated the foster kids, wishing they would go back to their own families.

'My stepmother ran our house like a boarding school with rules and timetables. Roast on Sunday. Leftovers Monday. Fish on Friday . . . Dad was different, full of funny voices as though he'd been swallowing helium from a party balloon. He could have us all in stitches – except for my stepmum, who would tell him to "stop acting the goat".

'I think she imagined her life would be like an episode of *The Waltons* where we all said goodnight to each other. "Good night, John Boy. Good night, Mary Ellen. Good night, Jim Bob . . ."'

'They didn't think of adopting?' asks Joe.

'My dad wanted her to get pregnant.'

'Where is she now?

'They divorced ten years ago. I see her every few years. She lives in Spain.'

At the bottom of the page, Daniel has written a note to Marnie: *Start the DVD.*

Joe slides the disk into his laptop. The software boots and he turns up the volume. Letters appear, bouncing off the edges of the screen before forming into words:

Marnie Logan: This is Your Life.

Daniel appears, his face close to the camera as he presses the record button. He walks backwards to a sofa. Sitting. Leaning forward with his fore-arms on his knees. Marnie reacts as though stung. He looks so real, so reachable, so alive. A song is playing in the background. James Morrison. 'Love is Hard'.

Daniel flicks back his fringe.

'I can't believe you're thirty-six and we've been together six years. You're still that same brilliant, hot, funny girl I fell in love with – the one who can dress like a film star one night and enjoy a beer and pizza the next. I know we've had some ups and downs lately. The "downs" have been mine. But I couldn't do this without you. Your love makes me want to be a better man. You truly are the cleverest, funniest, most wonderful person I know.

'Remember how I always struggle to find something to get you for your birthday? You're a nightmare to buy for because you're so unselfish. You give so much to everyone else and take so little. Well, today that changes. Today we begin again.

'Marnie Logan, I love you. Everybody loves you. And I'm going to prove it to you. In the pages of the Big Red Book you will see interviews and comments from loads of friends who come blasting from your

past. So let's start at the beginning. I'm going to take you back to your childhood and your first house . . .'

A photograph of a large terraced house flashes onto the screen. Another voice takes up the commentary.

'This is where you spent your first three years, Marnie. Your bedroom was on the top floor, second window on the right.'

'That's my father,' says Marnie.

An elderly man appears on screen with a tangle of grey hair. He looks nervously at the camera.

'Happy Birthday, Marnella, I'm supposed to take you down memory lane. You were beautiful as a baby and terrible as a toddler. I remember when you hid from your mother in Safeways because she wouldn't buy you a sparkly tiara. She had them seal off the doors because she thought you'd been kidnapped. And then there was the time you covered your bedroom floor with two containers of talcum powder and mixed it with water before planting jelly beans and telling us you were trying to grow a baby because you knew we wanted another one.'

Marnie laughs.

'You were always making us laugh. Remember the foster kid you tried to sell? You dragged him through the village on his skateboard with a sign around his neck saying "half price". And what about that time your mother took you to the video store and you went up to the handsome young man who was serving and put your hand up his shorts? The man jumped away. "Did your mummy teach you that?" he asked. "Uh-huh," you said.

169

'*Your mum almost died of embarrassment.*'

Marnie looks at Joe. 'In my defence, I was only three.'

A home movie appears on screen showing Marnie running around a sprinkler in the garden dressed only in her bikini bottoms. The footage fades and is replaced by Marnie in a school uniform, ready for her first day at primary school. Her uniform is too big for her and she's standing pigeon-toed in front of a door, smiling widely, her dimples on display.

'*We moved to the farm in West Yorkshire when you were three. It wasn't much of a farm and I wasn't much of a farmer, but your mum loved that place. She was in her element, running around like a sixties flower child, always barefoot and hugging trees. We were going to grow our own food and make our own cider from apples in the orchard. You probably don't remember because you were so young, but she would have been so proud of you if she had seen how you turned out . . .*'

Joe feels Marnie shift beside him, turning her face from the screen. 'I'm sorry, I can't watch it – not if he's going to talk about her.'

'You said you barely remember her.'

'I know, but I can't watch this.' She kneads the front of her shirt. 'Can we fast-forward this bit?'

Joe does as she asks. 'Do you want to stop for a while?'

'No, go on.'

An elderly woman appears on screen. She has a blue-rinsed perm and wrinkles around her eyes.

Blinking at the camera, she seems to be looking at her own reflection in the lens.

'Hello, Marnella, do you remember me?'

'It's Mrs Gilmore. She taught me in years three and four,' explains Marnie.

'I retired after forty years of teaching, but I miss all of my students. You were a cheeky little thing. I remember when you convinced Toby Clement that he was adopted and that his real father was Michael Jackson.'

Marnie laughs. 'He wasn't even black.'

Another woman appears on screen.

'That's my drama teacher, Miss Bonnie.'

'I know it's been a lot of years, Marnella, but somehow your wonderful husband tracked me down. You and Jessica Glenn were my two stars. You both wanted to be Snow White in the end-of-year concert. You were supposed to take it in turns but Jessica came down with food poisoning, remember? She missed both performances. I hope you're still singing and dancing.'

Marnie's father comes back on screen.

'When you were thirteen, we almost lost you. Remember Mr Slipper? You were riding him through the village and a dog spooked him. I got the call at work and went straight to the hospital. You had internal injuries and bleeding on the brain. They had to operate to relieve the pressure. You were in a medically induced coma for five days. I'd never been so scared.' He blinks wetly at the camera. 'You didn't ride again after that. I think Mr Slipper died of a broken heart.'

Marnie turns a page of the album and points to

a photograph of the pony. Then she drops her head and parts her hair, showing Joe the scar. 'You can only see it when my hair is wet.'

Daniel appears on screen again. *'You're allowed to shed a few tears, but only nostalgic ones. There's plenty more to come . . .'* He adjusts the camera and talks to someone else in the room. *'I can edit this later and take out all the mistakes.'*

Penny appears. They're filming in her sunroom.

'Happy Birthday, best friend, I can't believe you're as old as I am, but don't tell anyone our age. You don't want to hear me sing, so I thought I'd tell you a story.' Penny does a pirouette. *'You see what I'm wearing? Once upon a time, many years ago, this was my favourite top. Then we went to Italy in the summer of 1995 and you couldn't read the Italian label on the washing liquid and bought bleach instead. You ruined all our clothes. Remember? I kept this as a souvenir.'*

Marnie nods her head, acknowledging the memory.

'You are such an important person in my life and I really hope you realise that. You never give yourself enough credit. You are so strong, intelligent and you amaze me every day. And you have a hot husband – so look after him. Ciao.'

The recording continues. Daniel has interviewed old teachers, lecturers, colleagues and friends. The footage is unedited. Truncated. Blurred. A new face emerges. A man is sitting on a stool.

'Is it running?' he asks.

'Yes,' Daniel replies.

Marnie let's out a squeak of recognition. 'Oh, my God, that's Eugene Lansky!'

The man on screen is in his mid to late thirties with a receding hairline and ponytail. He's wearing a paint-splattered shirt rolled up past his elbows.

'Marnie Logan, I hope you're listening. You're the bitch who ruined my life! You're a vindictive, conniving, heartless piece of shit . . .!'

Daniel's voice comes from off-camera. *'Hey! You can't say that . . . What are you trying to do?'* He fumbles for the controls, knocking the tripod. The camera topples and he catches it again. Eugene Lansky is still talking.

'I used to wish you were dead. I wanted it. And I'm not the only one—'

The screen goes blank.

Marnie looks stunned. Mouth open. 'Why would he say something like that?'

'Who is he?'

'Eugene was my first real boyfriend. He took my virginity in the back of a Mr Whippy ice cream van. It's where he used to work. I could never get the melted choc-ice stain out of my dress.' Marnie scans the photographs. 'That's him.'

In the picture she's wearing a cocktail dress and Eugene has a suit, which looks a size too small.

'This was taken at our graduation ball – the biggest night of the year. All the girls bought new dresses. That's also the night Eugene ran off with Debbie Tibbets. We called her *Debbie Bigtits*. It hurt, but I was more embarrassed than heartbroken.'

Marnie pushes back her fringe and stares at the blank screen. 'It was eighteen years ago. Why would he say that I ruined his life?'

Joe doesn't answer. Marnie has her head down as though distracted by something on the floor. She excuses herself and goes to the bathroom. Bracing her hands on either side of the sink, she looks at herself in the mirror. Baffled. Hurt. It's a shock to realise that someone in the world hates you. What had she done to Eugene? *He* dumped *her*. Surely it's a case of mistaken identity or a practical joke?

Marnie looks at her watch. It's after eight. The library shut half an hour ago. Zoe should be home by now and Elijah in bed. She can hear him talking in the bedroom. He's sitting in her wardrobe with his toys spread out on the floor between his knees.

'Who are you talking to?' she asks.

'My friend.'

Marnie laughs. 'So he lives in the wardrobe – like in Narnia?'

'Huh?'

'I'll read you the stories one day. *The Lion, the Witch and the Wardrobe.*'

'I don't like witches,' says Elijah.

Marnie gives him a hug, lifting him onto the bed where he stands. 'Bedtime, big man.'

'But I'm not tired.'

'Well I am. Brush your teeth and choose a story.'

'Where's Zoe?'

'She's on her way home.'

'Can I wait up for her?'

'Nope.'

'Who's that man you're talking to?'

'He's a friend.'

Marnie knows that Elijah will keep asking questions if it delays bedtime. He brushes his teeth and goes to the toilet, concentrating hard as he balances on a step and aims a stream of urine into the bowl. Marnie tucks him into bed.

'Will Daddy be home tomorrow?'

'I don't think so.'

'What about the next day?'

'No.'

He nods. 'Maybe by the weekend.'

She turns off the light and rejoins Joe in the sitting room. Checking her mobile for messages, she's worried about Zoe. She's about to call when she hears the door opening.

'Where have you been?'

'At the library,' says Zoe.

'It's late.'

'I got talking to a friend.'

Zoe is holding her school satchel in both arms.

'Have you eaten?'

'No.'

She glances past Marnie and sees Joe on the sofa. He stands. 'This is Professor O'Loughlin.'

'Your psychologist?'

'He's also a friend.'

'You can call me Joe,' he says.

175

Zoe looks along the hallway. 'I'll just put this in my room.'

'I can make you something for supper,' says Marnie.

'I can do it.'

Zoe closes her bedroom door. A bolt slides into place.

Joe is holding Daniel's diary. It's open on a page with a list of names, some underlined, others crossed out. There are phone numbers and addresses. Other details are jotted in the margins: jobs still to be done.

Marnie takes the diary and studies the list. Most of the names belong to friends, former colleagues, old teachers or women she met at her mothers' group. A few she hasn't talked to or thought about in years.

'Penny must have helped Daniel put it together,' she says. 'She's terrible at keeping secrets, but she kept this one.'

Joe leans forward. Their knees touch.

'Are there any names on the list that you don't recognise?'

Marnie runs her finger down the page. It stops.

'I don't know anyone called Francis Moffatt.'

'Are you sure?'

'Yes.'

'What about this one – Dr Sterne?'

Marnie hesitates and shakes her head. She points to another name. 'Calvin is Zoe's father. We were married for about eighteen months.'

'Do you still see him?'

'He sends Zoe a card on her birthday when he remembers.'

'Where is he now?'

'He's been in prison, but he's out now.'

Zoe emerges from her bedroom. She's changed into tracksuit bottoms and a T-shirt. Opening the fridge door, she takes out a loaf of bread, butter and eggs, making more noise than necessary.

'We should do this another time,' says Joe. He holds up the diary. 'Can I borrow this?'

'You think it's important?'

'Daniel contacted these people. Maybe one of them knows what happened to him.'

Marnie is standing near the mantelpiece. 'What should I do?'

'Talk to your father and to Penny. Perhaps the Big Red Book will trigger a memory.'

When Marnie was a child I worried that she would fall out of a tree or get hit crossing the road or swim out too far beyond the waves. Look what happened with Mr Slipper, how close I came to losing her. She rode him every weekend, competing in gymkhanas and practising over jumps.

Then came the fall. She was riding through a village and a dog came snarling out of a yard, barking and biting at the hooves. Mr Slipper spooked. Marnie tried to hold on, but fell backwards across a railing fence, rupturing her spleen and causing bleeding on her brain.

I know she loved that pony, but I couldn't let her ride again. It was too dangerous. Once she was out of hospital, I collected green acorns from the fields, raking them into a hessian bag and carrying it over my shoulder to the stable. I could smell the horses. I didn't trust them any more. They were malevolent, ugly creatures that rippled and snorted.

Removing the chaff bag, I filled it with the acorns and hung it in Mr Slipper's stall. The pony died the next day. His kidneys had failed. They told Marnie that he didn't suffer; that he died in his sleep. That's not true, but I'm sure she appreciated the sentiment.

The dog was harder to find. I went back to the village for three weeks, looking for a dog that chased horses. Then I discovered the owners had taken the animal away, sent it to the farm, so to speak, which I hoped was a euphemism.

Don't get me wrong – I love dogs, I just love Marnie more. It's like when she was in primary school and wanted to play Snow White in the concert, but they made her share the role. Marnie accepted the decision, but I didn't think it was fair. I can barely remember the other girl's name now and neither can anybody else. She vomited both nights and couldn't go on.

Marnie was magnificent. I mouthed every line and took every bow with her. I wanted to show her that I had the power to save and protect her, to make her stairs less steep. And when she fell, I would pick up the pieces and put her together like Humpty Dumpty even when she didn't know she was broken.

CHAPTER 17

The shooting range is hidden away beneath railway arches and surrounded by factories and workshops in an area of East London that hasn't changed much in half a century. A small bronze plaque marks the doorway.

Ruiz buzzes and nods to the camera. The door opens. Upstairs, he goes through the protocol of having his licence checked and being made to read the rules.

1. Always keep the Firearm Pointed in a Safe Direction.
2. Always keep your Finger off the Trigger until Ready to Shoot.
3. Always keep the Firearm Unloaded until Ready to Shoot.

There are a dozen more. He doesn't bother reading them because he knows them by heart.

The range consists of six parallel twenty-metre lanes with a manual pulley system for varying the target distance. There are changing-room facilities and a small lounge with armchairs where members can make tea and coffee.

Detective Superintendent Peter Vorland is waiting for him at the lanes, wearing protective earmuffs hooked around his neck. Snowy headed, thinning on top, Vorland has a powerful handshake and an Afrikaans accent. He fled from South Africa with his family in the late seventies, after his lawyer father was arrested in Durban for representing a black political prisoner. The only person the Afrikaners hated more than an uppity black man was a white man who defended one.

Like his father, Vorland had proved himself to be a good man. Fair. Honest. Hard. He and Ruiz had both played rugby until their mid forties, throwing their bodies around muddy fields, trying to match it with younger men.

Ruiz is older by eight years. Vorland climbed higher. Both remember when policing required less bureaucracy and more common sense. Corners could be cut. Experience was considered valuable. Those times have passed.

Pistol shots echo through the cavernous range. The two men are side by side in the lanes, legs apart, arm outstretched. Steady. Squeeze. Fire. Vorland is methodical. Between each shot, he pauses, lowers his weapon, stares down the lane. Then he begins his build-up again.

Ruiz takes less time. He doesn't picture the pistol

as being an extension of his arm or reach inside himself for a Zen-like state of focus and calm. He points, aims and squeezes off six shots – a heartbeat between each of them – and every time the paper target rattles back toward him on the pulley, the cluster is a single ragged perforation.

Vorland grunts in disgust. 'I swear to God you don't even open your eyes. When's the last time you went shooting?'

'I can't remember.'

'You should teach people. You could start by teaching me.'

'Can't do that. Wouldn't know where to start.'

'Why?'

'You do *everything* wrong.'

'Fuck off!'

They check the weapons, emptying the chambers before signing them back into the armoury. In the locker room Ruiz washes his hands with soap and water, wanting to rid himself of the smell. Vorland is sitting on a bench, changing his shoes. He's not a big man, but solid, honed. He had a heart attack a few years ago and since then he's been pounding pavements and lifting weights as though death could come calling any day.

'You wanted to know about Niall Quinn,' he says. 'He was pulled out of the Thames four days ago. Throat partially cut. Hands bound with a cable tie. They found his car parked near Trinity Pier below the Lower Lea Crossing.'

Ruiz knows the place.

'His body was probably in the water for about twelve hours.'

'Who's handling it?'

'Eastern Division.'

'Who's in charge?'

'A newly promoted DI called Warren Gennia. He came out of Counter Terrorism Command. I've heard good things.'

'Did you talk to him?'

'No.'

'Any suspects?'

'They've been interviewing known associates and family.'

'What about Patrick Hennessy?'

'He turned up with his lawyer. Didn't say a word.' Vorland takes his watch from the locker and straps it on his wrist, checking the time.

'What's your interest in this, Vincent?'

'Hennessy has been putting the squeeze on a young woman – a mother of two. She was with Quinn that night.'

'Sleeping with him?'

'No.'

'Have the police talked to her?'

'Twice.'

Vorland gives him a prolonged noncommittal stare. 'You should have told me.'

'Told you what?'

'You've had me making inquiries on behalf of a murder suspect. You know how that looks.'

'I don't know if she's a suspect.'

'Don't bullshit me, Vincent. If she was with Quinn that night she's a suspect. I hope you're not protecting her.'

'I hardly know the woman.'

Vorland sighs, still not satisfied. 'What are you planning to do?'

'Talk to Hennessy.'

'You're going to warn him off.'

'I'm going to try.'

CHAPTER 18

Joe has spent two days looking for Eugene Lansky, finding him via a Facebook page and an artist's co-operative in South London. A woman tells him that Lansky has a pitch at Camden Market near the canal, an area Joe knows well. He and Julianne once owned a house less than a mile away and would walk to the markets on weekends, pushing Charlie in a pushchair or later letting her ride her bike.

Until the 1950s, the Grand Union Canal was a major transport link to the capital with barges bringing produce and coal from the Midlands, but then road transport took over and the warehouses and stables were no longer needed. In the 1970s artists and craftsmen took up the space, turning it into studios, workshops and galleries. Most of the artisans have since gone, priced out by the eighties property boom and replaced by stalls selling tourist tat and Chinese knock-offs.

Eugene is wearing paint-splattered jeans and a buttoned-up shirt with an antique tie-pin holding the collars together. His hair is pulled back into a ponytail and he's sitting beside a girl in customised Doc Martens and a short denim skirt. She looks half his age and impossibly bored.

Joe studies Eugene's paintings and prints, which are dark and macabre, featuring famous film stars whose bodies have been arranged to look like victims at a crime scene. One of the images shows Marilyn Monroe lying naked in a bed, with an empty pill bottle next to her head. Another shows James Dean's crumpled body draped over the bonnet of a wrecked Porsche 550.

'I can do you a deal on that one,' says Eugene, pointing to a picture of Katharine Hepburn being eaten by a pride of lions.

'I don't think Katharine Hepburn was eaten by lions,' says Joe.

'It's an allegory,' explains Eugene, making it sound obvious. 'I love watching old films: stuff from the forties and fifties, you know, but all those iconic actors are gone and they're just beautiful dead people. I'm trying to capture that final moment – the junction between life and death when immortality is born.'

Joe is glad Ruiz isn't with him. He once told Joe that modern art was an oxymoron like military intelligence or Australian intellectual.

'I'm not really in the market to buy,' says Joe. 'I wanted to ask you about Marnie Logan.'

Eugene glances around, suddenly nervous. 'Is she here?'

'No.'

He relaxes and looks at the girl. 'Get us a coffee,

babe.' He gives her a tenner. 'And don't forget the fucking sugar.'

She sulks and tosses her hair, walking with the strut of a catwalk model. Eugene licks his thumb and leans down, rubbing paint from the toe of his boot.

'Why would I want to talk about Marnie Logan? I've spent nearly twenty years trying to forget that bitch.'

Eugene leans over the railing and spits into the canal. Joe tries to picture him at eighteen – gangly, halfway handsome, trying to impress the girls.

'Daniel Hyland came to see you?'

'Yeah. He shoved a camera in my face and asked me what I thought of his wife. I said she was an evil vindictive bitch and I wouldn't piss on her if she was on fire.'

'Her husband is missing.'

'No surprise there.' Eugene scratches a bite on his neck. 'I told him to run a mile and keep going.'

'Why?'

Eugene chews the inside of his cheek, his eyes distant. 'How well do you know her?'

'I'm her psychologist.'

'I knew it! She's a complete fucking head-case!'

'What have you got against Marnie?'

'I used to go out with her. We had some fun. I got bored. Moved on. But after that a rumour went round the school saying I'd given Marnie herpes and the clap and genital warts, you name it. No girl would go within thirty feet of me.'

'Is that it?'

'You heard of Camberwell College of Arts?'

Joe nods.

'I had early acceptance, but they withdrew the offer because I didn't have an A-level. The deputy head raided my locker and found a bag of weed. I got expelled. Didn't sit my exams.'

'What's that got to do with Marnie?'

'It wasn't my weed. Someone put it there. A few weeks later I got a card through the post. Four words: *Payback is a bitch!* She diced me up into little fucking pieces and ate me cold.'

'Did Marnie sign the letter?'

'No.'

'Was it her handwriting?'

'It was typed.'

'So you can't prove anything.'

Eugene glances past Joe. A brightly painted canal boat is navigating beneath the hump-backed bridge. Tourists are taking photographs.

'OK, I'll tell you another story. I've got this mate, Devon Boucher. We went through school together. He created this fake yearbook with funny captions about the students. It was a joke, you know. Harmless. He called Marnie a professional virgin because she acted like such a princess. For the next six months somebody played porn soundtracks down Devon's home phone with lots of grunting and screaming orgasms. His parents had to change their number.'

'Did he confront Marnie?'

'She denied it. I know what you're thinking. No proof. But Marnie is too clever to let anyone trace it back to her.'

'You said she ruined your life.'

'Maybe I exaggerated a little. I didn't go to art school. Yeah, I could have sat my A-levels at another school or tried again, but I didn't. That's my fault. But what she did to Debbie was worse.'

'Debbie?'

'Debbie Tibbets. The girl I went out with after Marnie.'

'After you dumped her at the graduation ball.'

'Yeah, well, these things happen. Debbie got engaged a few years after we broke up. No hard feelings. I was booked to take photographs at her wedding, but someone rang up and cancelled the job a week before the event. They also cancelled the reception, the band, the honeymoon flights, the flowers and the wedding cake.

'It was malicious. Debbie didn't realise until the day before. Her entire wedding was ruined, months of planning. She was devastated. Finished up marrying in a registry office. A month or so later, Debbie got a card through the mail. Same message: *Payback is a bitch!*'

'And she thinks it was Marnie Logan?'

'We all do. Debbie, Dean, me, the others.'

'Did anyone ask her?'

'You don't believe me. I can see that. She's got you fooled. That's Marnie's gift. She comes across as all sweetness and light. When you're with her you feel stronger, cleverer, more capable. But when she turns, it's like winter setting in, the longest coldest winter of your life.'

The sun has passed behind a cloud, throwing shadows across the cobblestones. Nearby, a street mime dressed up as Mary Poppins unfurls her umbrella and curtsies. Eugene lowers his face again, watching from under his eyelashes.

Joe is trying to picture Marnie taking revenge on old boyfriends and past enemies, but he can't make the image stick in his mind.

'You mentioned there were others.'

Eugene squints at Joe, trying to decide how much to say. 'Talk to Olivia Shulman.'

'Who is she?'

'She works at a bookshop on Charing Cross Road. I bumped into her a few months back.'

'What happened to her?'

'It's not my business to tell you.'

His girlfriend is back. She's carrying two coffees. A digital camera is hanging from her wrist. Joe didn't notice it before. She lifts it to her right eye and takes a photograph. Lowers it again. Then she gives him a soulful, commiserating look, as though she understands.

Eugene takes the coffee and rips open two sugar sachets, tipping the contents into the cup. He looks at Joe, almost pleading with him. 'Do me a favour. Don't tell Marnie where I am.'

CHAPTER 19

On the train to Ealing Broadway, Elijah eats a sandwich from a Tupperware box and Marnie stares at the posters for West End musicals and insurance companies. The carriage is full of office temps, tourists and bored-looking people, capitulating to the mundaneness of the day.

Elijah is engrossed in a young couple sitting opposite.

'Why is that boy whispering in that girl's mouth?' he asks.

'They're kissing.'

'Can she breathe?'

'She can.'

The girl looks at Marnie, who smiles apologetically.

At Ealing Broadway, they emerge onto street level and follow the High Street as far as the common. Elijah watches boys playing park football and gets a hotdog from a barrow. He drips tomato sauce down the front of his best shirt, but Marnie doesn't get annoyed.

On the southern edge of Ealing Common, they cross a road and follow a terrace-lined street to a larger detached dwelling with lace-trimmed curtains and a brass plaque beside the door.

Marnie rings the doorbell and it opens automatically. Instantly her nose wrinkles at the smell of boiled cabbage, disinfectant and people crumbling with age. The nursing home belongs to a corporation with a name like Everglade or Evermore and is run by a Welsh couple, Mr and Mrs Herman. Mrs Herman has short, permed hair like a ball of steel wool and black-rimmed glasses. She wears a white coat and stands with her legs apart and arms crossed, guarding the nurses' station.

Signing the visitor's book, Marnie walks along the hallway, past different rooms. Most have beds with worn-out human beings propped on pillows, some with oxygen masks on their faces and catheters coming out from their bedclothes. A few are watching TV, mouths open, toothless. Occasionally one of them makes eye contact with Marnie, gazing at her like a prisoner peering through the bars of a cell.

Thomas Logan is in a different wing. His dementia is getting worse, but only affects his short-term memory. He loses track of his yesterdays, forgetting whether he's eaten or taken his medication. The gaps are like missing words in a conversation but the meaning can usually be determined.

Marnie finds him sitting in the courtyard, wearing a battered Panama hat. His legs are bony under the thin striped pyjama trousers and his cheeks are grey and sunken. A big man, fragile now in his illness, he spent twenty years working as a roughneck connecting pipes down the well bore on North Sea oilrigs. Two weeks on, two weeks off. No alcohol. No drugs. No women. His hands bear the scars and grease that seems to be ingrained around his fingernails.

When he quit the rigs Thomas set up a window-cleaning business and later worked as a warehouse manager and moved to London when Elijah was born because he wanted to be closer to his grand-children. He was single by then. Divorced.

'Best decision I ever made,' he said, talking about the break-up. He didn't take much with him apart from an old-fashioned record player in a wooden box, with a sliding lid on top of the turntable. He loves Bing Crosby and Sinatra and Sammy Davis Jr. The crooners, he calls them.

Marnie crouches next to him and kisses his cheek. He looks up at her almost merrily as Elijah crawls onto his lap. Thomas stares at the boy for a moment, trying to make the connection.

'How about a cup of tea?' she says.

The dining room has been set up for lunch, but they're allowed to use the big silver urn to make tea. The milk comes in small plastic pods that are difficult to open.

'Let me do that, Dad,' she says, using her finger-nail to lift the foil flap. Elijah is allowed to choose a biscuit from the metal tin.

Thomas opens a cupboard and stares inside.

'What are you looking for, Dad?'

He doesn't answer.

'The sugar is here.'

He shakes his head.

'Do you want a biscuit?'

Another shake. The skin along his hairline is shiny with perspiration and there are tiny black specks in the blueness of his eyes. He's worse today. The messages aren't reaching his brain or there are no fumes for his synapses to ignite.

He takes a spoonful of sugar and stirs for a long time, looking into the cup, then at the spoon. Meanwhile, Elijah has found his colouring book and crayons, setting them out on the table. Somebody has a radio cranked up. Thomas hums tunefully along, glancing occasionally at Elijah as though puzzling over his grandson.

'I need to ask you about Daniel,' says Marnie. 'He was making a book for me. Do you remember?'

Something seems to fire in the old man's brain. 'It was gonna be a surprise.'

'You gave him some photographs.'

'We went through them together. I told him all the old stories – about you growing up. You were always getting into trouble. Remember the time you told Jacinta that Santa had run out of Barbie dolls and she would be getting a Ken doll for Christmas?'

'Jacinta?'

'One of the foster kids.' Thomas has a rumbling chuckle. 'You also tried to sell little Duncan at a car boot sale.'

Marnie feels a pang of regret. She grew up resenting the children who came and went. More kids meant shorter showers, shared treats and fewer presents under the tree. Why should she have to cope with these interlopers, these cuckoos?

'I was a selfish little cow.'

'You were pretty normal.'

Thomas looks out the window and straightens, holding himself upright, as though dignity might be found at higher altitudes.

'How is Daniel?'

'He's missing, Dad.'

'Did he ever give you that big red book?'

'I found it.'

The conversation is going round in circles. Thomas finally remembers what's been bothering him.

'A detective came to see me.'

'When?'

'Yesterday . . . or maybe it was the day before . . . He reminded me of someone, but I can't think who it is.'

'What did he want?'

'He was asking about Daniel . . . and he wanted to know what happened to your mother . . . how she died . . .'

'Why?'

'He wouldn't say.'

Thomas studies Elijah for a moment. 'Is he yours?'

'Yes, Dad.'

'Who's the father?'

Marnie laughs. 'Daniel, of course, who else would it be?'

Thomas turns back to his tea with a sniff.

CHAPTER 20

A plastic bag flies high up into the sky, caught on the wind, snapping and slewing like a runaway kite before being pinned against the branches of a tree. Ruiz listens to the midday news on the car radio. Resting his hands lightly on the steering wheel, he leans forward and gazes at the façade of the modern apartment block.

The building has a doorman, key-controlled lifts, a rooftop pool, landscaped gardens and a view down the Thames as far as the London Eye. Sold off the plan, high-end, it's worth three, maybe four million. Joggers drift past him, feet slapping the pavement, along with flocks of brightly coloured cyclists waving bums in the air.

Up until two days ago, it had been ten years since Ruiz heard the name Patrick Hennessy, but some criminals cling to his memory like burrs. Hennessy is one of them. His old man, Ronan, used to run illegal casinos and brothels in the seventies – establishments that sprouted like weeds after the Kray twins were sentenced to life imprisonment. Various gangsters and crime families divided up London as though they were playing Monopoly. Hennessy took the north.

Patrick was still in short trousers, going to the best schools. He could have broken the family mould, but filled it instead. He branched out into loan-sharking. One of his favourite fiddles was to plant people into chapters of Gamblers Anonymous, who befriended problem gamblers, getting details of their debts and addictions. He found those who still had assets left to lose – cars, houses or savings. They were addicts. It was easy to sow the seeds of their destruction. Soon they were chasing more losses and Hennessy was happy to lend them money with the right security: deeds to their house, registration papers for their cars.

Ruiz takes out his tin of rock candy and chooses a square, sucking it back and forth over the top of his tongue, tasting the sour sweetness.

A large black Land Cruiser is idling out front of the apartment block, polished so brilliantly that clouds roll over the bonnet and tinted windows. A doorman stands sentry in a uniform. The automatic doors open and Patrick Hennessy emerges, glancing at the sky as though confirming the weather forecast. He's dressed in a lightweight suit and Italian loafers with sunglasses like mirrors.

Ruiz calls his name and crosses the road.

'Well, well, look what the cat dragged in.' Hennessy looks up from the open car door. 'How are things, Detective Inspector Ruiz?'

'I'm not a detective any more.'

'So they finally kicked you out.'

'I retired.'

'Same result.'

The driver has stepped out of the Land Cruiser. He looks like the sort of weight-room poser who drops free-weights in the gym to attract attention. Hennessy raises his hand a few inches, telling him it's OK.

'How can I help you, Mr Ruiz? Are you looking for a job? Security. You're a bit long in the tooth. Terrence here can bench-press twice his body weight.'

'Must make him useful around the house. Does he wear a pinny?'

The driver isn't sure if he's understood the insult. Ruiz gives him a wave.

'Be nice,' says Hennessy. 'You're too old to be making enemies.'

The Ulsterman steps out of the car, tugging at the cuffs of his jacket. He inclines his head, his face upturned, giving Ruiz a wide elastic grin.

'So why are you here?'

Ruiz wishes he could see behind the mirrored glasses. Hennessy has a sun-bed tan and whitened teeth, but like most narcissists, he has a hidden streak of self-doubt that can't be camouflaged by expensive clothes and a posse of flunkies. It's the Ulsterman's lips that most fascinate Ruiz. They look as if they're made of rubber and belong to a man with a physical appetite that is visceral and base; someone who knows the value of violence and how to bend people to his will.

Ruiz motions to the building. 'Nice place.'

'My old man always told me to buy in the inner city, never mind the price.'

'How is your father?'

'Dead.'

'I'm sorry to hear that.'

Hennessy looks for sarcasm and can't find any. Ruiz continues talking. 'I had my issues with your old man, but he had a streak of the squeak in him. He could do the right thing. You're different, Patrick. Not so much a chip off the old block as a splinter under a fingernail that's turned septic.'

Hennessy's nostrils dilate and he forces his lips to curl into an insinuating smile.

'I was trying to be polite and you've gone and done the opposite. My father had nice things to say about you, Mr Ruiz, although he said you had a Don Quixote complex – always tilting at windmills.'

'Have you read Cervantes?'

'Who?'

Ruiz smiles. 'It doesn't matter. I want to talk to you about Marnie Logan. She says you threatened her two days ago. Maybe you knocked her off her bike.'

'I wouldn't believe a word that cunning bitch had to say.'

'You know her then?'

'She owes me money.'

'Her husband owed you money.'

'Same difference.'

'Not unless you mix up your genders and your tenses.'

Hennessy frowns, growing impatient. 'I'm a busy man, Mr Ruiz, I don't have time to play word games. Marnie Logan is madder than a midget with a chainsaw, so don't put too much trust in anything she tells you.'

'What makes you say that?'

'I've heard stories.' Hennessy's face is empty of expression. 'My brother-in-law is dead and Marnie Logan was the last person to see him alive. She comes across as all soft and vulnerable, but I'm not buying it. She's a head-case – and I'm not talking about your typical female insanity, I mean seriously fucked up.' He pauses, lips peeled back. 'Are you bumping uglies with her?'

'What?'

'I wouldn't blame you. She's prime real estate. I mean, if I were you – and I'm not – I'd take her back to that little place of hers in Maida Vale and hump until she can't sit down for a week. Her daughter's not bad either, if you're in a Jimmy Savile frame of mind.'

Ruiz feels his molars grinding against each other. He can see his reflection in Hennessy's mirrored glasses, a tiny phantom version of himself who seems to be standing a long way away, struggling for relevance.

'But if you are going to fuck her, watch your back,' says Hennessy. 'She's a first-class babe, but she can cut a man's throat with a kitchen knife and pretend nothing has happened.'

'When was the last time you saw her husband?'

'What is this, twenty questions?'

Ruiz waits. Hennessy sighs. 'I loaned Mr Hyland certain monies, which he failed to repay. The man couldn't back a winner if it had twelve legs and was the only horse running.'

'Unlucky?'

'Didn't know when to quit.'

'Where is he?'

'Dead. Don't read too much into that – it's just my opinion.'

Ruiz can taste something bitter and cloying in his mouth, which seems to leak into the back of his throat. Hennessy picks up on the vibe.

'Why is it that you don't like me, Mr Ruiz?'

'You really want to me to answer that?'

'Enlighten me.'

'You're an intelligent man, but you're a narcissist and like most narcissists you destroy anyone who questions your perfect view of yourself. You think legitimate businessmen like Richard Branson and Alan Sugar should treat you as an equal, but nobody wants to break bread with you because the faecal stench is too much for them.'

Hennessy doesn't react. 'How can someone with your experience be so naïve?' he asks. 'You think you have principles. You think you're on the right side. Explain something to me. When a man like me lends money and seeks to recover the debt, I sometimes have to remind people of their responsibilities. When a bank is owed money, it throws a man out of his home, along with his wife and kids. They sell his furniture and his cars. You think I'm scum, yet you ignore the banker sitting in his fancy office, foreclosing on mortgages, gambling with other people's money, pawning risky products, getting bailed out by taxpayers, and not one of them ever goes to prison. They get knighted and fêted by politicians. The scum you should be complaining about is already floating on the top, Mr Ruiz, bobbing with the turds.'

Hennessy motions to the car and Terrence opens the door.

'I have people to see. May I suggest you make an appointment next time you want to talk to me? Don't be offended if I decline.'

'I'm taking an interest in Marnie Logan's welfare,' says Ruiz. 'Don't threaten her again.'

Hennessy smiles. 'I'll be sure to remember that.'

He raises a single middle finger and pushes his sunglasses higher up his nose. The finger stays in place. The door closes. The Land Cruiser accelerates away. A whiff of diesel catches in Ruiz's throat. The whole encounter bothers him. It's as though he's missing something – a major plot point or a turn of events, which means the story doesn't quite hang together. Why is he so concerned? It's not his fight. He's retired. He's settled for the easy life. No more criminals, gangsters, junkies, bent coppers, defence lawyers, terrorists, or victims. No responsibilities. Yet it doesn't seem like enough.

CHAPTER 21

The bookshop has a narrow frontage but deep aisles lined with shelves that reach to the ceiling and into the darker reaches of the store. The place is empty apart from a couple of browsers who are running their fingers along the spines of books, tilting their heads as they read the titles.

The woman behind the counter is helping a customer. Her name-tag is in the shape of an owl and written in an elegant script: *Olivia Shulman*. She taps the name of a book into the computer. 'We don't have it in stock, but I can order it for you.'

Watching people is second nature to Joe. He does it without even realising it: picking up on small details that accompany every interaction – the shrugs, nods, tics, twitches, jiggles and dips, the words spoken and unspoken, the subtexts and overtones. Olivia's clothes are shapeless and dark, but she's flying the flag for a younger version of herself with a pretty smile and sparkling teeth. She glances at Joe, not wanting to keep him waiting. She's an introvert. Sensitive. Quiet. Perceptive. She listens more than she talks. She doesn't draw attention to herself. She wouldn't know how to work a room. She's more comfortable in a shop full of books than a room full of people.

The customer says goodbye. Olivia turns to Joe. 'Sorry to keep you waiting. How can I help?'

'I wanted to ask you about Marnie Logan.'

Olivia's eyes widen and she steps back, reaching behind her as though looking for something to brace herself against. Whatever goodwill she harboured towards Joe has been replaced by something darker and more elemental.

'Please leave.'

'Why?'

'Did she send you?'

'No.'

Olivia rocks her head from side to side. 'Tell her I'm sorry for whatever she thinks I did to her. Tell her to leave me alone.'

'Relax, please, I'm not here to cause trouble. I'm a psychologist. I'm treating Marnie.'

The blast of a truck horn from outside makes Olivia jump. She looks at the windows where sunlight angles onto a display table of discounted books.

'Why are you here?' she asks.

'I'm looking for Marnie's husband.'

'I haven't seen him.'

'But you know who I'm talking about.'

'He came to see me last year. He wanted to film a message for Marnie's birthday. I told him to leave.'

'Did he ask you why?'

'Yes.'

'What did you tell him?'

Olivia begins rearranging stationery on the desk, as though the pencils and paperclips are suddenly in the wrong place. She describes how she and Marnie met in secondary school and became best friends. When they finished school they were both accepted by universities in London. Marnie went to Brunel and Olivia to King's College. They still saw each other regularly and invited each other to parties.

One Saturday night she arranged to meet Marnie at Piccadilly Circus. They were going to go clubbing but had no money so they went to a party instead. It meant travelling all the way to Millwall, but they took a bus and then walked the final mile.

The house was packed with bodies. People were in the garden and outside on the street. Olivia lost touch with Marnie during the evening. When she decided to go home she went looking, but couldn't find Marnie anywhere and she didn't have a mobile.

Olivia looks at Joe. 'If I'd known what was going to happen I would never have left her. Never.' She pauses, moving a pen from one side of the blotter to the other. 'I didn't hear about the rape until a few days later. I felt awful. I went to see Marnie. I tried to apologise. She told me it wasn't my fault. She said I wasn't to tell anyone.'

'Marnie was raped?'

Olivia nods. 'Her drink was spiked. She didn't press charges.'

'Why?'

'I don't know. Maybe she was scared.'

What happened then?'

'About a month later, I had a letter from a secret admirer. I know it sounds stupid, but it was really nice to think someone fancied me. Marnie was always the prettier one who could take her pick of boyfriends.'

Olivia trembles, smoothing the front of her blouse. 'He wrote such lovely things. He made me feel . . .' She doesn't finish. 'I wrote back and we began corresponding. It was like an old-fashioned court-ship by post. Romantic, you know. I wanted to meet him, but he said he was frightened because I was so beautiful. I thought he had mistaken me for someone else. Maybe he saw me with Marnie and got us mixed up. He sent me a picture. He was dressed in uniform. I thought he looked very rugged and handsome. Too good to be true.'

'Did you meet him?'

'He said he was due to go to Kosovo with the peacekeepers. He wanted to wait until he got back, but asked if I'd send him a photograph he could take with him. Something sexy, he said. So I borrowed lingerie and I took pictures of myself. Silly really, but I thought it was harmless.' She grimaces and glances at Joe and away again.

'Have you worked it out yet?' she asks.

Joe shakes his head.

'My secret admirer didn't exist. He was invented. A joke. My photographs and letters were printed up and stuck on noticeboards and on lockers and put under dorm-room doors and left on chairs in lecture halls.'

Olivia lowers her eyes, looking at the spot where Joe is standing.

'I couldn't walk the corridors without people pointing me out or whispering things behind my back. It went on for weeks. I wanted to kill myself, I really did . . .'

'And you think Marnie did this?'

'I received a letter – in the same handwriting that my fake boyfriend used. Someone had written: *See what happens when you leave a friend behind*?'

'Did you confront Marnie?'

'She denied it.'

'But you don't believe her.'

'I know she was behind the letters. She's been persecuting me ever since.'

'What do you mean?'

'I've missed out on jobs and had deliveries cancelled. Once I got a phone call from a hospital saying my parents had died in a car accident. Two people were actually dead, but they were someone else's parents.'

Stepping around Joe, Olivia begins stacking books onto a trolley. She pushes it along the aisle. Joe follows.

'Did you complain?'

'Who to?'

'There are laws about public nuisance and intimidation.'

'I have no proof. I called Marnie. I begged her. She denied everything.'

Olivia stops and turns, pleading, 'Please make her stop. No, I take that back. Don't even mention me. Don't tell her where I am.'

Joe doesn't know what to say. He wants to defend Marnie. He wants to believe she's still the sweet smiling waitress who helped him find a flat. At the same time, he imagines Olivia as a young student, shy and looking for love, whose memories of university will always by tainted by feelings of acute embarrassment and the loss of a friend. His own degradations came much later in his early forties, when Mr Parkinson began tripping him up, freezing him in mid-stride or sending him sideways or backwards.

When he looks at Olivia he sees a searing frailty and the shakiness of an accident victim who can't be freed from her torment by a few comforting words. It doesn't matter that she's older now. She's like a walking bruise with eggshell defences, waiting for the next blow to strike.

As Joe says goodbye, he keeps his eyes closed so he doesn't have to look at her face and see the hole in her heart.

CHAPTER 22

Rhonda Firth lunches most days at an American-style diner on Edgware Road: one of those places where the milkshakes come in tall metal cups with double malt and an extra scoop of ice cream. The waitresses are wearing Betty Boop dresses and little paper hats that are red, white and blue.

Sitting at the main counter, Rhonda's buttocks swamp the vinyl stool and her police belt rattles against the metal edge of the Formica table. Ruiz takes the stool next to her and orders a black coffee, looking at the laminated menu.

'The specials are on the board,' says a waitress, whose antecedence is nearer Bangladesh than Bayswater or Brooklyn.

'I'll have a burger.'

'Which one?'

'Just a normal burger.'

'You want Cajun-style, Creole-style, with or without cheese, double cheese, bacon, double bacon, chilli con carne, jalapeño or egg?'

'Just give me your regular cheeseburger.'

'Swiss, cheddar, Mozzarella or pepper jack?'

'Cheddar.'

'Rare, medium or well done?'

'Medium.'

'You want chilli cheese fries, taco fries or French fries?'

'French fries.'

'You want a drink?'

'I want you to stop asking me questions.'

Rhonda's milkshake has beads of condensation running down the metal mug, leaving a moisture ring on her newspaper. She reaches for another handful of chilli fries.

'Excuse me, officer,' says Ruiz.

She turns. Her dreadlocks have been pulled tightly against her skull, showing paler skin on her scalp.

'I don't want to interrupt you while you're eating,' he continues.

'Don't then.'

She goes back to her newspaper.

'My name is Vincent Ruiz. I used to be with the Met.'

Rhonda spins her stool, her breasts heavy on her stomach, her stomach heavy on her lap. 'I've heard of you.'

'I doubt that.'

'No, I have. You're the guy who busted that terrorist cell in Swindon.'

'Luton.'

'Yeah, that's the place.' She wipes her hands on her thighs before gripping his outstretched hand, pumping it firmly.

'I know you're not allowed to talk about cases, but I was hoping you might make an exception. I wanted to ask you about Marnie Logan.'

'I thought you'd retired.'

'I'm helping a friend.

'Not Marnie?'

'Hardly know the woman, but my friend says she's had a rough time.'

Rhonda frowns and glances out the window at the passing traffic. She pushes her plate of fries towards him. Ruiz declines.

'So you're working as a private detective?'

'I'm trying to find out what happened to her husband. Marnie needs the insurance money, but the company won't pay out unless she can prove that Daniel is dead.'

'It's only been a year.'

'You think he's alive?'

'Didn't say that.'

'Foul play?'

Rhonda seems to smile at his old-fashioned terminology. 'They had a blazing row about a week before he disappeared, a real humdinger, screaming and throwing stuff. Neighbours told me all about it.'

'What was the fight about?'

'Gambling losses.'

'You sound like you don't believe her.'

'I keep an open mind.'

Ruiz waits for her to explain. Rhonda takes a toothpick and works it between her molars and her gums. 'Little Miss Tight Bod has a history.'

'Meaning?'

'She cried rape when she was twenty. Someone found her wandering the streets and took her to hospital. They ran a tox-screen, which came back positive for Special K.'

'Ketamine.'

'The police took a statement. Marnie gave them a name. A suspect was picked up and interviewed. He said he drove her home from a party and she jumped out of his car at a set of lights. Swore blind he didn't touch her.'

'Forensics?'

'Nothing useful. Police were trying to make a case, but Marnie Logan withdrew the allegations.'

'A lot of rape victims get cold feet.'

'Agreed. But how many rape suspects are dead within a month? Water police pulled Richard Duffy's body out of the river. Could have been a coincidence. Could have been a contrivance, a god loose in the machine – know what I'm saying?'

'You're not suggesting . . .?'

'I'm just telling you the facts, Jack. Marnie Logan cried rape, then withdrew the complaint and the dude was dead within a month. Maybe it's got no bearing. Maybe people disappear around her.'

Ruiz's burger has arrived. It looks like half a cow has been minced and flame-grilled.

'You might want to wash that down with something,' says the waitress.

Andrews, thinks Ruiz.

'Tell me about the day her husband went missing.'

'She came home. He wasn't there. She waited. He didn't show up. We interviewed family and friends. Monitored his bank accounts. Checked the borders. Nothing. He hasn't so much as signed for a library card.'

'So what's the thinking?'

'Like I said, I'm keeping an open mind.'

'What about suicide?'

'He didn't leave a note – not one that we could find. Maybe his old lady got rid of the note because he wrote some cruel things about her. Been known to happen.'

'And the gambling debts?'

'We looked into that. Didn't take us very far.'

'Patrick Hennessy isn't famous for his patience when people fall behind in their payments.'

'Dead men don't pay their debts. Hennessy is a businessman – and I use that term in the loosest possible sense.'

'He's been putting the squeeze on Marnie.'

'She should make a complaint.'

'Will that do any good?'

Rhonda sighs. Her chins shake. 'Not a lot, unless she can produce some evidence.'

'Witnesses disappear around Hennessy.'

'Nature of the man.'

'Scumbag.'

'I'll drink to that.' Rhonda drains her milkshake in a rumble of bubbles.

'Did the name Niall Quinn ever come up?' asks Ruiz.

'Who is he?'

'One of Hennessy's drivers.'

Rhonda shakes her head. 'What's he got to do with Marnie Logan?'

'Hennessy had her turning tricks to work off her husband's debt. Quinn was driving her around.'

'You're shitting me.'

'I shit you not.'

'I knew the lady was desperate, but that's a stretch . . .'

'Quinn's body was pulled out of the Thames last week.'

Rhonda's mouth is open. The pinkness of her tongue is almost fluorescent. 'Men get waterlogged around that woman. Where was the body found?'

'Wapping.'

'That'll be the Eastern division. Is Marnie a suspect?'

'Apparently.'

'And you're still trying to help her?'

'Like I said, I'm helping a friend of mine.'

Rhonda hooks her thumbs into her belt. 'Well, I'd be careful about involving myself in a police investigation.'

'Thanks for the advice.'

Ruiz has barely touched his burger. He gets up and reaches for his wallet.

'Are you going to eat the rest of that?' asks Rhonda, not waiting for his answer. 'I hate seeing food wasted.'

CHAPTER 23

Marnie can't find her keys. She searches the same drawers again and the pockets of her jacket. Zoe follows her to the bedroom and back to the kitchen, complaining.

'But I have homework to do.'

'You're looking after your brother. It's only for a few hours.'

'Why can't you take him?'

'I have to go out.'

Zoe knows the argument is lost, but continues because the unfairness warrants an adequate protest. When Daniel was around she could sometimes persuade him to see her point of view. He enjoyed the cut and thrust of an argument, wanting Zoe to be passionate and articulate. It was like when they played Scrabble and Daniel would find a way of guiding Zoe to the best squares or the highest-scoring words, never letting her settle for something mediocre. 'I'm a journalist,' he'd say. 'Words are my tools.' With her mother it was different. She'd changed in the past year, becoming tougher, harsher, intransigent.

Elijah is in Marnie's wardrobe, deep in conversation with himself.

'Listen to him,' says Zoe. 'He's a freak!'

'Don't talk about him like that,' scolds Marnie.

'He's always talking to himself.'

'He has an imaginary friend.'

'Which can't be healthy.'

'It's just a stage.'

Marnie kisses the top of her head. 'Even to the post office,' she says, offering her cheek. Zoe grudgingly returns the kiss. Her mother leaves. Standing in the bedroom doorway, Zoe watches Elijah, who is lying on his stomach with his feet sticking out of the wardrobe. He's such a baby, she thinks. She shouldn't have to spend her weekends looking after him. Ryan Coleman plays park football at two. If she hurries she might still get there. And say what? It doesn't matter. Anything is better than staying home.

She pulls Elijah's coat over his arms, being too rough with him. He squawks and she tells him to shush. She laces his trainers and holds him at arm's length, talking sternly. 'OK, we're going to the park, just you and me, but we have to hurry.'

'Can I go on the swings?'

'If you're good.'

'Can I have an ice cream?'

'You're not allowed to have ice cream.'

'Only if I'm good.'

'OK, but don't tell Mum.'

Once outside, she stops Elijah running ahead by

holding the hood of his jacket like a leash. They pass the bank of shops near the tube station and Elijah waves to Mr Agassi, the dry-cleaner, and Judy, the florist. Zoe is thinking about Ryan. Maybe he'll want to hang out with her. She has her babysitting money. They could go to Westfield Centre at Shepherd's Bush.

The bus takes them down the Edgware Road as far as the M40 flyover and they catch another along Euston Road past Madame Tussaud's and the Planetarium. Elijah presses his face to the window, talking to himself.

'Why do you always do that?' asks Zoe. 'Talk to yourself.'

'I don't.'

'What about your imaginary friend?'

'What does imaginary mean?'

'Made up. Make-believe.'

'He isn't make-believe.'

'He lives in the wardrobe.'

'So?'

'Does he have a name?'

'Malcolm.'

'Your friend is called Malcolm.'

'What's so funny?'

'Nothing.'

Elijah pouts. He doesn't like to be laughed at.

'Don't worry about it, squirt,' says Zoe, giving him a hug.

They get off the bus at Regent's Park near the southwest gate. Dodging the slower pedestrians and dog-walkers they reach the playing fields just after three. Impromptu football games are underway, shirts versus skins, with clothing marking the boundaries and goals.

Ryan is shirtless and barefoot. He lopes across the grass like a loose-limbed red setter puppy, calling for the ball, passing it with one touch. Zoe has never been very interested in football. Daniel once took her to a big game at the new Wembley stadium. Zoe tried to follow the action, but mostly she stared at the people in the stands who treated every near-miss as if it were a life-and-death occurrence. They cried, swore, abused the referee and chanted insults at opposing fans.

'Why is it so important?' Zoe asked.

'Supporters belong to a tribe,' Daniel explained.

'A tribe?'

'People want to belong. They want to be part of something bigger.'

'Why?'

'It means they're not alone.'

Across the grass, Ryan notices her and waves. Some of his mates look over, checking her out. Zoe pulls back her shoulders and wishes her cut-off shorts weren't so obviously old jeans that her mother had cut down when Zoe wore holes through the knees.

Dean Hancock smirks and makes some comment. He's playing for the 'shirts' because his pudding-shaped body embarrasses him. The game hasn't finished. They kick off again.

Zoe wanders back and forth in the shade of a tree. Meanwhile, Elijah crouches on his haunches and pokes twigs into bare patches of mud between clumps of turf. Like a magpie, he collects anything shiny or brightly coloured.

'So what brings you outside on such a nice day?' asks a voice.

Zoe turns. The man from the library is leaning against a park bench. He's wearing jeans and a light cotton shirt, buttoned at his wrists. A long stalk of dry grass is balanced between his lips like he's a farmer.

'Are you following me?' asks Zoe.

The man laughs. 'What other reason could there be? It's a sunny day. This is a public park. I *must* be following you.'

Zoe feels foolish.

'I managed to find that spare laptop,' he says. 'If you're interested.'

Zoe doesn't answer. Elijah is watching them. He runs to Zoe and takes her hand, resting his head against her hip.

The man crouches down. 'Is this your little brother? Hello, little big man.'

Elijah frowns at him.

'Say hello,' says Zoe.

'Hello.'

Someone has scored a goal. There are high-fives all round. Zoe looks across and hopes she hasn't missed Ryan doing something impressive.

'So which one is your boyfriend?'

'Nobody.'

Ruben smiles. 'So about that laptop?'

She hesitates. 'I'm not allowed to.'

'Suit yourself.'

He turns to leave, ambling away, not looking back. At the last moment Zoe calls out and meets him halfway, still holding Elijah's hand.

'I'll be at the library tomorrow afternoon . . . if you want to bring it.'

'Fine.'

He raises two fingers in a casual salute. Then he glances up at the sky, as though expecting rain. The clouds float across his eyes for a moment until he blinks them away.

After he's gone, Elijah tugs at her hand, trying to attract her attention.

'What is it?'

'What was the man's name?'

'Ruben.'

Elijah frowns and goes back to poking a stick into the damp earth.

CHAPTER 24

Penny opens the door barefoot, dressed in a T-shirt and shorts.

'Thank God! Adult company.' She hugs Marnie and holds her at arm's length, as though studying her. 'Abigail is sleeping. Twelve more years and I can send her to boarding school.'

'It can't be that bad,' says Marnie.

'Oh, you think? Madam woke eight times last night. I thought I was in Guantanamo Bay. Sleep deprivation, waterboarding, motherhood. I gave up the lot – my age, Osama's last hiding place, who killed J.R. . . .' Penny looks past her. 'Where are your brood?'

'Zoe is looking after Elijah.'

'Perfect, a live-in babysitter, I'll buy her from you. How much do you want?'

'Right now you can have her.'

'Why?'

'Someone kidnapped my sweet little girl and replaced her with a princess bitch-face.'

'Mmmm,' says Penny, 'you're not selling parent-hood to me.' She pulls Marnie into the kitchen and automatically opens the bar fridge, pulling out a bottle of wine without bothering to read the label. Glasses are found and filled. Clinked together.

Penny leads her to the conservatory, where she puts the baby monitor on the windowsill, adjusting the volume. 'No more talk of children,' she says. 'I'm more concerned about you. When's the last time you shaved your legs? You look like a Wookie.' She notices the graze on Marnie's arm. 'What happened?'

'I was knocked off my bike.'

'Who?'

'It doesn't matter. We need to talk.'

'That sounds serious.'

Penny pours herself more wine. Marnie hasn't touched hers. She glances around the room. There's a fern drooping in a glazed pot, shedding dead leaves onto the floorboards. This is where Daniel filmed Penny for the birthday DVD.

Marnie pulls the big red album from a cotton shopping bag and sets it down on the coffee table.

Penny's eyes crinkle. 'I wondered when you'd find that.'

'Why didn't you tell me?'

'Daniel made me promise.'

'But even afterwards . . .?'

'I thought it would just make you sadder.'

'Sadder?'

'It was such a beautiful idea – for your birthday. He spent weeks working on it. I went through my stuff and found him photographs from university.'

Penny opens the album, turning the pages.

'That's one of mine . . . and that one. He wanted me to track people down so they could film messages. I contacted the usual suspects and gave the details to Daniel.'

'Did he discover anything unusual?'

Penny's eyes widen. 'What do you mean?'

'I'm trying to find out what happened. I thought if I could trace his last movements . . . ' Marnie looks around the room. 'This is where he filmed you.'

'Yes.'

'Did he come here often?'

'Three or four times.'

'Why so often?'

'He was going to a lot of effort.' Penny gazes at Marnie with a mixture of pity and sadness. 'He wanted to make it up to you.'

'Really?'

Penny frowns. 'Tell me what's bothering you, Marnie.'

'On the DVD that Daniel was making, one of my old boyfriends said he hated me and that I'd ruined his life.'

Penny laughs. 'Talk about a sore loser.'

'I'm being serious.'

Penny glances at her painted nails. 'Daniel did say that you'd made a few enemies.'

'What do you mean enemies?'

'I wouldn't lose sleep over it – I'm forever pissing people off.'

'That's you, not me.'

225

'Don't be nasty. We can both be quite vindictive.'

'Not me.'

'What about that lecturer you slept with at university – Mr Hatch?'

Marnie cringes at the memory. James Hatch had been late thirties, married. He smoked and drank to excess, coughing phlegm that gurgled in his throat. At nineteen Marnie had fallen for his rumpled charm, sharing glasses of red wine in his rooms and listening to the silky words he borrowed from the poets. His own verse – a slim volume published a decade earlier – had set nothing on fire except his own ego.

In the beginning their affair had seemed exciting and dangerous, until it became sleazy and infantile. It involved sex in his rooms, sex in his car and sex in the house when his wife was away. Hatch wasn't attractive with his clothes off: all skin and bone and stretched out like a lemur.

Marnie didn't do it for better marks or preferential treatment. The opposite happened. The lecturer belittled her in class and picked apart her essays so that nobody could accuse him of showing favouritism. When Marnie complained, he accused her of not being adult enough to handle such a relationship. Marnie ended it then, refusing to answer his text messages and emails. Her marks fell further. She thought about complaining to the vice-chancellor's office but feared the ramifications. Instead she changed her course, dropping English literature. Hatch was suspended soon afterwards, accused of plagiarism and 'excessive borrowing' from a student's work.

'Somebody told his wife,' says Penny.

'And you think it was me?'

A swatch of Marnie's hair has come loose from its pins and hangs down by her ear, swaying as she shakes her head.

'Well, he blames you,' says Penny.

'How do you know?'

'I bumped into him a few years ago. He looked like a completely different man.'

'And he mentioned me?'

'He said somebody sent photographs to his wife. He also believed the same person had stitched him up in the plagiarism case. He blamed you.'

Marnie feels her stomach spasm. There is something wrong inside her; she can feel it slipping and swelling, rising into her oesophagus. She rushes to the bathroom and vomits bile and yellow water.

Penny knocks on the door. 'Are you OK?'

'The wine,' says Marnie. 'I'm out of practice.'

I can't always protect Marnie, not unless she acknowledges my existence. And I can't help her if she makes bad decisions. Naïvety can be attractive, but it's also dangerous. That's when hearts are bruised and knickers are stained.

In her second year at university Marnie went to a party in Millwall – a rough area of south-east London where the Thames curls around and comes back on itself, bringing to mind a dog's bollocks when you see it on the map. She wore a little black dress, the only one she owned, and went along with a friend. The house was full of strangers, but she found her groove, drinking and dancing. Her friend drifted away. At the end of the night Marnie needed a lift home. A guy offered. Have one more drink, he said. She took the glass from his hand.

She could barely stand when she walked to his car. She clung to his arm and his hands were groping her already, fondling her breasts and sliding up her thighs.

A factory worker came across Marnie at 6.00 a.m. the next morning, wandering the streets of Shepherd's Bush. Crying. Cramping. She couldn't remember anything at first, but the flashbacks came soon enough, the feeling of pressure between her legs, her arms like lead weights. This is what she told the police. She could remember the party, the music, the wine, but not the name of the man who spiked her drink and drove her to his bedsit; the one who raped her and made her shower afterwards.

Doctors took samples. They gave her the morning-after pill and antibiotics in case of infection. Then she went home and spent three days in bed. Embarrassed. Traumatised. Scared.

The police interviewed a man called Richard Duffy. Marnie identified him in a line-up, but withdrew her allegations when she realised what came next – the criminal trial, the questioning, the laying bare of her character and her sexual history.

I traced Duffy through his number plate, telling the DVLA that I worked for an insurance company. I watched him for a few weeks, following him to work and home, seeing a man who was dumb with certainty and nurturing an ingrained sense of entitlement. Private school will do that to you. So will a mother's unconditional love.

He lived in Hammersmith and worked as a telecom engineer, although he told women he was a freelance journalist and war correspondent. He saw himself as a real man in a world where limp-dicked metrosexuals were being fêted. He was a rower. Single scull. Five mornings a week, he skimmed up and down the Thames, looking at his torso afterwards to see how the sessions were chiselling his physique.

One morning I waited at the rowing club, watching

the sun rise and the mist float on the water like soap-scum. The rowing club had a small dark door painted black, scarred and chipped by graffiti carved into the paintwork. Duffy had a key. He arrived early and lifted his scull from a rack along the wall.

Beyond the bend in the river, I could see broken wooden pallets washed up on the shore. Low tide. Mud flats. A rowboat canted sideways and crusted with barnacles. Duffy turned around, surprised to see me. 'What are you doing here?'

'I wanted to talk.'

'Why?'

He carried the scull easily to the ramp, placing it down gently with the nose facing the water. Is it called a nose, I wondered. Maybe it's the bow and the back is the stern. Do rowers use nautical terms?

Duffy turned to collect his paddle. He brushed past me and I plunged the needle into his thigh, injecting 100 milligrams of Ketamine directly into his muscle. He spun around, rearing away from me, staring at his leg. The drug took hold quickly. He staggered on unstrung knees and leaned against me, his sour morning breath on my cheek.

'Why are you doing this?' he slurred.

'You don't remember the rape?'

More puzzlement. Maybe he had drugged and raped so many women he couldn't recall every name and face.

'Marnie,' I said.

Again nothing.

'The party in Millwall.'

The penny dropped. He was slurring his words. 'What did you give me?'

'Your drug of choice.'

'I can't feel my legs.'

'They're still there.'

His knees buckled and he sat like a ragdoll on the edge of the sloping ramp. He tried to stand. Fell. Tried again. Nothing worked.

I could feel the cool dawn on my cheeks. Any moment the others would arrive. Duffy looked at the door, hoping for help. Then he gazed across the river to where a council truck was collecting bins, chomping on bags of rubbish with stained metal teeth.

'What are you going to do?' he slurred.

'I'm going to watch you die.'

'No, please. I'm sorry. I'm so sorry. I'll make it up to you.'

'How are you going to do that?'

'I don't know.' He was crying. 'I'll make things right. I'll move away. I'll give you money. Please, you don't want to do this.'

'That's where you're wrong.'

'For the love of God, show some mercy.'

'Are you really calling on God?' I looked up into the brightening sky. 'I don't think he's listening. Wait?' I paused. Listened. 'Nope.'

He looked into my face and saw his death lurking there. He made promises. He would do, say, undo, unsay whatever I wanted. He would go to the police and confess. The drug had reached his lips and he dribbled his last pledges.

I moved forward and raised my foot onto his shoulder. I kicked him gently and he toppled backwards into the water, bobbing once or twice, his face showing as he rolled and gulped for air. His limbs wouldn't obey. His head went under last.

The current carried him away. The cold carried him down. They found his body four days later, eleven miles downstream. Only the river knew where it would resurface but the Thames seems to favour the U-bend around the Isle of Dogs. He wasn't pretty any more. The river is tidal, the water cruel. Bodies are hit by boats and barges and attacked by seabirds. Not much evidence is left behind. Inquests are inconclusive. Deaths unexplained.

CHAPTER 25

Joe walks along the river towards Chelsea Bridge, listening to the sound of water slapping against the granite walls. His shadow shortens and lengthens as he passes each streetlight. On the southern approach to the bridge he notices flashing lights. Fire engines and ambulances have surrounded the base of an apartment building on the edge of the water. A police launch is trawling that stretch of the river, looping back and forth. In the uppermost apartment he sees a flashgun firing and figures moving behind the glass.

His mobile is vibrating. He recognises Julianne's number, but knows that Emma will be calling. She rings him every evening before she goes to bed and tells him about her day and asks when he's coming home as though 'home' is with her and Charlie and Julianne in the cottage in Wellow. He can only wish.

Joe stops and sits on a bench, listening to Emma's news.

'My friend Sadie says that if you kiss a boy you have to marry them and have babies,' she says with a slight lisp.

'Not exactly.'

'Good.'

'Have you been kissing boys?'

'Ew! Yuck!' She giggles, but grows serious again. 'Is it hard to fall in love?'

'That's a pretty big question for someone who's only seven.'

'I'm seven and a half.'

'Why do you want to know?'

'I just do.'

'Well it depends. It was very easy to fall in love with your mother and very hard to fall in love with anyone else.'

'Is it harder than learning to read?'

'For some people.'

'Does it take that long?'

'Sometimes.'

'I don't think I'll ever fall in love.'

'I'm sure you will.'

Joe has to blow 'sloppy kisses' down the line and say goodnight a half dozen times. Sometimes he talks to Charlie on these same calls, but tonight she's doing homework. And if he's really lucky, he might get a few minutes with Julianne before Emma calls out to her. He likes those moments. He tries to think of funny stories to tell her because he's convinced that laughter will win her back. When she stopped laughing she stopped loving him.

She comes on the phone.

'Charlie had a nice time in London.'

'Good.'

'She said you had Vincent over for dinner.'

'We did.'

There is a slight pause. 'Charlie said you'd also found a new friend.'

'Who?'

'Your neighbour.'

'Oh.'

'Apparently she's very pretty.'

'She's married and she's a patient.'

There is a pause. The statement was too abrupt. Joe softens his voice. 'Her husband has gone missing. I'm trying to help her.'

'That's nice,' says Julianne, embarrassed now. 'Charlie didn't mention that. I thought you might have found someone.'

'I did find someone. I married her twenty-four years ago.'

Julianne sighs. 'That's not what I meant.'

'Maybe we should make one of those pacts,' says Joe.

'What sort of pact?'

'If neither of us has found someone after a certain amount of time, we get back together.'

'How long did you have in mind?'

'Next weekend.'

She laughs. He loves to hear the sound. That used to be enough. He was never the most handsome or the richest or the best lover, but he could always make her smile.

Julianne says goodnight. Joe puts the phone away

and gazes across the water at the flashing blue lights, wondering what crime has touched another set of lives.

At the edge of his vision, he notices someone on the bridge, standing away from the streetlights. Silhouetted against the soiled light, frozen in a pose, the figure looks flat and two-dimensional, like he's been cut out of cardboard.

Joe's left arm is jerking spasmodically, his medication wearing off. He should have taken a pill earlier. Feeling in his pocket, he searches for the small white plastic bottle. Managing to get it open, he swallows the pill dry, waiting for the chemicals in his brain to rebalance.

From further along the footpath, he hears voices; young men, drunk, laughing and jostling each other. Two of them pass. The last is metal thin with black hair and fuzz on his chin. He pretends to trip, spilling his beer.

'What did you do that for?'

Joe looks up. The man is dressed in a Chelsea football strip, jeans and thick-soled work boots.

'Excuse me?'

'You spilled my fucking beer.'

'No I didn't.'

'Are you calling me a liar?'

Joe stands with difficulty. He can't stop himself rocking from side to side like he's a sea captain standing on the bridge of a ship. His left arm spasms.

'I don't want any trouble.'

This seems to amuse the man. 'You think I'm looking for trouble?'

'I didn't say that.'

The others have turned back. Joe's right hand opens unconsciously and his white pill bottle bounces across the asphalt and rolls towards a grated drain. One of them places his heel on the bottle. Joe's tongue has grown fat and lazy in his mouth making his words thick and wet. 'Please don't do that.'

'You a retard?' asks one of them.

'No.'

'I hate retards.'

The smallest of them has dreadlocks and eyes like black glass beads. 'Maybe you're one of those perverts who hang about waiting to flash women who walk by. Are you a pervert?'

The boot presses down, crushing the bottle and grinding the contents into a powdery dust that seems to glow in the darkness. The footpath has become a dangerous place with bitter air and sour light. Joe glances in both directions. Nobody is coming.

'I'll buy you another beer,' he says to the ringleader.

A finger pokes him in the chest. 'You didn't answer the question – are you a pervert?'

Joe's fists have closed, stopping the tremor. He can feel his nerves fizzing and popping under his skin like bundles of electrical wires.

'Can I ask you something?' he asks, his words

clearer, addressing the Chelsea supporter. 'What are you trying to prove?'

'Huh?'

'Who are you trying to impress?'

'What are you talking about?'

Joe has found his voice again. Medicated. On. 'You're mid twenties, unemployed, still living at home because you can't afford to move out. You do odd jobs, getting your hands dirty so you can buy cheap lager, cigarettes and the bags of white I can see crusted around your nose.'

The youth's eyes have widened, but he doesn't know how to react.

'You can't get a girlfriend, so you hang out with these losers, trashing bus shelters and rolling drunks, because it's always someone else's fault that they're richer and better looking and more successful with a pretty girlfriend and a nice car. So you go out and get pissed and you come across a man with Parkinson's Disease and you decide to pick on him. You want money? Take my wallet. You want respect? Give a little.'

There is an echoing silence, a tremor in the air. The ringleader runs his tongue over his upper lip. The dreadlocked one keeps looking from face to face, as though waiting for a signal.

For a moment, Joe thinks he might have shamed them into leaving him alone, but they're too drunk or stupid to understand.

'You're gonna fucking swim for that,' says the Chelsea supporter, letting out a roar and driving his shoulder into Joe's chest, sending him backwards until he hits the stone wall guarding the river. Someone picks up his legs, tipping him upwards, arching his body over the water. He hears another sound. *Ooomph!* Air leaking. Punches landing. Groans. The fight only lasts a few seconds before the young men are running, their boots echoing into the night.

A man is crouching next to Joe. 'You OK?'

'Can't breathe!'

'Wind got knocked out of you.'

The stranger helps him stand and brushes dirt from his coat.

Joe feels for his wallet. It's still in his pocket.

'Do you want to call the police?' asks the stranger.

'Won't do any good.'

'All the same, you should report it.'

'I'll call from home.'

Joe's left hand keeps opening and closing, adrenalin overriding the drugs. He concentrates on trying to slow his heartbeat.

Across the water, a police helicopter is hovering above the apartment block. The stranger walks with Joe to the bridge, climbing the stairs to the main road.

'Thank you.'

'It was nothing.'

'No, I mean it, I owe you my thanks, I don't even know your name.'

Joe fishes a business card from his wallet. A cab slows. The door opens. He wants to shake the man's hand and thank him again, but the cab door is already closing and the vehicle moving away, leaving behind the faintest aroma of petrol and bleach.

Ruiz is waiting for him in a pub where the barmaid has thick black eye shadow and spiky blue hair that angles like a sundial from the top of her head. She looks intimidating until she opens her mouth and lets slip a posh St Trinian's school accent.

He likes this place. It has clean pipes and real ale and he knows most of the regulars – by sight, if not by name. The skinny ex-jockey at the end of the bar once rode a Grand National winner, while the red-nosed accountant does Sudoku puzzles all day, waiting for closing time so he can go home and wait for opening time.

'What do you mean, you got beaten up?'

'Just what I said.'

'They didn't rob you?'

'No.'

'Are you all right?'

'Shaken not stirred.'

Joe tells him the whole story of the confrontation and rescue.

'Who was the guy?'

'No idea, but if it weren't for him, I'd be swimming.'

'You'd be drowning.'

'Maybe.'

Ruiz can't understand how Joe can be so

philosophical about it. The professor is always making excuses for mindless violence, blaming it on deprivation, boredom and neglect, but these people don't deserve to be defended. They're animals. They ape, they parrot, they hunt in packs, picking on the weak because they're cowards. And when caught, they stand before judges while their defence lawyers make impassioned speeches about their clients' shitty childhoods and terrible luck. And they walk free, grinning and chest-bumping each other, ready to fuck up someone else's life.

Ruiz buys Joe a shot of whisky and insists he drink it. Then the two men take a table outside near the river, smelling the briny pong. Ruiz belches quietly, gazing up at stars that are barely visible in the ambient light from the city.

'I miss looking at the night sky,' he says. 'When I smoked, I used to do it a lot . . . sit outside and contemplate the great unknowns.'

'God?'

'He's a little too unknown for me.'

Ruiz blows his nose on a handkerchief, which he folds and puts into his trouser pocket. 'How well do you know Marnie Logan?'

'Why?'

'I'm concerned we might be working for the wrong side.'

Joe waits for an explanation.

'People have a habit of disappearing or dying around her. Maybe she killed her husband. Maybe she murdered Quinn.'

'I don't believe that.'

'Something doesn't smell right.'

Ruiz tells Joe about Richard Duffy – Telecom engineer, rower, date-drug rapist and ultimately Thames flotsam.

'She withdrew the complaint and within a month the guy was found floating in the river.'

'Was she questioned?'

'The coroner came in with an open verdict.' Ruiz empties his Guinness and wipes his lips. 'I hate to say I told you so, but I always had doubts about that woman.'

Joe doesn't answer.

'You like the lady, I get it.'

'It's not that.'

'What then?'

Joe talks of his sessions with Marnie. Despite her remoteness, she had never seemed dangerous or prone to violence. She was more like an open wound who shied away from being touched or examined too closely. The past twenty-four hours had revealed different opinions and perhaps another side to her personality. Psychopaths and narcissists can bear grudges for years because it challenges the way they see themselves. Their hatred is so pure it sustains them. It cleanses them of wrongdoing and justifies their worst behaviour, but Marnie Logan isn't a psychopath or a narcissist. She's damaged and vulnerable, yet unselfish and fiercely protective of her children.

'What about the break-in?' Ruiz asks.

'Marnie wouldn't steal her own clinical notes. What reason would she have?'

Ruiz stares at his empty pint glass, studying the way the foam is drying in patterns. 'I went to see Patrick Hennessy today. Showered twice and still feel dirty.'

'What did he say about Marnie?'

'Said she was madder than a midget with a chainsaw. He warned me to be careful.'

'Of him?'

'Of her.'

Pulling Daniel's diary from his pocket, Joe looks down the list of names. So far he's spoken to Eugene Lansky and Olivia Shulman, who both claimed that Marnie had 'ruined their lives'. People exaggerate. Old scars are slow to heal. Petty feuds get blown out of proportion.

'We still haven't spoken to Calvin Mosley,' says Ruiz, 'although from experience ex-husbands are rarely unbiased.'

'Are you speaking from personal experience?'

'My second wife is going to squat over my grave instead of dancing.'

Joe wants to laugh, but he's too exhausted.

'I'll take the ex-husband,' says Ruiz. 'What are you going to do?'

'Marnie didn't recognise two names on the list – a Dr Sterne and a Francis Moffatt. I'll start with the doctor.'

The two men say goodbye and Ruiz watches the professor crossing the road and hailing a cab. He's hunching more these days. Perhaps the Parkinson's is accelerating. Ruiz had never paid much attention to his own health. As a rugby player he'd been fearless, charging into rucks and mauls, unconcerned about his personal safety. As a detective he knew how to physically intimidate, but rarely had to test himself. Disease, like old age, is something he dreads having to fight because he can't see it in front of him. He can't tackle it into the mud or lock it in a police cell.

How would he shoulder a burden like Joe's? Would he cope as all sufferers cope – because he had no choice – or would he crawl into a hole and never come out?

The breeze swirls around him, whispering in his ears, but the answers do not come.

CHAPTER 26

Marnie has a dream of being awake. A man is straddling her body, sitting on her chest. She can't open her eyes or move her limbs, but she can smell him. His head is directly over hers. Nose to nose, forehead to forehead, he's breathing into her mouth, but she can't scream or cry out.

Concentrating hard, she tries to open her eyes. *Wake up. Wake up. Wake up.*

Her body rises into the air and she hears a violent rush of wind. Jumping so violently, she expects to bump heads with the figure on top of her, but the weight has gone and she's staring into the darkness, listening to her own heartbeat.

Is she really awake, or dreaming of being awake? How can she be sure?

She lies still for a minute more, breathing slowly, soaking up the certainty of the room. Staring upwards, she sees stars twinkling above her on the ceiling. They swim before her eyes and disappear in the blink of an eye.

Something crawls over her leg, the last remnant of the dream. She shudders and sits up, looking out the window at the tops of trees and the mansion blocks on the far side of the garden. Tree branches thrash in the wind and raindrops hit the glass like grains of sand.

Sleep has always been Marnie's retreat from the world, one of life's few pleasures. But now these dreams make her fear it. She's frightened of not waking up and being caught in a parallel world that seems so real and physically solid she can actually feel the weight of a man sitting on her chest and smell his breath.

Her own mouth tastes sour and metallic, as though she's vomited. Going to the bathroom, she splashes water on her face and stands woodenly in front of the mirror, letting droplets fall from her nose and chin.

Sometimes, she has a sensation of breaking loose from herself, as though stepping out of her body. Either that or she senses there is another better version of herself trapped inside or walking in the world. Braver. More deserving. This *other* Marnie is waiting for her to slip up so they can assume control. Professor O'Loughlin has said it could be post-traumatic stress, but he doesn't know the cause.

When Marnie was a child, after her mother died, she had an imaginary friend. Doctors told her that this friend was another part of her personality, trying to help her cope, but Marnie didn't believe them. How could somebody else live inside her without her knowing? Surely she'd see the evidence

– a marker of this other 'self' – a shimmer at the edge of her vision or something half-glimpsed in the shadows of her mind. She had never told anyone – not the professor, or Daniel or any of her friends – because it embarrassed her and she denied its existence.

Wiping her face with a towel, she goes back to the bedroom and hears a sound near the wall, a tiny muffled sob. Elijah has curled up next to her bed, cuddling a battered rabbit he calls 'Bunny'. Marnie scoops him up onto her lap.

'C'mere, baby, what's wrong?'

Elijah chews on his lower lip and the underside of his chin quivers. 'I saw a monster.'

'That's silly. There aren't any monsters.'

'He was in the hallway.'

'You saw me. I went to the bathroom.'

Elijah sniffles. 'Who were you talking to?'

'Me?'

'You were talking to someone. You were saying, "Wake up, wake up."'

'Was I?'

He nods.

'That was a dream talking.'

'How do dreams talk?'

'They just do sometimes.'

The flat is quiet now, everything amplified by the darkness. Green numbers glow on the digital clock: 3.37.

'You can sleep with me,' says Marnie, tucking him into her bed.

'What if I fall asleep and forget to wake up?' he asks.

'I'll wake you,' says Marnie, getting into bed beside him, holding him close. 'We'll wake each other.'

'What about Bunny?'

'We'll wake him too.'

Some time later she hears a scream. Zoe is yelling in the kitchen, bashing a saucepan with a wooden spoon.

'Muuuum!'

'What?'

'I saw the mouse. It's under the fridge.'

'It's only a mouse.'

'It's disgusting.'

Marnie drags herself out of bed. Elijah follows, rubbing sleep from his eyes. He peers under the fridge. Marnie tucks her dressing gown between her thighs. Zoe is still brandishing the saucepan, holding the handle with both hands, ready to swing.

'I'll buy some mousetraps today,' says Marnie.

'You can't do that,' says Elijah.

'Why?'

'It could be Stuart Little.'

'It's *not* Stuart Little,' says Zoe, exasperated.

'How do *you* know?'

'He's not white and he can't talk.'

'He could be related,' pouts Elijah. 'He could have a family.'

Marnie looks in the crack between the fridge and the cupboards, contemplating what to do. She won't call Trevor. She doesn't like him coming into the flat. Instead she phones Mr and Mrs Brummer, her landlords. Mr Brummer answers the call, sounding bright and chirpy like he's been awake since VE-Day. He tells Marnie the adjoining building had to be fumigated because of mice. 'Now they've come to us – seeking refuge,' he says, making it sound like the Jewish diaspora.

'What should I do?' asks Marnie.

'Buy a cat.'

'You don't allow pets.'

'I will make an exception.'

'I don't want a cat.'

'Suit yourself.'

CHAPTER 27

Ruiz hammers his fist against the large metal door. It opens and a blast of warm air escapes, wet with steam and dry-cleaning chemicals that hook the back of his throat and squeeze tears from his eyes. A man's face appears, as grained as a cedar shingle. Flecks of dandruff have settled on his overalls.

'What do you want?'

'I'm looking for Calvin Mosley.'

'He in some sort of trouble?'

'Not from me.'

The door opens further. Ruiz is pointed along a corridor between massive stainless-steel driers that rumble as if they're washing rocks. Above him sheets, towels and tablecloths are pinned to hangers that are being pulled along a conveyor belt. Lint and dust are caught in the heated air, sucked into the vortex created by extractor fans.

The commercial laundry is in the East End, just off Brick Lane, where it cleans table linen and bedding for some of London's finest hotels and restaurants. The majority of the employees are Bangladeshi or Pakistani. Women. Veiled. Wearing saris. Most will never dine on the tablecloths or sleep on the sheets they launder every day.

Ruiz follows directions between the rows of driers. Calvin Mosley is wheeling a trolley and pushing armloads of linen into the machines. He's wearing overalls and scarred leather boots that remind Ruiz of what his stepfather used to pull on every morning before working on the farm. Perspiration rings are half-mooned beneath his arms.

Ruiz shouts over the driers.

'We need to talk.'

'Who are you?'

'I'm a man seeking information.'

'A copper?'

'Not any more.'

'I'm working.'

'It's about Marnie Logan.'

'Not interested.'

Mosley pushes the trolley past him. Ruiz shoots out his hand and grips the handle.

'Tell me something, Calvin,' he says. 'Who actually gives a kid a name like that? What were your parents thinking? He'll be a fashion designer or maybe a cartoon character. Instead they got a drug dealer and an ex-con.'

Anger flares in Mosley's eyes. He breathes deeply. Deflates. 'Don't tell my boss.'

'You bucking for employee of the month?'

'I need this job.'

'I'm not looking for trouble.'

Mosley glances at a delivery entrance at the rear of the factory. He walks. Ruiz follows. Red vans with the laundry logo are backed up to the ramp, some delivering, others collecting. An open drain runs down the centre of the loading dock where water trickles through a metal grate.

Mosley pulls a crushed packet of cigarettes from his pocket, his eyes dull with fatigue, hands shaking. The skin on his face is stretched tightly over his bones creating angles and shadows. Putting a bent Marlborough to his lips, he thumbs a plastic lighter. Smoke curls in wispy threads from his fingers, which are scarred below the knuckles. Homemade tattoos. Prison. Regretted.

'Is she after money?'

'Not unless you're offering.'

'I don't owe that bitch the sweat off my balls.'

The words are punctuated with a rasping cough. Mosley covers his mouth, coughs again. 'Is Zoe OK?'

'When did you last see her?'

'Years ago.'

'Maybe you should get back in touch.'

'Bit late for that.'

Dragging on his cigarette, he savours the smoke moving across his tongue and into his lungs.

'Did he send you?'

'Who?'

'The new husband.'

'You've met Daniel Hyland.'

'He came to see me. Said something about

Marnie's birthday and wanting to do something special for her. He wanted me to film a message to her.'

'What did you do?'

'I told him to run, to go somewhere far away. Change his name. Buy a gun. Get the hell out. Otherwise it's only a matter of time before she turns on him.'

'Marnie?'

'She won't just plant the knife, she'll twist it a few times or use it like a joystick.'

Mosley talks with a warped smile, one side of his mouth higher than the other, as though he's suffered nerve damage to the left side of his face. Two of the Bangladeshi workers pass, lowering their eyes and wrapping veils across their faces.

'Daniel Hyland is missing,' says Ruiz.

'I hope he's hiding.'

'The police suspect that he's dead.'

Mosley hesitates and seems to shake off an unspoken fear. His shoulders are sharp beneath the heavy cotton.

'I've been married three times,' says Ruiz, 'but I don't hate my ex-wives.'

'You weren't married to Marnie.'

'What did she do to you?'

'She fucked me over. She chewed me up and spat me out. She's like that girl in *The Exorcist*. I'm not talking about her head spinning around and vomiting green shit, but she's possessed by something evil.' He pauses and lights a second cigarette with the remains of the first. 'I know what you're thinking. How can a man blame a woman for putting his life in the crapper? But she's not normal.' He waves smoke away from his eyes. 'You want to hear the story? I had an affair, OK? I screwed up. I shagged one of our friends. She'd been a bridesmaid at our wedding, but I knew her from before that. We'd always liked each other. Kept in touch. Then one weekend I told Marnie I had a work conference in Brighton, which wasn't lying. I went with Patrice. Marnie stayed at home. She was still breastfeeding Zoe.'

Mosley leans on a downpipe, flexing his fingers. 'I'm not making excuses, but things hadn't been great between Marnie and me. She hadn't lost her baby weight and we weren't doing the conjugal tango very often, if you catch my drift. I don't know how Marnie found out about Patrice. Someone must have told her.'

'She threw you out.'

'On my arse . . . and I deserved it. I fucked up, I accept that.'

He wipes his sleeve across his mouth. A grey tube of ash clings to the end of his cigarette.

'We separated. I collected my shit and went to live with Patrice. About six months later, we drove to Austria for the ski season. Patrice got work as a chalet girl and I fitted boots and skis. We were away four months. I sent back money to Marnie when I could, but we aren't talking about much. I was earning fuck-all.

'Patrice and me didn't last the season. She ran off with a ski instructor who took her to New Zealand. I drove the van back. Caught the ferry at Calais. Customs pulled me over in Dover. They found fifty grams of heroin in one of my bags. I swear on my Mum's grave it wasn't mine. I swear on my daughter's life. I had no idea.'

The ash falls onto his chest. He brushes it away.

'The police didn't believe me. I had a few problems when I was at university, small time stuff, you know. I got picked up selling pills at a party and received a suspended sentence. That sort of shit counted against me, but none of it made any sense. If I was going to smuggle heroin, why only bring in fifty grams? That's not how the prosecution saw it. They said it was probably a test run. My brief told me to plead guilty. Said I might get three or four years. I didn't *do* anything. I was fucking *innocent*. So I pleaded not guilty and I got seven years. Served five.'

He holds back tears, gazing into space.

'You want to know what's truly fucking ironic?'

'What's that?'

'I didn't have a drug problem until I went to prison.'

He blinks at Ruiz, who recognises the sallowness of Calvin's skin and the jaundiced tint to his eyes. A dirty needle. A drop of blood. A slow death sentence.

'How long have you got?'

'Eighteen months, maybe a little longer. My liver is fucked.'

'Are you clean?'

'Wouldn't make any difference.'

Ruiz catches a whiff of his body odour, a smell of sour milk and yeast. 'Why blame Marnie Logan?'

'I didn't – not for a long while.'

'And then?'

'About a year after I got banged up, I read a story about a British girl being arrested in Bali. It was Patrice. Customs officers found a kilo of cannabis in her suitcase. She's serving twenty years at Kerobokan Prison.' He takes a ragged breath. 'Now I can accept that coincidences can happen, but Patrice says she's innocent. We were both set up the same way. You want to know what else? She got the same postcard as me.'

'What postcard?'

'It arrived about a month after I started my sentence. No name, no return address, postmarked from London. It said, *Payback is a bitch!*'

Mosley rubs at his bloodshot eyes.

'Did you tell Daniel Hyland all this?'

'Yeah, I told him.'

'What did he say?'

'He tried to defend Marnie, but I know he was having doubts.'

'Why?'

'I think he'd talked to some other people. The scales were falling from his eyes. Marnie Logan comes across as being all sweetness and light, but she's like an angel of vengeance, believe me. Nobody escapes.'

CHAPTER 28

Joe's last patient of the day is leaving – a middle-aged woman who is so frightened of the dark that she carries two torches with her everywhere in case her tube train plunges into blackness. The condition is called Nyctophobia and Joe has traced it back to Betty's childhood, but no one single event. For her the darkness is like a virus that will consume her if she steps out of the light.

After writing up his notes, Joe takes Marnie's Big Red Book from the top of the filing cabinet, along with Daniel's diary and his list of names. Studying the pages again, he tries to decipher the cryptic shorthand of half-sentences, addresses and dates. Marnie recognised all but two of the names: 'Francis Moffatt' and 'Dr Sterne', both of which are underlined. Perhaps Daniel couldn't find these people, or he dismissed them as unimportant, or he found them and underlined the names for another reason.

Dr Sterne has an initial, which has been scrubbed out or overwritten by one of the notes that Daniel jotted in the margin. Joe holds the page up to the light. He can read the outline of the letters beneath the scribbles. The letter 'W' is legible. Joe types

W Sterne into a search engine and comes up with nearly six hundred results. He tries putting 'Dr' in front of the name. Nothing.

Medical practitioners must be licensed with the General Medical Council. Joe searches the list of the organisation's website but comes up empty. Anyone with a PhD can call himself a doctor. W. Sterne could be an engineer or a physicist or a mathematician.

An idea occurs to Joe. From the moment he began treating Marnie, he had sensed that she might have been in therapy or psychoanalysis before. She seemed to predict so many of his questions before he asked them. And she knew how to avoid most of the obvious 'tells' that would let slip her true emotions or reveal that she was holding something back.

Working on this hunch, Joe looks up the British Psychological Society and then the Royal College of Psychiatrists. There is a Dr W. Sterne living in Chiswick in West London. A telephone directory reveals the number. An elderly woman answers on the fourth ring and Joe asks for Dr Sterne.

'He's in the garden.'

'Am I right in thinking he is a psychiatrist?'

'Retired, but you have the right man.'

She fetches him. Joe can hear a dog barking excitedly.

'That is the stupidest dog in England,' says a man's voice, before he picks up the phone. 'Hello, can I help you?'

'I'm Professor Joseph O'Loughlin. I'm a clinical psychologist based in London and I'm making some enquiries about a man called Daniel Hyland.'

'What about him?'

'You know him.'

'No, not really, he came to see me.'

'When?'

'Last summer.'

'I'm treating his wife, Marnie Logan. Daniel Hyland has been missing since August of last year.'

The doctor has gone quiet. After a long break he clears his throat. 'How is Marnella?'

'You know her?'

'Yes.'

Joe squeezes the phone tighter in his fist. 'Is that why Daniel came to see you?'

'Marnie was one of my patients many years ago. She was just a child.'

'What was wrong with her?'

'You know I can't discuss that. How did you get my name?'

'It was in one of Daniel's notebooks. I've been treating Marnie for almost a year and she hasn't mentioned seeing a psychiatrist as a child. I showed her your name. She said she didn't recognise it.'

'She was lying.'

There is a long pause. 'Can I come and see you, Dr Sterne?'

'I don't see what good that would do.'

'Marnie Logan is in trouble. I'm trying to help her.'

The doctor is about to argue, but something makes him change his mind. A memory. He gives Joe his address and suggests that he bring his clinical notes.

Joe remembers the break-in. 'Someone stole Marnie's file from my office six days ago.'

'How very strange,' says Dr Sterne. The tremor is audible in his voice.

'Why is it strange?'

He takes a deep breath. 'Perhaps we should wait until you get here.'

CHAPTER 29

As she reaches the bottom of the stairs, Marnie hears a door open. Trevor is watching her, his pale face stark against the shadows behind.

'Why do you always do that?' she asks.

'Do what?'

'Listen for people coming and going.'

'I'm the caretaker.'

'You're not a guard. You don't have to monitor when people go in and out.'

Trevor licks his bottom lip. 'I wanted to talk to you.'

'I'm pretty busy.'

'It won't take long.' He opens the door wider.

'Can't we talk here?'

Although Marnie had never felt intimidated by Trevor, she usually avoided being alone with him. Occasionally he had fixed things for her or allowed her to use his computer, but she had never liked his hopeful, hungry stare. It reminded her of her adolescence, when she began to develop breasts and boys started taking an interest. One boy in particular, she can't remember his name – it might have been Declan – was always trying to look at her bra and seemed obsessed with the colour of her underwear. She took to charging him fifty pence for the privilege, counting to 'three Mississippi's' before pulling her skirt down and tucking it between her knees. She shouldn't have been so stupid, but they were all of twelve.

'It's about Zoe,' says Trevor.

'What about her?'

'Come.'

Marnie glances at her watch. Elijah is at a birthday party until four-thirty. She doesn't need this now. Trevor steps back as she enters. He leads her to the sitting room, which is so airless and hot that the furniture seems to be sweating. He points to the sofa. Marnie perches on the end nearest the door.

'Would you like a cup of tea?'

'I really can't stay. You mentioned Zoe.'

He glances at his hands. 'Will you have dinner with me tonight?'

'No, I can't do that.'

'What about tomorrow?'

'You're very nice, Trevor, but I'm not interested. Is that why you invited me here?'

He opens his mouth and pauses as though the words are hovering on the tip of his tongue. 'I phoned the agency. I tried to book you, but they said you weren't available.'

Marnie blinks at him rapidly, trying to recover. 'I don't know what you're talking about.'

'I can pay . . . if that's what you want.'

She shakes her head from side to side. 'You've made a mistake. I don't know anything about an agency.'

Trevor opens his laptop and the webpage refreshes, showing a gallery of women dressed in skimpy clothes: lingerie, corsets, camisoles and sheer night-dresses. The main picture is Marnie wearing a black bustier that barely covers her nipples. She's sucking on a strand of pearls, half leaning over a chest of drawers. Pixilation blurs her eyes, but she can recognise herself. She remembers the photograph being taken. The man with the camera was about sixty and sniffled through the session, telling her to look slutty, when all she wanted to do was go home to her children.

Blood has drained from Marnie's face and the walls seem to shiver. 'It's not me,' she whispers.

'I can take away the pixilation.'

'No!'

'You shouldn't be ashamed. You look beautiful. See what it says: *An English beauty not to be missed.* They fudged your age, but everything else is true. Eyes: hazel. Height: five-seven. Vital statistics: 34C-24-34. *Gracious and elegant*, they call you.'

'I was desperate,' says Marnie. 'We needed the money.'

'I can pay.'

'You don't understand.'

'I *want* to pay. The agency tried to send me someone else, but I expressly told them it had to be you.'

'I don't do it any more.'

Marnie wants him to shut the computer. How did he find the webpage? Why was he looking?'

Trevor moves closer to her on the sofa. 'I can understand you wanting to keep it private. I won't tell anyone.'

'Thank you.'

'I've seen how lonely you are, Marnie. I can help you.'

'I don't need your help.'

'You take money from complete strangers. Why not take it from me?' He puts his hand on her knee. Marnie lifts it away. She gets to her feet, moving towards the door. A sudden change comes over Trevor. It's as though an invisible switch has been flicked and his shapeless body transmogrifies into something more grotesque and aggressive. 'I've tried to be nice to you.'

'What?'

'I've been your friend, but you treat me like shit. Why are you such an arrogant bitch?'

'Fuck you, Trevor.'

'Does Zoe know?'

Marnie is almost at the door. She stops. Turns. Any softness in Trevor's voice has gone. The transparent irises of his eyes seem to whiten for a moment.

'You're not proud of it, I understand that,' he says. 'A mother does what she has to.'

'I shouldn't have insulted you,' says Marnie. 'I'm going to pretend this hasn't happened.'

'I've printed out the page.'

'Pardon?'

'The website – I've made copies.'

'Why?'

'I can email the link to Zoe or I could just post it on the noticeboard and put a printout in everybody's mailbox. I don't suppose Mr and Mrs Brummer will like a prostitute living in one of their flats.'

'Why would you do that? Please, I'm begging you . . .'

Marnie's hands are pressed together. Trevor drops a cushion onto the floor.

'If you're going to beg, best get on your knees.' He unzips his fly. His narrow erect penis is scribbled with purplish veins. His hands are on Marnie's shoulders, pushing her down.

'I thought you were my friend.'

'I've tried to be.'

'Why then?'

'You fuck for money – you can fuck for mine.'

His penis smears a thread of seminal fluid across her cheek. His fingers grip her hair. Marnie opens her mouth. Trevor shuts his eyes, waiting for her lips to close. She drops her arms to her sides, bunching her fingers. Then she drives her right fist into his testicles, forcing his scrotum into his bladder. Trevor's body goes rigid and doubles over. He crumples to the floor, unloading a strand of semen along her thigh.

Marnie stands over him and kicks him twice in

the stomach, not wanting to stop. It feels better than it should. Empowering. Fundamental. Gratifying.

'If you threaten me again, I will tell the police that you tried to rape me.'

Trevor is lying curled in a ball, clutching his genitals.

'Don't ever come near me again,' Marnie spits. 'Don't come near my daughter. You leave us alone.'

She reaches the door. Trevor is trying to say something, pain etched around his eyes.

'They'll all know,' he moans.

Marnie is crossing the foyer.

'Your daughter, your father, your friends, they'll all know . . .'

Marnie isn't conscious of running, of her legs carrying her, or her feet striking the wet pavement, or tears being pushed across her cheeks. She dodges pedestrians and prams, sprinting along the asphalt paths until her lungs are hurting. At the same time she has a sensation of floating like a fish in a stream, swimming to stay in the one place as the world rushes past her on all sides, dense, clear and swift.

The bastard! The fucking bastard!

Stumbling to a halt, sucking in air, she wipes her cheeks with her sleeve. A couple of old women come out of the Post Office, giving her a look of practised sympathy, as though tut-tutting and patting the back of her hand. A man walking a dog drops his head and hurries past, pulling the animal.

Having run blindly, Marnie now recognises her surroundings. She's near Little Venice, close to the Warwick Avenue Bridge over the Regent's Canal. The wind has sprung up, shaking the trees and sending leaves scuttling to quiet corners or pinning them against the railings. In the distance she can see the A40 flyover and beyond that the curving rooftop of Paddington station. A thought occurs to her. For a split second she contemplates getting on a train and running away. Maybe this is how Daniel felt. He ran from his family and his mounting debts, leaving her to face the music.

Marnie looks at her watch and thinks of Zoe. Soon she'll be getting home from school, walking past Trevor's door. Maybe she'll go to the library first. There's still time.

Ten minutes later she's waiting opposite the bus stop. Catching sight of her reflection in a nearby window, she wipes her eyes and brushes back her hair, looping an elastic band over her ponytail.

Students spill from the bus, some rushing for home, others in no hurry. Zoe is sitting near the back, next to a man whose face isn't visible. She gets up and walks down the aisle, jumping down the last two steps.

'What are you doing here?'

'I thought I'd meet you.' Marnie gives her a hug.

'I'm going to the library.'

'I'll walk you there.'

More rain clouds are rolling across the sky. Thunder rumbles like a distant train. They cross the road and follow Elgin Avenue, past the station and shops.

'Have you been crying?' asks Zoe.

'I do that sometimes.'

'Is Elijah OK?'

'He's at a birthday party.'

Marnie shivers as sweat dries on her skin. 'We need to talk.'

'If it's about what happened the other night, I'm sorry. I didn't mean what I said.'

Marnie makes her stop. She blinks two or three times, building up her courage. 'The job I used to do – I told you I was a waitress – that wasn't true.'

'What do you mean?'

'I was doing something else.'

Zoe is waiting.

'We needed the money and I couldn't see another way.'

'Do I want to hear this, Mum?'

'I promised to tell you the truth.'

'Why now?'

'I'm afraid you're going to find out anyway. I don't want you to hate me.'

'I could never hate you.'

Zoe shifts her school satchel from one shoulder to the other and pushes her fringe from her eyes.

'Your dad owed people a lot of money. Dangerous people. That's why I joined an agency.'

'What sort of agency?'

'I worked as an escort.'

Zoe's jaw slackens and her eyes widen in a fusion of surprise and disbelief. 'You were a prostitute?'

'An escort.'

'You slept with men for money.'

Marnie sighs. 'Please don't make this harder.'

'Pardon me. I'm so sorry. Did I hurt your feelings?'

Her sarcasm stings, but the look on her face is worse. It's as though Zoe wishes she could expunge Marnie from her life, brush her away like something nasty on her shoe.

'You should have told me we needed money,' says Zoe. 'I could have done a bit of drug-dealing at the bus stop or given blow-jobs behind the half-pipe.'

'Please don't say things like that.'

Marnie reaches out for her. Zoe shrugs her away. 'What are you going to tell Dad when he gets back?'

'He's not coming back.'

'You don't know that. I can't believe you'd fuck for money.'

'Please don't swear.'

'Who did you do it with?'

'It doesn't matter.'

'Is that why Mr Brummer waived the rent?'

'No.'

Zoe drops her head. Hurting. 'Why did you have to tell me? Why couldn't you keep this bit to yourself?'

'Trevor found out. He threatened to tell you.'

'Oh, Jesus! Were you fucking Trevor?'

'No.'

'Liar!'

'I'm not lying. That's the whole point – I'm telling you the truth.'

'Now! You're telling me now! I'm fifteen, Mum. Don't lay this shit on me. I don't deserve it.'

Zoe turns away, brushing Marnie aside. She doesn't want to hear any more. She doesn't *have* to listen. Instead she blocks her ears and yells, 'La, la, la, la, la,' drowning out the sound.

CHAPTER 30

The police constable standing outside Ruiz's house has a boyish haircut and an eager expression, tipping his hat whenever someone walks by, wishing them a good afternoon. He reminds Ruiz of himself forty years ago, full of expectation and pride in the uniform.

Ruiz opens his gate and strolls up the front path.

'Detective Inspector Ruiz?'

'You can drop the rank. I'm retired.'

'I'm here to collect you, sir.'

'And who might you be?'

'PC Banks.'

'You got a first name?'

'Robert.'

'Really?'

'Yes, sir.'

'You're a copper called Rob Banks?'

'It causes some merriment, sir, but I've learned to live with it.'

The turn of phrase makes Ruiz want to laugh but he decides not to double down on the mockery. Instead he glances at the threatening clouds and reaches into his jacket for his keys.

'Where are you going, sir?'

'This is where I live.'

'My guv wants a quiet word. He sent me to get you.'

'Tell him I'm open to house calls. I'll put the kettle on.'

'He's at the station, sir. He's conducting a murder investigation.'

'Then he'll probably want a biscuit.'

Half an hour later, the doorbell rings. Ruiz can see a figure silhouetted behind the frosted glass, shaking an umbrella. A wet strand of hair is curved against his forehead.

'I'm Detective Inspector Gennia,' says the man, hanging the umbrella across his forearm. 'I believe you're expecting me.'

Ruiz opens the door wider.

'I'm not coming inside,' says Gennia. 'You wanted a personal invitation. Here I am.'

The detective is a big man who might have played rugby except his nose is too straight and his ears are too pretty. Ruiz won't hold it against him. He recognises something in the younger man's face. 'Have we met before?'

'You knew my mother,' Gennia replies.

'That doesn't narrow it down a whole lot.'

'Katie Sylbert.'

Pieces fall into place. Kate Sylbert was one of the first female police officers recruited into the Flying Squad back in the eighties. She died almost thirty years ago, executing a search warrant on a drug den in Brixton. A junkie called Cullen McCurtie opened fire through the door. Later he claimed that Katie had failed to identify herself as a police officer.

'You came to the funeral,' say Gennia.

'You must have been all of ten.' Ruiz can remember a young boy standing next his mother's open grave, holding his little sister's hand, flinching during the three-volley rifle salute. Only a handful of female police officers have been killed in the line of duty in Britain. Katie was the second of them. She was from a police family. Her father and brother had been officers. And now there is another generation.

'How is your father?' asks Ruiz.

'He's moved to Norfolk to be closer to my sister.'

'She's married?'

'Three kids.'

'What about you?'

'Just one boy.'

The pleasantries have been exhausted. A car is waiting.

'You want to tell me what this is about?' asks Ruiz.

Gennia opens the car door for him. 'We're not going far.'

Fulham Public Mortuary is in Sands End at the southernmost part of the borough of Hammersmith. It used to be a solid working-class area until the property developers bought up the terraced houses and factories, replacing them with retail parks and luxury flats overlooking the Thames.

Gennia drives into a small internal courtyard behind the coroner's court.

'I thought we were going to the station,' says Ruiz.

'Call it a detour.'

The two-storey building is protected by soot-stained brick walls that are topped with jagged glass and security cameras. Ruiz can't imagine why anyone would want to break into a morgue, but can think of a few reasons to break out. The post-mortem rooms are on the ground floor, past a swipe-card barrier, through a series of swinging doors. They follow a long corridor deeper into the building.

Ruiz glances through an open door and sees a familiar face. Dr Gerard Noonan, a Home Office pathologist, is scrubbing his hands and forearms over a deep metal sink.

Known as 'the Albino' on account of his pale skin and snow-white hair, Noonan has cut up more bodies than Wes Craven, but with far greater finesse. He's also rumoured to favour the dead over the living because they talk less, but tell him more.

Noonan wipes his hands on a paper towel.

'Vincent – not dead yet.'

'I'll keep you posted.'

'You should consider donating your body to science.'

'I've seen what you do to the dead.'

'But I'd be gentle with you.'

'You really should get yourself a girlfriend.'

Noonan laughs and signs a clipboard with a flourish. He addresses Gennia. 'What can I do for you, Detective Inspector?'

'The post-mortem.'

'Finished.'

'Photographs?'

'On a disk.'

Further along a corridor, a door opens. A woman emerges with red-rimmed eyes and a middleweight backside squeezed into a short skirt. Her hair has been scraped into a bun revealing unbleached roots and fiercely pink little ears. The woman spies Gennia through the glass and her mouth twists out of shape.

'You wanted this!' she screams, her whole body shaking, including breasts that seem to defy gravity and age. She jabs her finger at the detective. 'You're happy he's dead!'

A WPC tries to lead her away. Gennia closes the vertical blinds.

'Friend of yours?' asks Ruiz.

'We found her husband floating in the Thames a week ago and last night her brother was murdered.'

'Who is she?'

The detective doesn't answer. He takes a seat in front of the screen and his fingers flick at the keyboard. Moments later, a printer begins humming behind him.

'I am going to ask you five questions. I know the answers to most of them, so I'll know if you're lying. Do you know a man called Patrick Hennessy?'

'What about him?'

'Answer the question?'

'Yes.'

'When was the last time you saw him?'

'Yesterday morning.'

'Where?'

'Outside his address.'

'Did you threaten him?'

'I gave him some advice.'

Gennia screws up his face as though suffering from gastric reflux or piles.

'Where were you between nine and eleven last night?'

'I was having a drink with a mate.'

'Where?'

'The Duke's Head on Lower Richmond Road.'

'I'll need your mate's name.'

'Why?'

Gennia ignores the question. Ruiz loses patience. 'By all means ask for my help, Detective Inspector, but don't piss on my porridge and tell me you're cooling it down. Either you tell me what this is about or I'll bring a lawyer in here and you can play charades with him.'

Whatever friendly connection existed between them has faded like an FM station on the drive through the Dartford Tunnel.

'What did you say to Hennessy?'

'I told him he was a parasite who feeds off problem gamblers – taking their homes, destroying their families. I said he should be scraped off the pavement with steel wool.'

'No loss to the world.'

'None whatsoever.'

Gennia places a series of printed pages on the desk, lining them up side by side. The images look like something from a torture museum. Patrick Hennessy seems to be facing one way and looking the other as if he's wearing a mask on the back of his head. His entire skull has been twisted one hundred and eighty degrees so that it faces in the wrong direction. The hands that are taped behind his back are also directly beneath his chin.

Ruiz sits in silence. The visual impact of the images makes something shift in his stomach. There are close-ups showing Hennessy's face, the swelling and bruises. His eyes are closed and those strange rubbery lips are peeled back in a grimace or a scream.

Gennia continues talking. 'There is a service entrance via the underground parking area. We believe that somebody followed a car through the automatic gates. This person then pushed a bin full of paper and cardboard near the lift-wells and forced open the doors. The bin was set alight, triggering the smoke alarms and the sprinklers in the basement.' Pausing, he places a new sequence of pictures on the desk showing a soot-covered ceiling and a metal bin twisted and crumpled by heat.

'Residents were evacuated. The fire doors lead to the street outside. Two fire engines were at the building within eight minutes.' The next photographs show Patrick Hennessy standing with other residents at one of the evacuation points. He seems to be arguing with a fire officer, giving him the pointy finger for upsetting his evening. 'The all-clear was given after thirty minutes and residents allowed to return. We believe that during that time the same person who lit the blaze took the stairs to the penthouse level.'

Another sequence of pictures is placed before Ruiz. These show a figure in a darkened stairwell, dressed in overalls with a baseball cap pulled low to hide their features. The angle of the camera doesn't give any indication of the person's age or gender.

Ruiz works his teeth along his bottom lip. 'What's this got to do with me?'

Gennia has one final series of photographs. These were taken with another CCTV camera situated outside the apartment block. The time-frame has changed. Ruiz recognises himself and Hennessy, nose to nose, exchanging words.

'You see how it looks?' says the detective. 'You argued with him. He's dead.'

Ruiz scoffs. 'I know fifty guys who'd give both nuts and two inches of cock to see Hennessy on a slab.'

'What did you say to him?'

'He was putting the hard word on someone to pay a debt that belonged to her husband.'

'Who?'

'A woman called Marnie Logan.'

The detective seems to chew on the name, holding Ruiz's gaze. From somewhere deeper in the building a bone saw starts up, growing louder as it makes contact with a torso.

'Her husband was a gambler. He disappeared more than a year ago.'

'How much did he owe?'

'Thirty thousand.'

'So this Marnie Logan asked you to talk to Hennessy?'

'Indirectly.'

'What does that mean?'

'I was doing my good deed for the day.'

His sarcasm grates on Gennia. 'Why didn't she phone the police?'

'Maybe she knows how the system works. A complaint is lodged. A record is kept. Fuck-all happens.' Ruiz gets to his feet, buttoning his jacket.

'I didn't give you permission to leave,' says Gennia.

The statement seems to ignite something between the two men. Ruiz's gaze turns inwards. 'Let me give you a piece of advice, Detective Inspector. I was doing your job before you were popping pimples and wanking over your mum's Littlewoods catalogue. When I couldn't solve a crime, I didn't cut corners, bend rules or fit people up. You think I'm good for this? Gather your evidence and lay a charge. Until then, I'm going home.'

Hailing a cab outside, Ruiz slumps in the back seat, closing his eyes against the images of violence. Maybe it was easier to handle such things when he was on the job. He remembers a retirement party for his first station sergeant – warmed-up sausage rolls and cloudy beer at a pub in Wapping. Ducking outside for a cigarette, he found the sergeant sitting on a low brick wall.

'What am I going to do now?' he asked.

'I thought you had it all planned – the caravan, touring . . .'

'Yeah, but now it frightens me. I feel as though I rushed through life, trying to save time, and now I've got too much of it. I want to give it back, do it over, only more slowly.' He looked at Ruiz. 'Remember that, son. The total of a man's days eventually become a circle not a sum. And when it's all over and you're back where you started, you'll wish you did it slower.'

CHAPTER 31

Joe O'Loughlin stands on the footpath, studying the address. Large well-established trees have created a green tunnel to the front door, making it look like a fairytale cottage in a forest instead of a semi-detached house in West London. A brief shower has passed and the sunshine returned. Walking across a layer of wet leaves and husks, he stops at a brightly painted red door and presses his thumb against the doorbell.

Shapes move behind the frosted glass. The door opens and an elderly man blinks at him over the wire rims of his spectacles. Dr Sterne is dressed in baggy trousers, a short-sleeve shirt and sleeveless woollen jumper that stretches over his belly. His wife is a hoverer, making small talk as they negotiate the narrow hallway and find a neat study overlooking the back garden where a man is raking leaves and trimming the hedges.

The weather is discussed. Traffic. Tea and biscuits are offered. The doctor talks to his wife sweetly. They are good together. Joe can imagine them finishing each other's sentences until one of them dies and their conversations will be forever left hanging.

Joe scrutinises his surroundings. The study had seemed small at first glance because of the dark salmon walls and the amount of furniture: a desk, filing cabinets, bookcases and a TV. Medical journals and texts are stacked on a side table, along with microcassettes around a micro-recorder. Framed citations and certificates hang on the walls.

'I hope you don't mind,' says the doctor, packing the bowl of a polished wooden pipe. He presses down the tobacco with the discoloured ball of his thumb. 'It's my one vice. Angie won't let me smoke in any other room.'

Joe notices a photograph behind the desk. It shows Dr Sterne standing thigh-deep in water, casting a rod. The fishing line shimmers like a golden thread as it curls through the soft light. There are other pictures of a boy, growing into a teenager and then a man.

'That's my son, Roy,' says Dr Sterne. 'He's grown now, of course. He's around today . . . working in the garden.'

'He lives at home?'

'No. He's a very successful IT consultant. Has his own business. He comes back to help with the lawn and keep his mother happy.'

Tucking the pouch of tobacco in a drawer, he lights the pipe and deposits the spent match into an ashtray, watching the wisp of smoke rise from the blackened tip.

'I really shouldn't be talking to you without

Marnella's permission. I told her husband the same thing.'

'You said it was last summer.'

'Late July, I think.'

The doctor makes a popping sound as he sucks on the pipe and then bites the stem as he talks. 'After Daniel visited me, I went looking for Marnie's file. That's what I didn't mention over the phone.' He motions to a filing cabinet on the far side of the room. 'That's where I kept all my clinical notes, including Marnie Logan's file. I don't know how long it's been missing. We had a burglary about six years ago. They took most of the usual things – electronics, cash, jewellery – but I didn't even think about the possibility of a file being stolen until you mentioned the break-in at your office.'

'And now?'

Dr Sterne shrugs. 'I can't remember ever misplacing a file, let alone losing one. I don't know what to think.'

'When did you last see the notes?'

'It would have been a decade ago. Under health guidelines they should have been destroyed after twenty years.'

'Why didn't you?'

The doctor pauses, trying to decide how much to say. He swivels towards the window. Roy emerges from the trees, pushing a wheelbarrow. His hair is cut close to his skull, which seems to bob above his shoulders as though it belongs to a bigger person. Propping the barrow near a flowerbed, he begins spreading mulch around the base of the roses.

'What I'm going to tell you is highly privileged information. I'm doing this because you're a fellow mental health professional who is treating Marnella. Do you understand?'

Joe nods.

'You have to be very careful about using any of this information without her permission.'

'Of course.'

Satisfied, the doctor leans back and closes his eyes for a moment, gathering his thoughts. 'Marnella was rather unique,' he says, sounding almost in awe of her. 'She came to me when she was eight. She lived with us for a while, became part of the family. She and Roy were very close.'

'She lived in *this* house?'

'When she wasn't at the hospital or allowed to go home, I often brought her here. It meant she was closer to the unit in case of relapses.'

'Relapses?'

Nursing his pipe, he peers through the curling smoke, as though summoning the details from the spirits. 'I was the senior consultant child and adolescent psychiatrist at the Mildred Creak unit in London – an in-patient facility for children with behavioural problems.'

Joe had heard of it.

'Marnie spent nearly four years at the unit as an in-patient, but came home with me on holidays and weekends. She was a pretty little thing. She liked old-fashioned dresses and wore ribbons in her hair. But she was also very difficult. Abusive. Violent.'

'What was the cause?'

'Before she arrived, she had seen a dozen different therapists and psychiatrists who had diagnosed her with everything from PTSD to schizophrenia. Over time I became less convinced by these conclusions. I thought her problems stemmed from her mother's death.' Dr Sterne looks up. 'I'm sure Marnie has told you about it?'

'She said her mother died in a traffic accident.'

'Did she go into the details?'

'No.'

Dr Sterne nods and uncrosses his legs. He brushes a strand of tobacco from his lap into the palm of his hand and carries it to the window where he releases it like it's a butterfly.

'Her car ran off the road, hit a tree and crashed into a swollen stream,' he says, blinking sadly. 'Marnie's mother wasn't wearing a seatbelt and was thrown clear. She was heavily pregnant, possibly in labour. Marnie was also in the car, strapped in a booster seat. Police think somebody pulled her free, but nobody ever came forward.

'Her mother gave birth before anyone could reach her. Marnie must have helped to deliver the baby, but mother and newborn died during the night. Marnie was found lying next to their bodies the following morning.' He stares at the roses, which look like they're rusting in the sunshine. 'It was a terrible thing for a child to endure, truly awful.

'Marnie was very young. For the first few years she seemed to cope with the tragedy. Her father remarried. Marnie started school. Then her behaviour began to change. Her father and stepmother took in foster children, whom Marnie seemed to resent. She tried to sell one little boy at a car boot sale and put another in a tumble drier. She set fire to her bedroom. She stole a car.

'There were similar problems at school. Her swearing and sexual precociousness set off warning bells. She drew lewd images of a teacher and was accused of molesting a girl in her class. Marnie denied it. I thought she was lying at first, but slowly I came to have qualms.'

'You thought the school was mistaken?'

'Not exactly.' Dr Sterne relights his pipe, shaking the match. 'No doubt you're aware of dissociative identity disorder.'

'Split personality.'

Dr Sterne nods. 'The condition is rare and often misdiagnosed. It involves the existence of two or more separate personality states within one person. Each "alter" has a distinctly different way of thinking, feeling and behaving.'

'And you're suggesting . . .?'

'I know it for a fact: Marnie had a separate personality.'

'And you *met* this alter?'

'Eventually, yes. Perhaps I should have realised sooner. Marnie complained of having blackouts and missing periods of time. Some lasted a matter of minutes and others for hours. She couldn't remember anything of these fugues – not where she'd been or who she'd spoken to. On one occasion, aged eleven, she escaped from the clinic and I called the police. She turned up, covered in blood. She had no scratches or cuts and she couldn't tell us the circumstances. It's still a mystery.'

The doctor pauses, aware of how his story is being received. 'I know you're finding this hard to believe, Professor. Trust me, so did I. Such a rare condition – such a landmark case . . .'

'This other personality—'

'Would you like to hear him? I taped some of our sessions. I still have the recordings.' He steps around his desk and goes to the side table and the pile of microcassettes. Reading the labels, he discards them one by one until he finds the one he wants.

'I had been seeing Marnie for almost a year with little progress. To control her anxiety I was teaching her deep relaxation techniques, but it was difficult with a child her age. She was lying on the sofa and I asked her to close her eyes and let her body relax and concentrate on my words . . . Marnie rarely could sit still for more than half a minute, but this time the world seemed to fade away and I thought she'd fallen asleep.' He presses the play button. 'Maybe this will give you some idea.'

Without warning, a deep howl fills the room like an animal in pain.

'*You're not going to take her away from me. Who do you think you are? I've spent years looking after her. She's mine.*'

Joe looks at Dr Sterne. 'Who is that?'

'Marnie.'

'But that sounds nothing like . . .'

'I know, I know. You should have seen her – her whole posture changed, her back arched off the couch as though some creature had become trapped inside her and was trying to rip out of her chest. The muscles in her face twisted and her jaw seemed to lengthen. I thought it was a seizure. I was reaching for the phone.'

They listen to the tape again. Dr Sterne is trying to communicate with the 'alter'.

'*So tell me about yourself – do you have a name?*'

'*Fuck off! I'm not going to talk to you.*'

'*What are you doing here?*'

'*Protecting my property.*'

'*Are you talking about Marnie?*'

'*She belongs to me.*'

'*Why her? What's so special about Marnie?*'

'*I chose her.*'

'*Why?*'

'*Because she's mine.*'

'*Nobody owns Marnie. She has come to me for help . . .*'

'*She doesn't need your help! You're trying to fuck with her head.*'

Listening to the tape, Joe is almost convinced that two men are arguing. Marnie's voice is harsh and guttural, as though she's speaking with her head inside a tin bucket. Joe struggles to picture a child making these sounds, particularly a nine-year-old girl.

A dissociation as dramatic as this one normally manifests itself in a person with a history of being abused or someone under extreme stress. The mind reacts by splitting off, creating a separate alternative personality, a different part of themselves to deal with the trauma. This fracturing can be so deep and fundamentally complete, there isn't a crack or wedge in the wall between the divided aspects of personality. Neither half will recognise the other or know of his or her existence.

The tape is still running. A string of invective fills the room.

'Bastard! Arsehole! Cunt! Leave her alone. I found her first. She's mine.'

Dr Sterne is trying to talk to Marnie's 'alter', pushing back against 'him'.

'What sort of man are you, preying on a young girl? Why don't you pick on someone your own size?'

'Don't insult my intelligence, you arrogant prick, I can crush you. I can crush her.'

'Why would you want to do that?'

'Because she's weak and stupid.'

'What makes you say that?'

'Look at her, always crying and whining about her mother. It's pathetic!'

Dr Sterne turns off the tape. 'It's more of the same,' he says, almost apologetically. 'I didn't always manage to talk to Malcolm.'

'Malcolm?'

'That was his name.' Dr Sterne swaps the micro-cassette tape for another one. 'I was twice Marnie's size, yet still this voice could intimidate me. He called me a dirty old man and a paedophile. He punched me . . . not just once. He was out of control. I had to force Marnie's arms behind her back. Then I did something I'm not proud of. I slapped her. I have never hit a child . . . or a patient.' He looks at Joe, hoping for understanding. 'When Marnie returned to me,' he holds up his fingers, putting the phrase in inverted commas, 'she had no memory of the incident. She was exhausted but bore no outward signs of having had been controlled or influenced by another personality. Of course, I questioned her, but she appeared to be completely unaware of Malcolm's existence.

'Clearly a case like this was extremely rare. If I'd been a younger and more ambitious man I might have published a paper, but I'm afraid I have little time for therapists and psychiatrists who treat unusual cases as opportunities to advance their careers. Instead, I focused on helping Marnie. Rather than trying to reach *her*, I tried to reach *him*. I spoke to Malcolm maybe two dozen times over the next three years, picking up clues. Initially, I put him at fifteen, possibly sixteen, but later I realised he was older. Uncouth. Wild. He swore and scratched his crotch and spat on the floor. He talked about sex incessantly.' Dr Sterne lowers his voice. 'He asked about my secretary and wanted to know if I was sleeping with her. He didn't seem to like women very much.'

'Was Marnie being abused?'

'I have no evidence of that.'

'What about her father?'

'He doted upon her.'

'And the rest of her family?'

'I met the new Mrs Logan many times and don't doubt that she loved her stepdaughter. They were a very caring selfless couple who looked after foster children, dozens over the years.'

'Could one of the children have abused Marnie?'

'She made no complaints.'

'Then why did she *need* Malcolm?'

'I think he arrived when Marnie watched her mother miscarry and bleed to death. She lay with those bodies all night. God knows how she survived, but somehow Malcolm helped her cope.'

The tape is still running.

'She's nothing without me. She's fucking useless. I can make her hurt herself. I can destroy her.'

'It's coming up now,' says the doctor.

The tape has ten seconds of silence. Then a little girl's voice becomes audible. She's crying in broken, breathless sobs. Dr Sterne tries to comfort her.

'Did I fall asleep?' she asks.

'Don't you remember?'

'No.'

'Why are you crying?'

'I don't know.'

'I talked to Malcolm.'

Marnie doesn't answer.

'Do you want to hear him?'

'No, no, no,' She is almost hyperventilating. Dr Sterne has to calm her down. There is a long period of silence.

'Did you tell him to go away?' she asks.

'Yes.'

The recording ends. Dr Sterne resumes his seat.

'Whenever Malcolm let go and Marnie came back, she had no recollection of what had happened. Her personality had fragmented so completely, she might as well have been unconscious.'

'Did you ever manage to play the tape to Marnie?'

'She didn't believe the voice was coming from her.'

'What about filming a session?'

'It might have traumatised her.'

Dr Sterne taps the pipe against the rim of a glass ashtray and begins packing the bowl again.

'How did you treat her?'

'It was like negotiating the release of a hostage,' he says. 'I attempted to confront Malcolm, draw him out, find out his reasons for choosing Marnie . . . I tried to face him down, order him to leave her alone, but he was manipulative and deceitful.'

'In what way?'

'He threatened to harm Marnie. He cut her arms when he was in control. She couldn't explain the injuries.' The doctor hesitates. 'He sexually abused Marnie, penetrating her with objects. Her stepmother found blood on her underwear and it led to an investigation by social workers.'

'How did you know the injuries were self-inflicted?'

'Malcolm bragged about taking her virginity. At one point I was under suspicion. It could have ended my career.' Dr Sterne blows smoke from the corners of his mouth. 'Marnie saved me. She denied I had ever touched her.

'As I said, Marnie had no knowledge of Malcolm. The division of her personality was faultless, but operated like a one-way mirror. Marnie could only see herself reflected in the glass, whereas Malcolm could look inside her mind.'

'Tell me about him.'

'He was clever. Manipulative. He learned to second-guess my line of questioning, but slowly I gained the upper hand.'

'How?'

'As our sessions continued, he began showing up less regularly. I attributed this to Marnie getting stronger and needing him less. He claimed to be protecting her, but was really the cause of her problems. He stole Mr Logan's car and crashed it. He sexually assaulted the girl in her class and set fire to Marnie's bedroom.'

'And one day Malcolm just stopped showing up?'

'That's about it.'

'How old was Marnie?'

'Twelve. I didn't want to press her too hard because I didn't want to call him back.'

'Do you think she outgrew him?'

'I honestly don't know. Marnie had managed to talk about her mother's death, although she remembered very little. By reliving the events, she learned to cope with them.'

Dr Sterne stands and stretches. His joints creak. Sunlight bounces off the transparent roof of a greenhouse.

'Perhaps Marnie didn't need him any more and she integrated the two elements of her personality.' He says the words as though trying to convince himself, but then wavers. 'I would have been happier if he had said goodbye.'

'Malcolm?'

'I know it sounds stupid, but he didn't deliver a final statement or make any last show of defiance.'

'And that bothers you?'

'No, yes, well, it's just . . .'

'What?'

'I didn't expect him to give up so easily.'

W atching a woman bathe has a poetry that is far more intoxicating than watching a woman undress. It's like a dance without music, every movement so practised and graceful, her breasts rising and falling as she breathes. This is a real woman doing something so matter-of-fact and everyday, rubbing a washcloth down her arms and along her legs. Squeezing water over her shoulders.

Even through the steam Marnie looks beautiful. Devoid of make-up and blandishments, stripped back to the basics, naked as the day she was born. Flesh. Blood. Family. A fragile package of flesh and bone, yet so cleverly put together. So beautifully designed.

But she has bruises and grazes. People keep hurting her and she's not strong enough to fight back. She's weak. Pathetic. That's why she needs me.

Now she's staring into the bathroom mirror, colluding with her other self, deciding what to wear and how much make-up to use. I love the way her bottom lip curls when she concentrates. I love her upturned nose and dimpled cheeks and her round ears attached at the lobes. She chooses her nicest outfit: the pink cami-knickers from Helene's and the skirt and top she bought from Zara for her last birthday but two. Daniel went with her to the shop and sat outside the changing room, texting while she tried on outfits. How she agonised over her choices.

Why is it that women think they look lovely when they're all dolled up, elegant as a champagne flute, when in reality they look just as beautiful when they're home from the gym wearing black leggings and an old T-shirt? They doubt their natural beauty and rely too much on blandishments and tricks.

A radio is playing somewhere, or perhaps it's a TV in a nearby room. When I was younger I used to lie in bed and press my ear to the wall, listening to the sounds of the people living next door. They were foreigners. Iraqis. Mr Khan ran a panel-beating shop and Mrs Khan cleaned hotel rooms. Their grown up daughter, Fariba, was still living at home. She told people she was going to beauty school to be a make-up artist, but spent most days watching TV and reading diet books.

Fariba didn't like me very much. I once lost a homemade kite over their fence when it crash-landed in their back garden. I knocked on their door. Fariba answered. I told her about my kite. She stared at me.

'Can I have it back?'

'No.'

'It's sitting on the grass.'

'So?'

She picked at her painted nails and leaned on the

door-jamb, challenging me. Her hair was wrapped in a towel. She had bleached it a lighter colour, but I could see where she'd missed some of the roots. I went back inside, through the house and climbed the back fence, using the trellis to get my footing before climbing onto the roof of their garden shed and jumping down onto the grass. The kite was beneath the clothesline.

Fariba guessed what I was going to do. Head down like a horse in a harness, she charged along the back path still with the towel wrapped round her hair. She beat me to the kite and crushed it with a single stomp, turning the spars into wooden wafers. She was bigger than I was. Fatter. Stronger.

'You're trespassing,' she said. 'Climb this fence again and I'll tell my daddy.'

'Why?'

'Because you're a freak.'

I went home and tried to glue the kite back together. I could hear Fariba through the wall, playing her record player, listening to Madonna singing 'Like a Virgin', which I thought was 'Like a Persian' until Rebecca Mortimer explained virginity to me. The idea of a girl safeguarding her virginity was a foreign concept to me when I was eight.

Fariba was a secret smoker. Her parents didn't know that she sneaked cigarettes into the house, hiding them behind the drainpipe outside her bedroom window. At night I would hear the sash cords rattle as she slid the window upwards. She leaned out over the yard, propped on her elbows, blowing smoke into the darkness and singing along with her record player. Afterwards, she sprayed her room with air freshener and left the window open to clear the smell.

I waited until evening, when I heard her summoned downstairs for dinner. Crawling out of my window, I swung across the gap, jamming my toes against the bricks and using the downpipe to reach her window-sill. I had always been good at climbing. In those days I could wedge myself into a right-angle corner, bracing my arms and feet on each wall, and shimmy up to the ceiling. My mother would sometimes come looking for me, calling my name. She had no idea I was perched above her head, splayed out like a gecko. This one day she started tidying my room and I couldn't hold on any longer. I dropped like a shot bird and almost gave her a heart attack. She smacked me so hard across the head I thought my left eardrum had ruptured.

Fariba's window was still open and her bedroom messy, draped in clothes and towels. I took one of her cigarettes and placed it between my lips, breaking two matches before I got one to light. I swallowed the smoke. My eyes watered. I wanted to cough. Once it was alight, I put the cigarette on the edge of her mattress. Then I hid her cigarettes and matches inside her bedside drawer.

Smoke was billowing out of her window when I raised the alarm, hammering on the Khans' door and yelling fire. They called the fire brigade and ran outside. Mr Khan looked at Fariba.

'Were you smoking?'

'No, Daddy.'

'Are you sure?'

'I never smoke.'

Firemen dragged the smouldering mattress outside onto the footpath and doused it properly. The cigarettes were found in Fariba's drawer. She tried to concoct a suitable excuse, but Mr Khan wasn't buying her sweet little angel routine. They were renting . . . without insurance. Fariba wore a black eye like a badge of resistance for the next few weeks before they moved out of the neighbourhood.

CHAPTER 32

One corner of the brown envelope is poking out from under the door. Reaching cautiously to pick it up, Marnie wonders why nobody knocked. She hasn't seen Trevor since yesterday. She never wants to see him again.

This envelope is large and flat, stiffened by cardboard. Like the last time, it has just her name written in block capitals. No address. No stamps or postmark. No details of the sender.

She thinks about the money. Two thirds of it has already been spent and the rent will be due again next week. Even if she's careful, she won't have enough to last another month.

Taking the envelope to the kitchen, she sits at the table and tears open the flap. A note flutters from inside. Handwritten. Unsigned.

Stop trying to trace your husband. He's gone. He didn't deserve you. From now on, listen to your heart.

A dozen photographs slip from the envelope. She studies the first one carefully. Taken with a long lens, it shows a blurred couple sitting outdoors at a café, chairs pulled close, whispering to one another. The photograph is part of a sequence. The remaining images show the same couple leaving the café and walking along the footpath, getting closer to the camera. Clearer. Marnie recognises Daniel. He's dressed in his leather jacket and baggy jeans. They stop at a car. The woman turns and kisses Daniel. Marnie can see her face. Penny. Something delicate seems to shred inside her.

He's alive! This is the proof. In the same breath she realises that the leather jacket is still hanging in Daniel's wardrobe. These are old pictures. This is evidence of an old assignation. Her husband and her best friend are kissing at the side of a road. Holding hands.

Marnie turns the photographs, hoping to find time-code or a date.

'Put on your shoes,' she says to Elijah.

'Where are we going?'

'To see Aunt Penny.'

Adjusting Elijah's hat, she tucks a water bottle next to him in the pushchair and sets off along Elgin Avenue. Crossing Maida Vale, they climb Abercorn Place into St John's Wood where the trees grow taller and the houses are grander. Marnie's mind keeps racing ahead and she can picture herself arriving at Penny's front door, demanding answers, explanations, perhaps even vengeance. A photograph doesn't reveal how long

301

a kiss lasted or how much passion it contains. Frozen by the blink of a shutter, a peck on the lips can seem like a fervent embrace. An accidental brush of the hand can look like a loving squeeze.

There's no answer at the door. Marnie's anger has nowhere to go. She sits on the front step, holding the envelope, letting Elijah wheel the push-chair up and down the path. She calls Penny's mobile.

'Where are you?'

'On my way home.'

'I'm waiting for you.'

'Did we arrange something?'

'No.'

The black Audi convertible pulls into a gravelled off-street parking bay. Penny waves and grabs polished paper shopping bags from the back seat before the roof closes and automatically clips onto the windscreen with a satisfying suction sound.

'Is everything all right?'

Marnie doesn't answer. Penny keeps talking.

'Come, come, I have a house without shitty nappies. Keegan has taken Abigail to his mother's.'

They go to the kitchen. Penny opens the back door and Elijah runs outside, skipping across the garden to a set of swings. Marnie puts the envelope on the stripped pine table. Penny hasn't seen it yet. She unwraps a bunch of flowers and begins cutting the stems, arranging them in a vase. She looks older today, like a piece of polished bone or stick of driftwood, thinned and hardened by the sun and sea. Outside Elijah has found a stick and is thrashing the branches of a willow tree. He lies across the swing seat and turns in circles, winding up the chains before letting go and spinning in the opposite direction.

'Coffee? Wine? Tea?' Penny opens and closes cupboards as though she's forgotten where things are kept. Marnie picks up the envelope and takes out the photographs, setting them side by side on the table. Penny stops. Turns. She picks up two of the images. Her fingers smudge the glossy surfaces. 'Who took these?'

'I don't know.'

'Were you having him followed?'

'No.'

She drops the photographs dismissively. 'We were meeting to talk about your birthday.'

'You're kissing him.'

'I gave him a peck on the lips. I kiss everyone on the lips, you know that.'

Marnie feels it inside her, a tiny quiver of certainty that exposes the lie. Penny is still talking. 'I didn't take you for the jealous type.'

'Tell me the truth.'

'Let this go. He's not worth it.'

'Were you sleeping with my husband?'

'Daniel abandoned you. He's an arsehole.'

Marnie collects the photographs and puts them into the envelope. She goes to the back door and summons Elijah. Penny blinks at her, shocked by her reaction. The thought had never occurred to her that her friend might not believe her. Behind her a lead grey cloud is edging across the window. She sighs impatiently, a memory stirring in her mind, a moment of stupidity. Lust.

'It happened once,' she whispers.

Marnie turns. Penny has her hands outspread in a gesture of supplication.

'He turned up here one night. You guys had had a fight. He said you threw him out. It was late. Keegan was away in Geneva. I put Daniel in the spare room. He was drunk. I told him to sleep it off. He started crying, saying he'd let you down, lost your savings . . . He was hurting.' She blinks rapidly, her head dropping in a penitent's pose. 'I'd been drinking. I'm so sorry, Marnie, it just happened.'

Marnie has been moving closer, wanting to see Penny's face. Without thinking, she swings her hand, slapping her hard across the left cheek. The violence surprises her, along with the noise.

'Nothing just happens,' says Marnie, shaking her stinging palm.

Penny is cradling one side of her face. 'I fucked up.'

'No, you *fucked* my husband.'

'I would never do anything to hurt you.'

'Really?' Marnie points to the envelope. 'So what was this – a favour?'

'I'm so, so sorry. How can I prove it to you?' Penny opens a drawer and takes out a chequebook.

'You think I want your money?'

'I'm trying . . . please . . .'

'You want to do something for me?'

'Anything.'

'I'm going to have Daniel declared dead. I need you to sign an affidavit.'

'Of course.'

'You have to say that you think he's dead.'

'I do.'

Marnie ushers Elijah to the front door. Sensing something is wrong, he stays quiet. Penny begs them to stay but Marnie leaves quickly, knowing she's about to cry and that some tears aren't meant to be wiped away by others; they're meant to fall.

Elijah falls asleep in the pushchair on the way home. Marnie doesn't want to wake him and he's too heavy for her to carry him up the stairs to the top floor. She sits on the front wall outside the mansion block, letting him sleep, while she contemplates a marriage that is becoming less golden as each day passes.

Children are riding scooters up and down the pavement. Marnie closes her eyes and watches the dappled light play behind her eyelids. She can picture them having sex, Penny pretending to be coy and naïve until she twigged that Daniel wanted her best *Pretty Woman* routine. She had always been very good at giving men the impression they were in charge when, in reality, she pulled the strings.

Penny made it sound as though Marnie had pushed

Daniel away and should accept some of the blame for what happened. Why? She hadn't let herself go. She had never withheld her body from Daniel. She was a loving wife. Supportive. Patient. Faithful.

Then she tries to remember the last time they made love. Daniel had come up behind her as she changed sheets on their bed and flipped her as easily as turning a pillow, burying his face between her legs. Then he turned her again, entering her from behind, pursuing his own pleasure, pushing into her until he was done. He went to the bathroom and back to the TV. Lying on the rumpled sheets, Marnie wondered when their sex life had become so artless and crude.

A shadow falls over her face. Marnie opens her eyes, shielding them against the glare. Craig Bryant is wearing dark glasses and carrying his suit jacket over his shoulder, his tie at half-mast. Even his shoelaces look laundered and pressed.

'I was hoping I'd run into you,' the lawyer says, glancing into the pushchair. 'I could carry him upstairs for you.'

'He won't sleep for much longer.'

Marnie doesn't realise how hard her jaw has been clenched until she tries to smile. Dimples dot her cheeks. A long silence follows.

'Is everything all right?' he asks.

Marnie shakes her head, fighting her tears.

'What's wrong?'

'Daniel was sleeping with my best friend.'

The lawyer sits on the low wall, folding his jacket

over his knee and putting one arm around Marnie. She sobs into his shoulder.

'I'm sorry.'

'You don't have to apologise.'

Mrs Brummer passes on the footpath, taking an interest because this is gossip-worthy: Marnie crying on the shoulder of a strange man. The story will spread through the building within hours. That's what Marnie despises. Her tragedy isn't private and it isn't public enough. With more headlines, perhaps Daniel would have been found.

'You were too good for him,' says Bryant.

'You didn't even *know* him.'

'I know you.'

Marnie pulls away and wipes her eyes. She doesn't want anyone sympathising or feeling sorry for her. Even worse, people seem to model her pain as though trying it on for size and then hand it back to her, making her feel even sadder and emptier. Why should *her* shitty life help others appreciate what they have?

'Why are you here?' she asks.

'I've been looking into this issue of probate. The law changed after the Asian tsunami disaster. Nine hundred Britons were missing and their relatives were in limbo. The UK government allowed them to be declared dead after twelve months.'

'So we can do that?'

'That was a natural disaster. I've made an application for a court hearing. It might take a few weeks.'

'I've waited this long.'

Bryant pulls a loose thread from his folded jacket.

'Would you like to have dinner with me?'

'Me?'

'Eleanor has taken Gracie to the country for the week. I hate dining alone and you look like you need cheering up.'

'I have Elijah.'

'Your older daughter could babysit. Zoe, isn't it?'

'How do you know her name?'

'I've bumped into her at the shops.' Almost as an afterthought, he says, 'We could discuss the case.'

'What is there to discuss?'

'I contacted the insurance company.'

'Did you talk to Mr Rudolf?'

'No, he's off work. He fell down two flights of stairs and fractured his skull.'

'Really?'

'So I was told.'

Marnie remembers her last words to Mr Rudolf, her anger and violent thoughts. Instead of being shocked or saddened, she feels strangely vindicated and has to admonish herself.

'About dinner?' he asks. 'I could pick you up at seven-thirty.'

'I can't tonight.'

'Maybe tomorrow?'

She doesn't answer. Elijah has woken, rubbing his eyes with balled fists.

'I have to go,' she says, unbuckling his harness. She folds the pushchair and follows Elijah up the stairs. Craig Bryant has gone when she finds her keys. What was she supposed to tell him? *My husband slept with my best friend, so I'm not in the mood for dinner.*

Upstairs she runs a cool bath for Elijah and helps him undress, trying not to be shocked by how much weight he's lost. She makes him dinner, which he barely touches. Washing up the dishes in the plastic sink bowl, she glances at the knife-block and notices an empty slot in the wood. She checks the cutlery drawer and benches, trying to remember when she last used the knife.

Her mind flicks to something the detective said when they first met. Niall Quinn had been killed with a kitchen knife. Marnie pushes the thought away. There are lots of explanations for a missing knife, all of them more plausible than the one she can't bring herself to picture.

CHAPTER 33

Ruiz is sitting at a pavement café in Chelsea waiting for his ex-wife, Miranda, who will be twenty minutes late because 12.30 means 12.50 and everybody knows that except men like Ruiz. They've been divorced for eight years, but Miranda still acts like they're married, choosing Ruiz's clothes and occasionally letting him sleep with her. The sex is better since they divorced – dirtier and more spontaneous. She's a good stepmother to the twins, who are grown up now, but still need someone to remind them about family birthdays and anniversaries.

Ruiz scours the menu for something with a carbohydrate. The salads will come drizzled in balsamic and feature strange leaves that look like nettles. The 'wedges' are sweet potato and advertised as a 'healthy treat'. Why is everybody so determined to help him live longer?

Miranda skips across the street. She's wearing a mid-length floral skirt and dark blue top with shoestring straps. Her hair is cut shorter than he remembers, brushing her pale shoulders. She moves with such grace and sensuality, her feet barely touch the ground.

The sun is slanting across half the table. Miranda chooses the shade, dropping her handbag on the chair. Leaning forward, she accepts a kiss to each of her cheeks, then holds Ruiz's face and pecks him on the lips.

As she lowers her arms, he gets a glimpse of exposed skin below her navel before her top slides over her flat stomach. Instantly, he conjures up images of running his tongue down her torso.

'Did you just smell me?' she asks.

'Might have done.'

'That's creepy.'

'Well, don't smell so good.'

She rolls her eyes and takes a seat. A waiter appears as if by magic. She contemplates the wine list. He's looking at the edge of her silken top where it loops beneath her breasts. Ruiz distracts him.

'Do you have any lager on tap?'

'No, sir.'

'Well then, bring me something foreign and over-priced in a bottle.'

Ruiz notices how women at the other tables are taking an interest in him now, whereas five minutes ago he'd been invisible. Why is it that men become more interesting to the opposite sex when they're with a beautiful woman, but that same woman is treated with suspicion by her peers because she's considered to be fishing with too much bait in the water?

Miranda orders a New Zealand Sauvignon Blanc and a chicken salad. She can't stay long. She's meeting a friend at John Lewis to help choose a set of curtains.

'How have you been?'

'Good.'

'What have you been working on?'

'Why the sudden interest?'

Miranda runs the tip of her tongue over her upper teeth. 'I had a strange phone call this morning. I don't know how this person got my number.'

'What do you mean "strange"?'

'He said he was a friend of yours. I'm supposed to give you a message. Stay away from Marnella Logan.'

'Is that it?'

'The gist of it.'

A basket of bread has been delivered to the table. Ruiz breaks the warm bun apart and decides that not everything about modern restaurants can be faulted.

'Are you sleeping with this woman?' asks Miranda.

'No.'

'So it's not a jealous husband?'

'I'd like to meet her husband. He's been missing for more than a year.'

'Who is she?'

'One of the professor's patients.' Ruiz chews slowly on the bread. 'Tell me about this caller?'

'He sounded insolent. Angry.'

'Threatening?'

'Worrying.'

'Did you take down the number?'

'It didn't show up on the screen.'

Ruiz doesn't like the idea that somebody knows about the people in his life. It's something Hennessy would do, but he's no longer in a position to threaten anyone.

Their meals have arrived. Miranda toys with her salad, occasionally picking up a morsel of chicken or a green leaf. Ruiz looks at his tiny lamb cutlets and wonders if the animal ever gambolled.

Miranda talks easily, asking about the twins, wondering if Claire is thinking about starting a family.

'That would make you a step-grandmother,' says Ruiz.

Miranda frowns momentarily.

'A glamorous one,' he adds.

'Thank you.'

She reaches across the table and picks up one of Ruiz's wedges, biting it in half.

'I have to go.'

'This is my treat.' He takes out his wallet.

'I'm a cheap date.'

'You were *never* cheap.'

Her laugh is drier than a martini. Ruiz hugs her and holds on this time. 'I want you to tell me if you get any more calls.'

'Should I be worried?'

'Just be careful.'

Something fragments in her eyes. Ruiz strokes strands of hair off her neck. Miranda looks directly at him. 'Do you ever take your own advice?'

'I'm always careful.'

'Don't get hurt.'

'I won't.'

'And don't hurt anyone.'

'If you say so.'

Ruiz decides to walk home along King's Road, past boutiques, brand stores and galleries. This is a different world from most of London, full of beautiful people who are beautifully dressed with no word for austerity in their phrasebook.

He cuts north through Parsons Green, stopping at the White Horse for a palate cleanser. His phone is ringing. He doesn't recognise the number.

'How is your ex-wife?' asks the voice.

'Do you know her?'

'*Everybody* knows her.'

Ruiz is outside, glancing across the green, scanning the street. There is a man with a briefcase and a black umbrella. He's talking on a mobile phone. A young black kid is waiting to cross at the lights. A motorbike with a broken exhaust waits for the green signal. A white van is parked on the corner.

'She has incredible tits, Miranda. Are they real?'

'All natural.'

'And you divorced her. Are you gay?'

'No, but I could make an exception for you. I'll

shove my foot up your arse. I bet you don't even jump.' Ruiz is moving, looking into cars, studying pedestrians. He hears a horn sounding: once in his left ear and again through the phone. 'How about we talk this over? I'll buy you a drink.'

'I'm not a drinker.'

The voice is a gentle monotone. Cocky. High-pitched.

'How was your lunch?'

'If you're hungry . . .'

'No, I've eaten.'

'What should I call you?'

'You don't need to know my name.'

'Make it easier.'

'That's not on my list of priorities, you just need to listen. I want you stop putting your nose into other people's business.'

'Pot, kettle, black,' says Ruiz, who is walking towards Parsons Green station.

'I'm only saying you should look after things at home before you insert yourself in someone's life. A pretty ex-wife, a daughter in Primrose Hill, retirement, you have a nice thing going. Leave Marnie Logan alone.'

'Is that a threat?'

'Why so antagonistic? That time of the month?'

'Full moon.'

'You should tell your friend the psychologist to do the same. He's not helping Marnie.'

Ruiz can hear a train rattling above his head. Scratching steel. He looks up at the overhead bridge.

A train is pulling into the station. Swirls of graffiti cover the windows. That's where the voice is coming from. The platform.

He leaps the barrier and sprints up the stairs, forcing his way past the people streaming towards the exit. He stumbles, holds out his hand. Someone steps on his fingers. He wrenches his hand free and rights himself. The doors are closing. He can't get his fingers in the join. He hammers on the glass. The train is moving. He runs along the platform, trying to keep up, peering into the windows.

The last carriage passes him and disappears towards Putney Bridge and onwards to Wimbledon. Holding his mobile to his ear, he listens to the dead air.

He calls Miranda. She's shopping in John Lewis. He can hear laughter and voices.

'Are you missing me already?' she asks.

'That call you got this morning – the guy who said he was a friend of mine?'

'Yes.'

'He called me when you left.'

'Who is he?'

'I don't know, but I don't think you should go home.'

She chuckles down the line. 'Are you trying to get me to spend the night with you?'

'I'm serious. He knows about you and Claire.'

There is a long pause. 'I thought you retired from all this.'

'What?'

'You know what I mean.'

'I'm doing a favour for Joe O'Loughlin. I owe the guy.'

'No you don't. You owe me. You owe your family.'

'It seemed harmless.'

'And now it's not . . .' She makes an audible tut-tut sound. 'I was a parole officer, Vincent. I've dealt with my share of freaks. I have deadlocks on the doors, locks on the windows, mace and a panic button. I think I can handle myself.'

Ruiz remembers the post-mortem photographs of Patrick Hennessy and wants to argue, but he decides not to frighten Miranda. She's angry with him, but at least she'll be careful.

'Can you talk to Claire?' he asks.

'Why not you?'

'She'll take it better.'

'Coward.'

'Guilty as charged.'

She hangs up. Ruiz clenches the phone in his hand and descends to street level. He retraces his steps and stops at the White Horse, nursing a pint in the outside courtyard. He has had his cage rattled by pros, but it's been years since a disembodied voice on the other end of a telephone made his pulse quicken and mouth go dry. For some reason this caller has struck a discordant note that hums in his mind, making him feel uncomfortable. Vulnerable.

His mobile rings again. His heart skips. He sets

down his pint glass and looks at the screen. Answers.

'Hey, pal, where have you been?'

'We need to talk,' says Joe.

'You just read my mind.'

CHAPTER 34

Zoe sits on the steps of the library, her thumbs moving on a mobile phone that is nestled in her cupped hands. Dressed in a black skirt, white blouse and black school blazer, the knot of her tie is pulled down and her top button undone.

She looks at the time. He's late. A bus pulls up opposite. A dozen students pile out, pushing between shoulders. They go to another school. Belong to another tribe. Zoe doesn't make eye contact, but watches just the same. Ruben is the last person to get off the bus. He crosses the road and stands two steps below her. She keeps her knees together, tucking her skirt beneath her upper thighs, self-consciously.

'Hi.'

'Hello.'

'Have you been waiting long?'

Zoe shakes her head.

'You seem upset. Is everything all right?'

She nods, not wanting to meet his eyes.

'Any luck finding your dad?'

Zoe looks at him. 'How did you know . . .?'

319

'I saw you updating your website at the library.'

'No news.'

'How long has he been missing?'

'Over a year.'

Zoe takes a lip-gloss from the zipped pocket of her school satchel and paints the stick across her lips. She's trying hard to be cool, but doesn't like the way he looks at her. It's as if he knows what she's thinking or what she's going to say before she even decides to speak. And his eyes seem to be laughing at her, but not in a cruel way.

'Did you bring the laptop?'

He nods. 'Did you tell your mother about it?'

'No.'

He takes it from a pouch. It's not new or sleek, but neither is it old and boxy.

'It's got a fast processor and four megabytes of RAM. I've cleared my stuff off the hard drive. If you come across anything I missed, just delete it. It doesn't have a password. Where do you live?'

Zoe hesitates. 'Up the road.'

'You should be able to find an unsecured network, or you can use your mobile phone as a hotspot. Don't download any big files or surf the web for too long or your data bills are going to bankrupt your mother.'

'What do you do, Ruben?'

'I'm an analyst.'

'What do you analyse?'

'People. Companies. Countries.'

'Sounds interesting.'

'It has its moments.'

'Really?'

'No.'

Zoe laughs. She can't tell when he's being serious.

He changes the subject. 'I could move your page higher on the search engines so it reaches more people.'

'How do you do that?'

'I link it to other sites.'

'What would I have to do?' she asks.

'Let me be an administrator for the website.'

'That's all?'

'Yep.'

'Why would you do that?'

'I'm a dangerous pervert who preys on teenage girls.'

Zoe looks at him. 'Yeah, right!'

When she gets home, Zoe goes straight to her room and slides the bolt across her door. She opens the laptop on her bed and waits for the operating system to load. Then she searches for an unsecured wireless connection. There are so many flats in the vicinity she discovers nearly twenty wi-fi networks. Two of them are open. Zoe thanks them for their generosity and gets herself online, calling up her Facebook page and updating her status, before setting up bookmarks for her favourite sites. The laptop has a built-in webcam. Zoe turns it on and poses, pulling funny faces and taking photographs.

She posts one on her Twitter page, telling people that she's 'plugged in and connected'.

A message pops up on screen from her friend Steph, who has been teasing Zoe about Ryan Coleman, but not in a nasty or jealous way.

> Welcome to the twenty-first century. Want to do my history essay for me?

Zoe types back:

> In your dreams.

CHAPTER 35

The consultant has maroon-coloured trousers, two-tone shoes and tight coppery clown hair. A bright red bow tie completes the ensemble. His name is Dr Cole and he moves across the consulting room like a robot, jerking his mechanical arms. Elijah laughs and wants him to do it again.

'Only if you tell me what you had for breakfast,' says the doctor, talking like an android. 'And how often you poop? And if it hurts?'

Elijah laughs at the word poop.

Dr Cole lifts the boy's arms and legs, looking for skin rashes on his elbows and knees. He presses Elijah's abdomen, making him giggle.

'Open your mouth.'

Elijah opens wide, dimples creasing his cheeks.

'Wow, I can see all the way to your toes. Wiggle them for me.'

Elijah wiggles.

'Now jump down and step on the scales.'

Elijah looks down at the glowing red digits between his feet. 'How much do I cost?'

'It tells me how big you've grown.'

'Am I bigger?'

'You're getting there.'

Marnie is sitting on a chair next to the desk, feeling as though she's holding her heart in her clammy hands. She can see the river from the window. It triggers a memory of Niall Quinn. She pushes it away and concentrates on the doctor's face, trying to read his thoughts.

Dr Cole produces a bag of jellybeans from behind Elijah's ear, making it seem like a magic trick. Afterwards, Marnie takes Elijah to the reception area where they keep a box of toys and books. She goes back to see the doctor, preparing herself for bad news.

Dr Cole begins using medical terms and Marnie tries to concentrate. Then she hears the word biopsy and her mind starts to scream.

'We'll take a tissue sample by inserting a long thin tube called an endoscope through Elijah's mouth and stomach, into the small intestine. We'll sedate him first. The results will tell us if the villi in his small intestine are still being damaged.'

'But I've changed his diet.'

'It might be something else.'

'Like what?'

'That's what we'll try to find out.'

'When?'

He studies his desk calendar, turning the pages. 'How about the twenty-fourth of October?'

'But that's weeks away.'

'It's the best I can do.'

Marnie stares at him glumly. She doesn't want cheerful reassurance. She wants a healthy little boy. The consultant has another patient waiting. Elijah gets a helium balloon as an extra reward. Marnie ties it to his wrist so it won't drift away. On the journey home, she tries to pretend that everything is normal when she fears nothing will *ever* be normal again. Her life is crumbling and she's holding it together like a child protecting a sandcastle from the waves.

Halfway down Elgin Avenue she senses someone following her. Gripping Elijah's hand a little tighter, she crosses the road. When he stumbles on the kerb, she lifts him upright before he falls. Someone calls her name. She turns. Penny's husband is standing beneath a tree, waiting for a break in the traffic.

'We need to talk,' he shouts.

Marnie has been squeezing Elijah's hand too tightly. He wants to pull away. She bends and kisses his fingers.

Keegan catches up to her. Short and overweight with the makings of an extra chin, he has a mouth that creases permanently downwards. He has always struck Marnie as the sort of man who suspects that everybody else is happier than he is, with more money, better friends and more fruitful lives.

Instead of kissing Marnie on each cheek, he grabs her arms, pushing Elijah aside, spilling his sweets. The Winnie the Pooh balloon bobs jerkily on his wrist.

'Is she *my* daughter?' he yells.

A fleck of spit lands on Marnie's cheek. 'What?' she asks.

'Abigail . . . Is she mine?'

'I don't know what you're—'

'Please tell me.'

His bottom lip is quivering and his voice sounds almost comedy posh. Penny must have told him about Daniel. Maybe she feared that Marnie would say something first. Payback. Friendship means nothing any more.

'Penny said she was drunk and Daniel took advantage of her. I'd kill the bastard if he was still around.'

'Grow up, Keegan,' says Marnie. 'It takes two to have an affair and we both know what Penny used to be.'

'And we both know what *you* are now.'

Marnie wants to slap him like she slapped Penny, but Elijah is watching. His jellybeans are scattered on the concrete path among the acorn husks. Marnie bends and begins picking them up. They'll have to be thrown away.

'I'll get you some more. You don't like the black ones anyway.'

'I was going to give them to my friend.'

'He doesn't need your sweets, baby.'

Despite being matron of honour at Penny's wedding, Marnie barely knows Keegan. Once or twice she and Penny had organised weekend breaks to the country, but Daniel and Keegan usually hung out together while Penny and Marnie enjoyed spa treatments. Keegan once invited Daniel on a shooting weekend at a Scottish estate. Daniel didn't like guns, but Keegan wanted to impress the host by bringing a hotshot journalist along.

'I warned Daniel to stay away from Penny.'

'What?'

'He was always flirting with her. Undressing her with his eyes. Brushing up against her.'

'That's a lie.'

'You think he's so perfect.' Malice curls the corners of his words. 'On our hunting weekend, Daniel bragged about shagging some photographer at the paper whenever they went abroad. Said she went off like a firecracker.'

Marnie remembers a photographer called Jill Edridge who often travelled with Daniel. Small, pixie-faced, she dressed like a man and was always lurching around under the weight of her camera bag. Daniel talked about her being gay. Marnie can't picture them together: Penny, yes, but not Jill Edridge.

Keegan is trying to hurt her because he feels betrayed. *Join the club, you arsehole, we've* both *been betrayed!*

Straightening up, Marnie wipes her hands on her jeans. 'Is that why you came here, Keegan, to hurt me? Or maybe you just like beating yourself up.'

They look at each other, sharing a moment of

bleak futility. Elijah tugs at Marnie's hand, wanting to go home. Keegan seems to deflate, sitting on a low wall, his anger having blown out like a passing squall. 'Can you tell me something honestly,' he asks. 'Am I really that hard to like?'

'Penny loves you . . . so does Abigail.'

'How do *you* feel about me? Do I make your skin crawl?'

'No.'

'You didn't remember me,' he says. 'We met years ago . . . way before I started seeing Penny. You were interning at the advertising agency. One of my friends was opening a bar in Covent Garden. You came along with one of the account managers.'

'I remember the bar,' says Marnie.

'I talked to you. It was before you met Daniel. You came right out and told me about Zoe. I thought you were testing me – to see if I was the type of guy who would run at the first mention of you being a single mother. I asked for your phone number.'

'Did I give it to you?'

He smiles sadly. 'You gave me a fake one. I thought maybe I just had a digit wrong, but I tried a dozen different combinations. Then I realised what you'd done.'

Marnie grimaces slightly. It's the sort of thing she used to do. 'I'm sorry.'

'Don't sweat it,' he shrugs. 'I was just another guy in a bar trying to chat you up.'

'It wasn't like that. Why didn't you say anything before now?'

'Say what? I once bought you a drink and you blew me off.'

'I don't remember it.'

'That's exactly right. I bet you were the same when you were at school – just like Penny: pretty, popular, cruel . . .'

'I wasn't like that,' says Marnie.

Keegan chews at the inside of his cheek as though trying to draw blood. 'She married me for my money, I know that.'

'Penny loves you.'

'She loves the lifestyle I provide: the holidays, the Botox injections, the frocks and spa treatments.'

'Have some faith.'

'Faith in what?'

'People.'

'I would have looked after you.'

'I don't *need* looking after.'

CHAPTER 36

Joe has spent most of the night reading and studying the literature on dissociative disorders – the latest research and case studies. He has also been wrestling with a dilemma. How much can he reveal of Marnie's mental history to the police or to Ruiz? He has a duty to protect her privacy or to seek her permission before breaching patient confidentiality. Trust lies at the heart of the relationship between a patient and a clinical psychologist. Without it, there is no way he can help Marnie.

At the same time, he's aware of the Tarasoff precedent – the duty to warn. Tatania Tarasoff was a Californian university student stabbed to death in October 1969. Her boyfriend, a paranoid schizophrenic, had confided to his psychologist that he planned to kill her, but the warning was never passed on to the girl or her parents because of the 'duty of confidentiality' between a mental health professional and a patient. The parents sued. The psychologist lost. The precedent was created. Joe has a duty to divulge confidential information if a client communicates a plausible intention to do serious harm to a third party. But Marnie has never communicated such a desire. She's never shown any evidence of dissociation or an alternative personality . . . not to him.

In twenty years of clinical practice, Joe had never come across a patient with a dissociative identity disorder – a condition more common in fiction than the real world. The most notorious case involved Sybil Dorsett – a girl with sixteen separate personalities – who had a book and film made about her in the seventies, but was later exposed as a fraud. Her therapist had invented her story, with the help of a journalist.

A colleague of Joe's once wrote a paper about a woman called Caroline who dropped out of university and disappeared for two years. She was discovered working at a laundromat in Battersea, but didn't call herself Caroline any more. She was Hannah, aged twenty-eight instead of twenty, with a Scottish accent. Psychologists interviewed her for months, uncovering a pattern of drug and alcohol abuse, along with frequent blackouts, depression and two suicide attempts. It was during one of their sessions that Caroline reappeared, asking her therapist to help her because Hannah wouldn't leave her alone.

Hannah hated Caroline, despising her weakness, whereas Caroline feared Hannah was taking control and pushing her out of her own mind. Her 'alter' had a completely different accent and body language to Caroline. She was older and more sexually promiscuous. She took drugs and got into fights.

Childhood abuse appeared to be the trigger: a stepfather prone to random acts of violence that seemingly came from nowhere and vanished just as quickly. Hannah emerged as an antidote – someone who could stand up to the abuse because Caroline was too passive and accepting; too beaten down.

Marnie Logan's dissociation is different. According to Dr Sterne, she had never acknowledged Malcolm's existence, which means she had either suppressed the knowledge or lied to him. Why? What are the chances that Malcolm has survived – a separate personality existing concurrently, harboured since childhood? Slim to nothing – vanishingly small. Marnie was twelve. Her clinical files should have been destroyed years ago, along with the tapes. That's the law.

Joe has arranged to meet Ruiz in a pub near Paddington. On the walk through Little Venice, across Westbourne Terrace Bridge, he goes over the details again. Up until a few days ago, everything he knew about Marnie had been based upon what she'd told him. Her marriage was good. Daniel was happy. Even her story about the gambling debts and Patrick Hennessy had no independent verification. Could these be elaborate cover stories to explain her bruises and blackouts?

Ruiz is sitting on a high stool with his back to the door, looking at the passing parade of drunken football fans as though he'd like to make a mass arrest. One of them has a snare drum and is hammering out a brainless tattoo while the others chant.

The two men hug, which is something Joe does rarely with other men. Ruiz buys him a lemon, lime and bitters and himself a Guinness. Settled. Heads together. Joe tells him the story about Marnie Logan and the mysterious Malcolm.

Afterwards there is a long silence. Ruiz shakes his head. 'I hate this psycho crazy-arsed shit. No offence.'

'None taken.'

'So what you're saying is that Marnie Logan – or this Malcolm side of her personality – could be acting independently, without her knowledge?'

'In theory.'

'Why only in theory?'

'In my sessions with Marnie she mentioned suffering blackouts and fugues, but nothing beyond a few minutes. As a child her blackouts lasted for hours, sometimes days.'

'So she's been lying to you.'

Joe doesn't answer.

'I think we should stay away from this woman. People have an unhealthy habit of dying around her.'

'What do you mean?'

'Patrick Hennessy is dead. Someone tried to unscrew his head like a cheap bottle of wine. You could argue the world has been vastly improved by his passing, but two wrongs don't make a left turn. And if you're thinking Marnie Logan isn't strong enough to do something like that, I've seen arrests where it took six officers to bring down a female schizophrenic or a meth addict.'

Joe doesn't show any emotion. Mr Parkinson will sometimes rob him of facial expressions, leaving behind a fixed vacant stare like he's mentally left the building.

Ruiz continues talking, describing his meetings with DI Gennia and Calvin Mosley.

'Where would Marnie get fifty grams of heroin?'

'I'm just telling you what he told me.'

'How long did he spend in prison?'

'Five years.'

'And he's sure it was Marnie?'

'Yep. That's not all. The woman he was banging, Patrice Heller, was a bridesmaid at Marnie's first wedding. Now she's serving twenty years in Kerobokan Prison for drug possession, which I wouldn't wish upon my least favourite mother-in-law. Calvin and Patrice both swear the drugs weren't theirs. No history. No accomplices. No witnesses.'

Ruiz leans back and takes a lingering look at the curves of a woman encased in a sheath dress.

'Should be a crime,' he says.

'The dress?' asks Joe.

'The body.'

The woman sneaks a glance over her shoulder, aware that she's being watched.

'How is Miranda?' asks Joe.

'I had lunch with her today. She's looking very fine.'

'You're the most married divorced man I've ever met.'

'I'm in a healthy relationship. No strings attached.'

'A pensioner with benefits.'

'Fuck off!'

Ruiz stares into his empty pint glass. 'Something else happened today. I had a phone call about Marnie Logan. Somebody tried to warn us off.'

'Male or female?'

'Up until five minutes ago, I would have said definitely male. I've got a question. Hypothetically speaking, if this Malcolm character is a separate personality, does he lead a separate life? Does he have his own clothes? Could he have identity papers, bank accounts, or a different address?'

'She's not likely to dress up as him.'

'How do you know?'

'I'm basing it on what I've read.'

'So how different is he?'

'Some "alters" have exceptionally high tolerance for physical pain. They split off physical sensation, which becomes encapsulated in their alternative personality, thus avoiding the pain. They also have dramatically different skills and abilities. One "alter" may be able to drive a car, the other may not.'

'And she could have no idea?'

'It's possible.'

'But you don't believe it.'

Joe doesn't answer. He glances outside at the

footpath full of backpackers, tourists, street traders and commuters. There are eight million people in London – each one of them unique yet similar enough that their behaviour can be charted and predicted with reasonable certainty. Yet there will always be individuals who don't conform to any pattern, just as there are rare neurological disorders and genetic mutations. For every rule there is an exception. Perhaps Marnie is one of them.

Sometimes he gets tired of watching people, unconsciously picking up on the details around him. Take the couple in the corner: she's in her mid twenties, brunette with pale ankles and bitten nails. He's ten years older with a tankard-shaped head and a job in an engineering firm whose name is sewn onto his shirt pocket. Such potential written over them, yet guilt holds them back. She's Catholic. He's married. They're holding hands. She's pregnant, nursing a soft drink, shame written all over her face, looking for certainty.

Joe's mind drifts to back to Marnie.

'Someone must have known. You can't have blackouts when you're raising two children.'

'Maybe her husband covered for her,' says Ruiz.

'I think he realised something was wrong. That's why he contacted these people. He listened to their stories.'

'That's enough to give a man doubts.'

CHAPTER 37

The heat of the day is still radiating through the western wall rendering the kitchen the hottest room in the flat. Marnie is trying to make it up to Zoe by cooking her favourite meal. The bolognaise sauce is bubbling, the lasagne sheets are layered and the cheese sauce is cooling. She's also rented a DVD from Mr Patel's shop (*Les Misérables*) and will tidy up Zoe's room.

A movement catches her eye. She studies the gap beneath the fridge and the bench. A mouse appears, nibbling at a toast crumb. It glances around disdainfully as though deciding whether to rent the place.

Elijah chooses that moment to dash along the hallway. He's wearing a tea towel as a cape and brandishing a plastic ray gun. Sometimes Marnie wonders if she should take away his crime-fighting paraphernalia – the cowboy guns and Spiderman outfit. Penny thinks Elijah is being gender-stereotyped, which explains why she gave him a Care Bear for Christmas, which he's barely taken out of the box. Penny can go to hell!

The mouse has gone.

'You missed seeing Stuart Little.'

'Where?'

Marnie points to a spot on the floor.

'Are we going to get a cat?' he asks excitedly. 'My friend has a cat.'

'Does he?'

'Yep.'

Elijah takes off again, running down the hallway to her bedroom where he's playing in the wardrobe. Marnie goes to Zoe's room and begins tidying, hanging towels and folding clothes. She has to move the single bed away from the wall to change the sheets. If Zoe didn't have so much rubbish under her bed, it would make things easier.

Marnie pushes the bed back into place and notices a soft computer case that she's disturbed in the process. She picks it up and unfastens the zipper. When did Zoe get a laptop? Maybe it belongs to a friend. She could have borrowed it from school. But why keep it a secret? Why keep it hidden?

Sitting on the bed, Marnie's finger hovers over the power button. A mother should respect her daughter's privacy. A mother should be concerned. She presses the button and waits for the hard drive to boot. The screen lights up. The desktop background is a photograph of Daniel, Marnie, Zoe and Elijah. It was taken at the Queen's Diamond Jubilee concert outside Buckingham Palace. Elijah is perched on Daniel's shoulders. It's the last photograph they have before he went missing.

Marnie calls up the history directory. A list drops

down showing the sites that Zoe has visited in the past twenty-four hours. *Facebook. YouTube. LinkedIn. Pinterest. Wikipedia.*

One page stands out above the others. Marnie clicks the link. The page opens with another photograph of Daniel smiling from the screen. Cotton wool seems to fill Marnie's throat.

She reads Zoe's last message.

> It has been over a year since my stepdad disappeared and now my mum wants to have him declared dead. I know something horrible must have happened, but I believe my dad is still alive and he's trying to get home. Can you please share this page and email the link to all your friends.
>
> And if you're reading this, Dad, please come home or send me a message. I miss you so much . . .

There are dozens of comments posted below. Marnie doesn't recognise the names. People are sharing similar stories or offering their prayers; complete strangers from all over the world. 'Randoms', Zoe would have called them, but now they're her friends.

A message pops up in the lower right-hand corner of the screen.

WHERE HAVE YOU BEEN, GIRL?

The curser blinks, waiting for an answer. Marnie waits.

RYAN COLEMAN IS WORKING AT APOLLO'S TONIGHT. YOU SHOULD ORDER SOMETHING HOT, HOT, HOT . . . GET IT HOME DELIVERED . . . ROFL. SERIOUSLY, TALK TO HIM.

Another secret, thinks Marnie. Who is Ryan Coleman? A boyfriend? Zoe doesn't talk to her any more. It's like living with a foreign exchange student who doesn't speak English or chooses not to because conversation would mean answering questions.

Marnie closes the screen. Elijah is watching from the doorway.

'Have you been crying, Mummy?'

'I'm having a sad day.'

'Did I make you sad?'

'No, of course not.' She opens her arms. 'How about a hug?'

CHAPTER 38

The doorbell. Marnie presses the intercom and hears Joe O'Loughlin's voice.

'I know I should have called ahead.'

'Is everything all right?'

'We need to talk.'

Something soiled and faint fills her nostrils. She waits for Joe to climb the stairs. Opens the door. He's not alone. The former detective is with him, not saying a word. Elijah is in the bedroom playing in the wardrobe. Zoe hasn't come home yet.

Marnie takes them through to the kitchen, clearing a space, offering tea, coffee, a cold drink . . .

'I spoke to Dr Sterne,' says Joe.

There is a pause. Marnie won't look at him.

'You told me you didn't recognise his name in Daniel's notebook.'

Marnie doesn't respond. She avoids his eyes.

'Why didn't you tell me about Malcolm?'

'He doesn't exist.'

'He was once part of your personality.'

'No.'

Joe waits. Marnie can't sit still. She paces the kitchen, looking out the window. The darkness is different now. Softer. Diffuse. Her hands are clutching at the front of her blouse, kneading the fabric.

'Malcolm was Dr Sterne's invention, not mine.'

'I heard the recording.'

'That voice didn't come from me.'

'There was nobody else in the room.'

Marnie shakes her head, refusing to believe him.

Joe keeps pressing. 'You spent four years in therapy and didn't mention it.'

'I was a little girl.'

'Your mind split off, Marnie. You unconsciously created an alternative personality.'

'I know what they say happened. I accept that I had problems. But even if what Dr Sterne says is true – even if Malcolm existed – he's gone. He left a long time ago.'

Ruiz hasn't said a word. He doesn't trust her. Worse still, he doesn't *believe* her.

'Patrick Hennessy is dead,' he says. 'The police will want to talk to you.'

'Why?'

'You're a suspect.'

'That's ridiculous!'

'When was the last time you saw him?'

'When he almost fucking killed me,' she spits, surprised at the aggression in her voice. 'Do you want to see the grazes? Oh, that's right, you've seen them. Hope you got a good look.'

Ruiz ignores her. 'Have you ever been to Hennessy's apartment?'

'No.'

'First Quinn, then Hennessy – what did you do to your Daniel?'

Marnie looks at him incredulously. Joe studies her reaction, looking for any telltale signs that she's lying. He once saw something in Marnie that he described as being coiled and caged; something she didn't want to come out. He can see it now.

She drops her voice and glances along the hallway to the bedroom door. 'Can't we talk about this another time?'

'No,' says Ruiz, ignoring her concerns. 'I talked to your first husband.'

'Calvin?'

'You got him sent to prison.'

'Why would I do that?'

'He says you fitted him up – you planted drugs in his van.'

'That's crazy.'

'He says you were punishing him for screwing one of your bridesmaids.'

'He's lying.'

'Is Patrice lying?'

'What?'

'She's rotting in a Balinese prison. And what about the others? Eugene Lansky, Debbie Tibbets, Olivia Shulman, Devon Boucher, Richard Duffy – did they deserve to be punished as well?'

Marnie looks from face to face, feeling the room shrink around her. The fever in her eyes gives them a polished, almost bottomless light.

'*Payback is a bitch* – remember the line?' says Ruiz. 'You don't take hostages, do you, lady? Everyone is your enemy.'

Marnie's mouth opens but no words emerge. She puts her hand on her forehead, massaging her temples, searching her memories.

'I hardly remember them.'

'They remember you,' says Joe. 'Olivia Shulman told me what happened when you were at university. Somebody spiked your drink at a party. You were raped. You blamed her for leaving you behind.'

'That's not true.'

'You punished her with fake emails from a secret admirer.'

Marnie raises her hands to the absurdity of it all. She can see herself reflected in the polished chrome tap over the sink. She looks like a twisted figure in a funhouse of mirrors.

'Why didn't you see her again?' asks Joe.

'I was embarrassed. I did a stupid thing.'

Ruiz makes a guttural *hmmmph* sound, expelling air through his nose. 'Why did you withdraw the rape allegations?'

'I know what happens at rape trials,' says Marnie. 'The victim goes on trial. My reputation would have been trashed. The defence would have dragged up my sexual history – how many partners, how many one-night stands, my sexual preferences; how much I'd had to drink, what drugs I'd taken, the clothes I was wearing. They'd try to convince

344

the jury I was a slut . . . that I *wanted* to have sex. I wasn't strong enough to go through that.'

'You were strong enough to kill Richard Duffy.'

Marnie blinks at him. 'They said it was an accident.'

'The inquest was inconclusive.'

'I didn't *want* him dead.'

Ruiz laughs.

Marnie's eyes flick from Joe to Ruiz, more agitated now. Disconcerted. Tearful. Her skin feels clammy and crawling with questions that have impossible answers. She wants to flee, to run down the stairs, along the street, out of the city itself, away.

'I'm sick of people blaming me or using me,' she says angrily. Her eyes are fuller and sharper, illuminated by something that entered the world centuries before civilisation began. 'Yesterday it was Trevor trying to blackmail me. Today it's you. What do you want from me?'

'The truth,' says Joe.

'I didn't do anything to these people. I haven't seen them in years. I didn't kill my husband. I didn't kill my rapist. I'm the victim here.'

'I'm not saying it was *you*.'

Marnie raises her chin. 'What *are* you saying?'

'You told me you were suffering blackouts . . . missing periods of time.'

'Minutes.'

'What if it was longer than that?'

'It wasn't.'

345

'What if Malcolm is back? What if you're dissociating?'

'I'd know.'

'Your husband has gone. You've been under enormous pressure.'

'I'd know,' she says again, louder this time.

'I'm trying to help you, Marnie.'

'I want you to leave.'

'Listen to me.'

'Get out!' Her anguish seems to use up the air in the room. Her voice grows louder. 'GET OUT! GET OUT!'

She raises her fists, beating at Joe's chest, hitting him repeatedly as though trying to fight her way inside his body. He hugs her tightly until her arms drop to her sides. She presses her face into his shirt, incoherent in her anger.

Ruiz is standing at the door. 'You heard the lady. She told us to leave.'

'You go,' replies Joe. 'I'll stay.'

Marnie shakes her head. 'Leave me alone.'

Joe takes her to a chair and crouches in front of her, resting on his haunches. 'I had to challenge you, Marnie. I need to know if Malcolm still exists.

'I didn't do these things,' she whispers. 'I didn't hurt anyone.'

They're gone. The good cop, bad cop routine is over. It was quite a show. They think they've discovered the truth, but they have no idea what I'm capable of . . . what I've done for Marnie and what she's done for me.

I move downstairs, unlocking the rear door to reach the garden. Few residents use the grassy area unless they have kids. Elijah and Daniel used to kick a ball against the wall and play hide and seek. Skirting the side of the building, I follow a concrete drain that smells of weeds and wet masonry. The basement windows are barred. Crouching beneath one of them, I raise my head and peer through a crack in the blinds, one eye painted by a smear of light coming from inside.

I can see the caretaker moving back and forth behind the glass. He's pulling at a rowing machine, his knees and elbows working like pistons. I run my fingers over the windowsill. He has an alarm system, but it's not back to base. No dogs to worry about. These things must be checked.

Bees are buzzing in my head, but they are quieter now. Waiting. Retracing my steps, I enter the rear door and cross the foyer, glancing up the stairwell to make sure nobody is coming. I knock. The door opens a crack.

'What do you want?'

'We need to talk.'

CHAPTER 39

Zoe pushes her finger through the ring of condensation on the plastic tablecloth. The pizzeria is busy, but mostly doing takeaways. Few people bother dining at the Apollo, which has no air conditioning and only a handful of tables. The heat from the pizza oven has plastered a lock of Zoe's hair to her forehead and the air is thick with the smell of baking cheese and fresh cardboard.

Occasionally, Zoe glances at the door, waiting for Ryan Coleman. The chef, Ricardo, is an older man with liver spots like dark freckles on the back of his hands. He works the dough under his palms, fashioning it into balls.

He glances at Zoe. 'Your boyfriend is on a delivery.'

'He's not my boyfriend.'

'You could do worse,' says the chef.

Zoe blushes.

What is she doing here, she asks herself. How will Ryan react? They'll both be embarrassed. Awkward. Searching for something to say.

A girl at school called Steph Gables had bragged

about having been all the way with a boy, but nobody believed her. Zoe didn't want to do anything like that, but she wanted to talk to someone. It's not as though she hadn't kissed a boy. At Ruth Kasmauski's birthday party they played spin-the-bottle and her turn stopped on Toby Hendricks. They were sent to the cupboard for five minutes with the door closed. It was a broom cupboard with cleaning supplies, and everything smelt of bleach and disinfectant that made her eyes water. They stood in the dark, pressed against the opposing walls, listening to each other breathing. Eventually Zoe could stand it no longer and leaned forward, mashing her lips against Toby's, tasting soft drink and potato chips. Their teeth clicked together. She pulled away. Toby kept his hands at his sides. The buzzer sounded. Someone hammered on the door and they emerged to a chorus of wolf whistles and cheers. Toby grinned at his mates and adopted a swagger that teenage boys seem to perfect.

Zoe didn't understand what the fuss was about. Sex was everywhere – on TV, in magazines and online, but nobody Zoe knew was actually *doing* it. They were groping their way through adolescence, literally and figuratively, waiting for the accidental right time or wrong time.

Her can of Pepsi has grown warm in her hands. A scooter pulls up outside. Ryan swings his leg off the seat and unclips the helmet strap, hooking it over his forearm. He brushes hair from his eyes and opens the door backwards, only seeing Zoe at the last moment. He stops.

'Hi,' she says.

'Hi.'

'Is everything all right?'

She nods, feeling foolish. 'I was in the neighbourhood.'

'Oh. Do you want a pizza?'

'No.'

'OK.'

'What time do you finish work?'

'Ten.'

'Oh.'

The chef has been watching them. 'You can take ten minutes,' he tells Ryan. 'Eric can do the next run.'

Ryan leads her through the kitchen and outside to the rear alley where there are plastic chairs arranged around a cut-off drum full of sand and cigarette butts. Zoe sits and presses her hands between her thighs.

'Did you listen to the CD I burned for you?'

'Yeah, it was good.'

She nods.

A minute passes.

'What do you want to do?' he asks.

'What do you want to do?' she counters.

Ryan shrugs.

'Do you want to kiss me?' asks Zoe.

'Yeah, I guess.'

He leans forward. She does the same. It only

lasts a few seconds, but for that brief moment Zoe seems to float, barely breathing, outside her body. She feels his tongue between her lips and lets it rest there. A strand of Ryan's hair brushes against her eyelids. She doesn't push it aside.

Ryan pulls away and takes a breath. 'I have to get back to work.'

Zoe looks at her watch. She doesn't want to go home. She wants to sit with Ryan and float outside her body again.

The chef opens the kitchen door. Orders have to be delivered. Zoe collects her schoolbag from inside and follows Ryan to his scooter. He puts a pizza satchel in the rear carrier box and waves, doing a U-turn and fishtailing the scooter's back wheel as he disappears around the next corner, heading towards Westbourne Grove.

Lowering her head, Zoe gives a skip and starts walking home.

CHAPTER 40

Elijah has taken a blanket from the bed and draped it over the handle of the wardrobe, making a cubby house with a woollen door. Sitting in the wardrobe, he presses his ear against the back and listens. He knocks his knuckles against the smooth wood. It echoes. He puts his eye to the crack and listens again.

He can smell his mother's clothes hanging above his head. Other smells belong to his father, a man he can barely remember. Sometimes he wonders if he existed at all, yet he has memories that he can't explain, of riding high on a man's shoulders, yelling that he was king of the castle. He has other recollections of funny voices and belly button farts and kicking a ball in the garden.

Elijah calls out from the bedroom. 'Mummy?'

She doesn't answer.

Elijah presses his ear against the wall again. Hooking his fingers into the crack, he pulls the wooden panel back and forth. The edge of the plywood pinches his fingers. It moves sideways an inch. A black and white paw sweeps across his fingers. A cat. The paw comes through the crack again.

'Mummy? There's a kitty.'

No reply.

Elijah leans against the wooden partition, pushing his fingers further into the gap. They touch a metal hook that pivots. The panel falls away and the cat jumps backwards, running off.

Elijah crawls forward. 'Here, kitty, kitty . . .'

Marnie is worried about Zoe. She should be home by now and she's not answering her mobile or responding to texts. She tries again, leaving her a message.

Elijah has been quiet. She goes looking for him.

'Are you hiding from me?' she asks, peering under his bed. She looks behind the door. 'Am I getting warmer? Where are you?'

She checks the living room, looking in the obvious hiding places, behind the sofa and the door. Then she moves along the hallway. 'You know you're not allowed in Zoe's room,' she says, peeking under the bed, spying the laptop again. 'Elijah? Please come out. I'm getting worried now. I don't want to play any more.'

She returns to the main bedroom. The wardrobe door is open. Elijah has dragged a blanket off the bed and hooked it over the door handle. She crawls towards his cubby, hoping to surprise him.

'Ha ha!' she says, lifting the blanket. The wardrobe is empty except for shoes and hanging clothes and assorted toys. Something is different. Wrong. Instead of a rear panel there is a hole where one shouldn't exist. Someone or something has broken through the double-brick wall between the two buildings.

'Elijah?'

Marnie crawls forward, her skirt catching on her knees and then the jagged bricks. Her hands feel a smooth surface. Another floor. Another room. The curtains are closed. The darkness seems to coat Marnie's lungs and fill her mouth.

'*Kitty, kitty.*'

It's Elijah's voice. She can't see him. 'Where are you?'

'In here,' he says. 'There's a pussy cat.'

'Come to me.'

She stands. The carpet is threadbare and sticky underfoot. She can see the outline of what could be furniture – a bed or a sofa – but the place smells closed up. Abandoned.

'Leave the kitty alone, Elijah.'

'But he's all by himself.'

'He doesn't belong to us.'

The floorboards creak beneath her. The room is so dark she holds out her hands, feeling ahead of her. She touches a wall and searches for a light switch. It flicks upwards, but nothing happens. Glancing at the ceiling, she can just make out the empty light socket. Someone has removed the bulb.

'We have to go, Elijah. Come to Mummy.'

The hallway has more light. Marnie peers into a second bedroom. The curtains are open. She can see a tall single bed with a chamber pot beneath the springs. Women's clothes are draped on the bed. Support hose. Worn shoes. Above the fireplace there are Lladro figurines, girls in pastel dresses holding parasols and bunches of flowers. Marnie knocks over a hat stand, catching it before it topples. A wig is displaced. It looks like a squashed animal. Roadkill.

Moving along the hallway, she finds a light switch that works. The wallpaper seems to be hanging in ragged strips. Then she realises that photographs and pieces of curling paper have been stuck to the wall. Her eyes scan them quickly before settling on something familiar. It takes her a moment to recognise herself in one of the images . . . then another . . . and another. There are pictures of her weddings, her graduation, her mother's funeral; Zoe on a merry-go-round in Brighton, riding a scooter, walking to nursery, Marnie at her gym class, sanding a cabinet, painting a bedroom, sitting in a deckchair, shopping, riding her bike, having coffee with Penny . . .

Arranged haphazardly between these images are receipts, ticket stubs, business cards, photocopies of bank statements and telephone bills, a street map, a library card, a parking notice, shopping lists, registration papers for the car . . . The wall is a scrapbook, a ragged wallpaper of clippings, images and ephemera that document her life.

Marnie gazes in wonder, letting her eyes travel from the ceiling to the skirting board. Fear, like a small animal, scurries around her chest, looking for a place to hide. Once when she was a young girl, she went to the movies with one of the foster kids, an older boy. They were supposed to see *Never Ending Story*, but it was sold out so they sneaked into *Nightmare on Elm Street*. Even when Marnie covered her eyes she could hear the music and the screams. If she covered her ears, she could see the shiny blades that were Freddy Krueger's fingers.

It was dark when the film ended. They caught the bus home and walked to the farmhouse from the main road. The boy ran ahead of her. He turned off the porch light and all the other lights inside the house. Then he crouched in the darkened hallway as Marnie opened the front door and reached for the switch, but touched his hand instead. Marnie screamed and wetness ran down her legs into her boots. That's how she feels now.

She turns her head towards the kitchen. A cat is sitting in front of the fridge, wanting to be fed. Elijah is kneeling on the floor. There is a coffee cup in the sink. Toast crumbs on the counter. A plate.

'Go back home, Elijah.'

'But the kitty?'

'Go!'

Something in her voice frightens the boy. His bottom lip trembles. He does what he's told.

A cupboard is open. The jars are labelled. Flour. Rice. Pasta. The cat curls around her ankles, rubbing the side of his head against Marnie's bare feet. There is a note on the fridge beneath a magnet. She recognises the handwriting as Zoe's.

I want to thank you for the laptop and for helping me with my dad's Facebook page. I'll try to meet you tomorrow at the library.

Elijah yells from the other bedroom. 'Are you coming, Mummy?'

'Stay in your room.'

'Did you find Malcolm?'

A question gets caught in her throat. She tries again. 'Who?'

'My friend, Malcolm.'

'Just stay there. Don't come in here.'

Marnie notices the ladder. It stands in the middle of the kitchen, rising to a hole in the ceiling. She stares up at the dark square. Taking hold of the cross spars, she climbs, hand over hand until her head rises above the hole and she's peering into the ceiling cavity. A torch has been left next to the opening. Finding the switch, she points the beam of light ahead of her, revealing a crawlspace that stretches the length and breadth of the ceiling. The air is hot and stale below the tiles. Insulation squares are squashed between the beams and ceiling joists. Boards have been placed across them, stretching to the far end of the sloping roof where it narrows as the angle disappears.

She can see bedding. A thermos. Tissues.

Crawling forward, she keeps her weight on the beams, holding the torch in her right hand. Ten . . . fifteen . . . twenty feet, crawling deeper into the cavity.

This is a bad idea, she thinks, *a bad, bad idea.*

She stops at the bedding. The insulation batons have been removed. Pinpricks of light create thin beams that brighten her fingertips. She leans down and places her eye to the light. She's staring down at her bedroom. She can see her duvet and the pillows and her dressing table.

Shuffling sideways, she finds another pinprick of light. This one is over Zoe's bed. Another looks down into Elijah's room. The kitchen. The living room. This is someone's vantage point . . . a hiding place.

Beneath her a key rattles in a lock and the door opens, changing the air pressure. It's not *her* door . . . not Zoe . . . Marnie crawls across the ceiling and peers through the hatch. A shadow passes beneath the ladder. Something heavy hits the table. A tap is turned on. Soap squeaks from a dispenser. Hands are washed.

A voice screams inside her head.

Run!

Where?

Just run!

Her mobile phone is digging into her hip. Rolling onto her back, she pulls it free, her hands shaking. Joe O'Loughlin has left her a message. She doesn't read it. She types a reply:

HELP ME!

It's not enough. She presses 999, cradling the phone in both hands. The person below her is moving. He's gone into another room. She's at the top of the ladder. Somebody answers her call. She cups the phone and whispers.

'I need the police. A man has been watching me.'

'What man?'

'I'm trapped in his ceiling.'

'Please can I have your name and address?'

Marnie gives her the details. 'Just send the police.'

'You say you're trapped. Do you need the fire brigade?'

'He's here now.'

'Who?'

The man below her has walked back into the kitchen. She can see his shoes. Marnie stops talking and tries not to breathe. She can't see his face. He's standing at the base of the ladder.

The operator is still speaking. 'Hello . . . hello . . .'

He's climbing. Marnie scans the crawlspace, looking for a means of escape or a weapon or somewhere to hide. She moves across the ceiling on her hands and knees, wincing with each shuffle, trying not to make a sound.

Stupid cow! Stupid cow!

He's been talking to Elijah through the wall. He's been watching them from the ceiling . . . giving presents to Zoe.

The ladder creaks again. Marnie closes her eyes for a moment, sipping on the darkness. Then another sound reaches her. It's further away yet closer in every sense that matters.

'Mummy?'

BOOK II

'It's not spying when you care about someone.'

Broadway Danny Rose

CHAPTER 41

Zoe dodges the cracks on the pavement by elongating her stride or doing a quick shuffle. Cranes are silhouetted against the sky and look like stairways to unfinished buildings or extension ladders to the clouds. Zoe can still feel Ryan's tongue against hers. Taste it. Nothing her mother can do or say could possibly spoil that memory or take it away from her.

Climbing the front steps, she searches for her keys. She finds the gold one and slides it into the lock. Turning her head, she gazes along the street. Something caught her eye, but it's gone now. Inside, she glances at the mailbox and takes the first two steps. Stops. On the far side of the entrance hall Trevor's door is slightly ajar. She half expects him to be watching her but there's nobody peering through the opening.

She continues climbing, reaching the flat, kicking off her shoes and dumping her schoolbag. Normally Elijah hears her coming and barrels down the hallway. This time she doesn't get a welcome.

'Mum?'

She walks to the kitchen.

'Elijah?'

Bolognese sauce is bubbling on the stove. It's almost boiled dry, sticking to the bottom of the pan. She turns off the burner. Lasagne sheets are on the bench. The cheese sauce has solidified. Where are they? She stayed out late to punish her mother and now she's not even here.

Zoe wanders through the flat to the darkened living room. Before she can flick on the lamp switch, she notices something – a tiny pinprick of light on the ceiling that looks like a lone star on a dark night. She turns on a lamp and the 'star' disappears. Curling up on the sofa, she checks her mobile. There are two texts and a voicemail message from her mother, nagging her to come home. She spells out a reply.

I'm home, where are you?

Waits.
Nothing.
Maybe she's downstairs at the Brummers or with Trevor. No, she wouldn't talk to Trevor. Zoe slips on her shoes and goes downstairs. She reaches the second floor landing when a voice makes her jump. Mrs Brummer peers from her door. Her eyes are so pale they look like white marbles and her skin is wrinkled and pitted like the bark of a tree.

'Zoe dear, I thought you were Trevor. His door is open.'

'Have you knocked?'

'He didn't answer.'

'Did you go inside?'

The old woman shakes her head. 'I didn't think it was right. Trevor promised to unblock my sink.'

'I'm not very good with sinks,' says Zoe. 'Have you seen my mum?'

'No, dear.'

Why do old people's mouths always hang open? thinks Zoe. It's like they can't hear without gaping. She continues downstairs, knocking on Trevor's door. Listening. Crossing the threshold, she calls the caretaker's name, hugging her arms to her chest. The small living room is crammed with odd furniture and jumbled shelving. An old navy locker doubles as a coffee table. DVDs are stacked in haphazard piles against the walls. She notices naked women on some of the covers.

'Trevor? Can you hear me.'

Her voice catches in her throat. Somewhere inside her head, Zoe hears a rumbling sound like a bowling ball spinning down a lane. She moves along the hall and stops outside a bedroom. Big dark pieces of furniture are huddled in the gloom.

She can see the outline of a person, sitting upright in an armchair, staring at the wall.

'Trevor? Are you OK?'

Silence.

'Your front door was open. Mrs Brummer was worried.'

Zoe steps into the room. She reaches for the light switch and turns back towards the seated figure. Trevor has tape wrapped around his chest and forearms. His mouth is stretched out of shape by a gag, which is darkened by the blood that has seeped past the corners of his lips and down his chin. His bowels have emptied, the smell insulting the air.

Zoe takes a moment to comprehend the scene because there's so much to digest and so little she wants to. Her eyes move downwards, looking for Trevor's hands . . . not finding them. Then she sees them, palms open, facing upwards, pinkies touching, lying on the floor between his feet.

Holding her mouth, she reels away, her stomach sliding, cramping. Stumbling into the bathroom she vomits into a stained bowl. Once. Twice. Nothing left. She scoops water into her mouth. Blinks tears.

What to do? Not touch anything. Call the police. Maybe he's still alive. She punches 999.

'There's been a murder,' she whispers, glancing over her shoulder. What if she's not alone?

An operator wants her name and address. She has to describe the scene.

'Is he breathing?'

'I don't know.'

'What are his injuries?'

'He doesn't have any hands.'

'What do you mean?'

'Somebody cut them off.'

'How old are you, Zoe?'

'Fifteen.'

'Where is your mother?'

'I don't know.'

'Do you know the man in the chair?'

'He's our caretaker, Trevor.'

'You should check if he's breathing, Zoe. Can you do that?'

'OK.'

'If he's not, then leave the flat. Don't touch anything. Is it safe outside?'

'I don't know. Mrs Brummer is there.'

'Who is Mrs Brummer?'

'Our landlady.'

'You stay with Mrs Brummer. The police and paramedics are coming.'

Zoe glances at Trevor. He looks almost mummified, like something has sucked the moisture from him and left him desiccated and crumbling. His mouth has been pried apart by the gag and blood crusts his nostrils. A low moan escapes from his chest. Air escaping. Maybe he's alive. Zoe moves behind him and loosens the knot, pulling the gag away. Trevor's eyes are wide with terror and he's staring at her as though pleading for help, but he's not breathing.

Zoe hears a sound behind her. Mrs Brummer is standing in the doorway with her hand halfway to her gaping mouth.

'Oh, dear, what have you done?'

CHAPTER 42

'Please don't hurt him,' says Marnie, hearing her voice echo through the empty ceiling.

The man has one hand cupped on Elijah's neck and the other resting on his shoulder where the blade is pointed towards the young boy's right ear. Marnie isn't looking at the knife, but at the man's face. It's not that he's particularly memorable, yet she remembers. He said his mother had died. He had her funeral the next day. He had a suicide note and a will. Marnie talked him out of it. He called her the next day to say thanks.

Owen looks up at her now, acknowledging her concern. He sets the blade down on the kitchen table and drops his chin, placing a kiss on the top of Elijah's head. He's dressed differently, wearing a tight sweater, dark jeans and needlepoint boots. His skull is clean-shaven and oiled. He must have been wearing a wig when she first met him.

'Come down the ladder. Nothing in your hands.'

Marnie has to turn around. Descending the ladder, she tries to hold down her skirt against her legs. She glances at the table and the knife.

'I wouldn't if I were you,' he warns.

368

She looks along the hallway to the spare room; the wardrobe; the hole in the wall.

'I've sealed it off,' he says, as though reading her mind.

'Who are you?'

'Surely you remember me?'

'Why have you been watching us?'

'I've been looking after you.'

Elijah looks up at her excitedly. 'This is my friend, Malcolm.'

Marnie shakes her head, struggling to fathom the circumstances as much as the name.

Owen is still holding the boy. 'I didn't want this to happen . . . not yet.'

Marnie doesn't understand.

'Now we'll have to go.'

'Go where?'

'Somewhere safe.'

She can hear sirens in the distance. The police. They're coming. Thank God!

'They're not coming to rescue you,' he says, studying her closely. 'There's been an accident downstairs.'

'What sort of accident?'

'Perhaps I should use another word.'

The man has a strange light in his eyes, almost trembling with excitement, soaking up every detail.

'What are you staring at?' asks Marnie.

'You.'

CHAPTER 43

Joe has almost reached his flat when he gets Marnie's message. He tries to call her but she's not answering her mobile. There are police sirens in the distance. They sound like bleating lambs from this far away. Retracing his steps, Joe turns into Elgin Avenue, making sure his arms are swinging naturally in the same direction as the opposite foot.

Police cars come hurtling past, skidding to a halt. Blocking the street. Officers burst from the doors and mount the stairs. Moments later Zoe emerges, escorted down the steps by a constable. A foil blanket is wrapped around her shoulders.

Joe has reached the mansion block. From across the road, he makes eye contact with Zoe. Something in her gaze is greater than fear.

'Where's your mother?' he asks.

'She's not home.'

'Elijah?'

She shakes her head.

'Who then . . .?'

'The caretaker.'

A policeman confronts Joe, demanding to know what he's doing.

'I'm a friend of the family,' he says, looking at Zoe for confirmation. She nods. 'I had a message from Zoe's mother.'

'What message?'

'She said she needed help.'

The detective glances back at the mansion block. 'Stay here.'

Joe takes a moment to realise that the orders are directed at him. More officers have arrived, along with paramedics. The entrance hall is crowded. People have begun spilling out of surrounding buildings. There are faces pressed to windows and peering from doors.

He calls Ruiz.

'You'd better get here quickly.'

'What's she done?'

'I don't know.'

The back of the patrol car smells of hamburgers and disinfectant. Zoe is huddled in the foil blanket, shivering, but not cold.

'What happened?' Joe asks.

She shakes her head and tries to get her tongue to work, forming words and sentences. She describes coming home to the empty flat . . . looking for her mother . . . finding Trevor. Joe wants her to describe the caretaker's injuries.

'Who would do something like that?' Zoe asks.

Joe doesn't answer. In some cultures cutting off a man's hands is punishment for theft or rape – an archaic ritual like stoning and crucifixion, but nothing else about the scene that Zoe had described would indicate a ritualistic killing.

'Did you see your mother?'

Zoe shakes her head. 'She's not answering her phone.'

Joe remembers the text message. Marnie needed help. He also recalls the last words she spoke to him, her eyes glistening, protesting her innocence.

Zoe exhales and Joe feels her breath against his skin and sees the tremor in her eyes. She's looking at him expectantly, craving reassurance and answers, but more importantly a happy ending.

There was always a possibility that Marnie would find me. Despite the precautions I took and my efforts to disguise my presence, I knew that one day she would see my fingerprints on her life. I can pinpoint my errors, but it makes no difference. I was careless and let her cross the divide. Now she's here next to me. I can smell her. I can touch her if I want. My face is no longer pressed to the glass or watching her from the ceiling.

Marnie wasn't the first. There was another before her. One day I'll tell her the whole story and she'll get to appreciate the synchronicity of our lives; our one degree of separation. My first real love was the woman who lived next door to me – not the horrid Fariba but the one who came after, when the Khans had moved out.

Christina was the first real hippy I'd ever met. She wore translucent cheesecloth tops without a bra and sometimes sunbathed topless in the garden. Her husband was a little older with long hair and a beard. I couldn't tell if he wanted to be Jesus Christ or Charles Manson. Their house was always full of people: dropouts, acidheads and new-agers;

373

girls in printed kaftans whose arms jangled with bangles; guys with long hair and sideburns. They drove around in brightly painted Combis and grew dope in the back garden, telling neighbours they were tomato plants. And they talked about wandering the world, visiting communes and ashrams, discovering the true meaning of life, as though life had a true meaning.

Over the months, the drifters drifted away. They went travelling or found somewhere else to squat or went corporate and 'sold out to the man'. The seventies were disappearing like an outgoing tide, leaving some of them washed up on the beach, rotting like dead fish.

Eventually, Christina was alone most days. I would lie in bed and hear her singing along to the radio or her record player while she made beaded wall hangings and sewed lace hems on dresses to sell at the markets. She was also making money as an artist's model, taking her clothes off for art students at the university.

Her husband was away most weeks. I figured he worked on the trains or in the Gulf. When he was home I could smell dope drifting from the garden and parrot their arguments, listening to them in bed or having breakfast. Sometimes I would sneak into their garden and through the laundry door into the basement, which ran the full length of the house, with varying headroom. I could stand upright and look into the kitchen, but had to crawl on my stomach to reach the living room. Some of the floorboards were so old and bowed that the gaps were wide enough for crumbs and keys to drop through. I could look right up through them and see Christina, who often wore no underwear beneath dresses that floated around her thighs.

The basement was full of old furniture, including an armchair with lion's paws as feet. I could sit down and lean back, watching Christina as she cooked. This one day – it was my fifteenth birthday – she collected her dirty washing and carried the basket on her hip to the back door and down the side steps to the laundry. I hid behind the old boiler as she sorted the clothes. She must have noticed a movement or heard me breathing because she knew I was there. She didn't call the police or march me back home to my mother. Instead she carried on loading the machine, bending lower and showing me the full majesty of her posterior. What dreams I had of holding those hips in my hands; touching places in between them.

'How long have you been spying on me?' she asked.

I didn't answer.

'I'm going upstairs now. Would you like to come?'

I followed her to the kitchen. She pulled out a chair. She talked to me as she did her chores. It wasn't a conversation. I hardly said a word.

'I'm going upstairs to vacuum. You can come and watch me, if you want.'

I hesitated.

'It's not the same is it?' she asked. 'Now that I know you're there.'

I shook my head.

'I can't change that.'

She went upstairs. I sat in the kitchen, listening to the clock ticking and the fridge rattling and music playing. I climbed after her. I sat on the bed and watched her vacuuming. I listened to her talk about how the Beatles and the Rolling Stones had sold out their principles. She liked Dylan and Woody Guthrie and Joan Baez. She said the secret to happiness was to share what you have and build a community spirit. She talked about Buddhism and enlightenment, most of which I didn't understand.

She didn't eat meat, but she didn't call herself a vegetarian. She had another word that I can't remember. She said she made her own soap and candles and grew vegetables in the summer, but wouldn't use insecticides, which were poisoning the planet and giving everyone cancer.

I listened and watched.

The next day when she came to the laundry she didn't bother looking for me. She went about her work, knowing I was there. She didn't wear a bra or cover herself when she walked about the house after a shower. And she didn't stop wearing dresses or start wearing underwear.

I was nervous around her. I had never really had a woman friend. The girls at school were more interested in shopping and older boys and I was an outsider because I rarely stayed long enough in any school to make friends or become a fixture.

The first time she took me to her bed, I was terrified.

'We're just going to hold each other,' she said, but I wasn't used to being held. I tried to shut down my mind, but her hands made that impossible and I was amazed at how different it felt when someone else's hands were doing the touching.

'You've had an accident,' she said, mopping up the discharge. 'No use crying over spilled milk, but it really shouldn't be wasted.'

I didn't know what she meant. I thought she was giving me a gift, but she was taking from me as well. She locked my fingers over hers and rolled onto her knees, wanting me to slip into her from behind so she could watch us in the mirrored door of the wardrobe. My legs were spread, my stomach distended, as my back arched and I drove into her. I thought I was being violent, but she told me to do it harder.

She explained things to me. Why her nipples hardened and what parts I should stroke, whispering the words softer, or harder.

She seemed to concentrate, searching for the pleasure as though we had dropped a needle on a carpet. There it is! Just there! Yes!

I had never kissed a girl before then, but I knew all about the dynamics of sex. My mother was a prostitute. I spent my first four years, locked in a cupboard, daring not to breathe, peering through a crack in the door and listening to flesh slap against flesh. But this was different. Christina pushed me back on the bed. She swung her hips over my head and pressed her sex against my mouth.

I didn't hear her orgasm because her thighs were

covering my ears, but I felt her body shudder and roll and vibrate against my tongue. Afterwards, she arranged herself beneath me, pulling me inside her, urging me on until I was done.

The first time was in her bedroom. Later we used other rooms in the house and once we did it on the armchair in the basement as the tumble drier rumbled out the tempo.

This happened when her husband was home. He called out for her.

'Where are you?'

'In the basement,' she answered.

'What are you doing?'

'Laundry.'

I thought I was going to go soft inside her, but stayed hard. She kept moving her hips, smiling to herself.

This is her legacy. This is the moment I return to again and again when I try to remember the first time I was truly happy. I can summon up the darkness of the basement, the warmth of her body, ejaculating deep inside her, as I looked up through the gaps in the floorboards and watched her husband move around the kitchen. The affair (can I call it that?) went on for six months and I remember every assignation. My urgency. Her ambivalence, until I entered her. Redoubling my efforts. Fastening onto her breast. I would glance up and catch her smiling at me with a fond benevolence rather than lust. When I came she would push me away, grunting for me to 'Get off!'

She would straighten her dress. I would try to pull her close, walking my fingers up her thighs, kissing the heart-shaped mole above her right breast. And she would close her eyes and moan helplessly, offering her lips to me.

How did it end? She was twenty-nine. I was fifteen. For me it was love. I liked to imagine that Christina was in love with me, but in reality I sensed she was bored and seeking pleasure and it suited the times.

Her husband found me in the basement one Sunday morning. He thought I was stealing her underwear. I was hauled down to the police station. They read my file and sent me to see a psychiatrist – a woman with a shrink-sounding name like Dr Weiss. She had a hot-looking receptionist called Nigella, who talked in this up-speak voice like everything was exciting and unbelievable and amazing.

Dr Weiss told me to be candid, to open myself up. She wanted to know if I liked girls.

'Sure.'

'What do you like about them?'

'Their smell.'

'What else?'

'Watching them.'

'What about touching them?'

'I guess.'

Dr Weiss asked about my relationship with my mother, angling to get my whole fucked-up family life on the table. I told her I didn't want to go there, so she accused me of being emotionally stunted, whatever that meant. By then I was almost sixteen: old enough to join the army.

The recruitment officer had a scar on his top lip that made him look like he was permanently sneering. He told me that girls would 'drop their knickers' when they saw me in uniform. Then he slapped me so hard on the back that I spat my chewing gum onto the floor.

'Pick that up, soldier,' he said.

It was my first order.

CHAPTER 44

Ruiz marches through the police cordon, ducking under the crime-scene tape as though it doesn't apply to him. He surrendered his badge six years ago, but still has the countenance, if not the authority, of a detective. Reaching the police cars and ambulance, he pauses and seems to inhale the scene as though the air might provide him with answers.

'Who's in charge?'

'The boss is inside,' says a sergeant.

Ruiz spies the professor in the back of a police car with a teenage girl. It must be Marnie's daughter. DI Gennia emerges from the mansion block. He fixes his eyes on Ruiz. 'Who gave this man permission to be here?'

Blank faces among the officers. Mumbles.

Gennia addresses Ruiz. 'Go home, Vincent. This isn't your concern.'

'What happened?'

'You can read about it in tomorrow's paper.'

The detective is moving away. Suddenly, he stops and turns. 'Do you know where Marnie Logan is?'

'No.'

He motions to the police car. 'Friend of yours?'

'He's Marnie's psychologist: Joe O'Loughlin.'

Gennia seems to roll the name over his tongue before walking away.

'You're making a mistake,' yells Ruiz.

'Won't be the first time.'

'The professor can help you.'

'He'll have plenty of time to talk. I can hold him for forty-eight hours. And If I find out he's been withholding information from the police, I'll charge him with obstructing justice or being an accessory to murder.'

'What murder?'

At that moment paramedics emerge from the house, carrying a stretcher down the stairs and setting the wheels onto the pavement with a rattling finality.

'The caretaker,' says Gennia. 'And I'm betting we find Marnie Logan's DNA all over the murder scene.'

The DI barks an order at one of the constables stringing crime-scene tape around a railing fence. A white marquee is being erected over the front steps to shield the entrance hall. Floodlights burst through the edges of the curtains on the ground floor.

'Answer me this,' he says, focusing again on Ruiz. 'Is Marnie Logan dangerous?'

'What did the professor say?'

'I'm not asking him – I'm asking you.'

Ruiz lowers his head and looks at the toes of his

leather shoes. Gennia's eyes are fixed on his, and his face a mask of disgust.

'I'll take that as a yes.'

Harrow Road police station is an elegant old building with Georgian windows and decorative mouldings. It used to be Ruiz's old stomping ground when he headed the Serious Crime Squad a decade ago. Little has changed, certainly not the décor, which is public service grey except for the occasional splashes of pastel in the interview suites to soothe the savage beasties who are dragged in off the streets and questioned.

DI Gennia keeps them waiting. Ruiz paces the room like he's circling a cage, whereas Joe could be measuring for new carpet. He wants Ruiz to be quiet. He needs time to put the details into context and assign them a weight. Dissociative disorders. Malcolm. Marnie. The caretaker. Trevor threatened her. He lost his hands.

Ruiz is still pacing. 'Did she do it?'

Joe looks up.

'Marnie – did she cut off his fucking hands?'

'I don't know.'

Ruiz seems to react under his breath. 'Is that the best you can do?'

Joe apologises, knowing that Ruiz expects more. In the ten years the two men have known each other, Joe has never felt so lost or grasping helplessly for answers. Normally, almost instinctively, he understands human behaviour – the good, the bad, the

383

weird and monstrous; psychopaths and sociopaths, people on the fringes of sanity and society – but this time it's different. It's as though the entire process of human interaction is a farce of misperception. We get people wrong before we meet them, while we're anticipating meeting them, when we're with them and when we go home and tell somebody else about the meeting. Yet Joe has based his career on getting people right, even if the more interesting path is getting them wrong.

DI Gennia shows up in the early hours. Transparent bubbles of exhaustion seem to be bursting in front of his eyes. He picks up a chair, spinning it around and straddling it backwards. Joe notices the freckles on his nose, which make him look younger, like a schoolboy caught unawares in a camera's lens.

'How did you let a nutjob like Marnie Logan get past you?'

The question is deliberately provocative.

'I don't believe she is a nutjob.'

'You say tomato, I say fuck you.'

Joe ignores the insult. 'How is Zoe?'

'She's being looked after.'

'You're holding her?'

'Child protection will find her accommodation until we locate her mother or father. Tell me about Marnie Logan?'

'What do you want to know?'

'Where is she?'

'No idea.'

'Does she have family?'

'Her father is in a nursing home in Ealing.'

'Friends?'

'You can check her phone records,' says Ruiz, growing impatient.

'We're doing that,' replies Gennia. 'We're also watching the airports, train stations and bus terminals. She's with her boy. How old is he?'

'Four.'

'Is he in any danger?'

Joe hesitates and glances at Ruiz.

'What was that?' asks the DI. 'That look you gave each other. What aren't you telling me?'

Joe makes a decision. 'Two days ago I talked to a psychiatrist who treated Marnie Logan when she was a child. What he told me was confidential. It can't be used in a court of law.'

'Don't lecture me on the law, Professor.'

Joe glances at Ruiz again, who nods. For the next fifteen minutes the professor explains his meeting with Dr Sterne and the details the psychiatrist revealed about Marnie's mental history. He describes the emergence of a second personality, who co-existed in Marnie's mind until slowly becoming integrated and disappearing.

'And you think this Malcolm is back?' asks Gennia.

'It's a remote possibility, yes.'

'And this *other* personality might have killed Niall Quinn and Patrick Hennessy and the caretaker?'

Joe doesn't answer.

385

Gennia looks at Ruiz. 'Do you buy into this bullshit?'

'I think you should listen.'

The detective stands up so suddenly his chair topples over. 'This woman is playing you, Professor. She's angling for a cushy stint in a secure psych unit with lots of coloured pills and art classes. Then she's out again, free as a bird. Three men are dead and we found Marnie Logan's DNA at two of the crime scenes. I'll bet you London to a house brick we find traces of her at the caretaker's flat. That woman is a cold-blooded killer and I'm all over her like a fat kid on a Happy Meal.'

CHAPTER 45

The floor of the car is littered with Styrofoam food containers, cups, chewing-gum wrappers, hamburger cartons and old newspapers. Marnie's wrists and forearms are taped behind her back, forcing her to sit sideways in the passenger seat or lose feeling in her hands. From side-on she can keep an eye on Elijah, who is sleeping across the back seat. Occasionally, she sneaks a glance at Owen's profile as oncoming headlights sweep over his face, barely registering in his eyes. His eyelids, lips and nostrils are tinged with pink as though inflamed and the corners of his mouth are dimpled.

'Is Owen your real name?'

'Yes.'

'Elijah called you Malcolm.'

'That's a game we played.'

'Why did you choose that name?'

'You know the reason.'

Marnie narrows her eyes, trying to fathom how he could know the significance of the name. Only Dr Sterne knew about Malcolm . . . and her father. Who else?

They are driving on the North Circular, near Wembley, past car yards and fast-food restaurants. The BMW has heavily tinted windows and a brightly lit display panel. His wrists are relaxed on the steering wheel.

'Why are you doing this?'

'You gave me no choice.'

'You could have left us behind. You could drop us off now. I wouldn't tell anyone.'

'It's too late for that.'

Marnie's mind is so full of questions that she struggles to put them in order. The photographs. The ceiling. Zoe. Malcolm. She contemplates trying to kick the steering wheel, but fears killing them all in a fiery crash. Instead she tries to memorise the road signs.

'How long have you been watching me?'

'Longer than you think.'

He glances at her and grins, knowing she won't believe him.

'When did you move next door?'

'Six years ago. It took me a while to get the flat. The previous tenants wouldn't leave. I tried mice but they called in a pest controller. So I haunted them instead, making weird shit happen. They even organised an intervention, a proper séance. A priest came to the flat and said prayers, sprinkling holy water. Seriously.'

The memory amuses him.

'You were in our ceiling?'

'Yes.'

'Why?'

'Isn't it obvious?'

'No, not to me.' Marnie shifts her body, flexing her fingers, testing the strength of her restraints. 'You rang the agency and hired me, what was that about?'

'I thought maybe . . . ' He hesitates and begins again. 'I was going to take you then. I couldn't let you sell your body to strange men.'

'The suicide note . . .'

'Yours not mine.'

Marnie doesn't understand.

'I wrote the note for you. I was going to leave it by the river, along with some of your clothes.'

'Why didn't you?'

'I wasn't ready.'

'Ready for what?'

'You'll see.'

He looks at the dashboard. The fuel is running low. Pulling into a lay-by, he parks away from the overhead lights and flips the interior latch that unlocks the boot. He walks around the car, opens Marnie's door and pulls her out, dragging her to the rear of the vehicle.

'Get in.'

'No, please.'

'I have to get petrol. If you stay quiet I'll let you out again afterwards.'

'What about Elijah?'

'He stays with me.'

'I don't want to.'

'Get in.'

Marnie rolls into the boot. He takes his belt and puts it between her teeth, buckling it around her head. The leather cuts into the corners of her mouth. The boot shuts. Darkness fills her world. Her cheek is pressed against a rough nylon floor mat. She smells the faint reek of unleaded petrol. Her hands are still bound behind her back. She squirms, trying to straighten, feeling the confines of her prison, touching the walls with her feet and forehead.

The car starts moving again. Minutes later it pulls into a petrol station and stops at the pump. Raising her head, she puts her eye to the boot latch and can see the forecourt. An eighteen-wheeler is parked nearby. The driver walks across her vision, heading back to his cab. Marnie kicks her feet against the inside of the boot. He stops, looking behind him.

Owen answers him, 'You got a problem, pal?'

'Thought I heard something.'

'How long you been on the road?'

'Too long.'

A shadow steps in front of the latch. Owen whispers, 'Another sound and you'll never see your boy again.'

Marnie's heart shrinks back into the bottom of her stomach.

It is past three in the morning when Ruiz and Joe leave the station. Zoe is with them. Despite the arguments of social services, she refused to go with a foster family or police liaison officer. She asked to stay with Joe because he was a known among the unknowns, a familiar face who understood what she'd endured in the previous eight hours.

Gennia agreed, too exhausted to argue, but demanded that Zoe be returned to the station by midday for further questioning.

Ruiz drives them home. 'There's more room at my place,' he says. 'You should both come and stay until we sort this out.' Zoe says nothing. Joe isn't sure if it will ever be sorted out.

When they reach the house in Fulham, Ruiz organises the spare bedrooms and gives Zoe a shirt to use as a nightdress. After a shower, she comes downstairs and tries to listen to them talking, but falls asleep on the sofa with her head resting on the crook of her arm and her legs curled beneath a cushion.

'I keep forgetting how young she is,' says Ruiz.

Joe glances at the teenager. 'She's older than her years.'

'Should we wake her?'

'Let her sleep here.'

Ruiz unfurls a blanket and drapes it over Zoe, who inhales a ragged breath and mumbles something before settling down. He studies her for a moment, pondering her porcelain face, bouncy curls and mouth like a scarlet rosebud. She's an introspective young thing. Clear skinned. Blue-green eyed. Not as pretty as her mother, but that's probably because she fights against it. Dressing down.

Another stray, he thinks. The professor has a habit of picking up waifs and lost souls. That's why Julianne left him. That's most likely why she fell in love with him. How's that for one of life's tragic absurdities?

Joe is sitting at the kitchen table, holding his left hand to stop it trembling. Ruiz pours another drink and takes a seat, rubbing at the nub of his missing finger. It's an old injury – a high-velocity bullet tore through Ruiz's upper thigh and another obliterated his wedding ring. Ruiz says it's another reason not to remarry.

'What did I miss?' asks Joe.

'She had a second personality.'

'No.'

'But Dr Sterne said . . .'

'I saw no trace of a second personality.'

'You said yourself that Malcolm could exist independently of Marnie. Dr Sterne only met him sporadically. You saw her, what, twice a week?'

Joe rubs his eyes and tries to picture another face in Marnie's mirror – a separate personality, isolated, caught between worlds, as though dropped from the heavens or rising from the underworld; an avenging angel, a killer who chose to protect her from anyone who had hurt or threatened or disappointed her.

The level of cruelty in each of the murders had

bordered on sadism and included touches of macabre theatre. Whoever did this enjoyed the act of punishing and killing. They were aware how others would react to finding the victims, their shock and revulsion. Hennessy had his head almost twisted off. The caretaker was partially dismembered. That takes a particularly deviant personality; someone driven by a certainty of purpose and a lust for revenge. Strength. Pitilessness. Anger.

The last killing was more compulsive, reckless, less in control. The caretaker didn't die immediately. If Zoe had arrived earlier, Trevor might have still been alive. He could have talked. The killer was rushed. Something made him panic. What changed?

Joe is staring at a spot on the wall, but looking at the problem internally, rearranging the facts to support a different premise. 'What if there is someone else?' he says out loud.

'What do you mean?'

'Someone avenging Marnie . . . protecting her.'

'Other than Malcolm?'

'I mean a real person.'

Ruiz blinks at him, not understanding.

'Somebody phoned you and warned you off. You said it was a male voice.'

'You said a split-personality often takes on a different voice.'

Joe remembers the tape he heard in Dr Sterne's office, but he's still not convinced. His left arm jerks

393

in a strange rhythm. Pressing his thumbs into his eye sockets, he searches for the words. 'A dissociative disorder is rare. The chances of Malcolm sharing her mind and acting independently are infinitesimally small.'

'So she's a freak.'

'Marnie sometimes talked about having a sense that she was being watched. I put it down to paranoia, but let's accept for a moment that she was right and somebody was following her, someone close to her, a friend or a confidante, a neighbour or a colleague. It could be someone hiding in plain sight.'

Ruiz is staring across the table in that sombre way he has when expecting a better explanation. 'You're always accusing people of ignoring the obvious answer, Professor. Now you're bending over backwards to exonerate this woman.'

'I'm just saying there are too many questions.'

'So what? You think I knew every answer when I solved a crime and caught the perpetrator? It didn't matter. I knew the answers that counted: who, what, where, when and, if I was lucky, why. Usually, I didn't give a shit about the motive as long as I had the rest. You can look at the nuances and white noise, I'll stick to the facts.'

Ruiz lifts his glass and swallow the last of his Scotch, sucking air through his teeth. 'Sleep.'

'And then what?'

'We see how things look in the morning.'

CHAPTER 46

The Motor Court motel is a hundred metres from the M1 on the edge of a desolate industrial park on the outskirts of a northern town. The rooms are a collection of cinder-block cottages built around an asphalt parking area that circles a yellowing patch of grass and a naked flagpole. The swimming pool is empty, covered, collecting leaves.

Three hours before dawn, traffic hurtles past the motel, desperate to be somewhere else. Marnie has been left in the car with her hands and feet bound. Owen has gone inside to pay for the room; he signs the register and counts out cash. The receptionist gives him a tired smile and glances at the woman in the car, wondering how someone like Owen could pull a bird like her.

Parking outside the most isolated of the cottages, Owen scoops Elijah in his arms and carries his sleeping form inside, depositing him on one of the beds. He goes back to collect Marnie, keeping his hand tucked into the waistband of her skirt as he nudges her inside the room. Bags of shopping are dumped on the bed. The contents spill out:

HobNob biscuits, juice boxes, scissors, a bottle of hair dye, toothbrushes, toothpaste . . .

Elijah stirs, snuffling, settling again.

The masking tape is chafing at Marnie's wrists.

'I have to go,' she says, motioning her head towards the bathroom.

Owen studies her for a moment and pulls a knife from a worn leather scabbard hitched to his belt. Inserting the tip of the blade between the tape and her pale inner wrist, he flicks his hand upwards. The masking tape falls onto the carpet and curls like a severed snake.

'Don't lock the door.'

The bathroom smells of matted hair and disinfectant. The only picture on the wall is a foxhunting scene with men in red coats jumping fences on horses with unusually small heads and elongated bodies.

Marnie talks to him through the closed door. 'What do you do, Owen?'

'What do you mean?'

'What do you do for a living?'

'I don't want for things.'

'Did you leave the money?'

'I couldn't see you starve.'

'The photographs?'

'You deserved to know the truth.' He is standing outside the bathroom door. 'Are you finished?'

The toilet flushes. The door swings open. 'Stay there,' he says, carrying a chair to the sink. 'Sit.'

'What are you going to do?'

'I'm going to cut and dye your hair.'

'Why?'

'I don't want you to be recognised.'

He is running a tap, feeling the water.

'I'll do it myself.'

'I can't trust you. You should take off your blouse so it doesn't get stained.'

Marnie shoots him a look, clutching her buttons.

'I don't have any other clothes for you,' he explains. 'You're wearing a bra and there's nothing I haven't seen.'

Undoing the buttons, she slips the blouse off her shoulders and Owen hangs it on a hook behind the door. Marnie sits with her arms folded across her chest. Owen brushes her hair, running the brush backwards from her forehead to the nape of her neck. Picking up the scissors he uses his opposite hand to judge how much to take off, slicing it quickly, letting the cut locks rock to the floor like wood shavings from a lathe. Marnie watches the haircut, feeling nothing, as though gazing at a stranger in the mirror.

Owen opens the box of hair dye and reads the instructions, setting out the contents on the edge of the sink: a plastic bowl, a tube, a bottle, a brush and gloves.

'You empty the tube into the bowl,' says Marnie. 'Then you mix it with the liquid in the bottle. Use the gloves.'

Owen pulls on the plastic gloves and picks up the bowl, smearing the dark paste across Marnie's scalp.

'Start at the roots,' she says. 'Do the front first, then work it in with the brush and then your fingers.' He does as he's told. 'We have to wait now,' says Marnie.

'How long?'

'Twenty minutes.'

Goosebumps dot her arms.

'Are you cold?'

'No.'

He puts a towel around her shoulders. 'I remember when you had short hair. It was after your riding accident. They had to shave part of your head and afterwards you had the rest shortened to even out the kinks.'

'How could you know that?'

'You were in hospital for five weeks.'

Marnie looks at him incredulously. 'Did you visit me?'

Owen shakes his head.

'I remember how jealous you were of your friend Andrea Heaney because she had long straight hair and had breasts and a boyfriend before anyone else did.'

'She wore skater dresses and wedge heels,' says Marnie.

'She was such a bitch to you when you came back to school with your short hair and scars. She said those cruel things to you. Then she had that accident with the hot oil. She didn't wear short dresses after that.'

'Why are you telling me this?'

'I did that for you.'

'What?'

'I made sure she didn't bully you any more.'

The information sinks in. Marnie can't answer.

'It's time,' he says, motioning her to lean back with her head over the sink. His hand brushes over her eyelids, urging them to close. Scooping water from the sink, he wets her hair. Inky darkness swirls into the porcelain bowl, disappearing down the drain.

When the dye has been rinsed out, he shampoos her hair and uses the special conditioner from the box. She doesn't flinch any more when he touches her scalp. When he's finished, he combs out her wet hair, which is now a dark brown bob. She looks younger by ten years, like a punk, like that girl with the dragon tattoo in the movie, but without the piercings and the attitude.

Marnie looks in the mirror. Owen is standing behind her, waiting for her opinion. She can smell his fleshy heat and the testosterone ironed into his clothes. The hair dye has left a mark on her forehead like a fake hairline, but she doesn't care. She wraps her head in a towel and puts another around her body then crawls into bed next to Elijah.

'I have to do this,' says Owen, hooking her wrist with a plastic tie and securing it to his own. 'I don't want you getting away.'

The sun rises pale and weak beyond the motorway. Headlights sweep across the flyover, heading north. A car door slams. An engine starts up. Marnie sleeps lying on her left side, one arm above her head. Her chest rises and falls, her eyelids flutter, but it's not the same . . . not the same.

During the night, before I sank into my own shallow sleep, I saw it over and over, that moment she shattered the glass wall between us. She doesn't yet understand what I've sacrificed for her. How I've lived in crawlspaces away from the light; how I've subordinated my own desires and mortgaged my past and the present to make us a future. There is no end to what I've done.

The dawn has come and gone. The ochre and pinks have succumbed to faded blues and corpulent clouds. Marnie stirs next to me. It's like we've never been apart. I know so much about her: how her mother grew up in Bannock Street, Gorton, which doesn't exist any more. It's where Myra Hindley used to live with her gran before she met Ian Brady and they began kidnapping and killing children. Marnie's mother regarded herself as one of the lucky ones because Myra had asked to take her out one day, but her parents said no. She moved out of the area when she met her first boyfriend – not the one she married, but the one before that. I can tell Marnie all of these things. I can fill in the gaps.

I have not robbed Marnie of her freedom or spontaneity. I have only ever sought to play the role I was meant to play. The one I was denied.

She's frightened, but time will make her see me differently. I have seen her change for others. She has become what they wanted her to be. She watched football, drank beer and ate cheap curries. She gave blow-jobs and worked as an escort. I hated seeing her alter herself to satisfy the desires of others. Why couldn't she stand up to them? Why couldn't she be herself? I will teach her the lessons that she should have learned earlier. A man has to be worthy of her love, not the other way around.

I didn't have a role model in my life, anyone to teach me lessons or pick me up when I stumbled. My mother, dead now, drowned in her own bile, or whatever toxic fluid filled her lungs until they bubbled and gurgled into silence. She had been sick for a long while. I nursed her. Fed her. Bathed her. Wiped her arse. It's more than she did for me. When she died they asked me if I wanted to have her cremated. 'Yeah, I'll watch her burn,' I said.

I once worked out how many years I spent with her in my childhood. I counted six of sixteen before I joined the army, which means I spent ten years in foster care, being raised by other people. Strangers.

My aunt Pat came to the funeral, but left straight afterwards. She was my mother's older sister and I hadn't seen her since I was a child. My mother was her family's black sheep, which is not surprising given her addictions and arrest record – and me, of course, her bastard son.

I have never discovered why my mother was so ostracised by her family, although my cousin Jenny once told me (when we were kids, in a quarrel) that my mother ran away from school with a foreigner who took her to France and introduced her to drugs and sex. I went straight to Aunt Pat and asked if it were true. She told me I had a filthy mouth and threatened to wash it out with Fairy Liquid. Cousin Jenny smirked from the doorway.

After that I didn't believe anything Jenny told me. I liked being with Aunt Pat and Uncle Hank and my cousins. I used to go on fishing holidays to the Lake District until Uncle Hank had a stroke. Nobody could understand a word he said after that.

All I ever wanted was a proper family. Once or twice more I got a taste of what it might be like. I went to foster homes where people sat around a dinner table, eating and talking, saying please and thank you, would you like some more potatoes, how about another sausage? Mum. Dad. Kids. It was like being in a TV commercial for Bisto gravy.

Mid-morning, the birds are singing, telling me the world goes on as normal, even though it's different now. My feet are cold. I wish I'd worn thicker socks. I wish I could put them against Marnie, but I don't want to wake her. Instead, I use the knife to slice the plastic that tethers us. I go to the bathroom and try not to make a sound as I urinate. Shave. Then I fill the kettle and plug it into the socket.

Her eyes open.

'I've made you a cup of tea.'

I put it next to the bed, along with a sandwich. I take a chair and sit down.

'You should eat something.'

'I'm not hungry.'

'You will be later.'

'The police are going to be looking. You should just let us go.'

'Why would I do that?'

CHAPTER 47

Z oe is sitting at the kitchen table, sipping on a can of high-energy drink. Caffeine. Sugar. She's wearing the same clothes as yesterday but has washed her hair and pinned it differently. Ruiz, already dressed for the day, is beating eggs in a bowl.

Joe is the last to arrive. His buttons are done up unevenly. 'What have you given her to drink?' he asks.

'It's what she wanted,' says Ruiz.

'And if she'd asked for tequila?'

'Bit early in the day.'

Ruiz tips the eggs into a heated pan, adding salt and pepper. Bread pops out of the toaster.

Zoe looks at Joe hopefully. 'Have you heard any news?' For a moment her eyes seem to shiver, but she's not going to cry. She's holding all her emotions in her fists, which are squeezed tightly shut.

Joe shakes his head. Zoe looks at her hands, feeling somewhat cheated. She had prayed last night. She knew this wasn't a guarantee, but given all that has happened in the past eighteen hours and the thirteen months before that, she thought God might have owed her some good news.

Ruiz offers her scrambled eggs. She declines. He gives her some anyway. Joe takes a seat opposite. 'Can I ask you a few questions?'

Zoe nods.

'Does your mum ever suffer blackouts or absences?'

'What sort of absences?'

'Does she wake up and forget where she's been?'

'She can be forgetful, but that's just little stuff.'

'Does she ever go out without telling you?'

'No.'

'What about at night?'

'She stopped working nights,' says Zoe, wanting to change the subject.

'I know what she used to do,' says Joe.

Zoe's shoulders rise and fall in an exaggerated shrug.

'Have you ever noticed anyone hanging around her? Someone who's always in the background – a neighbour or a friend.'

'Penny.'

'Anyone else?'

'Not really.'

'The police think your mother killed Trevor.'

Her eyes swivel from face to face. 'That's crazy!'

'That's why they think she ran away.'

Zoe rocks backwards and forwards, staring at the uneaten eggs. She has fought so hard not to cry, but now her fists open and big childish tears slide down her cheeks, dropping off her chin and landing on her jeans where the denim is most faded. She wipes her eyes and sniffles. 'I didn't kiss her and say the words.'

'What words?'

'Even to the post office – that's what we say. We always kiss each other goodbye and say, "Even to the post office", just in case we don't come back.'

'From where?'

'From anywhere! That's the point. Mum says you should always say goodbye as though it's the last time.'

'That's macabre,' says Ruiz.

Joe shoots him a look. 'I think it's touching.' He hands Zoe a tissue. 'Do you still have your key to the flat?'

'I gave them to the police, but there's a spare set in the meter box.'

Ruiz interrupts. 'Hey, you're not thinking of going back there. Gennia will go bat-shit crazy if you contaminate the crime scene.'

'Forensics will have finished by now.'

'And I need my laptop,' says Zoe, 'and some clothes.'

Ruiz grunts in disgust. 'So that makes me the getaway driver.'

A police caravan is parked opposite the mansion block with a sign asking for public help. Ruiz drives slowly along Elgin Avenue beneath trees in full leaf but beginning to turn.

'Is there a rear entrance?'

Zoe nods. 'We can go along the back lane and through the garden.'

He parks the Range Rover opposite a row of lock-up garages with padlocked shutter doors. Joe walks along the alley and into the garden where he spends a few moments, turning slowly and gazing up at the surrounding windows which seem to look down on him like indifferent witnesses.

'Which is your flat?'

Zoe points to the top floor. 'That's the kitchen window.'

Joe studies the buildings opposite, seeing if any overlook or provide a vantage point to watch Marnie. Meanwhile, Ruiz has walked along the lane and stopped in front of an open lock-up containing tools and boxes. A patch of oil stains the concrete where a car must have been parked. Somebody forgot to close the roller door. Maybe they left in a hurry.

'The keys are this way,' says Zoe. They follow her along a rear path to a heavy wooden door set several feet below the level of the lawn. The electricity meters are housed in metal boxes bolted to the wall. Zoe runs her fingertips along the top of a box until she finds the spare keys. One of them opens the outside door.

On the top floor, Ruiz pulls away the crime-scene tape, which flutters like a busted piñata. Zoe enters first, searching the rooms as though possessing some vague absurd hope that Marnie and Elijah might have come home. But the flat is unchanged except for a dusting of fingerprint powder on the polished surfaces and a sense that everything has been slightly disturbed by the search.

Joe moves more slowly through the rooms, looking for something that Zoe wouldn't comprehend – the psychological 'mind traces' left behind at the scene, the indicators of human behaviour that is out of character, or unexpected or inexplicable.

Zoe has gone to her bedroom and retrieved a laptop from beneath her bed.

'Is this how you found the flat?' asks Joe, standing at the door.

'Yes.'

'You didn't move anything?'

'No.'

'Or touch anything?'

She thinks about this.

Ruiz is standing in the living room, gazing at the street below. 'Are any of your mother's clothes missing?'

Zoe shakes her head. 'The police asked me to check.'

Joe wanders into Marnie's bedroom. The bed is untouched. Bottles are lined up neatly on her dresser. Towels are folded on the towel rails. The wardrobe door is open. Clothes have been pushed to the far ends of the railing. Shoes have fallen from a rack. A blanket lies on the floor, along with Elijah's matchbox cars and trucks.

He goes to the window. 'Did your mother sleep naked?'

'No.'

'Did she ever wander around the house naked?'

'No.'

'Did she draw the curtains before she undressed?'

'She always told me to.'

The bedroom overlooks part of the garden and the adjoining building. Someone with a telescope could look into the room, particularly at night if the curtains were open and the lights were on.

'It doesn't smell right,' says Ruiz. 'She didn't take anything with her.'

Joe sits next to Zoe on the bed. 'When you came in yesterday, what did you notice?'

'What do you mean?'

'I want you to picture coming into the flat. Lie down on the bed. Close your eyes if it makes it easier. Relax. Think back.'

Zoe does as he asks. She listens to Joe's voice. He asks her about meeting Ryan at the pizza parlour and then walking home . . . up the stairs . . . opening the door.

'What can you see?'

'The hallway.'

'What lights were on?'

'The kitchen, the bathroom, the bedroom . . .'

'This one?'

'Yes.'

'What else did you notice?'

'Mum left a saucepan on the stove. She was making lasagne. It's still there.'

'So you turned off the stove?'

'Uh-huh.'

'Then what?'

'I tried to call her.'

'Where were you?'

'Sitting on the sofa in the living room.'

'So you walked from the kitchen along the hallway to the living room?'

Zoe nods.

'Were the lights on?'

'In the hallway, yes.'

'What about the living room?'

Zoe frowns.

'What?'

'I was about to turn on a lamp when I noticed the ceiling.'

'What about it?'

'The star.'

'Star?'

'There was a pinprick of light on the ceiling. It looked like a star, but when I turned on the lamp it disappeared.'

'And you'd never seen that before?'

'No.'

'Show me.'

Zoe takes Joe's hand as he pulls her up from the bed. In the living room she points to the high ceiling with its ornate cornicing and a plaster rosette around the light fitting. 'It was just there – a tiny white light.'

'What's above us?' asks Joe.

'Nothing. We're on the top floor.'

Wrestling an armchair to the centre of the room, Joe stands and reaches above his head, still shy of being able to touch the light fitting.

'Is there any way to get into the ceiling? A manhole or hatch?'

Zoe shakes her head.

Joe looks at Ruiz. 'We need a ladder and a hammer.'

'You're not thinking of . . .'

'Renovating.'

CHAPTER 48

They leave the motel late in the morning after Marnie has given Elijah a bath and combed his hair, putting on his clothes from yesterday.

'We'll buy him some more later,' Owen tells her.

'He needs gluten-free food.'

'I'll arrange that.'

Owen has an answer for everything. Nothing seems too much trouble – not kidnapping two people or holding them hostage.

At first Elijah had been shocked by Marnie's new hairstyle. 'You don't look like a mummy,' he said, running his fingers through her ragged bob where the edge of her hair brushed against her neck.

'I'm still me,' she told him.

They're driving on back roads, avoiding motorways and police patrols and CCTV cameras. Reaching the outskirts of Manchester, Marnie begins to recognise places, particular landmarks and buildings from her childhood. McAlister's, the carpet warehouse, had terrible radio commercials with a man screaming about crazy prices going down, down, down. She remembers the Chinese restaurant in Princess Street and the Old Quay swinging bridge over the canal.

The car doesn't have air conditioning and Owen won't open the windows because he's worried that Marnie will yell for help. The heat reminds her of her childhood trips to Blackpool in the summer with whatever foster kids were staying. They'd walk on the beach, eating ice-cream cones or taking donkey rides. Blackpool is where she first rode roller skates and let a boy kiss her. She went in a talent show and sang a Cyndi Lauper song about girls just wanting to have fun.

She looks at Owen and wonders if he knows about her kissing the boy. Was he watching her then?

'Why me?'

'Huh?'

'Why have you been watching me?'

'It's what I'm supposed to do.'

'I don't understand.'

'You were so afraid.'

'Of what?'

'Just about everything.'

Marnie is sitting in the front passenger seat with her knees drawn up and her hands still taped together behind her back. The seatbelt holds her in place. Elijah has the rear seat, his head bowed over a cheap colouring book that Owen bought him when he filled up with petrol.

'Why couldn't you just pant down the phone or flash me in the park?' Marnie asks.

Owen looks hurt. 'I'm not a degenerate.'

'No, you just get your jollies spying on women.'

Elijah looks up. 'I'm hungry, Mummy.'

She glances at Owen.

'Give him a biscuit.'

'He has a special diet. You can't just feed him anything.'

'He'll have to wait.'

Dust and broken plaster covers the floor of the living room and the shoulders of Ruiz's jacket. His hair has also turned a shade greyer and dust sticks to his nose and forehead. Standing on a ladder, he launches a ball-headed hammer into the jagged hole, tearing off another chunk of ceiling.

'Are you sure you're allowed to do that?' asks Zoe. 'We only rent.'

Ruiz motions to the professor. 'Ask him. He's paying.'

He launches the hammer again. Another piece of plasterboard falls away, but something comes with it – a flashlight with a rubber grip. It bounces twice and rolls in a circle.

Joe picks it up. Presses the button. The batteries are flat. He glances at Ruiz, something unspoken passing between them. He has opened up a hole wide enough to pull himself up, using the crossbeams to take his weight.

'What can you see?'

'It's too dark.'

'Hence the torch,' says Joe.

Ruiz reaches forward and feels a blanket and thin mattress. His eyes are still adjusting. The roof cavity stretches the width of the room and beyond.

'Somebody has been up here. I need more light.'

Zoe says her mum keeps a torch in the kitchen in case of power cuts. She fetches it and climbs the first two rungs of the ladder, handing it up to Ruiz. He pulls himself higher, bracing his forearms, slithering upwards until his legs disappear. A moment later his head appears in the ragged hole. 'Don't go anywhere.'

He's gone again. Joe climbs the ladder and peers into the roof space. He can make out Ruiz's torch about twenty feet away. It sweeps over the ceiling cavity and then drops from sight. Minutes pass. They hear a voice. It's coming from Marnie's bedroom. Zoe runs along the hallway, not waiting for Joe. Ruiz's upper body emerges from her mother's wardrobe. Zoe peers past him and sees a passage through the bricks. Her eyes go wide. 'Where does it go?'

'Another flat.'

'Next door?'

Ruiz nods and looks at Joe. 'We have to call Gennia.'

Joe takes out his mobile and punches the number. Zoe is still asking questions. 'So someone lives there?'

'By the looks of it.'

'And they were in our ceiling?'

'There are spyholes. Somebody left a torch on. That's the light you saw.'

'Spyholes. How many?

'Six, maybe seven.'

'In the bathroom?'

'Everywhere.'

The knowledge sinks in.

'How could anyone do that? We would have heard?'

'They put insulation between the beams.'

A cat appears behind Ruiz. Zoe calls to it, sitting back on her haunches. The cat comes to her, sliding against her thighs as though trying to soak into her body.

'Gennia is on his way,' says Joe, peering into the wardrobe. 'I need to see it.'

'Don't touch anything,' says Ruiz. 'We don't have long.'

Joe crawls through the hole scraping his back on the jagged bricks. The first room is so dark it takes a moment for his eyes to adjust.

'The light doesn't work,' says Ruiz, who has followed him through the hole. 'He unscrewed the bulb so that it wouldn't shine through the wardrobe. Come and see this.'

He guides Joe into the hallway that leads to a kitchen and two more bedrooms. Ruiz points to the wall. Joe's gaze travels from the skirting board to the cornices above his head. From floor to ceiling, the surface is papered with photographs, newspaper clippings and documents. Marnie Logan features in all of them. Some of the pictures are posed and formal, others are more candid and off-the-cuff.

416

Stolen moments. Keepsakes. Souvenirs. Particular shots must have been taken with hidden cameras and telephoto lenses. There are also phone bills, bank statements, invoices, reminders, shopping lists and credit card receipts.

Ruiz looks at his watch. 'Five minutes.'

In the main bedroom Joe uses a handkerchief to open the wardrobe and finds four pairs of jeans, two black, two blue; a cashmere overcoat, a dozen business shirts, predominantly white. The occupant has a thing for shoes. There are six pairs arranged in neat rows. Oxford brogues. Polished. Brown. Black.

A second bedroom belongs to an old woman. Her clothes are still in the wardrobe. Powders and perfumes line the dresser, along with bottles of pills. Medications. Beneath the bedsprings, he notices a bedpan and an oxygen bottle with a mask. She'd been sick.

There are cracks in the linoleum floor and rust stains on the enamel in the bathtub. In the kitchen a frying pan is soaking in the sink. Egg yolks, hard and black, are stuck to the heavy base. A pine ladder is angled over the small table, providing access to the roof space. Using the tip of a pencil, Ruiz separates envelopes on the bench, looking for a name. He glances out the window. The police are out front.

'Time's up.'

'Gennia?'

'On his way up.'

'How much trouble are we in?'

'On a scale of one to ten – I'd say fifteen.'

Zoe is waiting for Joe on the far side of the wardrobe, eyes wider than before. She's holding her laptop across her chest.

'Who was living there?' she asks.

'I was hoping you might know.'

She shakes her head. Ruiz has gone down the other stairs, knocking on doors, hoping one of the neighbours will provide him with a name.

Joe and Zoe wait on the landing.

'Was your mother seeing anyone?' he asks. 'An old boyfriend . . . a friend she knew from school . . . someone she used to work with?'

Zoe blinks at him, wanting to have an answer. 'Elijah used to play in the wardrobe. He used to talk to his imaginary friend.' Her pupils dilate and she wraps her arms tighter around herself. 'He called him Malcolm.'

CHAPTER 49

On the drive through Manchester, Owen had been hunched over the wheel, glancing in the mirrors, worried about being pulled over by the police. Now in the countryside, he has relaxed and cheered up, looking for music on the radio.

'Not far to go now, little man,' he says, doing a drum roll on the steering wheel.

'I don't want you talking to him,' says Marnie. Her arms are cramping. She can't shift her weight to relieve the pain.

'I have been a very good friend to Elijah,' says Owen. 'You neglect him. You've spent too long fretting about your husband.'

'Don't talk about my husband!'

Marnie realises in the same breath what question she should be asking. 'Where is Daniel?'

Owen takes a hand off the steering wheel and waves it vaguely. 'We'll have plenty of time to talk.'

'What happened?'

'It was his own fault.'

Marnie's eyes are fixed, anguish in them. 'Is he alive?'

Owen sighs.

'Answer me, you son of a bitch!'

He hits her so suddenly that she doesn't have time to duck her head. It's a backhanded slap that strikes her across the cheek. Marnie turns her face away, sucking on her lip, tasting for blood.

Owen's voice doesn't change. 'Show me some respect and I won't have to hit you again.'

Elijah looks up, wondering what happened. 'Mummy, why is your hands tied?'

'It's a game,' says Owen.

'Can I play?'

'No!'

'But I want to play.'

'I said no.'

Elijah flinches.

'You don't have to shout at him,' says Marnie. 'He's just a little boy.'

Owen relaxes. 'You're right. Sorry, sport. We used to have great fun in the wardrobe, didn't we?'

'I saw you in the park,' says Elijah. 'You were talking to Zoe.'

'Do you want to play now?' asks Owen. 'Come sit on my lap. You can drive for a while.'

'No, please, leave him,' says Marnie.

'He wants to play. Come on, partner. You can do the steering.'

'Stay where you are, Elijah.'

Owen reaches back and grabs Elijah by the arm, pulling him between the seats onto his lap. 'Hold it like this,' he says, taking the boy's hands and putting them on the wheel. Elijah's head barely reaches above the dashboard.

'Put him back!' yells Marnie.

'We're coming up to a corner. Do you know right from left? We're turning left. That's it. Not so far.'

The car swerves to the right and crosses the centre lines. Owen straightens the wheel. 'Nice try.'

'I's doing it, Mummy. I's driving.'

It's a winding road down a steep decline. The car drifts again, crossing onto the wrong side of the road. An oncoming car swerves.

'You idiot!' yells Marnie. 'You'll kill us all!'

Something alters in Owen's eyes. He puts his left hand on the wheel and tells Elijah to let go. Then he opens the car door. The change in air pressure lifts rubbish from the floor. The next corner is a sharp left. Owen accelerates and steers hard. Elijah's body sways toward the open door.

Marnie screams. Begs.

'What did you call me?' asks Owen.

'I'm sorry.'

'I didn't hear you.'

'I'm sorry, please, please, don't hurt him.'

A car is approaching. Owen pulls the door shut and pushes Elijah onto the back seat. He's crying.

'Tell him to shut up.'

'He's a little boy.'

'You're his mother. Keep him quiet.'

'Let me hold him.'

'No.'

Marnie turns her head to look at Elijah. 'Shhhh, sweetie, just be quiet . . . If you're a good boy, you'll get a treat. Next time we stop, I'll get you a chocolate. You love chocolate.'

'I want Bunny.'

'Bunny is at home.'

'Can we go home now?'

'Soon.'

Gennia stands in the entrance hall, his chin jutting forward and teeth clenched so hard his molars might crack. The crime scene examiners seem to enjoy making him wait, smiling privately to each other as they set out evidence tags and take samples. His every conversation is tense – the calls to his superiors, the questioning of his team and the issuing of orders. Twelve hours ago the detective was so certain of Marnie Logan's guilt and her imminent arrest. Now he feels foolish. Stupid. Amateurish.

'You broke into one crime scene and contaminated another,' he says, unclenching his jaw. 'If my investigation has been compromised I'm going to chew you up and shit you out – and I mean shit not spit.' He glares at Ruiz. 'How did you know about this place?'

'We didn't.'

'What made you come back?'

'Curiosity.'

'Are you taking the piss?'

'No.'

Gennia stabs his finger at Joe. 'You're staying here. The rest of you – wait downstairs.'

Ruiz retreats with Zoe and Rhonda Firth. Gennia takes a stick of gum from his pocket and studies Joe while unwrapping the foil. He doesn't like psychologists. In particular, he doesn't like criminal investigations where psychology serves a purpose. Most crimes are straightforward and easy to understand. People steal and cheat because they're greedy or lazy or both. They kill for money, power or revenge – simple yet ancient motives that don't require a psychological profile to unravel or comprehend.

Gennia glances through the door at the broken ceiling. 'I'm not sure what level of reality I'm supposed to be operating on here, Professor. I work, I eat, I shower, I sleep; occasionally I take a dump, which is the best five minutes of my fucking day. Quality time.' He swaps the chewing gum from one cheek to the other. 'Yesterday, you told me Marnie Logan had a second personality. Now you say she has a stalker. Why should I believe you?'

'The evidence.'

'How did you find the room in the ceiling?'

'Zoe saw a pinprick of light.'

'When?'

'Last night when she came home.'

'Why didn't she say anything?'

'She didn't think it was important.'

Gennia looks into Marnie's flat again. 'So this guy was in her ceiling.'

'Yes.'

'Is he a voyeur or a stalker?'

'You've seen the photographs in the hallway.'

'Is she in danger?'

'Yes.'

The atmosphere between them alters. It's as though a tiny screw holding something vital in place has been given a small twist to ratchet up the tension.

'There were two 999 calls from this address last night,' says Gennia. 'One came from downstairs. That was Zoe. The other was made from Marnie Logan's mobile. The operator logged it as the same incident because police were already on their way to this address. Nobody listened to the tape until this morning. Marnie said some man had been watching her and that she was trapped in his ceiling. Then she hung up. It didn't make any sense until I saw this.' Gennia glances at the jagged hole again. 'OK, so this guy is obsessed with her. Why?'

'I don't know.'

'I need more than that, Professor.'

'This level of infatuation is usually a form of paranoid delusion. He thinks he's in love with Marnie and they're destined to be together. It can be triggered by the most prosaic of things. He could have passed Marnie on the street or sat next to her on a bus. Stalkers fall in love with people

424

they see on TV or hear on the radio. I don't know enough yet to say why he chose Marnie, but he *thinks* he has a special connection with her, either real or imagined.'

'What about her ex-husband or former boyfriends?'

'Possibly.'

'Who else?'

'You're looking for someone who has watched Marnie for a long time – perhaps since her childhood. The photographs will give us clues.'

'What will he do now?'

Joe has been pondering the same question, trying to picture this man's mind.

'He'll have imagined this moment – meeting her, telling her how much he loves her, showing her how much he's done for her. He thinks Marnie will fall in love with him.'

'And they'll live happily ever after?'

'Or die trying.'

CHAPTER 50

The nursing home worker has prominent teeth and a sharp widow's peak that looks painted onto her forehead. She's wearing a tunic dress and chunky shoes that squeak on the floor tiles as she leads Joe and Ruiz along the corridor, past kitchens and a dining room.

'I haven't talked to Thomas today. I don't know if he's having a good one,' she says.

'How long has he been here?' asks Ruiz.

'Four years and eight months.'

'Why so certain?'

'The police asked me that.' She waves to a colleague behind a desk. 'Have they found his daughter and grandson?'

'Not yet.'

She nods sadly and notices Ruiz's missing ring finger. 'What happened?'

'It's an old gypsy tradition,' he replies. 'When you've been divorced three times, they cut it off.'

Her eyes widen ever so slightly and then narrow just as quickly.

They have arrived in a cluttered lounge with a large bay window overlooking the garden. The room smells like an old railway carriage and has brown lumps of furniture, sofas with knobbed legs and sprawling armchairs. A second door opens and a man enters, dressed in plaid pyjamas and a dressing gown. He has comb marks in his hair and has cut himself shaving. A torn piece of bloody toilet paper is sticking to the cleft of his chin.

His eyes brighten at the sight of Joe and Ruiz. He comes forward quickly and holds out his hand, smiling, surprised to have visitors.

'It's been ages,' he says, shaking their hands. 'Far too long.'

'Too long for what?' Ruiz asks.

Thomas frowns, realising his mistake. He doesn't know if he's met them before, but his coping mechanism for his dementia is to smile and assume some prior contact, hoping not to cause offence.

'These gentlemen have come to ask about Marnie,' says the nurse, separating her words, as though speaking to a child.

'Is she coming?'

'She and your grandson are missing.'

'They normally come on a Wednesday. What day is today?'

The nurse turns to Joe. 'His long-term memory is better.'

Thomas has taken a seat opposite Joe. Ruiz is more comfortable standing at the window because nursing homes make him nervous.

'When did you last see Marnie?' Joe asks.

'It would have been . . .' He pauses and searches

for the memory. 'I can't remember. She normally comes on a Wednesday.'

'How did she seem?'

'Fine. She brought Elijah. Such a good boy.'

'Did she ever talk about somebody following her?' asks Joe. 'An old boyfriend, maybe, or someone from her past who might be infatuated with her.'

Thomas shakes his head. His fingers are toying with the bow of his pyjama bottoms.

'What about Malcolm?'

Thomas's mouth opens slowly and he hesitates like an actor stranded mid-monologue, gaping at the audience, having forgotten his lines.

'I've talked to Dr Sterne,' says Joe. 'He told me about what happened to Marnie.'

'Then you know the story.'

'Did you ever meet Malcolm?'

'I heard the tapes. Didn't sound much like Marnie.'

'But you accept that he existed – this other personality?'

'You trust the doctors, don't you? They're the experts.'

'According to Dr Sterne, Marnie's problems dated from her mother's death.'

Thomas seems to sink further into the lumpy sofa. In the silence that follows, Joe recognises a man who remembers too much rather than too little. His mind is abandoning him, leaving by degrees, yet he's condemned to relive the tragedies while forgetting what he had for breakfast this morning.

'I was working on the rigs, commuting out of Aberdeen,' says Thomas, blinking at them sadly. 'Away two weeks, home two weeks. I was planning to quit and get a job closer, but then my wife fell pregnant. We'd been trying for a baby for years – a brother or sister for Marnie.'

'How old was she then?' asks Joe.

'Just turned four. I signed on for another year on the rigs. We needed the money. That's why I was away when it happened. My wife went into premature labour. She tried to drive herself to hospital. Crashed. Miscarried. Marnie was in the car. Somehow she managed to get out.' He looks at his hands, dizzy for a second. 'It was a boy . . . the baby. *My* boy. We had his name picked out: Malcolm.'

Ruiz turns from the window. 'You were going to call the baby Malcolm?'

'After my grandfather,' says Thomas.

'Did Marnie know that?'

'We didn't keep it a secret.' Thomas closes his eyes and his breathing grows long and shallow. For a moment Joe thinks the old man might have fallen asleep, but he stirs suddenly and clears his throat. He describes getting the news and being airlifted from the rig to Aberdeen and then travelling south to collect the body of his dead wife and dead son and to console his traumatised daughter.

'They say that life can turn on the length of an

eyelash and that's what happened to us, Marnie and me. But we started again. We had no choice. I remarried. A good woman. Caring. Patient. We fostered kids, dozens of them.'

'Did any of these foster children get close to Marnie or develop a special bond with her?'

His lips make a popping sound. 'Marnie didn't like them. She preferred her own company. I used to hear her arguing with herself of an evening behind her bedroom door, having conversations, trying not to be heard, as if she'd done something shameful.

'That's when the trouble started. Marnie must have been seven or eight. She began telling lies and making up stories, blaming the other kids. We took her to see a shrink, the first of many. Initially, they said that Marnie was acting out her frustration because she lost her mum. The next therapist claimed she was reliving her traumatic experiences. Others said she had schizophrenia or was bipolar, or suffering from post-traumatic stress. Then Malcolm showed up. I had my own theory. I think she invented Malcolm because she was pining for the brother she never had.'

Joe takes Daniel's notebook from his jacket pocket and opens a page at the list of names.

'Do you know anyone called Francis Moffatt?'

'He used to place foster kids with us.'

'He's a social worker?'

'Yeah.'

'Did he spend a lot of time around Marnie?'

'Depends what you mean by a lot. He came to the house every few weeks.'

'Do you still have any contact details?'

Thomas shakes his head and seems to remember something else. Reaching into the pocket of his dressing gown, he pulls out a photograph that is worn with age and handling. It's a picture of Marnie aged about two, squeezed between her parents on a wicker sofa. It looks like a posed family portrait, but something has made them all laugh exuberantly with mouths open and eyes shining.

'Doesn't she look like her mother?' says Thomas.

Joe notices the oval faces and cupid-bow lips. Marnie has a narrower nose and dimples on her cheeks that look like thumb prints.

'She was her mother's daughter, never mine,' says Thomas. 'That's why I wanted a boy.' He looks at Ruiz. 'What day is it today?'

'Friday'

'Marnie won't come until Wednesday.'

CHAPTER 51

The car pulls into the entrance of a muddy farm track. Owen gets out to open the gate, which swings inwards on stiff hinges. The rutted track, dotted with puddles and cowpats, is overgrown at the edges with blackberry bushes. Crouching near the gate, Owen checks for fresh tyre tracks. Satisfied, he gets back behind the wheel and follows the track, wrestling hard with the wheel as the car bucks and rocks over the potholes. Marnie can't stop herself being thrown left and right. Elijah laughs.

The car crosses a small stream where rocks have been arranged to form a solid base beneath the water. The foundations of a washed-out bridge are fifty metres downstream. They pass through a grove of blighted trees and then begin climbing towards a farmhouse surrounded by orchards that look overgrown and diseased. The wooden dwelling has shuttered windows and a water tank squatting to one side. A lone oak tree is shading the front garden, etched so starkly against the sky it could have been cut out of black cardboard and pasted onto the scene. Behind the house, nestled into the

432

ridge, a barn seems to be leaning against the wind, the worn timber planks turning grey with age.

Marnie snatches a breath, feeling woozy. This is where she used to live. The barn, the house, the windmill and the oak tree are all relics of her childhood. When she was a little girl her father would hold her wrists and spin her round and round until her feet left the ground and she seemed to be flying. When she stopped and tried to stand, she'd lurch and stagger. She loved the feeling of flying, but hated when the world seemed to shift and buckle beneath her like an invisible earthquake. That's how she feels now, as though she's been spinning in circles and suddenly come to a stop.

'Look, Mummy, cows,' says Elijah.

'Yes.'

'Can I go see the moo-cows?'

Owen nods. Elijah pushes open the door and runs across the grass to a fence.

Getting out of the car, Owen stretches. Yawns. He surveys the overgrown fields as if he knows every inch of this place. Walking up the front steps, he crosses the front veranda and reaches up into a hanging basket to retrieve a key. The air in the house is musty and stale. He opens the shutters. Throws back the curtains. From the outside the house had looked almost derelict, but inside it is freshly painted and newly furnished. There are large comfortable sofas, side tables, a TV and woollen rugs on the floorboards.

Marnie sits in an armchair, swamped by memories from long ago. There used to be a bureau next to the window and a painting of a Tuscan villa. They would put the Christmas tree in that corner and hang stockings over the fireplace. There were shelves full of books and her stepmother had a sewing table. Her father was away for weeks at a time, working on the rigs; coming home with sweets and chocolate.

'Why did you bring us here?'

'You always liked this farm.'

Marnie walks from room to room. When she closes her eyes, she can hear her father and stepmother shouting at each other. Impossible love. Coolness. Arguments. Apologies. Regrets. What can a child do? What can a child know? She sees images of foster children. Shared rooms. Beds. She has a familiar feeling of not being good enough.

'Who owns this place?' she asks.

'We do.'

'What does that mean?'

'It's ours.' Owen turns in a circle, holding out his hands. 'I did it for us. You should have seen this place when I found it. Rats in the ceiling. Rain leaking through the roof.' He motions Marnie to follow him. She glances behind her at the open door.

'Elijah will be fine.'

Along a narrow hallway there are doors on either side. Bedrooms. The first is a large room with a queen-sized bed and a chest of drawers. For a brief moment Marnie feels as though she's back in the flat. The furnishings are identical to her bedroom, the duvet cover, cushions and curtains. The dressing table has her make-up and moisturising cream – the brands she could afford to buy before Daniel took redundancy.

Owen opens the wardrobe. 'I couldn't get everything,' he says, apologetically, yet pleased with his efforts. 'Some pieces weren't available so I had to approximate. The sizes are right.'

Marnie recognises blazers, skirts, blouses and silk scarves; a dress that Daniel bought her, her favourite boots (she bought them in the post-Christmas sales two years ago.)

'They're all new,' she whispers.

'Of course.'

'How?'

'When you bought them, I bought them.'

Marnie backs towards the door, feeling her throat tighten.

'There's more,' he says, brushing past her. She flinches, holding up her hands. Owen ignores her and walks along the hallway, pointing to another bedroom.

'This is for Elijah.'

The single bed has a Thomas the Tank Engine duvet, along with 3D posters and wall art and a toy box shaped like a train engine. There are dozens of books, toys and a painting easel cum blackboard.

'It's not exactly the same,' he says. 'I thought Elijah would like some new toys.'

'Why did you do this?'

'For us.'

'But why?'

'We're a family now.'

Marnie feels her stomach cramp and vomit rising, scalding her oesophagus. She swallows hard but can still taste it in her mouth.

'You can't expect us to stay here. People are looking for us.'

Owen touches her forearm. 'You want to hope they don't find you, Marnie.'

She doesn't understand.

'They think you killed Trevor and Patrick Hennessy and Quinn.'

'Trevor?'

Owen nods. 'Your kitchen knife was used to kill Quinn. Your fingerprints are on a glass in Hennessy's apartment. They're going to find Trevor's semen on your clothes.'

Marnie's mouth opens, but no sound emerges. She tries again.

'Why?'

'This way I can protect you. Leave here and you'll go to prison. Stay, and I can look after you.'

'I can't stay.'

'You have no choice.'

Elijah comes running into the house and along the hallway. He stops suddenly outside his bedroom.

'Wow!'

He looks at Marnie.

'I never want to go home.'

CHAPTER 52

Gennia is eating and talking to Ruiz on the phone. Each time he takes a mouthful, he catches a whiff of his shirt, which stinks of failure and yesterday. He hasn't been home. He hasn't slept. The sandwich is his first food in sixteen hours. He brushes crumbs from his paperwork.

'The flat was rented by Martha Cargill, aged seventy-five. She died of lung cancer two weeks ago. She'd been bedridden for months. People rarely saw her. She took over the flat six years ago. Neighbours say there was a younger man living with her. He told people he was a carer from the local authority, but social services have no record.'

'Do we have a name?'

'Called himself Owen.'

'What about the old woman's pension?'

'Somebody collected it every month. Scrawled a signature. The GP who signed the death certificate is on holiday in Benidorm. We're trying to reach him now.'

Gennia takes another mouthful and chews slowly.

'How did she pay the rent?'

'Cash, up-front, a year in advance, lodged in a Barclays account. The utilities are paid the same way, cash again at various Post Office branches, never the same one twice in a row.'

'It must have been the carer. What do the neighbours say about him?'

'Late forties, early fifties, he kept to himself. He normally used the rear door. The old lady had a lock-up and a car. He may be driving it. We're going over footage from CCTV cameras in the area.

'We're also canvassing the other crime scenes and talking to neighbours to see if any of them can link this guy to Quinn, Hennessy or the caretaker. All the principal suspects are being re-interviewed, including her ex-husband, who hasn't been co-operating.'

'Calvin isn't a fan of the UK police,' says Ruiz. 'The professor wants you to check another name – a social worker called Francis Moffatt. Could be retired. He used to work for Social Services in Manchester – the Child Protection Team.'

'What's the connection?'

'Marnie's parents were foster carers. Francis Moffatt organised the placements. He was in and out of their house. Maybe Moffatt developed an unhealthy interest in Marnie, or one of the foster kids became fixated on her.'

Gennia scrawls a note. 'Has Zoe remembered anything else?'

Ruiz glances at the teenager, who is sitting

cross-legged on his sofa with her laptop resting on her thighs. She's listening to something on earbuds, watching TV and typing. Multi-tasking in the modern age.

'I'll need to talk to her again,' says Gennia.

'I can bring her in.'

All my life I have lied. I lied to escape, I lied to be loved, I lied for power; I lied to lie. These falsehoods gave me a story more palatable than the truth and people swallowed it without chewing and asked for more. Yet I do not regard myself as a dishonest man. I have sought only what belongs to me and what I have been denied.

So much has happened to Marnie since our lives intersected: two marriages, two children, one divorce and countless moments of hope and joy and sadness. I know her worst fears and her greatest secrets. I know how she got that little scar on her shin, which she scraped on a rusty valve on an old inner tube. And that pale, almost invisible, mark above her left eyebrow where she tripped over and hit her head on the window seat and needed four stitches.

I know her favourite clothes are jeans and baggy sweaters. She votes Liberal Democrat. She reads novels rather than non-fiction. She likes modern art but hates shopping. All of this is background noise – necessary, but irrelevant – but the small things bring us closer, our similarities not our differences: how she leads with her left leg when she pulls on her jeans; how she sticks out her tongue when she concentrates; how red wine gives her headaches and cabbage gives her wind and how she puts on a different voice on the phone and whimpers like a blind kitten when she orgasms. I have seen her hungover, heartbroken, pregnant, frightened, joyful and lost.

Now the past and present have collided and I am sitting here at this scrubbed pine table watching Marnie wash the dishes and wipe the benches. This is how I imagined it would be. After all the years of waiting, here she is, barefoot, pale and beautiful. It has changed everything, transfigured everything.

I used to worry that I would love Marnie more in the moments before she knew about me, before she knew the truth, but I love her even more now that she's here, standing at the sink, putting washed dishes in the drainer. It is as though she has been formed by my desire, every piece fashioned from nothing and made to perfection, from the fine hairs on her legs to the scarp of dried skin along the edge of her foot. And somehow, just by being herself, she has added a drop of colour to a drab and dreary world; colour that is leaking into every corner, bringing brightness and joy.

My motives were always honourable. I have to make her believe that. I have to show her that I have made her stairs less steep, I have shielded her and protected her and smoothed her path. When she knows the truth she'll forgive me.

Marnie turns. 'Please don't stare at me.'

'I'm sorry.'

The table has been wiped clean. She folds the dishcloth and hangs it over the tap in the sink, pausing for a moment to look at her reflection. What is she thinking? She's trying to remember who I am? Ever since we arrived at the farmhouse, she's sensed some connection between us, but she can't work out what it is.

Elijah is in bed. I heard her singing him a lullaby to help him fall asleep. It's a song her mother used to sing to her. Marnie goes to her own bedroom without excusing herself. It annoys me how she cringes when she passes close to me, but I will content myself with the fact that she is here.

Night has fully taken hold now. When I finish my coffee, I wash the cup and walk past her bedroom. I knock on the door. Enter. She hasn't changed her clothes. She's sitting on the edge of the bed, her knees tight together.

'Goodnight, Marnella.'

She looks at me uncertainly.

'My room is just down the hall. If you need anything let me know.'

'I'm worried about Zoe.'

'You want to see her?'

'Can I?'

'I can get her for you.'

'No, don't do that. I didn't mean . . .'

'What did you mean?'

'Nothing. It doesn't matter.' She has one more question. 'What happened to Daniel?'

'We can talk about that tomorrow.'

'Tell me now.'

'No.'

The door closes and I move along the hallway, glancing in at Elijah, who is curled up against the wall. I will have to tell Marnie about Daniel. What will I say? I thought he was a keeper, but she was too soft, too forgiving. She gave him second chances and he gambled them away. He said he was going to make it up to her, but the more he looked into the past, the closer he got to me.

It had never occurred to Daniel that another man might love Marnie more than he did. And when he finally confronted me, he kept asking me to explain and pleading to talk to Marnie as though I could conjure her out of thin air.

'We are not the same person,' I told him, 'we just share the same story.'

CHAPTER 53

Elijah has wet the bed. Marnie changes his pyjamas and pulls the sheets from the mattress. She holds her fingers to Elijah's forehead, checking his temperature, and puts her hand on his chest, feeling for any rattle in his breathing. It's not until she turns around that she notices Owen in the doorway. Shirtless. The ammoniac smell of urine seems to ignite something in him.

'He's too old to be wetting the bed.'

'He had a nightmare.'

'He's too old for nightmares.'

Marnie ignores him and continues tucking fresh sheets beneath the mattress.

She smiles at Elijah. 'You can sleep in my bed, baby.'

'No he can't,' says Owen. 'He sleeps here. This is *his* room.'

Marnie can see how angry he is, his mouth twitching at the corners and his forearms knotted and scrolled with veins. She can't decide what's more frightening, his rages or the way they abruptly end, as if nothing has happened, or worst of all the way he silently stares at her.

Marnie kisses Elijah goodnight and goes back to her room. Owen has followed her. Marnie washes her hands in the en suite, eyeing him in the mirror. She turns and crosses the room until she's standing directly in front of him. Taking his hand, she pushes it under her nightdress, between her legs.

'Is this what you want?' she whispers. 'Then will you let us go?'

He pulls his hand away as though scalded.

'No, not for that,' he says, stammering, stepping away. 'I'm not a p-p-pervert!'

Marnie gawks at him incredulously. 'You were watching me from my ceiling – that *makes* you a pervert.'

'You don't understand.'

He looks distraught, uttering a quavering complaint halfway between a wail and a denial. He leaves, storming down the hallway. She can hear him slamming a door and his body hitting a mattress.

Marnie's skin feels dirty. Soiled. She draws a bath and tries to scrub herself clean. Slipping beneath the surface, she stares up through the water, trying to remember what she can't remember. She was just a little girl when she arrived at the farm. Four when her mother died. Thirteen when she was thrown from her horse. They moved to the farm because her mother wanted to be closer to nature. She grew vegetables and made candles and apple cider, which she sold at the growers' market. Her father didn't care where they lived, although he missed the pubs in Manchester and his mates who talked about football like experts although rarely went to Old Trafford or Maine Road to see the local derby games. Thomas was away a lot, working on the rigs, and when he came home his booming voice would make cups jump and plates rattle.

The oak tree in the yard is smaller than Marnie remembers. It used to be an ogre that threw shadows against her bedroom wall at night. And the big old-fashioned bathtub is half the size, which means she has to concertina her knees to get her head beneath the water.

How did Owen know about the farm? Why can't she remember him? Normally she hates recalling her childhood. Her bullying and disobedience created headaches for her father and stepmother. And she was forever being taken to various doctors and psychiatrists. She spent four years at a psych unit in London being treated by Dr Sterne, living with his family on weekends. He told her about Malcolm – a figment, a ghost, the supposed 'other' half of her personality – but Marnie's own mind was always clear. Malcolm didn't exist.

Out of the bath, she checks on Elijah once more before crawling into bed and listening to the water slowly draining. At some point she falls asleep, but doesn't dream.

CHAPTER 54

Still in darkness, Joe orders a cab and returns to the mansion block. The sky is clear but heavy grey clouds are gathering in the west as though waiting for daybreak before beginning their march across London.

Joe signs in at the police caravan and is given latex gloves and plastic covers for his shoes. Forensics officers have swabbed, dusted, scraped and vacuumed, but the crime scene will remain a crime scene until all the samples are tested.

Joe climbs the stairs and waits for the constable to unlock the door and pull away the police tape that warns CRIME SCENE. DON'T CROSS.

Once inside, he waits for his eyes to adjust to the light. For some reason he thinks of Julianne, who will still be asleep, curled up on her side with one hand beneath her pillow. She hates him doing work like this – delving into the minds of psychopaths and sociopaths – because she fears it like a contagion that will infect everyone around him.

For his part, Joe feels guilty for having doubts about Marnie. Yes, she withheld information from him, but not for personal gain. She didn't believe

447

in Malcolm, or she regarded him as a figment of her imagination, best forgotten, purged from her history.

Starting in the hallway, Joe studies the wall of photographs and clippings, looking for unusual patterns or gaps in the chronology. Some of the photographs must have been stolen but others have been taken with hidden cameras or telephoto lenses. What did he focus upon? None of the images are graphically sexual. He didn't take pictures of Marnie or Zoe undressing or bathing.

According to Daniel's Big Red Book, Marnie was born in Manchester, but grew up on a farm. Most of her childhood photographs are in a rural setting, but there are no shots of her as a baby or before she started school. The earliest images show her aged about seven or eight. There are pictures of her riding a bike along a narrow country lane and sitting on a tractor and squatting next to a narrow stream. It's not easy to watch someone when they live in a small community. Perhaps her stalker belonged in this place, which is why he could blend so easily into his surroundings.

Continuing to study the collage of images and ephemera, Joe notices how the fashions changed and Marnie's body developed. She graduated from tomboy clothes and began wearing dresses, short blouses and figure-hugging jeans. There are pictures of a school speech day, an outdoor ceremony with dignitaries summoning prize-winning students onto a stage. These images were taken with a long

lens and the edges are slightly blurred by shrub-
bery. He must have been hiding in the undergrowth
or in a tree.

There are photographs from university, snatched
between lectures or while Marnie ate in the cafe-
teria. Others were taken in Italy on a holiday. She's
wearing a crop-top, beneath a big hat and
sunglasses. Joe notices her youth and beauty. He
remembers Marnie hugging him and can almost
feel the warmth of her body against his and can
picture the sprinkle of freckles in the curved hollow
of her pale, melancholy breasts. She is his patient.
Off-limits. Married. Vulnerable. There is no future
for such thoughts.

Joe can't find any shots of Marnie's first wedding
and Zoe being born. 'Where were you?' he asks
out loud, as though speaking to the man with the
camera. 'Why did you disappear?'

There are also relatively few photographs of Marnie
between the ages of eight and twelve when she spent
long stints at the psych ward in London and living
with Dr Sterne. 'Is that when you met her?' Joe asks
out loud. 'Were you working at the hospital? Is that
why you didn't need to take photographs or hide in
ceilings, because you were already so close to her?
What other explanation could there be? Maybe you
were sick . . . or in prison.'

Joe walks into the second bedroom. Mrs Cargill
spent her last months here, terminally ill with
cancer. An oxygen bottle stands next to the bed;
a mask and plastic tubing are looped around the

valve. The man who cared for her claimed to work for social services and called himself Owen, but no record exists of a palliative care nurse being assigned to Mrs Cargill.

Did he win this old woman's trust to get close to Marnie or did he have another reason to care for her? Somebody paid for the funeral in cash and told the undertaker he was related, but didn't give his surname or accept a receipt.

Joe leans against the window frame, gazing through the dirty glass, imagining an old woman dying, sipping her last breath, pale as candle-wax, her world slowly going dark.

The police constable has waited for him on the landing. 'Seen enough, sir?' he asks.

Joe nods and thanks him. Outside he takes a deep breath, savouring the fresh air. The wind blows his coat open and he decides to walk for a while, stretching his legs. Hampstead Heath is as good a place as any. Catching another cab, he gets dropped off near Jack Straw's Castle and sets off across East Heath towards Kenwood House. A heavy shower has been and gone, before the sun prevailed again, turning the puddles to silver. Now a breeze sweeps wetly through the leaves sending droplets cascading over his head. Some of them trickle down his face and fall from his chin.

Clearing his own mind, Joe tries to focus on that of another, looking for some kind of architecture in the details, along with mental footprints that he can follow. He has always been fascinated by why things happen; how small occurrences keep adding to each other, layer upon layer. Human behaviour seems so random, yet can be plotted and graphed. The man who watched Marnie is someone from her past. It takes time and money to devote oneself so completely to another human being. He won't work a normal job. He will have a source of funds or work part-time, possibly from home.

He has an invisible quality – an ability to see but not be seen – but rather than use technology such as microchip cameras and surveillance equipment to watch Marnie, he chose to be physically close to her, only metres away.

Voyeurism is a psychosexual disorder where a person derives sexual pleasure and gratification from looking at the naked bodies or observing the sexual acts of others. It is a form of paraphilia that can range from peeping through bathroom windows, to eavesdropping on erotic conversations, or filming up skirts at shopping malls. It is the act of observing that excites the voyeur. He may fantasise about having sex with the subject of his infatuation, but such fantasies are rarely consummated.

Stalking is different. Most stalkers imagine their victims are secretly in love with them – or would be, given the opportunity. These delusions of romance and a grand love affair tend to become more and more 'real' as the stalking continues. It's only a matter of time, the stalker thinks, before she reciprocates. Once she knows me, she'll love me.

There are stages to the obsession. The attraction phase can be instantaneous and the urge immediate. Most stalkers will find elaborate ways to be close to someone – joining the same gym, going to the same church, shopping at the same supermarket . . .

The anxious phase is when a stalker begins to believe the subject of their obsession feels a mutual attraction. The slightest contact – a sideways look or a smile – is seen as evidence of their 'relationship', proof of their love.

In Marnie's case, it's different. This man has watched her for decades, yet hasn't acted upon his desires until now. He hasn't sought to be at the centre of her life. Instead he's chosen to watch, to oversee, to protect, but more importantly to stay hidden. It's almost as though he skipped the anxious phase and graduated straight to the obsession stage – the onset of tunnel vision, full of neurotic and compulsive behaviours.

The final phase is the destructive one, which can happen when the victim rejects or maligns the stalker. Anger turns to rage, which turns into a desperate need for revenge. Either that or the idealised victim fails to live up to the fantastic expectations of the stalker and must be punished for falling short.

Joe pauses at the top of the ridge and looks south across London. He can see the dome of Primrose Hill and the Post Office Tower. Further south the London Eye circles lazily and the skyline slowly disappears into the haze.

Stop generalising, he tells himself. Be more specific. How could this person have watched Marnie for so long without revealing himself? He was in her ceiling. He saw her marry twice and twice bring babies home. He used the name Malcolm, which means he knew about Marnie's 'other' personality. Was he there when her mind split off? Did he steal her case notes from Dr Sterne's study . . . from Joe's office?

If Joe could sit in front of this man, what would he ask him? He would try to move back through his life, drawing a picture of his family, friends, relationships and schooling. What sort of relationship did he have with his mother and father? What is it like now? How did he get on at primary school and secondary school? Has he had many girlfriends? Has he done this before? What work does he do?

Stalkers like this man are rare, but not unknown. They can be found in prisons, special hospitals and regional secure units, as well as in the community. They have been written about, studied and interviewed. They tend to be socially anxious and to suffer from low self-esteem or the fear of being rejected. Their life is dominated by the pursuit of the 'one', the subject of their obsession, the only person who will bring them true happiness and make their life complete.

Joe takes a notebook from his pocket and clicks the pen against the back of his wrist. He jots down several bullet points.

- *Loner with few male friends.*
- *He will have a history of perfectionism and obsessive relationships dominated by jealousy.*
- *Women will interest him, but none will match up to Marnie.*
- *He has sacrificed his career and social relationships for her.*
- *He has watched women before.*
- *Above average intelligence, but no evidence of extensive formal education.*
- *Possible military training (high degree of planning and discipline)*
- *Good local knowledge. Ordinary appearance. (He didn't draw attention to himself and disappeared quickly from the crime scenes.)*

Joe reads the list again, aware that it's not enough.

CHAPTER 55

Waking before dawn, Marnie puts on the same clothes and opens the curtains. The sky beyond the ridge is beginning to brighten and the stars are fading. She goes to the kitchen and hears an axe thudding into wood. Owen is up and working. When does he sleep?

Marnie checks the back door. Unlocked. Quickly, she wakes Elijah, experiencing an odd sense of déjà vu – a fleeting memory of being woken and bundled into clothes. She pulls up Elijah's trousers and ties his laces, tucking in his shirt, straightening his fringe.

'I'm hungry.'

'We're going to eat later,' she whispers. 'First we're going on an adventure.'

'Where?'

'Away. You have to be very brave.'

Marnie strips a pillowcase from the bed and fills it with a sweater and socks. She goes to her bedroom and looks for something sturdy to wear on her feet. Yesterday she noticed a pair of heavy work boots in her wardrobe.

The axe is still falling outside. She can hear Owen

whistling as he drops logs into the wheelbarrow. Opening the back door, she checks the porch and slides along the wall until she reaches the edge of the house. Peering around the corner she can see the garden and half the barn, but not the woodpile or Owen.

She goes back to Elijah. 'When I tell you, we're going to run really fast.'

'Like a race?'

'That's right, but you're going to hold onto Mummy's hand and be very quiet.'

Marnie ties a knot in the top of the pillowcase. She opens the kitchen door. Once they're on the grass, she starts to run, skirting the side of the house and heading down the slope, half dragging and half carrying Elijah. Marnie isn't conscious of her legs carrying her, or her feet striking the ground. It's too dark to make out the hollows and mounds, which make her stumble and almost fall.

She doesn't look back. Elijah is asking her to slow down. It's two hundred metres to the nearest grove of trees. She stops. Breathing hard.

'You hurt me, Mummy.'

'I'm sorry, but we have keep moving.'

The sound of an engine makes Marnie turn her head. Not a car. She glances up the slope towards the house and the barn. A single headlight emerges from the barn. The motorbike leaps over the mounds and potholes, the engine roaring.

Marnie is up and running again. Her field of vision is like a shaky hand-held camera with the image lurching back and forth. They come to a cattle grid where parallel metal bars cover a trench to stop cows moving between fields. Marnie makes her way across, balancing on the narrow bars. Elijah slips and his leg wedges between them. Marnie tries to lift him. He cries out. She reaches through the tubes and turns his foot, pushing as well as pulling.

The motorbike is getting nearer.

It won't move. She undoes the laces and slips off his trainer. His foot slips free. She carries him to the side of the track and they slide down an embankment. The motorbike swings around the nearest corner and rattles across the cattle grid. It stops. The front wheel pivots from side to side, as Owen uses the headlight to scan the trees. Marnie is lying on top of Elijah with her hand over his mouth, her mouth to his ear, hushing him. The engine dies. She holds her breath. The beam of light swings back and forth over her head. Seconds tick by. The engine starts again and she listens as it rumbles away.

Marnie rolls onto her back, hearing the soft gasping of the breeze in the trees . . . and water. The stream must be nearby. It triggers another memory: an early morning just like this one, with the same emotions, the same thudding heart, running. Elijah whimpers. She lifts him onto her lap. He clings to her like a baby marsupial looking for a pouch to crawl into. Cradling his head, she rocks him from side to side, humming a song. The tune sparks another recollection and she pictures a child sitting in the front parlour of the farmhouse. The wheels on the bus went round and round. The people on the bus stood up and sat down . . .

Her mother was pregnant. Struggling with the weight of it. Her father was away working. They heard a motorbike engine coming up the track, getting closer. Marnie ran onto the front veranda. A man climbed off the bike. Holding his hat. Wearing a uniform. Her mother walked across the lawn to the gate. She talked to the man, told him to leave, but he didn't seem to be listening. Instead he came into the house and sat at the kitchen table, too big for the room, his legs stretching out, his boots leaving marks on the linoleum.

He wanted to dance. Marnie's mother said no. He forced her up and they moved around the kitchen, bumping into furniture. Every so often, the man looked over her shoulder and stared at Marnie.

The man stayed for supper. He slept on her daddy's side of the bed. During the night her mother woke Marnie and made her put on her dressing gown and slippers before they tiptoed through the house, out the door trying not to make a sound. They went to the barn. Marnie's mother strapped her in the car seat.

The car wouldn't start first time. She tried again and again. A light came on in the house. The soldier came out and chased them down the driveway, wearing his singlet and dungarees.

It was still dark. They couldn't travel quickly on the track. They had to slow down at the cattle grid and to cross the stream. She heard the motorbike engine and saw the single headlight reflecting from the rear-view mirror, lighting up her mother's eyes.

There was a bang and the car shuddered. It left the road and crashed through a wall of brown reeds at the edge of a stream. The first tree ripped off the driver's door. The second tree spun the car in the opposite direction, scooping water through the open window and spewing mud onto the windscreen. Marnie didn't see what happened to her mother. She wasn't behind the wheel when the car came to a stop, axle-deep in water, sinking at the front. The engine cooled with a series of pings and knocks.

The soldier waded into the stream and unbuckled Marnie from her seat. Water swirled around his thighs as he lifted her onto his back and carried her to dry land.

Marnie's mother was lying broken in the reeds, sticky with blood and glass. She moaned and her legs spread automatically and she tried to push, gritting her teeth. Her eyes opened and fear lived in them like an animal caught in a trap.

'Help me,' she whispered.

He licked his palms and smoothed his hair. He walked away.

Marnie can see the scene behind her closed lids as clearly as if she had taken a photograph or recorded it on film: her mother moaning, her back arching, the baby coming . . . not moving.

There is a sound on the track above her. Owen is on foot now, carrying a torch, looking for their footprints. The sky has grown brighter as the light gathers behind Marnie. Her blouse is soaked in sweat and the breeze has found a way through the fabric to make her shiver.

Elijah has stopped crying, but his breathing is shallow. He's not strong enough for this. She should have stayed at the farmhouse; found another way.

'I know you're there, Marnie,' shouts Owen. 'I can see your footprints.'

He waits.

'I found Elijah's shoe. It's time to come home.'

Marnie stands and steps out from behind the tree, holding Elijah. Her legs wobble for a moment. Owen slips down the bank and takes Elijah from her. He slides a plank of timber over the cattle grid to help them cross. Marnie follows him up the track to the farmhouse, where he unlaces her muddy shoes.

'Porridge for breakfast,' he says. 'Warm you up.'

CHAPTER 56

Zoe has spent all morning at the police station going over CCTV footage. After the first hour the images began to blur into each other until she doubted whether she could recognise herself if she appeared on the screen. Rhonda Firth has been keeping her primed with giant cups of cola and crushed iced that give her an ice-cream headache if she drinks them too quickly.

The past twenty-four hours have been full of phantoms for Zoe. Last night she woke with a scream caught in her throat and a man leaning over her bed with bloody stumps instead of hands. The shadows were only shadows, she told herself, but she didn't sleep again. She sat by the window in the attic room and wondered whether her mother was looking out at the same rain that beat on the leaves and dripped from the wires and gurgled in the pipes.

Now she's sitting outside Gennia's office, waiting to go home. Where is home? She misses her mother and Elijah. She misses Daniel. If he were here, he'd know what to do.

Later, on the drive to Ruiz's place, Zoe stares out the car window, watching London in the rain. She's sick of people telling her how brave she is and how everything is going to be all right.

At the house Ruiz makes her a coffee with a machine that makes diarrhoeal noises. Zoe wants to ask him about his missing ring finger and why he limps, but that would mean engaging in a conversation, which might require her answering questions. She opts instead for silence.

Ruiz brings her the coffee. It's too milky.

'Have you eaten?'

'I'm not hungry.'

'I can make you something. How about a sandwich?'

She looks at him. *Which bit didn't he understand?*

He opens the fridge. 'I don't have any bread . . . or cheese.' He's silent for a moment. 'I'll go out and pick up a few things. Do you want to come?'

'No.'

'Will you be OK by yourself?'

'Yes.'

'Anything in particular you want?'

'No.'

'Answer the phone if it rings?'

'OK.'

She hears the front door close and opens her laptop. It finds the wireless signal and opens on the Facebook page that she set up for Daniel. She glances down the list of recent comments, answering some of them or pressing the 'like' button.

A dialogue box pops open in the lower right corner of her screen.

Zoe?

There is picture of a cartoon character next to the message – a squirrel with a mask over its eyes. Zoe types a reply:

Who is this?

Are you alone?

Yes.

I've been looking at the photographs you posted. I can't believe you used that one of me sitting on the cannon. I look like such an idiot.

Dad?

Hi, Dimples, it's been a while. I've been reading your postings. You sound so sad.

Only Daniel ever called her 'Dimples'. She types:

How do I know it's you?

Good point. That's my girl – always ask for proof. For your thirteenth birthday Mum and I gave you a hair straightening wand and tickets to see Jessie J at the Hammersmith Apollo.

Zoe stares at the screen, reading the message twice, wanting so much to believe. She types a reply:

What does Mum keep at the back of her underwear drawer in the old sunglasses case?

You shouldn't know what she keeps in that case.

What is it?

You know what it is, Zoe. You shouldn't be touching your mother's things.

I don't touch it.

Zoe feels her heart thumping in her chest. She types another question:

What did we do for my twelfth birthday?

We went to Paris for the weekend and stayed in that hotel near the Moulin Rouge that looked like a brothel.

OMG. It's really you! Where have you been? Can you call me? I want to hear your voice?

I can't call, Zoe. Not yet.

Zoe keeps typing, trying to convince him:

Mum and Elijah are missing. They say some guy has been following her. You have to come back and help find them.

I'm going to sort everything out. The man who took your Mum is a friend of mine. He's been keeping an eye on you.

But he was in our ceiling. He could see into my bedroom.

He wouldn't have hurt you.

So Mum and Elijah are with you?

Not yet, but we'll be together soon.

Someone killed Trevor. They cut off his hands.

See how dangerous it is? That's why you have to do exactly what I say. You can't tell anyone that I've been in contact. You can't show them these messages or reveal to anyone that you've heard from me – not the police or your friends. Nobody. It's really important. Do you understand?

No. Why can't you come home?

I owe some people a lot of money. Dangerous people. They were threatening to hurt us. That's why I went away . . . to keep you safe. Where are you staying?

In Fulham with Professor Joe and Vincent: they're helping the police look for Mum and Elijah.

Where are they there now?

Vincent has gone to the shops.

Do you have any money?

Not much.

You need to get £25. Can you do that?

I think so.

Go to King's Cross station. I want you to buy a train ticket to Walsden in West Yorkshire. You'll have to change trains in Leeds. Don't pack anything. Don't tell anyone. You'll have to sneak away. Nobody can know.

Why?

Think of what happened to Trevor. Don't tell anyone. I've found somewhere safe for us. We can be together.

I've missed you.

Me, too.

CHAPTER 57

The police car pulls up outside a row of terraces in a run-down area of central Manchester. A group of black teenagers are milling around the corner shop as though guarding the neighbourhood. Smoking. Stopping cars. Talking to girls. The journey from London has taken over three hours under siren, weaving between traffic and semi-trailers that travelled in convoys with all the obstinacy and application of freight trains.

DI Gennia finishes a phone call and climbs from the patrol car. He brushes lint from his shoulders and puts on his hat, adjusting the brim. Joe O'Loughlin joins him on the footpath, glancing at a small neat terrace where someone has cared enough to plant flowerboxes and clean the flagstone step.

'Francis Moffatt worked for the local health authority for thirty years, mainly in child protection,' says Gennia. 'He left the job eight years ago. Since then he's been driving trucks for a courier company. This is his mother's house – his only listed address.'

He rings the doorbell. After a long wait an old woman answers, opening the door a crack.

'My gas and electricity are fine. I don't want a new plan.'

Gennia flashes his badge. 'We're looking for Francis.'

Her eyes light for a moment and her demeanour changes. 'Is everything all right? He's a good boy. He looks after me.'

She opens the door wider. Dressed in a floral print dress, boots and a sagging cardigan, she looks as if she's been pickled in vinegar like a small brown onion and topped with the sort of blue-rinse hairstyle they issue women with every pension card.

'Did he get a speeding ticket? I've told him not to drive so fast.'

'Is he at home?' asks Gennia.

'He's sleeping. He works nights.'

The detective pushes past her. 'You'd better wake him.'

Mrs Moffatt leads them along a darkened hallway to the kitchen where she shoos an overweight corgi from beneath the table. The dog waddles over to Joe and sniffs his shoes. She puts the kettle on and goes to wake her son.

There are photographs on a mantelpiece above an old stove and more in the drawing room, which is full of big, dark, vague furniture. The images are in tarnished silver frames and show several children and grandchildren, scattered now.

Mrs Moffatt reappears. 'He's getting dressed.' A toilet flushes from along the hallway.

She potters, taking out cups and putting milk in a small white jug. The kitchen smells of overripe fruit and the lone window is so dirty it gives the impression the house is completely submerged in water.

Floorboards creak. Francis Moffatt appears, a thin, dour man with a close-clipped white beard and an ugly scar beneath his left eye. His hair is receding at the front and long at the back, dragged into a greying ponytail. He takes a chair at the table, scratching his stomach through an unbuttoned shirt.

'This better be important, I didn't get home until five this morning.'

'When did you last see Marnella Logan?' asks Gennia.

Francis frowns. He has false teeth, which he pushes forward with his tongue and then sucks back in again. 'Why?'

'Answer the question.'

Francis sneaks a glance at Joe. 'Until last year, I hadn't heard her name in almost twenty years. Her husband came to see me.'

'Daniel Hyland?'

'Yeah. He wanted to know about her childhood. I couldn't really help him. Mostly I dealt with her folks.'

'Meaning?'

'They were foster carers. They had a farm in

West Yorkshire, about twenty miles from here. I used to place kids with them. Marnie was their only child. Started off being a real sweet kid, but then she sort of lost her way.'

Joe leans forward, wanting more. Francis shifts uneasily on his chair. He doesn't like the way the psychologist is staring at him, as though suddenly his mask has been pulled aside and his true character exposed, revealed in every wrinkle and tic.

The kettle has boiled. A thread of steam rises from the spout. Mrs Moffatt adds seething water to the leaves, jamming a lid on the pot. Everybody seems to respect the ceremony, waiting until the tea is poured, the pot raised and lowered, dark brown liquid filling each cup. Milk. Sugar.

Joe is still waiting. Francis raises a cup to his lips, taking a cautious sip.

'When Marnie was eight she stole her father's car and crashed it into a bus shelter, injuring two people. Her father had taught her to drive on the farm, but she could barely see over the wheel. She drove nearly all the way to Manchester. The police called Child Protection. I had to prepare a report for the MSCB. I interviewed Marnie and arranged for her to see a child psychologist. I also spoke to her father and stepmother. They were good people.'

'How many foster kids did you place with the Logans?'

'Christ, I can't remember. There were dozens of them.'

'Any of them develop an unhealthy interest in Marnie?'

The former social worker picks up on the sub-text. 'Has something happened to her?'

'She and her little boy are missing. We believe they may have been abducted.'

'And you think it's one of the foster kids?'

'We're investigating that possibility.'

Francis looks at them sceptically. 'That was a long time ago.'

'Did any of them cause you concern?'

He smiles wryly. 'Every last one of them.'

'Meaning?'

'These were kids who'd been abused, orphaned, abandoned or cut adrift. Some went back to their real families. A few were adopted. Others were in and out of care until they turned eighteen and were in and out of prison after that. Don't get me wrong. I'm not writing them all off. Some turned out OK.' He looks at Joe and Gennia, opening his palms as though stating the obvious. 'Marnie had more problems than most of them and she came from a loving family.'

'How well did you know her?' asks Joe.

'She was jealous of the foster kids – that can happen sometimes, particularly with an only child. She lost her mum and struggled after that. I remember the first Mrs Logan. I met her before Marnie was born.'

'Why?'

'They were living in Manchester back then. Mr

471

Logan called social services because he caught a kid hiding in his basement spying on his wife. I knew the boy. He was one of my cases. His mother had convictions for prostitution, drug possession, neglect . . .'

Joe sits up straighter. His tea has been forgotten. 'Tell me about this boy.'

'I'd known him since he was a wee sprog. Once or twice a week we'd pick him up from the cinema where his mum dumped him because she couldn't afford childcare. Owen didn't watch the films. He preferred looking at the audience. He'd hide beneath the screen and just watch them.'

'How do you know?' asks Joe.

'That's what Owen told me. He was always a bit odd. Quiet. Unemotional. He preferred to sleep under beds than in them. He could climb a wall with his bare feet like he was Spiderman, wedging himself into a corner of the ceiling; and you'd come into a room and not realise he was up there. Scare the bejesus out of you.' Moffatt scratches at his navel and examines his forefinger. 'Once or twice he got caught peering through people's windows. He got a slap on the wrist, but I don't think he stopped. He just got better at hiding. I've never seen a kid who could be so quiet. He simply faded into the background, you know, like he was one of those lizards that change colour.' He clicks his fingers.

'A chameleon,' says Gennia.

'Yeah, one of them.'

'What happened to Owen?' asks Joe.

'Every time we put him into care, his mother would clean up her act and get him back again. Went on for years.'

'When did you last see him?'

Moffatt blows air out of his cheeks. 'When Mr Logan caught Owen in the basement he wanted him charged with trespassing. The police called me because I was Owen's caseworker. He must have been sixteen 'cos he joined the army soon after that. I don't know what happened to Martha.'

'Martha?'

'His mum.'

Gennia has the teacup to his lips as though he's forgotten to sip. 'What was Martha's last name?'

'Cargill.'

CHAPTER 58

DI Gennia is losing his voice. His orders are raspy and thin, as he barks down the radio, gripping the handset like a grenade. 'If he joined the military, they should have his prints on file,' he says, thinking out loud. 'And do a vehicle search using his name. Also look for a mobile phone number.'

Joe is doing his own calculations. If Owen Cargill joined the army at sixteen, he'd be fifty now or thereabouts. As a child he had peered into neighbour's windows, already well known to social services, caught in the ragged net, slipping through it. He joined the army, which can straighten out some teenagers and give them direction. For others it exacerbates their problems, furnishing them with the skills and discipline to stay under the radar without ever getting help.

The old woman was his mother – a former prostitute and heroin addict. Owen survived his childhood despite her not because of her. He nursed her through her final days. She was family. Blood. These aren't the actions of a sociopath or a psychopath.

What is Owen looking for now? What does he crave more than anything else? Love. Affection. Respect. Understanding. It's as though he's been holding his breath for thirty years waiting for this moment. At the same time he's remained pro-active, intervening in Marnie's life, punishing those who wronged her, but never introducing himself or trying to make contact.

Staring into the sky, Joe sees a flock of small black birds lift raggedly from a rooftop as though emerging from a chimney. They circle the tattered sky and return to wherever they came from.

He's in a different part of Manchester now. The houses opposite are pastel-coloured, painted in muted shades of mauve and blue because some corporate body or residents' committee has decided to make the street look more upmarket.

This is where Owen Cargill lived. Flat 2, number 24. The Logans were in the house next door, No. 22. Forty years ago this was a poor area of Manchester full of cheap houses, bedsits and council flats. Now it's home to doctors, accountants, lawyers and other professionals who can afford the inner-city prices.

Gennia's mobile phone beeps. He slides his finger across the screen. The text message has a photograph attached. 'That's him,' he says, showing Joe the phone, 'Owen Ruben Cargill. We don't have anything more recent.'

The image shows a young soldier in dress uniform with a beret and short-cropped hair. He's barely out of his teens but Joe recognises him anyway.

'I've met him.'

'What?'

'I'm almost certain. About a week ago I was mugged near Chelsea Bridge. Three guys. Young. Drunk. Looking for trouble. They tried to throw me into the river. This is the guy who chased them off.'

'Owen Cargill?'

'I didn't know his name.'

Joe studies the photograph, remembering that evening; the police cars on the opposite side of the river, the briny stink of low tide and his own ineptitude. Patrick Hennessy died that night. These events must be linked.

'Did you report it to the police?' asks Gennia.

'They told me to fill out an incident report.'

'Did you?'

'No.'

The detective grunts in disgust. Joe goes over the details of the confrontation again. There was a man watching him from the bridge just before the attack. Was it Owen Cargill? He came to Joe's rescue, but wouldn't give his name. Joe tried to give him his business card. Wanted him to call. Why would Owen Cargill risk such a meeting? To what end?

Another message arrives on Gennia's phone. He reads from the screen.

'Cargill was discharged from the army in 1988.

We're asking the MOD for his military records. In the meantime, I want to get his photograph in front of Zoe Logan.'

Joe gets out of the car and stands beneath the stiff crown of a birch tree. He walks along the footpath and turns the corner, clambering onto a wall to look into the rear gardens. Martha Cargill worked as a prostitute. Later she sold drugs and operated other girls from various addresses, taking a percentage of their earnings. Social services took Owen away from her and put him in foster homes. He was a loner, hiding in basements, peering through windows, pressing his face to the glass. He lived in this street. He would have looked through these same windows; and climbed these trees.

Dogs are barking. Curtains move. Joe jumps down and retraces his steps. As he walks past number 22 the door opens and a middle-aged woman emerges carrying a plastic bag of rubbish. Opening her bin, she dumps the bag and squints at Gennia warily. 'Can I help you?'

The detective holds up his badge. 'Police.'

'Is something wrong?'

'We're investigating two families who once lived in this street.'

'In my house?' She's nosy rather than concerned. 'When was that then?'

'Late seventies.'

'We've only been here since 1997,' she says. 'Would you like to look inside?'

Joe accepts the offer. Gennia stays with the car.

'We've renovated,' the woman says, leading Joe through a reception room and open-plan kitchen, pointing out features as though she's selling the place. He can smell toast and microwaved food. Descending the side steps, he walks into the garden and sees the laundry door.

'That leads to the basement,' she says. 'It's a good storage area. Place was full of junk when we moved in.'

Joe dips his head and steps into the laundry, which has a polished cement floor. The basement extends further beneath the house, but the light only allows him to see fifteen or so feet.

'We had to redo the floors,' the woman says. 'You could see right through the gaps. Made it cold in winter.'

Barely listening, Joe tries to picture a teenage boy crouching in the darkness. Neglected as a child, perhaps abused, he learned how to immerse himself in imaginary games, in films and in books and fantasies. Instead of becoming gregarious with good inter-personal skills and sensitivity, he grew accustomed to being an onlooker rather than a participant.

According to Francis Moffatt, Owen was dropped at the cinema and told to hide between sessions. He would have soaked up the details of countless films, many of them highly inappropriate, but he wasn't old enough or sophisticated enough to understand that most of these high-impact storylines weren't real. He saw horror stories and sex shows and family dramas. He saw perfect families and happy endings and then looked at his own family and wondered what had happened to him. If he'd been an ordinary, robust, uncomplicated young boy, being trapped in this world between screen and audience might have made no difference, but Owen had a delicacy and sensitivity about him; and he had nobody to interpret or guide his understanding of these things.

Soon he began to create his own stories with extravagant plots full of secret agents and spies. He stole into houses or peeped through windows, watching people and collecting details of their lives. He was still trapped between worlds, watching without participating.

At sixteen he joined the army. Suddenly, this boy who craved solitude couldn't escape from people. Surrounded by recruits and officers, he lived in noisy barracks and mess halls with rarely a quiet moment. Initially, nothing marked him out as being different. He did the training. He learned how to protect, defend and kill. But he *felt* different. He had always been a voyeur, watching the world from the outside, but now people expected him to partake, to play a role. Owen didn't know how.

At some point in this process, he began to fixate upon Marnie Logan. Of all the people in the world he brushed up against – why did he become obsessed with her?

Joe's mobile vibrates against his heart, like a tiny

bird is trapped in his pocket. Ruiz's number is on the screen. He ducks out of the basement and takes the call in the garden.

'She's gone,' says Ruiz.

'Zoe?'

'She left a note on the kitchen table. She says her stepdad is still alive and she's going to meet him.' Joe's fingers tighten around the phone. Ruiz is still talking. 'I was only away for fifteen minutes. When I got back she wasn't here.'

Joe is moving back through the house. 'What did she take?'

'Her satchel and some cash I kept in a drawer.'

'How much?'

'Eighty quid.'

'Did she get a phone call?'

'I checked the call return number. Nothing.'

'What about her mobile?'

'The police took it from her.'

Joe's mind is racing through the possibilities. Her laptop. Someone must have contacted Zoe via email or in a chatroom.

'How long has she been missing?'

'Twenty minutes at most.'

'What was she wearing?'

Ruiz has to think: Jeans, a Clash T-shirt, a hoodie and white Converse trainers.

Joe is also running through the options. Somebody either picked Zoe up, or she's on foot, probably heading for the nearest tube station or catching a bus. She took money, which means she could be heading for one of the mainline hubs or a long-distance coach terminal.

Joe has retraced his steps through the house, emerging from the front door. Gennia is sitting in the passenger seat, talking on the radio. He looks up. 'What's wrong?'

'You're not going to like this.'

The patrol car weaves aggressively through heavy traffic, the siren sounding as if it's coming from somewhere behind them. The detective sergeant behind the wheel is concentrating hard on the road while Gennia yells into a two-way radio, issuing a description of Zoe Logan, aged fifteen, five-five, slim build, short dark hair, blue-green eyes, last seen at 12.30 p.m. in the Fulham area in London.

'Pull a photograph from her police interview. Don't make her look like a suspect.'

When he's finished he turns to Joe. His eyes are cold, annoyed. 'Why are you so sure it's not Daniel Hyland?'

'He's been missing thirteen months – why turn up now?'

'Zoe is a bright girl. She would have demanded proof.'

'Cargill has been watching them. He knows every detail about this family. That's how he convinced her.'

'You said he was obsessed with Marnie, why take Zoe?'

'I don't know.'

'Maybe he's doing it *for* Marnie.'

'She wouldn't put Zoe at risk.'

Joe grips the handle above his head as the car takes another corner. Why can't he see it? The logic. The motivation. Most human behaviour is shaped by social norms – the cultural conventions, how to dress, what to eat, how to interact with others, the right and wrong way to do things. Psychologists are like mathematicians, searching for the patterns in nature so they can predict outcomes. But this case involves people who don't lie in the middle of bell curves, but on the 'tails'.

Joe tries to put himself in Marnie's position. What will she do? Fight. Survive. Protect.

'Where else did she live?' he asks, hearing how ragged his voice has become.

Gennia looks over the seat. 'What do you mean?'

'Owen Cargill has been following Marnie for decades, waiting for this moment. He's likely to have prepared a place where they can be together – somewhere of special significance.'

'Such as?'

'A previous address.'

CHAPTER 59

'Look, Mummy, I made a picture.'
Elijah waves a page in front of Marnie's face. Her eyes open.

Curled up beneath a blanket, she's still dressed in her muddy clothes. She doesn't know how much of the day has gone or how long she's been lying on the bed. Each time she closes her eyes she can see a wrecked car sitting in the water, a splintered tree, her mother's broken body, blood between her thighs, the brother she couldn't save.

Marnie views the scene from above, as though floating, drifting away until the scene grows further and further away. She had the same feeling when she was hiding with Elijah, a sense of leaving her body and gazing down at herself. How pathetic she'd looked. How weak and useless. A better, stronger person would have managed to escape. A better, stronger version of her would be able to protect her family. Instead she ruined everything. That's why Daniel slept with Penny. It's why he gambled. It's why her first marriage failed and her mother died and she lost her baby brother.

Elijah tugs at her sleeve. 'Who is you talking to, Mummy?'

'Nobody.'

He pulls a plastic frog from his pocket and makes it jump across her pillow.

'Owen says there are frogs in the pond. He says we can catch tadpoles.'

'We're not going to be staying here.'

'But he said . . .'

'This isn't our home.'

Elijah flinches at her tone. Marnie looks at the door. 'Where is he?'

'Outside.'

'What's he doing?'

'Digging a hole.'

Marnie is silent for a few beats. She drags herself to sitting. Everything aches. Then she stands and goes to the bathroom, washing her face and hands before putting on fresh clothes. Her day begins again. She washes Elijah's sheets and hangs them on the outside line under threatening skies. Owen has left her the breakfast dishes. After scrubbing crusted porridge from the pot, she sits on the sofa and listens as Elijah explains *SpongeBob SquarePants* to her. He seems to have seen every episode.

Marnie laces on her muddy boots and walks up the worn track to the barn. She can hear a shovel digging into the earth. Owen has cut the turf away and is turning the soil beneath.

'We'll have a vegetable garden,' he says, leaning on the shovel.

'I remember you,' says Marnie. 'You were there when my mother died.'

Owen doesn't answer. He picks up a military-style canteen and unscrews the lid. The water runs over his chin onto the front of his shirt.

'Did you kill her?'

'No.'

'Could you have saved her?'

'I saved you.'

He goes back to digging, raising a hoe above his head and swinging it hard into the rich dark soil, breaking up clods and separating stones into a pile.

'You still haven't told me why.'

'Why what?'

'Why me? There are millions of people out there, but you followed *me*; you watched *me*. What was the point? So you're a voyeur, you like looking in people's windows. You watched me sleeping . . . showering. There's nothing you haven't seen. You've had your jollies, now leave us alone.'

'You don't understand.'

'Explain it to me.'

'You're not ready.'

Marnie's frustration makes her want to scream.

Owen pauses from his work. 'I have devoted my life to you.'

'I didn't ask—'

'Let me finish. I want you to know how much I've sacrificed and then you'll forgive me.'

'I'll *never* forgive you,' she says, but her voice

lacks the conviction of her heart. 'What did you do to Daniel?'

Owen hesitates. He rests the hoe on his shoulder and stares at mud on the toe of his workboot. 'He was a feckless spendthrift. He gambled away your future. He didn't love you.'

'What did you do?' Marnie's voice croaks and a rash creeps up her neck, splotchy and hot.

'He was unfaithful.'

'What did you do?'

'He got too close to finding me.'

Owen looks past Marnie and the edge of the barn. Almost hidden in a grove of fruit trees planted too haphazardly to be called an orchard, he can see a small enclosure with a handful of grave markers.

Marnie follows his gaze.

'He would have left you anyway,' says Owen.

'You killed him?'

Owen doesn't answer.

'How?'

'He didn't suffer.'

'How?' Her voice sounds thick and clotted with phlegm.

Owen closes his eyes for a moment, as though making a decision. 'He suspected I existed. He was asking questions, searching for people, but he didn't know I was so close. Then he went looking for your old wedding photographs in the wardrobe and discovered the false panel.' He glances at Marnie. 'I know what you're thinking, but his death was inevitable from the moment he betrayed you. I had overlooked so many of his indiscretions, but not that one.'

Marnie opens her mouth to speak and in the end says nothing. Her loneliness is almost complete. She can whisper a hundred words, scream a thousand of them, she can beg, pray, cry, fight or surrender but nothing will bring Daniel back. She has a final act.

Owen is wielding the hoe again. 'I'm going to fence this off so the rabbits don't steal our lettuces. It's a bit late in the season to plant, but we'll be ready for the spring.'

Owen doesn't look at her but he's aware that something has changed between them. He had expected insults, accusations and hatred, but not acceptance.

'I have to go into town,' he says. 'Is there anything you need?'

Marnie doesn't answer.

'I'm going to lock you in the house while I'm gone. Elijah is coming with me.'

'No.'

'I won't be long.'

'Please.'

'I can't trust you yet, Marnie.'

He's walking towards the house. She runs alongside him, tugging at his arm. 'Leave him with me. He's not been well. He's not strong enough. Please don't take him.'

'I'm not going to hurt him . . . unless you're not here when I get back.'

Elijah is playing on the veranda. 'You're coming with me, sport.'

'Where?'

'Into town.'

Marnie wants to fight. She pulls at his shirt. He pushes her onto the porch swing, which rocks with her weight and bashes into the painted wall. 'Don't be foolish. Get in the house.'

Inside, she hears him locking the doors. Moving from window to window, she keeps them in sight as they walk to the barn and disappear inside. Then she watches the car emerge and Owen shutting the barn doors before getting back behind the wheel and driving down the track, disappearing into the trees. Her last glimpse of Elijah is when he turns to look out the rear window.

Even if she could get out, what would she do? Where would she run? How would Elijah cope without her? Instead, she moves through the house, looking for a phone or a computer. She searches his bedroom, opening drawers and the wardrobe, going through his pockets, sliding her hand beneath the mattress.

Two drawers are locked. She searches for a key; upending jars of pens and paperclips, rummaging through the contents. She looks under the desk, pressing her cheek to the floor. The key is a bump on a smooth plane of floorboards. Inside the drawers she finds papers relating to the farm: purchase orders, rate notices, electricity bills, oil deliveries.

Every time she hears a sound, she expects to turn and see Owen in the doorway. There's nothing. No phone. No computer. She moves along the hallway to a part of the farmhouse that she hasn't explored. Another room. Her childhood memories don't extend this far.

The door handle is stiff. She turns it with both hands. The bedroom on the other side belongs to a teenager; it belongs to Zoe, with the same posters on the walls, the same duvet cover, clothes, shoes . . .

Fear and fury balloon inside her. She thought Zoe was safe.

Owen wants her too.

CHAPTER 60

Zoe has a window seat and can rest her head against the glass, watching the fields and farms slide past in a tapestry of browns and greens. A man keeps looking at her from the seat opposite. He's staring at her chest, but glances away each time she moves her head.

There is free internet on the train for thirty minutes. It's painfully slow, but she uses the time to update her status and send a message to Ryan. She tells him that she's found her stepdad and she's going to meet him.

Zoe hasn't eaten since breakfast when Ruiz made her have toast and eggs. She feels guilty about leaving the note. He and Joe had been so nice to her. They didn't treat her like a child. Now they're going to say she's done a childish thing.

The conductor is coming through the carriage, punching tickets. Zoe searches the pockets of her denim jacket. Where did she put it? He reaches her row. The man opposite hands over his ticket and takes it back again. Zoe is still rummaging through her satchel.

'I do have one,' she says.

'Where did you get on the train?'

'King's Cross.'

'Where are you going?'

'Leeds.'

She slides her fingers into the back pocket of her jeans. 'Here it is!'

He looks at the ticket and then at Zoe.

'What's your name?'

She lies. 'Georgia.'

'Are you travelling alone?'

'My mum has gone to the dining car.'

'How old are you?'

'Sixteen.'

'Do you have your student card?'

'Mum has it. I can go and fetch her.'

He hands Zoe her ticket and moves on without saying a word. A woman further up the aisle asks him, 'What was that all about?'

'Police are looking for a runaway, a London girl.'

Greater Manchester police headquarters is at Newton Heath on a new industrial estate, four miles from the centre of the city. The glass-and-concrete building looks like something a biotech company might lease. Clean. Modern. Functional.

Joe waits in the brightly lit atrium while DI Gennia talks to his Northern colleagues; collecting whatever details he can about Owen Cargill. Any juvenile records will have been destroyed, but he may have an adult criminal history and the Ministry of Defence will have his service records.

Joe calls Ruiz. He answers from a noisy location, shouting to be heard.

'Where are you?'

'A CCTV camera picked up Zoe at King's Cross station about three hours ago. She was on the concourse looking at the departure board.'

'Any idea which train she caught?'

'Any one of fifty.'

Joe looks at his watch. King's Cross services North and East England as well as Scotland. 'What time was she sighted?'

'Just after two-thirty.'

She could be as far north as Leeds by now or have stepped off anywhere in between. A station announcement is sounding in the background, warning people not to leave bags unattended.

Ruiz is still talking. 'They're contacting the trains and asking ticket inspectors to look for unaccompanied teenage girls.' He shouts to be heard over the announcement. 'Zoe has a boyfriend. She called him from my place last night. I'm going to see him now.'

On the far side of the foyer, DI Gennia emerges from a lift, his image reflected in the inner glass walls of the atrium that rises six storeys to the ceiling. His driver is alongside him. They march almost in unison to the main doors. Joe starts moving and falls over. He picks himself up and tries again. This time he takes a sideways step and one pace backwards. People are staring. Concentrating, he slides his right foot forward, then his left, then right. He's walking properly, although his left arm refuses to swing.

Gennia briefs him in the car. 'Cargill spent three years in military prison in Colchester for assault and breaching the peace. In 1985 he was convicted of stalking the teenage daughter of his CO, although he denied the charge. Prior to that he had a history of insubordination and disciplinary issues. He went AWOL for five days in 1983 and the following year faced charges of beating up a fellow soldier in a dispute over a girl.'

Gennia hands the page to Joe and continues reading from the next one.

'Cargill did a computer course in prison. He was dishonourably discharged from the army when he finished his sentence at Colchester, but they arranged a job for him at a market research company. After that he set up on his own business, registering domain names and selling them back to people and companies. Cybersquatting. Made a fortune.'

Joe can see the attraction of market research to someone like Owen Cargill. It meant he could study people and observe consumer behaviour. It gave him a reason to ask questions and infiltrate people's lives. Cybersquatting also fitted Owen's profile. He didn't have to invent or build or sell anything. He stood on someone else's shoulders, taking advantage of their neglect or tardiness, making them pay for names they had already turned into brands.

'This is interesting,' says Gennia, handing Joe another page. 'In 1994 Owen Cargill was picked up by police outside a secondary school in Manchester after teachers complained of a man hanging around the school gates.'

Joe does the calculation. 'In 1994 Marnie would have been about fifteen and still at school.'

Gennia is still talking. 'The police cautioned him and let him go.'

'What about his earlier conviction?'

'The MOD didn't pass on the details, which means Cargill was never put on the Sex Offenders Register. That's why we didn't have his fingerprints on file.'

The detective's mobile is ringing. He takes the call. Joe can only hear one side of the conversation. The DI turns to his driver. 'How far are we from Walsden?'

The sergeant reads the information from the satnav. 'Eighteen miles.'

'How long?'

'Half an hour.'

'Get us there. Now!'

Gennia picks up the two-way and radios West Yorkshire Police Control Centre, asking for cars to be sent to Walsden railway station. He checks his watch. 'Can they be there in fourteen minutes?'

'No, sir, we don't have any cars that close.'

He hammers the dashboard. 'Call the transport authority and get a message to the station. We need to stop that train.'

Gennia turns to Joe.

'Zoe Logan caught a train from Leeds station thirty minutes ago.'

'How do you know she's going to Walsden?'

'She sent a message to her boyfriend from the train.'

The walls of the waiting room are dotted with posters for holidays abroad, car insurance offers and job agencies. I check the timetable, trying to read the small print behind the scratched Perspex screen. Elijah is holding my hand. His whole palm can fit around three of my fingers.

I can't remember my mother ever holding my hand – not until she died. Even up until the last weeks she continued to complain. Her soup was too hot, or too cold or too salty or not salty enough. And then, miraculously, in her last hours she gripped my hand as though I could stop her slipping away.

'I'll do better next time,' she told me, although I don't know what she meant. Maybe she believed in reincarnation and was coming back to do it all again, as though this had been a practice run and next time she wouldn't fuck up so badly.

There was something viscous and cloying about her body in those last weeks, as though her blood had thickened and almost stopped moving. She swallowed one poison to kill another or to dull the pain. A lifetime of abusing her body had compromised her immune system, but she still drank every day – vodka

– her fist wobbling to her mouth and dribbling down her nightdress.

I remember thinking that she was mine now. I could do what I liked to her. I could have burned her with cigarettes – which she once did to me. I could have walked out and left her all day, lying in her own filth. I could have thrashed her with my belt or dumped her in a cinema and come back at closing time.

I did the opposite. I fed and bathed her. It was as though there was some sort of forcefield around her, or some curse that compelled me to care for her no matter how much I detested her.

On the night she died, I was in the ceiling. I didn't hear her last breath. I came down after Marnie had gone to sleep and found her, head lolling back, eyes open. I thought I'd go dancing down the street singing 'Ding, dong, the witch is dead', but instead I felt nothing.

I had always thought that you had to grow old before you died, but sometimes you grow old when you're still a child. You can grow old in three hours on a battlefield . . . or three years in prison, or three years in a cupboard watching your mother fuck for money.

At her funeral I remember rummaging around in my head for a feeling, but I couldn't even summon up hatred. There was only emptiness and an odd bubbling thought of what the devil might say to her when she arrived in Hell. I cremated her in her least favourite dress and a pair of shoes that pinched her feet. Petty, I know, but it felt like a victory.

The Metro line train pulling into the station has only three carriages.

'Do you like trains?' I ask.

Elijah nods.

'Let's take a ride.'

'Where are we going?'

'To see Zoe.'

CHAPTER 61

The train from Leeds to Walsden travels on the Caldervale Line through Bramley, New Pudsey, Bradford, Halifax and four more stops before reaching Walsden. The journey takes forty-five minutes. By rail it is a fairly direct route as the track tunnels under mountains and carves through valleys, but by road it is a snaking, dipping journey full of roundabouts and village speed limits.

The seatbelt bites into Joe's shoulder each time the patrol car corners. Ahead of them, vehicles give way to the siren, pulling aside resentfully. Something has been bothering him since they left Manchester. Why would Owen Cargill risk giving Zoe the name of her destination? Surely he'd suspect that she'll tell someone or be followed. Why not withhold the name of the train station and get Zoe to call him from Leeds? He could have directed her to a mobile phone, hidden in advance. This man is a planner. He doesn't make schoolboy mistakes. Unless . . .?

'He's not going to be at Walsden station,' Joe mutters.

Gennia's head jerks around. 'But she told her boyfriend . . .'

'He'll get her earlier, before she reaches Walsden. He'll watch her for a while, just in case she's being followed, and then intercept her early.'

'You think he's on the train?'

'Yes.'

Gennia looks at his watch. He picks up the two-way and radios the control centre.

'Where is the train?'

'The next station is Hebden Bridge.'

'I want it stopped. Nobody gets on or off.'

'We don't have anyone there.'

'What about station staff?'

'It's only staffed part-time.'

'Get the driver to stop before he reaches the platform.'

'We'll be disrupting the entire network.'

'I don't care. I want it stopped.' Gennia glances at Joe, his look saying everything: *I hope you're right about this.*

Zoe gazes out the window at another small village. Who lives in a place like this, she wonders. What sort of lives do they lead? How boring would it be? Nothing to do except walk in the fields or ride a horse. Zoe has never ridden a horse, not unless you count those pony rides at school fêtes where they lead the horse in circles around a playground and charge five quid for five minutes.

London is barely a big enough universe for Zoe.

She wants to see Paris and Rome and New York. The train is slowing, stopping at another empty platform where nobody ever seems to get off or get on. Why bother stopping at all?

The further she travels from home, the more unsure she's become of who she's going to meet. A part of her aches with anxiety, wanting to see Daniel. Another part of her keeps asking the obvious questions. Where has he been? Why won't he ask the police for help?

The train has started moving again, picking up speed. She can hear people moving down the aisle behind her and see a vague reflection in the glass. Before Zoe can turn her head, Elijah crawls onto her lap, wrapping his thin arms around her neck. She can smell his apple shampoo and candy on his breath. The man from the library sits down opposite her; the one who called himself Ruben and gave her a second-hand laptop.

He's smiling. 'Fancy meeting you here.'

Zoe holds Elijah defensively now, shielding his body.

'What are you doing here?'

'I've come to collect you.'

'Where's my dad?'

'Your mum is waiting. I'll explain everything later.'

Zoe finds it hard to breathe. 'Daniel sent me a message.'

'That's why I'm here. We have to get off at the next station.'

'He told me to go to Walsden.'

'Change of plan.'

The train is slowing. It's too soon to be a station. Owen peers out the window, trying to see further along the track. 'Were you followed?'

Zoe shakes her head.

'Did you tell anyone you were coming here?'

She hesitates for a moment too long. The train has come to a complete stop. Owen crosses over and peers out the opposite window, trying to see what lies ahead. They're near a village.

'Who are you?' asks Zoe.

Elijah answers. 'We met him in the park, remember? I thought he was Malcolm and you said he was Ruben. Mummy calls him Owen.'

'Where is she?'

'She wasn't allowed to come.'

Owen has visited both ends of the carriage, checking the doors. He returns to the seat.

'I want to talk to Daniel,' says Zoe. 'What have you done with Mum?'

'I'll take you to her.'

'No. I'm not moving.'

Owen's face distorts, twisting in anger. He reaches for Elijah. Zoe turns her back, protecting him. Owen grabs her forearm, digging his thumb and fingers into her muscle until they seem to touch her bones. Forcing her to her feet, he pushes her through the carriage, past an elderly couple.

'Help me,' pleads Zoe.

The man gets to his feet. Owen shoves him down. The woman's hand flutters to her mouth.

They're at the doors. Owen smashes the alarm button and forces them open, bracing his back against one door as he pushes Zoe to jump. He lowers Elijah into her arms. She tries to run down the tracks, but he reaches her in a stride, marching her across the rails and over the edge of the embankment.

A man in a uniform is walking down the track. He shouts and begins to jog. Zoe could probably reach him if she left Elijah behind and ran fast enough. Owen couldn't hold both of them. It's now or never.

He lifts Elijah over a barbed-wire fence, but the boy's shin snags on the upper strand. He screams. Blood leaks over his ankle. Zoe's opportunity vanishes in that moment. Owen grabs her around the waist and lifts her over the fence, dropping her unceremoniously in the nettles on the other side.

They're pushing through waist-high weeds. Her arms are itching and burrs are sticking to her jeans. Elijah is crying.

'Shut him up!'

'He's bleeding.'

'Just shut him up!'

They come to a narrow road with broken unkempt hedges on either side. Houses are ahead of them. A village. A car appears around a corner, a Land Rover Discovery with muddy wheel arches. The woman in control is middle-aged, ruddy-faced, wearing a striped rugby jumper. Pulling up, she looks concerned. 'Is there a problem?'

'My boy cut his leg on a fence,' says Owen. 'We ran out of petrol a ways back.'

'You poor thing,' she says, glancing at Zoe, who shakes her head. Fingers dig into her shoulder.

'Is everything OK?' asks the woman.

'She's just tired. It's been a long walk.'

'That cut might need stitches. The village doesn't have a doctor. You'll need to get to Halifax.'

'Can you give us a lift?'

The driver looks at Zoe again and then at Elijah's foot. His right sock is soaked with blood. The railway line is out of sight, but she hears voices. Shouting.

Zoe reacts first. She yells at the woman to get away. 'Drive, go, go, he's not our father.'

The woman is too slow to react. Her door is wrenched open and she's hauled onto the road. She tries to fight back, but Owen punches her in the face and she topples backwards, hitting her head on the asphalt with a dull thud. Zoe stares at the motionless woman, stunned by the violence.

'Get in the car.'

She doesn't react.

'I'll kill this boy. Get in the car!'

Owen bundles Elijah onto the back seat. Zoe is pushed in after him. The Land Rover slips into gear and accelerates away. Zoe looks out the rear window at the woman lying on the road. She hasn't moved. Maybe she's dead.

'You didn't have to hit her,' she says.

Owen's eyes meet hers in the mirror. 'It was your fault. Next time, do as you're told.'

CHAPTER 62

A dozen police officers are walking down either side of the railway tracks, searching the crushed stone ballast between the sleepers and the sloping embankments, which are thickly covered with weeds and brambles. The Metro line train has pulled forward to the station platform where passengers are being interviewed. Locals have gathered near the station area to monitor and discuss the incident. Joe grew up in a village not much bigger than this one and remembers how quickly news travels.

Clouds are massing in the west, above an assortment of trees – oaks, poplars, birch and others that Joe can't name. The branches shiver as the wind picks up.

Paramedics are treating the woman who had her Land Rover stolen. She's sitting in the back of an ambulance while they swathe her head in a white bandage. Gennia is with her, asking questions before they take her to hospital for X-rays.

Below, in the station car park, Joe notices a little girl with braided hair leading a woman by the hand, asking questions, excited by the strangeness of the scene. She spies somebody she knows and leaves her mother, running to a man who picks her up and holds her above his shoulders. Joe smiles to himself and thinks of Emma. She's too old now to be thrown in the air, or maybe he's grown too physically frail, which makes him feel even sadder.

A bubble of spit forms on his lips because his medication produces excess saliva. As the bubble breaks, he can almost hear a voice inside his head saying, 'Of course, of course.'

He remembers the photograph that Thomas Logan pulled from his dressing-gown pocket: Marnie, aged two, sitting between her parents on a wicker sofa; mouths open wide, eyes shining. Joe studied genetics for a semester in his first year at medical school – a part of the course he enjoyed because it didn't involve cutting up cadavers. They were taught about dominant and recessive genes and what family traits are passed on through each generation.

Already in motion, Joe walks along the platform, down the stairs, searching for Gennia. He finds the DI at the station office.

'Dimples are caused by a dominant gene,' he says. 'They're inherited from one or both parents. Marnie has dimples, but her parents don't.'

Gennia looks at him as though he's losing his mind. 'So what?'

'Owen Cargill has dimples.'

The headlights of the Land Rover sweep over the farmhouse, whitewashing the wall before swinging towards the barn. Pulling up outside the double doors, I get out of the car and lift the metal latch, pushing each side open. I will keep the vehicle out of sight until I dump it tomorrow.

Elijah has stopped whimpering. Zoe stemmed the bleeding with her sweatshirt. Now she's cradling his head and looking at me sullenly.

'I want Mummy,' says Elijah.

'We're here now, sport. I just got to park the car.'

Pulling into the barn, I turn off the headlights and kill the engine.

'What are you waiting for – an invitation?' I say, signalling Zoe to get out.

The clouds have closed in and the starless sky is black apart from the horizon, which is faintly etched against the distant glow of Manchester. Occasionally, streaks of lightning flare across the ridge.

There is a torch on the windowsill. Feeling along the dusty wood, my fingers close around the handle. When I press on the switch, it flickers for a moment and glows weakly. The batteries are almost dead.

They were used up this morning when I chased Marnie and the boy. Nothing is ever easy.

'Come on.'

'Where's Mum?'

'In the house.'

'I can't see where I'm going.'

'Stick close to me.'

'Elijah can't walk.'

'Then carry him.'

The torch casts a pale glow on the ground in front of us. Something scurries from our footsteps, a fox or a rat perhaps. I glance at the darkened farmhouse, wondering why Marnie has turned the lights off. She won't have escaped. I know her too well.

I find the gap in the hedge and uncouple the gate. The house is in front of us now, less substantial in the dark, but we don't need to live in a mansion. Marnie can plant roses under the big window at the gable end and grow herbs in the garden outside the kitchen.

I reach the porch.

'Wait here,' I tell Zoe, before veering away from the door and skirting along the side of the house, navigating my way around the corners, peering into the darkened windows. Marnie has pulled the curtains closed. I press my face to the glass, trying to see inside. I can't make out anything except my own reflection bouncing back at me in the weak glow of the torch. Standing on tiptoes I try another window. My breath steams up the pane of glass and the torch dies completely.

None of the windows are broken. Both doors are secure. Returning to the porch, I search for the right key.

'I'm hungry,' says Elijah.

'Keep him quiet,' I say.

I push the door open with my foot and reach for the light switch but nothing happens. A fuse has blown or Marnie has found a way of cutting the power.

'Are you there, Marnie?'

Silence answers.

'What are you up to? I know you're in here.'

The question seems to bounce back off the darkness.

'Don't play games with me. I have the children.'

As I scan the kitchen, I feel the pressure of things behind me or in front of me, imagining that she's waiting in the dark. I've been here before, steeped in blackness, a little boy with inky fingers and pink translucent ears, hiding in a cupboard while his mother earned her keep.

'You're being foolish,' I say, aware that I took the knives away from her. 'You have to understand, Marnie, I'm used to the dark. I've lived in your ceiling.'

Zoe's voice is close behind me. 'What have you done to her?'

I grab Zoe's arm. 'Call to her.'

'Mum?'

'Tell her to come.'

'Mum, are you there?'

We listen to a dripping tap and a cooling water heater. Before Zoe can back away, I push her ahead of me. She bumps into a chair that is lying in the middle of the floor. All of the chairs have been overturned, creating an obstacle course. I kick them aside. They slide across the linoleum and crash into the cupboard doors.

I keep another torch in the kitchen, along with candles and matches in case of a power cut. Opening the drawers, I feel for them. Gone. Clever, Marnie, clever. You've taken away the light, but I don't mind. I'm a connoisseur of the darkness. I don't need to see you to find you.

'This isn't funny,' I yell. 'Elijah is scared. He cut his leg. It could need stitches.'

We've reached the hallway. The drawing room is on the right, bedrooms ahead, a bathroom at the far end. Another light switch doesn't work.

'We'll wait outside,' says Zoe.

'No, I want you close. Call out to her again.'

'Mum, it's me . . . are you OK?'

I twist Zoe's arm. She cries out. No answer from Marnie.

Glass shatters in a muffled whop and tinkles like laughter. It came from down the hallway. She's in the bathroom. I push Zoe aside and run, tripping over something on the floor – a wire at shin-height stretched between opposite doorframes. I land heavily on something that shatters under my chest and forearms. Light bulbs. I can feel the shards embedded in my skin. That's what she's done, the clever bitch, unscrewed the light bulbs. The pain arrives: a thousand cuts. Bleeding.

I hear another sound, a gleeful, guttural chuckle. She's making fun of me.

On my feet, I grind the shattered glass into the floorboards. Turning. Calling for Zoe.

'Come here.'

She's backing away from me.

'Do as you're told.'

I can see her silhouette. She's holding Elijah on her hip.

'We'll wait outside.'

'No!'

I hear the laugh again. It doesn't sound like Marnie. She can't be with someone else. I wait, listening. A shadow moves across a doorway. Perhaps my eyes are playing tricks on me. I'm in the bathroom. Marnie must have shattered the mirror. The light switch is a hanging cord. I hear a dull click when I tug upon the cord. Nothing. I try again. This time something swings into the side of my head and sends me crashing into the opposite wall, my brain rattling, legs wobbling, dazed. Fury balloons inside me.

'This isn't a joke, Marnie. I'm going to hurt Zoe and Elijah. Come out now.'

Lightning flashes. For an instant the windows and corridor are lit up. I see the blood on the front of my shirt. I see the broken mirror. Thunder arrives, shaking the pictures on the walls and the plates in the kitchen. The door to one of the bedrooms is ajar. I imagine someone standing behind it. With one finger I push it open and step in sideways, staying close to the wall.

Lightning flashes again. In the moment before I'm blind again, I see a stark figure, more animal than human, crouched in the corner. The darkness returns like a dustsheet thrown over everything. The room had looked empty. She must have moved the bed. I stay close to the wall, hoping for another flash of lightning.

I hear the same rumbling laugh.

'Are you with someone, Marnie? You'll have to introduce me.'

I want to run forward, but stop myself. Instead I close the door. My hands are slick with my own blood and I need both hands to turn the handle.

'It's over, Marnie. You can come out now.'

She's no longer in the corner. My head swings ponderously from side to side, searching for her. I can see the barest outline of a person kneeling between the window and where the bed used to be. Trying to hide.

'This used to be your room, Marnie. Do you remember?'

She doesn't answer.

'I won't keep secrets from you any more. We're family. That's why I watched over you. That's what a father is supposed to do. Do you understand what I'm saying? You're my daughter! Elijah and Zoe are my grandchildren.'

Silence.

'I thought we could live here. We could be like a proper family. We have everything we need.'

My body is trembling, but not from the cold. How calm she is. I expected more. Tears. Denial. Outrage.

'I have never desired anything more than this – to have what I've never had. Your mother kept you from me. She tried to pretend that I didn't exist. I can tell you the whole story.' My eyes are stinging. My limbs are leaden. 'Say something, Marnie. Please?' I kneel on the floor next to her. 'No more games.'

She makes a noise deep in her throat. Toneless. Mournful. It may be acceptance. For a moment I feel pleasure flood through me. She's going to forgive me. She's going to be mine. Not scared. Not frightened. Mine.

CHAPTER 63

The rain starts falling around nine, a drizzle at first, mingling with the dirt on the windscreen and bleeding down to the wipers. Gennia parks at the entrance to the farm track. The windows are fogging up. He cracks one of them and rubs a viewing porthole in the condensation.

Thunder rumbles overhead before fading like a passing freight train. For the past half-hour lightning has been painting the landscape in brilliant flashes, turning the trees to skeletons and buildings into charcoal sketches.

'This is the place,' he says, peering through his binoculars.

Joe glances at the farm track. The stolen Land Rover had a GPS/GSM signal locator hidden on the chassis. The owner's husband had it fitted after he had a previous car stolen.

Gennia takes a stick of gum from his pocket.

'What are we waiting for?' asks Joe.

'Maps. A property search. Back-up.'

Every so often a fork of lightning detonates on

the hillsides to the north of them, getting closer. Joe counts down the seconds until the thunder. He can't remember the equation – how many seconds between the two – which estimates how far away they are from the lightning.

The detective tilts his head towards the track. 'So what's his body count?'

'Pardon?'

'If this is our guy, how many people do you think he's killed?'

'I don't know.'

'If we trace back through Marnie Logan's life, are we going to find more bodies? Some poor guy sideswipes her car and next thing his life is ruined. Some hairdresser gives her a bad haircut. She gets bad service at a restaurant. Where does it end?'

He rubs the stubble under his chin and stares out the window for another full minute.

'We found Marnie Logan's DNA in Hennessy's apartment.'

'Cargill could have planted it there.'

'Why?'

'He wanted to have leverage over her.'

'All because he wanted a family.'

'It's something he's never had.'

'Christ, he could have taken mine. I haven't talked to my sister in ten years and my two nieces think all police are pigs who pick on blacks and Asians and Moslems and take bribes from journalists.' Gennia leans back against the headrest for a moment, cracking his neck and stretching his back muscles.

The radio squawks. He picks up the handset. A tracking company has confirmed the location of the car – a quarter of a mile to the east. The farm is owned by a company registered in the Isle of Man with a post office box belonging to a firm of solicitors. Prior to the sale it was rented for nearly thirty years to various tenants, including Thomas Logan.

Gennia glances at Joe. 'That's good enough for me.'

Three more police cars have joined them. The DI gets out and opens the car boot. He puts on a heavy black vest and a rain jacket. Other officers check firearms and don helmets.

'Do you want me to stay here?' asks Joe.

'We might need you,' says Gennia. 'I want to avoid a hostage situation.' He tosses Joe a vest. 'Put this on and stay well back.'

The detective briefs his team, seemingly more relaxed to have reached this point and to be dealing with a different sort of uncertainty. 'We don't know if he's armed, but we do know he's dangerous. Check your radios. No heroics. There are children with him.'

The officers begin moving, three abreast down the track. Torches dance over the ground ahead of them. Joe stays well back, trying not to look directly at the lights. A luminous mist rises from the fields, blurring the ridge above them.

Gennia crouches and shines his torch at the edge of a puddle. 'Two different vehicles and a motorbike. Fresh.'

The track follows the contours of the land, finding the path of least resistance. They wade across a stream and begin to climb. Occasional forks of lightning mark out the horizon and leave white spots dancing on Joe's retina. One such strike reveals a farmhouse and a ruined barn clinging to the hillside. Both are in darkness.

Gennia looks at his watch. Ten-fifteen. They could be sleeping. He sends two officers to the barn, telling them to check for the Land Rover. The others are to surround the house.

'We're going to give this guy a chance to leave the house peacefully,' he says. 'But I don't want him slipping away like a thief in the night.'

He summons Joe. 'How is this Owen Cargill likely to react if we come bursting through the doors?'

'He's a former soldier.'

'That's what I thought. You stay here.'

Gennia moves off along the track. Soon he's lost in the darkness. Joe can see the barest of shadows as the officers surround the farmhouse, crouching and running between cover. The minutes pass slowly.

A gull's cry seems to bounce off the ridge. Harsh. Beseeching. It takes a moment before Joe realises how out of place it sounds, this far from the sea. It can't have been a gull. The wind has died with the rain.

Somebody is coming towards him. A detective. Two children. Zoe carries Elijah, stumbling under his weight, but she won't let go. She falls to her knees and Joe cradles both of them in his arms.

'I'm sorry, I'm sorry, I shouldn't have run away,' she sobs. 'I thought it was Daniel.'

'Where's your mum?'

'I didn't see her.'

'Is she in the house?'

'I don't know. He went inside. I decided to run.' Her hair falls over her eyes. 'It's the man from the library.'

'What man?'

'He called himself Ruben. I met him there. He gave me a laptop. He said he didn't need it any more. It's him, isn't it? He's been watching us.'

'Ruben is his middle name,' says Joe, removing the bandage from Elijah's ankle. He looks for any other injuries.

Gennia has joined them. He addresses Zoe. 'Does he have any weapons?'

'I don't know.'

'You didn't see any guns, or knives, or anything explosive?'

She shakes her head.

The detective seems satisfied. 'I've called an ambulance.' He turns back towards the farmhouse, jogging with a spring in his step, driven by whatever strange cocktail of adrenalin and desire makes a person want to risk their life to protect others. Joe has felt it before. It's not something you expect, it just happens. You react instinctively: you fight or flee or stand your ground.

'*Police! Open up!*'

The bellowed warning echoes from the ridge, amplified by the contours of the valley.

'*Owen Cargill, we know you're in there. Come out with your hands in the air.*'

There is another long silence.

'*Nobody has to get hurt, Owen.*'

Glass breaks. Wood splinters. Heavy boots are inside the house. Torches swing from room to room, glowing behind the curtains.

Zoe's breathing has slowed. Joe has checked Elijah's ankle. He's fallen asleep resting his head on Zoe's thigh.

'Professor!'

Joe glances up sharply. A younger detective is stumbling towards him, the torch bouncing over the ground.

'The boss wants you,' he says, out of breath. 'I'll stay here.'

He hands over the torch.

Getting to his feet, Joe pauses for a moment, willing his legs to move in the right direction. The turf looks almost white in the disc of light. The first thing that strikes him on the walk to the farmhouse is the quietness. He can picture himself as a little boy running through fields on the edge of Snowdonia pretending to be a superhero who was going to save the world.

Gennia is waiting on the veranda. His stare seems

to pass right through Joe, as though he's gazing from the depths of history or some dark place that he can't escape. Another detective is leaning over the railing, vomiting into the flowerbed.

Joe manoeuvres his way through the fallen chairs in the kitchen and follows his own torchlight down the hall, grinding glass into the floorboards with his shoes. He swings the beam upwards onto a bathroom mirror. Cracks radiate outwards from the point of impact like a child's drawing of the sun. He can see himself reflected in a dozen different ways. Tall. Short. Fat. Severed.

He hears the sound of running water. Marnie is kneeling in the bathtub, washing her hands beneath the tap. She rubs them over and over, splashing water up her wrists, cleaning between her fingers, scrubbing at her nails, muttering to herself. Rasping and deep, her voice makes little crowing sounds of delight that seem to be coming from the pipes through some trick of ventriloquism.

'Marnie?'

She lifts her face. 'Don't use that bitch's name to me. I told her what would happen. I told her, but she wouldn't listen.'

'We haven't met before, Malcolm. I'm Professor Joe O'Loughlin.'

She blinks at him through a fringe of matted hair.

'Can I come in?' He moves inside the door and takes a towel from the shelf, putting it around Marnie's shoulders. He notices her split lip and a blue pulsing knot above her left eyelid.

'Are you hurt?'

She doesn't answer.

'Why did you come back, Malcolm?'

'Why do you think?'

'I want to speak to Marnie.'

'That useless bitch is never here when you need her. It's always me – doing her dirty work.'

'Can I speak to her?'

She doesn't answer.

'I want to make sure she's OK?'

The bitter laugh makes the hair on Joe's neck stand on end. His own voice betrays him.

'We have something in common, Malcolm, we both care about Marnie and we both want to help her.'

'I'm sick of helping that bitch.'

'But you need her, Malcolm.'

'That's where you're wrong. I don't need anyone.'

'Let me talk to her. Marnie, can you hear me? I've just seen Zoe and Elijah. They're OK. They're worried about you. If you come back to me, I'll take you to them.'

She spins around and lunges towards Joe, spitting the words. 'Why don't you just fuck off! She's not listening. She only listens to me.'

'You can't even say her name, can you?'

No answer.

'Say her name for me.'

'No.'

'Marnie doesn't need you, Malcolm. She didn't need Owen and she didn't need Daniel. She's survived on her own.'

Hatred curls in the corner of her lips. 'I can crush her.'

'She's stronger than you think. She's learned to live without you once and she'll do it again.'

'She's pathetic.'

'If you're so strong and she's so weak, let me talk to her.'

'No.'

'What are frightened of?'

'I'm not frightened of anything.'

'I think you are. I think you're frightened of Marnie. I think you know she's stronger than you are. She pushed you out once – she'll do it again. You're nothing without her. You're a fucked-up teenage thug with a potty mouth.'

Marnie is on her feet, hurling herself towards him, her face twisted with hatred and loathing, trying to scratch out his eyes. Joe grabs her arms, pulling her from the tub. He forces his body onto hers, using his weight to press her to the floor. His mouth is near the shell of her ear.

'Don't fight me, Marnie, fight him!'

She twists and squirms, trying to burst out of his arms, but the effort exhausts her and energy leaks from her lungs like a spent breath. She curls into Joe's chest, no longer struggling, withdrawing into herself.

'He won't be watching me again,' she whispers. 'He'll never watch me again.'

CHAPTER 64

They say love and death are like two uninvited guests at the party of life – one takes your heart and the other takes the heartbeat. They are the essence of human experience, like two sides of the same coin, spinning through the air. Falling.

Joe watches the coin turn. Owen opens his hand and catches it, slaps it against his wrist and looks at the result. He rests the coin on his thumbnail and he flips it again. A court security officer takes a set of keys from his belt. Joe has to step back as he unlocks the heavy metal door.

The cells are below the courtrooms of the Old Bailey in a building that dates from 1902, when it replaced the infamous Newgate Prison, which for seven hundred years had housed prisoners and executed the worst of them. Many were hung on the street outside, making their final journey along Dead Man's Walk, where large noisy crowds threw rotten fruit, vegetables and stones.

Owen Cargill is sitting in a chair facing a small barred window, high on the wall, cocking his head as though listening to something. He's wearing a neatly ironed cotton shirt and trousers that are a size too small; his hair is shaved tight to his skull, revealing every bump and hollow.

He flips the coin again, but turns suddenly at the sound of the door. The coin drops and rolls on its edge in a slow circle before toppling and rattling into stillness. Owen's face twists into a crooked smile.

'Is that you, Professor?'

'Yes.'

'I thought you'd come today.'

No matter how often he visits Owen, Joe struggles to hide his shock. It helps that his reaction can't be seen, although he suspects that Owen realises what impact he has upon people.

'You sound stressed,' he says, resting his hands on his knees.

'I'm fine,' replies Joe, taking a seat on a narrow bench against the wall. Owen reaches down between his shoes and feels for the coin with his fingertips. He flips it again.

'Heads or tails?'

'Heads.'

Owen catches the coin and slaps it against his wrist. He holds it up for Joe.

'Did I win or lose?'

'You lost.'

'Best of three?'

Depending upon the light, Owen's eye sockets can look like bottomless holes that gape openly into his brain. It's only when he turns his face to the window that Joe can see the scarred pink and white skin in the sockets. His pupils were gouged out by something jagged and sharp rather than surgically precise. According to the surgeon who operated on him at the Royal Eye Hospital in Manchester, it was most likely a shard of broken mirror. His eyes were never found.

For the first few months of his hospitalisation and recuperation, Owen fell apart. Joe witnessed the disintegration. He didn't wash or shave. He barely slept. His stubble grew thick and dark and the bandages over his eyes made him look like an emaciated panda. Joe could smell his nightmares and rancid hatred and hear the despair in his voice. All that changed when the trial began. He arrived each day at the Old Bailey, stepping from the prison van, looking more like a defence lawyer than a defendant. It's the same today. His suit jacket is hanging behind the door because he doesn't want to crease the sleeves.

Joe took advantage of Owen's presence at the trial to schedule meetings in the holding cells during meal breaks or when the judge adjourned early for the day. For a long time Owen played games with him, teasing out the details of when he began to follow Marnie. When he first joined the army, he had no idea that Christina Logan had fallen pregnant and given birth to a daughter. It was only later, when he tracked Christina to the farmhouse, that he put the pieces together and realised why a married woman would start an affair with a fifteen-year-old boy she caught hiding in her basement, spying on her. She and her husband had been trying for a baby for years, but Christina had miscarried or failed to fall pregnant. Thomas spent weeks away, working on the rigs, their marriage faltering.

'She didn't love me,' Owen said. 'She used me.'

Owen had written Christina letters, but they were always returned unopened. Eventually, he went looking for her and discovered Marnie.

'I had a daughter, but Christina kept denying it; telling me to leave. We could have been happy together, but the bitch told me to stay away. She didn't want me to see my daughter.'

'Is that why you killed her?' asked Joe.

'She killed herself.'

'You didn't save her.'

'I saved Marnie.'

Joe had a dozen such meetings with Owen during the course of the trial. He marvelled at the defendant's neatness and attention to grooming. In the months since that night at the farmhouse, he had mastered dozens of new skills, learning how to navigate around his room at the psychiatric unit and arrange things on the shelves so that he could find them without the aid of sight. He had also learned to walk with a cane and was studying Braille.

Owen rests the coin on top of his thumb and spins it again. He has become practised at throwing it almost to eye-height and catching it in the same palm.

'Is she here?' he asks.

'You know I can't talk about her.'

'But she's definitely here, isn't she? She'll come today.'

Joe doesn't answer.

'Has Malcolm come back?'

'No.'

'I like him. He's good for her. She needs somebody like him.' Owen smiles. 'Does that surprise you?' The coin is rolling over his knuckles between his fingers. 'Marnie should thank me rather than blame me for what's happened.'

'I don't think she's going to do that.'

'She could be in this cell with me. They found Marnie's DNA in the caretaker's flat and Hennessy's apartment, but none of mine.'

'You planted it there.'

'Can you prove that? I could have pleaded not guilty and made Marnie give evidence. I could have had her cross-examined. I could have claimed that she knew about me all along. We were working together . . .'

'The jury wouldn't have believed you.'

Owen looks up at the window. Joe can clearly see his empty eye sockets, which look like sunken craters beneath his brows. 'I hope she realises what I've done for her.'

He flips the coin and catches it in his palm, turning it onto his wrist. 'Heads or tails?'

Upstairs, Joe walks through the marbled anterooms and foyers that are crowded with black-gowned barristers, briefing solicitors, defendants, family, friends and random souls summoned to the lottery of jury duty and hoping their excuses might excuse them.

Marnie is sitting on a bench seat between DI Gennia and her lawyer, Craig Bryant. She looks up at Joe and smiles. Relieved. She's dressed in a mid-length skirt with a white blouse and navy blazer. Her hair has grown long again and she's wearing lipstick and mascara.

'You look terrific,' he says.

'I feel like a tranny on my first trip out as a woman,' she replies, forcing a smile. Then she apologises to Gennia. 'Did that sound terrible?'

He shakes his head.

Joe crouches in front of Marnie, taking her hands. 'How are you feeling?'

'I'm OK.'

'Do you want to have a quick chat before we go in?'

'No, I'll be fine.'

Craig Bryant is wearing a charcoal-coloured suit and a black robe over his shoulders. His horsehair wig is resting on a bundle of files that are sealed by red ribbons wrapped around a spool. 'I've just been explaining it to her,' he says. 'If she doesn't want to read the statement herself, I can read it for her. There is no jury any more, only a judge. Cargill has been found guilty. This is just a sentencing hearing.' Bryant turns to Marnie. 'If you get in the witness box and for some reason you feel overwhelmed or want to stop, just ask me. Take a drink of water. I can talk to the judge.'

She nods.

'I know you said you didn't want anyone to read your statement beforehand, but if you wanted a second opinion . . .?'

'No.'

Gennia interrupts. 'I thought your father was coming.'

'He's with Zoe. They're already inside.'

Bryant looks at his watch. 'We should go in.'

Climbing the steps, they pass through a second small waiting room and follow a corridor to Court 1. Joe and Gennia go to the public gallery, which is upstairs, overlooking the body of the court. Thomas Logan is seated in the front row, craning to look over the banister. Zoe is next to him, sitting alongside Ruiz, whom she treats like a favourite uncle. She has taken to visiting him on those days that she's isn't hanging out with Ryan Coleman.

'I saved you a seat,' she says, waving to Joe. She squeezes his hand excitedly. 'I've never seen the inside of a courtroom.'

'I hope it's the last time.'

'What if I become a lawyer?'

'Please don't do that,' says Ruiz.

'Why not?'

'They're like monkeys who get dressed up and fling poo at each other.'

Zoe laughs, not sure if he's joking.

The judge's bench is below them to the right of

them and the jury box directly ahead with the witness stand in between the two. A glass security panel surrounds the dock.

Joe glances over the railing. He can only see the top of Marnie's head. For weeks they've been preparing for this day. Talking about what might happen.

She chose not to attend Owen Cargill's trial and the prosecution didn't call her to give evidence once Owen had changed his plea to guilty. The jury found him guilty of murdering Patrick Hennessy, Niall Quinn, Trevor Waite and Daniel Hyland, whose body was discovered in a shallow grave near the farmhouse, between two gnarled apple trees. Owen admitted ambushing Daniel because the journalist had discovered his existence. He strangled him with a pair of women's tights and dragged his body through the hole in the back of the wardrobe. He dressed Daniel in his mother's clothes and used her wheelchair to transport him to the lock-up garage in the rear lane. No CCTV cameras. No blood. No clues.

After a three-month investigation and a public outcry, the Director of Public Prosecutions decided not to charge Marnie with any offence, particularly in light of what she and her children had been through. Marnie received the news on the day she was released from a psychiatric hospital in Kent and allowed to go home. Since then she's been seeing Joe three times a week, trying to deal with the creations of her unconscious and accept the existence of her dissociative disorder.

The professor has seen no trace of Malcolm since that night at the farmhouse. Marnie's voice, mannerisms and tone are all as before. Joe has tried to find the triggers, putting Marnie under pressure, making her relive those final hours, but no cracks have appeared in her psyche and no evidence has emerged of a second malevolent personality, an evil doppelgänger, a cuckoo in the nest.

Marnie no longer denies that Malcolm existed.

'I know what he did was wrong,' she told Joe, 'but I'm not sorry for what he did.'

'But he's inside *you*.'

'Not any more.'

'How do you know?'

'I can't feel him.'

'Could you feel him before?'

'No.'

Joe used hypnosis and deep relaxation techniques. He played word association games and took Marnie back to the morning her mother died, making her relive the tragedy. Throughout these sessions, she didn't fashion elaborate lies or try to evade his questions, yet there were times when she gripped the arms of her chair as though she felt suspended and weightless, ready to lift off and float away. It wasn't her body, but her mind that wanted to break loose.

'All rise,' announces the usher. A door opens behind the bench and the judge enters dressed in a black and violet robe. The wig on his head is perched high on his dome, barely covering his baldness. Moments later, Owen Cargill is led into the dock from the cells below. Flanked by two security guards, one holding each of his arms, he is turned to face the bench. Owen immediately reaches out and feels for the glass wall, judging the dimensions of his new surroundings. Turning his head, he scans the courtroom as though looking for Marnie. After several moments, he stops and stares in the direction of the prosecutor's table, where Marnie is sitting beside Craig Bryant. She has her head down, not looking at him.

Judge Baum asks the prosecution and defence counsel if they're ready to proceed.

'Yes, My Lord,' says the prosecutor, who begins by tabling a psychiatric assessment of Owen Cargill, which includes statements from three different psychologists and psychiatrists who have been treating him at a high-security NHS hospital. 'We also have Marnella Logan in the court today, who would like to present a victim impact statement.'

The mention of Marnie's name seems to ignite something in Owen, who leans forward on his bench seat, craning to get closer to her. Meanwhile, Marnie makes her way to the witness box. The lawyers are conferring. Owen tells them to be quiet.

Judge Baum interrupts him. 'Mr Cargill, please refrain from speaking.'

'They were talking,' says Owen. 'I wanted to be able to hear her footsteps.'

'Counsel are allowed to confer.'

'What is she wearing?' asks Owen.

Nobody answers.

Owen looks from side to side. 'Somebody, please tell me.'

'Pull yourself together, Mr Cargill, or I will have you removed.'

'Is she wearing the pencil skirt and white blouse, maybe with a blazer?'

'This is your last warning,' says Judge Baum, signalling to the guard.

'Sure. Right. I'm sorry.' Owen bows his head and puts his hands together.

Marnie is staring at him, appalled. Up until now she hasn't seen or acknowledged Owen's injuries. They were explained to her, but she claimed to have no memory of gouging out his eyes. For a fleeting moment she seems to waver, her body shaking. Then she looks up at the public gallery and sees Zoe and her father.

Stepping into the witness box, she unfolds a piece of paper that she has crumpled in her fist. She reads the first sentence to herself and then out loud.

'The man being sentenced today claims to be my father and says that he was protecting me. But a real father is someone who holds you when you have nightmares and kisses your scraped knees. He carries you on his shoulders when you're tired and pulls out thorns and drinks cups of pretend tea at pretend tea parties, surrounded by dolls and teddy bears. A real father reads bedtime stories and takes you swimming and to ballet and to drama classes. He waits up when you go on your first date. He wipes away your tears when you're jilted. He walks you up the aisle when you get married and cries when he holds his grandchild for the first time. A real father loves you unconditionally, not because your eyes are the same colour as his, or you share the same DNA. He loves you because he's the one who's always been there.'

Marnie looks up from the page. 'I have a real father. His name is Thomas John Logan and he's here today in the public gallery. Owen Cargill is not my father – he's the monster who killed my husband and my mother and my baby brother.'

Owen's head is swinging back and forth. Leaping to his feet, he roars, smashing his head against the glass.

'I'M YOUR FATHER,' he screams.

Marnie continues, her knuckles white on the page. 'I cannot forgive the horrors this man inflicted on my family. I *will not* forgive him.'

'I DID IT FOR YOU. I KEPT YOU SAFE.' Blood drips from Owen's nose down onto his lips, staining his teeth. 'YOU UNGRATEFUL BITCH! YOU FUCKING COW!'

Judge Baum yells for order and demands that the prisoner be removed. Owen is still screaming: 'WE'RE FAMILY, YOU CAN'T CHANGE THAT.'

Marnie folds her statement and steps down from the witness box, passing the dock as she walks towards the door. She stops opposite Owen, who is fighting with the security guards, his face contorted with rage. They restrain him, twisting his arms behind his back, forcing his face against the glass. In that brief moment, Marnie stares into Owen's sightless sockets and seems to fight an emotion that is ancient but still potent. Then she turns and walks out of the courtroom.

Joe finds her inside the main entrance. Judge Baum has given Owen Cargill three life sentences.

'You were amazing,' says Zoe, giving Marnie a hug.

'I'm still shaking.'

Thomas dabs at his eyes with a white handkerchief. 'You made your old man cry.'

'I meant every word.'

A restaurant has been booked, champagne on ice.

'Are you sure you won't change your mind?' Marnie asks Joe, picking up his hand and putting her fingers between his.

'I can't.'

'Why not?'

'You're my patient.'

'Can't you be my friend too?'

'I don't want to have to define those boundaries.'

Marnie pouts sadly, showing her dimples. She cups the back of his neck and kisses both his cheeks, leaving a smudge of lipstick. Then she hugs him close, pressing her face to his chest and her body against his loins. 'You can get mad if you want to, but allow me this.'

Joe can smell her perfume and the fragrance of her skin. She pulls away and waves goodbye as she takes her father's arm. Elijah and the nanny are waiting for them at the restaurant. Zoe falls into step beside Ruiz, who has also been invited to the celebration.

DI Gennia appears at Joe's shoulder. The detective takes a stick of gum from his pocket and unwraps it slowly. He spits out the old wad into the silver foil and wraps it in a tight ball. The new gum is concertinaed against his tongue and he chews it reflectively. Above his head a passenger jet is descending west towards Heathrow, leaving a thin vapour trail like a chalk mark on a blue board. 'Marnie Logan is your problem now,' he says. 'I hope you're up to it.'

'She'll be fine.'

'You sure about that?'

Joe turns to him, wanting an explanation. Gennia shrugs, giving the impression that he's simply making conversation, but Joe knows the detective isn't prone to asking pointless questions.

'Ever heard of Stephen Rudolf?'

'No.'

'He's an insurance broker; works at a place called Life General; has an office in Tottenham Court Road. He was the guy who was handling Marnie Logan's life insurance claim on her husband. A few days before Patrick Hennessy was murdered, Rudolf had a meeting with Marnie Logan and he rejected her claim. The next day he fell down a set of stairs at a car park in the West End. Fractured his skull. Broke his leg.'

Gennia pinches the gum between his teeth and pulls it into a long strand. 'Maybe the guy tripped. Maybe he's looking for a pay-out. Wouldn't that be ironic?'

'I don't understand,' says Joe.

'Owen Cargill confessed to pushing Rudolf down the stairs, but that's not possible. He wasn't in the West End that day. We have CCTV footage and mobile phone records that put him somewhere completely different.'

Joe doesn't respond. Gennia tugs the collar of his jacket around his neck and plants his hands in his pockets.

'Like I said, she's your problem now.'